THE GOSSIP COLUMNIST

NOVELS BY MARTYN BURKE

Laughing War
The Commissars Report
Ivory Joe
The Shelling of Beverly Hills
Tiara
The Truth About the Night
Music for Love or War

THE GOSSIP COLUMNIST

MARTYN BURKE

DARKSPUR PRESS

For my brother Edmund

Censorship had raised gossip to the level of official communication.

1933: The Year the Nazis Seized Power;
by Phillip Metcalfe

ONE

1

Sunday April 22, 1945

I HAVE NEVER BEEN BEAUTIFUL. Not like her.

And nor has there been that inner certainty that beauty conveys until age and the mirror eat into it, a fortress falling slowly into its own moat. Of course like most of us I have been bestowed with the usual assessments: Attractive. And also: Looking good. Medals second-class. And that worst of all for a woman: Handsome, as if you did not fit into any of the usual categories. But never beautiful. Like her.

Thank God.

Or so I tell myself.

Remember, we lived through an era that knew no restrictions and everything shocking was permissible, encouraged even. Before it ended fifteen years ago, faces and bodies were openly graded for sexual valuation. And those with the higher scores could open the darkest doors of the soul in the name of all that was supposed to be free and fun.

Many such doors were opened. Too many.

And Karin never needed a key.

In the most decadent of the wild Weimar years she lied, saying she was 18, and then went onstage at the *Himmel u Hölle* nightclub where she shed her clothes as naturally as a discarded chrysalis. In a way it made sense that nudity was her natural state. No clothing could improve on what lay beneath. Nor the stage makeup, the powders and rouges that she refused to use. In the whipping and spanking acts she was the only one of the female performers allowed onstage without makeup.

By the end of her first week, the club had to keep the older men from the audience away from the door leading to the dressing rooms. All of them reeking credentials from Berlin's wealthier classes. By the end of her second week Karin had become bored with the playacting on the stage. So in the middle of a bondage scene that she regarded as false and ridiculous, she got dressed and quit.

She just walked off the stage. Leaving two naked, bound and gagged men flopping like fish across it.

Silliness annoyed her. Even though everyone else was telling her it was all such fun! But the kind of fun that was being had in those days was relentless, the kind that only presents its bill when the laughter is the loudest. And for so many, that bill had to be paid wrapped in regret or even shame at what they had done.

And not merely because so many of those people seeking all that free and fun life soon became Nazis.

Even after the Weimar years ended, after the most depraved sex dens, clubs and lachtnokals were shut down by Nazi Storm Troopers, Karin was one of those whose face and body prevailed as they always had. In some odd way it might have been because she was so careless about how she looked. It was a carelessness that allowed her sexual qualities to remain unhindered. It was what saved her on so many levels.

She would have been uninterested to know that she was exactly what the Nazis wanted from its Nordic or Aryan women—that blonde wholesomeness of the Volk. The kind that in the years before the Nazis took over, had been the camouflage for the raw sexuality that lay below.

The Nazis decreed that feminine artifice like cosmetics were for whores and Slavs. But it was a decree that did not affect Karin. Nothing about her had to be enhanced. She had never needed the ladled face powder, the gashes of lipstick, the painted fingernails or the battle armour of corsets. Not for her any of it.

Or sometimes, even clothing.

The Russians and their big guns have moved closer. To us they are the Ivans. They are just over there, wherever over there is at any given moment. It could be Pankow or Neukölln, no one seems to know. So far we haven't seen them. But you hear them, these mad volleys of Katyusha rockets that sound like the sky is silk being violently ripped in a hundred places. We know the Ivans are encircling Berlin.

And it terrifies us that the twisted dwarf, Goebbels, might have been right. About us. And what will happen if the Russians get to us—the women.

But would she think about any of this? Would she understand the danger? Karin?

Which is why I am bicycling as fast as I can. A war-ragged woman too big for this bicycle, flapping foolishly through rubble like an ungainly bird that cannot take flight. To warn her. Maybe to save her? And again and again I ask myself: why? Because I promised I would, all those years ago as a girl when mother explained to me that some of us had roles in life? Roles we could never expect to comprehend. And this is my role, she said—saving your sister even though she could never understand she needed saving.

But during these years of war and terror I have come to understand that maybe it is not the real reason I am doing this.

I am cycling through the smoke and destruction of Berlin, believing now that mother was wrong all those years ago. It is Karin, not me who had a role thrust upon her, one she could not change. And it's her who has been sending out unspoken messages pleading for help.

And so I hurtle onward. This mad journey to the movie studio near Potsdam, bicycling through the wreckage of the Reich. As the Americans and British planes are bombing what is left of Berlin into splinters.

Yes bicycling. There is no other way now. Starting from Charlottenburg and then weaving through the wreckage of the Ku'damm, the once majestic Kurfürstendamm, a street so devoted to luxury and elegance that its current state of devastation is like a scar leading to the single jagged spire, looming ahead like a dagger plunged into the heart of fashionable Berlin. Still steaming in its death throes, that spire is all that is left of the Kaiser Wilhelm Church which once rivaled the great cathedrals. And all along my mad bicycling dash through the remnants of the Ku'damm, the outer walls of buildings stand roofless and windowless, naked structures having spewed their innards onto the road like dying creatures embarrassed to be seen holding their entrails in front of them.

The bridge across the Havel at Kohlhasen has been destroyed and the roads are full of shattered buildings and there is still the fear that the Americans will fill the afternoon skies with their bombers dropping treacly silver things that blow us all up. The Americans by day, the British by night. But that is not we fear the most now. No, it is the Russians—the Ivans, who terrify us. For a year or more, the twisted dwarf as he is called, has been haranguing us on the radio. He fills his speeches with horror stories of what the Russians will do: rape us, eviscerate us, slaughter us.

Did he think we were stupid? We knew he was terrifying us so we would keep fighting. And now: keep fighting? By sending children and old men against the military might of the Ivans? These Russians who would do awful things if they could get to us. As our soldiers apparently did to them.

We heard the twisted dwarf fled to Hitler's bunker yesterday. One can only hope. It is only a rumour. The stepchild of gossip.

But gossip long ago became the only truth we get. After the Nazis took over I had to write my newspaper columns in a kind of code.

Karin would have missed it.

For her, life is simply whatever she's decided it should be. When she decided she should be in the movies, it was simply a matter of showing up at the Berlin Film office on Unter den Linden and announcing that she was ready to be an actress. Just like in Hollywood. After the smirks subsided, the fearsome older woman in charge of the office looked at Karin like an appraiser inspecting a nugget someone had just brought in and unwrapped. And then told her to come back a day later to read from a movie script that had just been handed to her.

A day later, the smirks stopped.

Karin was an actress. It was that simple.

Which is why I am cycling through the smoke and destruction believing that mother was wrong all those years ago. It is Karin, not me who had a role thrust upon her, one she could not change.

And so I hurtle onward. But wondering: am I doing this out of love or fury? I have no idea.

All I know is that I must get to the movie studio.

Artillery shells are landing further to the west and when I stop by the riverbank I think God must be taunting us: Death is all around and yet this is what He surrounds us with? —delicate pink geraniums just budding into life? And clematis peeking above the ravages of winter? And tiny lilacs? Spring is here and for the first time in my life spring makes no sense. But then I am one of the lucky ones to think such a thing. Others before me have perished Millions of them who will never have that thought.

An old man is standing in front of me. Leathery face, a mustache that colonizes his upper lip; angry confused eyes. Standing on the riverbank holding a knife.

"What do you want?" I say. It sounds strange but that was all I could think of to say.

"I am here for my son," he says defiantly. "What do you want?"

"I am here for my sister."

"Why does your sister need you?"

"She's an actress. Over there." I point to the west. "Babelsberg."

"The movie studio?"

"Yes."

"Yes." He nods. "She definitely needs you." Then he walks into the delicate geraniums.

"You're trampling those little flowers,"

He looks at me as if I am mad. And when I look up, up to the tree on the hillside, I see that maybe I am mad. Little flowers? When a man hangs from a rope tied to the biggest branch of the tree. A young man. Dead, in civilian clothes dangling from the end of that rope strung around his neck. Tied to him is a piece of cardboard with a crudely scrawled piece of writing: *Coward! He refused to fight for Hitler and the Reich.*

"The bastards took him," he said. "Help me cut him down." When I don't understand, he turns to me angrily. "My son," he says with tears in his eyes.

The old man rows the little boat in silence with his back to me and my bicycle resting across the bow. He is ferrying me across the river. In front of him his dead son lies against the gunnels, his face angled up toward the sky. The stillness of the river as it runs into the small lake and the budding forests around it are broken by jagged artillery bursts in the nearing distance.

About halfway across the lake I hear him talking. At first I think he is talking to me. "Excuse me. I didn't hear what you said."

He doesn't hear me. "Oh Horst, Horst, Horst," he says his words pouring out: "Please, please forgive me. I am sorry. So sorry" His voice is rasping, breaking. "Forgive me."

In the middle of the little lake he is weeping.

He half turns toward me. "I am responsible for what happened to my son. My son! It was me, ten years ago. He was just a boy. I took him to see all those swine with their banners and parade and Nazi salutes. But really it was me—I was the swine. It was me who was thrilled by it all. It made me a man again. So what did I do? I made him want to be one of them. Until this February. Two months ago. When I told him not to die for what was already lost. To come home. I told him we could hide him.

"It was me who told him to throw his uniform away. What was there left to die for? So he came. As far as there. Where they caught him without his uniform."

He is pointing toward the shore we just left but his hand is shaking too much. "And now what have I done? I gave those bastards my son ten years ago and now they give him back to me like this." Something inside him buckles as he slumps, sobbing.

In the silence and stillness of the lake we drift.

And then we hear it.

At first it is like a distant insect buzzing, scraping against the sky. From the east it appears over the tree line, a single fat metallic bug bumping through the air.

"Russians," says the old man.

The fat bug sputters high above us, its engines tubercular and rasping. "The British only come at night," he says. I know this. We all know it. And have for two years, cowering in bomb shelters as the nights exploded around us. "And the Americans come in daytime. And in waves.; He must have been a teacher, like some I had who believed that dull pupils could only absorb their lessons by repetition. "Not single planes, So this is a Russian plane who is lost. Or in trouble."

The plane seems like it's swooping down right onto us. "He's checking us out." With a shuddering roar it skids through the sky right above us and then keeps going, soaring and turning until it again becomes a dot in the distance.

Then the dot turns. And becomes bigger. And bigger until it's not a dot any longer, it's back to being the fat bug. Which in turn becomes the plane, the Russian plane. "A Yak," the old man says.

"Yak?"

"The worst." They are the last words he has time to say before the bug stitches the water in front of us, jagged geysers erupting a meter or so into the air, one following so quickly after the other that I barely have time to put the rest of what happens into even a memory.

I do know that those little geysers race closer, too close, and so fast as they blow the old man into something bloody and jagged and he takes flight as rubble that lands in different places across the water. And all this must have happened in that particle of a second before the whistling bomb spiraled into the water sending this little lake, exploding as if something had punched the water so hard that it heaves. And sends my bicycle flying off the remnants of the little boat. The lake shudders and quakes, sending out rumbles that suck in my screams as the bug vanishes into the eastern sky from where it came.

I release my grip on the side of the little boat. There are no oars or paddles now. Except for a red stain on the water there is no sign of the old man. All I can do is drift on that tranquil lake, just me and the old man's dead son. After a while I swear he is looking at me. Which of course is ridiculous. I keep telling myself that. But it does no good.

2

BABELSBERG IS A HALF-CITY.

Buildings there are just movie-set facades propped up by scaffolds behind them. It seems to rise up out of the earth beyond the fields in the west like a mirage. But it's a different kind of mirage, one seen through the longing optics of dreams, always just beyond our reach. And filled with alluring, heroic and beautiful people we feel as if we know. And who would probably want to know us. Or so we tell ourself.

The eternal role of the movie star.

The UFA studios at Babelsberg have been our Hollywood, our magic place from where they came from, the famous movie stars, the people we wanted to be, the people knew we could be if only...if only.... The Marlene Dietrich's, the Emil Jannings and Zarah Leanders who took us away in *The Blue Angel, La Habanera* and all the other film fantasies shimmering out there just beyond all this death and war and the towering barriers between us and what we can remember of the lives we once led.

I see the UFA sign on the side of a distant building larger than most aircraft hangars. I recognize it as the sound stage which is sort of the castle at the center of the movie village. For years the studio was patrolled by the fearsome gatehouse guard Kruger, keeping the rest of the world from getting close to their idols. Several years ago I walked past Kruger into the studio on the day that Goebbels showed up in all his grisly grandeur amid a flotilla of Nazi limousines, jackboots and forced smiles.

But years ago there I was, walking almost side by side with this monster because my editors at *Vossiche Zeitung* wanted me to write in my gossip column about the Nazi takeover of the movie business.

That last trip to Babelsberg was over a decade ago. And it was a culturally historic moment: the Nazi as Hollywood mogul! Josef Goebbels, the rapacious Minister of Public Enlightenment and Propaganda was surrounded by anxious and puzzled movie people who were now totally under his control. And among those were the young actresses, from whom Goebbels would soon expect a different kind of performance.

As simply as can be expressed in polite company, Goebbels was a total pig.

And by the way, I have always wondered if he got to Karin. You know what I mean—got to her the way he did to so many girls like her. Basically ramming his thing into them until they couldn't walk straight. And god forbid they should ever complain.

That is probably why I have come all this way. Because for someone so decisive, Karin has almost always chosen the wrong places and people to trust.

Which is perhaps why I am here.

As far back as when Karin was twelve and I was almost twenty, I realized that it was because of the age difference that I might as well have been her aunt instead of her older sister. It was sometime during that year that I began to understand that I had truly become her protector. It is a terrible cloak to wear. It can smother the one who wears it. And also the one who comes close to it.

I really wasn't prepared for any of it.

But now, from the road UFA looks like a ghost town. There is none of the usual movie studio bustle. And Kruger no longer is standing at the guardhouse. It is shuttered and empty with barely even a gate protruding from it. But the stillness is deceptive; it is not as deserted as it first appears. Once you walk past the cloisters of the modern brick building and get around behind the big south studio, you come across the frantic scramble of a movie being filmed in urgently choreographed sequences.

In front of the façade of a plaster Bavarian castle are maybe a hundred people, mostly men, moving under piercing lights on tall poles as a big camera is being rolled backwards on a track, its lens pointing at a man and a woman who talk and then stop and kiss.

The woman being kissed is Karin.

From behind the camera another man, obviously the director, yells, "Cut! Let's do it again!" The director is a small bald man wearing a patched suit and a tie that has unraveled. He has intense, darting eyes and an aura of calm that cannot completely cover the tension that has thinned his voice.

Someone else yells "Fast! Fast! C'mon people! The planes are coming!"

Everyone hurries around, each in their own part of some spontaneous choreography. All of them but Karin. In the blur of sounds and reckless motion she is somehow not part of the rush. It is as she has always been ever since she was a girl, cheerfully apart from whatever urgency or even panic was overcoming others around her.

It's not that she is lagging behind—she moves as quickly as the actor who just kissed her, back to the marks on the ground beside the track. But he is obsessed with the sky, constantly looking up as if invisible strings are tugging at his fear of the planes that he is trying to conceal. Beside him Karin is the opposite. She's in her own world, gliding through thoughts of something that secretly pleases her.

The director hurries from behind the camera, talks to them both and then nods to another man who yells instructions to the others. But the actor can't stop looking up at the sky. "Goddamn it look at her!" yells the director. "You're not making love to the clouds!" The actor nods but looks like he's about to faint. "Action!" yells the director and it all starts again, Karin and the actor walking beside the long track on which the camera rolls. They only get a few meters when it happens—that little scraping sound in the sky. It is a faint noise of British bombers, a noise we all have come to know the way a herd picks up the scent of a predator that cannot yet be seen,

The actor's head swivels.

"No! No! No!" yells the director. He almost jumps up stamping his feet furiously. "Look at her!"

Instead, the actor now looks like someone is hitting him with a stick. He tries to look at Karin but that scraping sound gets louder. The director yells at him again. It does no good because the actor is shaking so much he can't hold his hands steady. "I'm not going to die for your stupid movie," he croaks.

Which enrages the director who turns and calls out: "Untersturmführer! Where is the Untersturmführer?" From behind the plaster façade of the imitation Bavarian castle a tall SS officer lurches forward unsteadily through a thicket of light poles. He is young and has what was once a handsome face but part of it is now missing. Beneath his thin blond hair the left side of his head is caved in and one eye is covered by a black patch.

The sleeve of the left arm of his uniform is empty and pinned to the side of his jacket.

"*Untersturmführer,*" says the director. "Please tell this actor how many men I am to give you to send to the front once filming this scene is finished."

"Five." says the young SS officer. "Heil Hitler!" But his wounds on his face and the scar tissue prevent him from forming an H so it comes out *Queile Kitler.*

The director turns to the actor. "Now do you understand? The SS are demanding we make a list of five men from this film to be sent into combat. And you talk about dying?—there you will definitely die!" he yells at the actor. "Because right now I'm putting your name on that list."

"Please. No."

"Then act!"

The actor is sinking into congealed panic that immobilizes him in his fear. But then Karin steps between him and the director. "A moment?" she says motioning with her hands like a traffic policeman. "Okay?"

The director nods impatiently. Karin puts her arm around the actor, walking him away from the camera. I know what she's doing. She has this power, a power that can pull others into her serenity. I've seen it since we were children. And ever since then, I've thought what a perverse gift it is not to see danger while being able to draw others into the comfort of that cocoon. Until of course, the real world vaporizes the cocoon.

The mists of her certainty and warmth settle invisibly around the actor who grows calmer and walks slowly beside her. He becomes not exactly serene, but calm enough to function like an actor is supposed to.

And not even noticing that the scraping sound has grown louder.

Karin nods to the director. In an instant everything starts again; the camera is turned on; marks are hit; the clapper is struck as sound is synched and *Action* is called. And the two movie lovers walk serenely through the thicket of movie illusions, whispering declarations of love.

But there's a problem: that scraping from above is suddenly very loud now. In an instant it becomes a roar, as if the sky's cover is peeled away. At ground level, what is a tapestry of a hundred or more people intently focused on specialized tasks unravels in seconds as everyone scatters. Lights topple, equipment carts are knocked over, the camera is abandoned, and the kiss does not happen. A bus and several trucks are quickly encrusted with clinging film crew while stragglers are running after them yelling for them to wait. But no one can hear anything in the howl of the air raid sirens and that roar from the clear, still sky.

A hand tugs at mine. It is Karin. Balancing two UFA bicycles, the bulky kind used for studio mail delivery. Nothing is said. Nothing has to be. It's as if we saw each other a day or two ago. She smiles, shrugs. And then we pedal as fast as we can, side by side out to the distant field where the rest of film crew and actors are lying in the trenches UFA has dug so that its people can protect themselves against blast waves.

Before we can even put the bicycles down, we are suddenly shoved into a trench by a man who hurls himself at us. It is the actor, who lands on top of us yelling something about planes. (This is when he chooses to be decisive?) Karin is beginning to sound offended when suddenly the air above our heads invisibly explodes in a battering ram of sound and shock waves that slam into anything they can find standing. Ripping, shredding everything in its path, it has a voice, a shriek that screams over our heads and vanishes into the distance. Leaving only an eerie alloy of silence and the sound of flames on something back from where we came.

I hear Karin say *Thank You...* to the actor... *for saving us.* Just from the way she says it I know what it means. She's about to be in love. For a day, maybe two.

Karin, Karin.

What is now known:

At that moment, just over thirty kilometers to the east, inside the Führerbunker under the wreckage of Berlin Adolf Hitler, in the last hours of his life is having what his closest military advisors believe is a nervous breakdown. It is almost May now and since the beginning of the year the Nazi officers have grown used to his rages and tirades. They are the furies of a man for whom delusion is being overwhelmed by reality as the news from the front grows worse.

In other words it is becoming obvious to Hitler that he must soon kill himself.

The Führerbunker is a huge underground complex of small rooms into which the Nazi high command has now retreated as the sound of Russian guns can be heard in the distance. Today the news is as grim as it was yester-day. Not far away, the Ninth Army with its 56th Panzer Corps is being anni-

hilated, the same German forces that were supposedly going to save Berlin from the Russians. And when Hitler is told, the spittle-flung wrath erupts in a man suddenly grown old, haggard, and oddly, for a man still with a rapidly fading power of life and death over others, pathetic.

The rages can be heard out in the hallway of the Führerbunker which confuses the six children playing there with the puppies that have just been born to Hitler's beloved German shepherd Blondi.

Soon all of them, the laughing children, the puppies and Blondi, will be put to death.

But for now there is just the laughter and tumbling of children and puppies amid the jackboots. The six of them, five girls and one boy, are the children of Magda and Josef Goebbels. They are, in a word, striking. Or, even beautiful in that way that the Reich wanted its German young to be: blonde, beaming and fine featured. Which is in contrast to their father, Josef Goebbels the feared Reich Minister of Public Enlightenment and Propaganda the misshapen, bulbous-eyed, lecher whose profile could have been created by Picasso with a face receding quickly from the nose toward both ends and stretched around a jagged slit of a mouth. And then of course there is his deformed right foot, called by the doctors a case of neurogenic clubfoot that had condemned him to a childhood of mockery and bitter solitude. And as an adult, a man of terrifying power, daring anyone to notice his deformity.

Unlike his laughing children, the Reich Minister is often seething. It is an almost genetic fury, so scalding, so deep and hate-filled that it can never be quenched by the deaths of the millions. The more deaths he orders, the more he needs to see death. But the children know none of this—not Helga the oldest who is twelve, nor Hilde, nor Helmut, nor Holde, nor Hedda, and especially not Heide who is only four. (How better to honor the Führer than to call all your children by names beginning with the letter H?) All they know is that they have just been brought here to the bunker from the serenity of their beautiful lakeside home in Schwanenwerder. There is neither daylight nor spring here in the vast bunker. There is nothing like the dappled light coming off the little lake or the flowers blooming near the marshes.

And "Uncle Führer" perplexes them now. Not only because of his rages that they hear through the door—so different from the chuckling way he has always talked to them, no it is how "Uncle Führer" looks. He is suddenly an old man with trembling hands and hair that has turned grey. He looks at them with eyes that sometimes see nothing and when the children ask their mother what has happened to "Uncle Führer", Magda Goebbels says merely that he is busy planning how to win the war.

When they ask why the awful noises from outside are getting louder, their mother tells them it is because the courageous German soldiers are outside protecting them all.

The planes have gone for now, their bombing run finished and there is this odd silence that seems to last too long. Even Karin senses that something is about to happen. She, who usually never pays attention to storm clouds on the horizon, shoots me an uneasy look.

And then, like waves breaking on rocks, comes the gasps as people see the Bavarian castle. It is in flames. Or what was pretending to be a Bavarian castle is in flames—eating away at the fake plaster stonework nailed onto a flimsy wooden frame. The fake plaster stonework burns faster than the wood behind it, leaving the impression that the castle is in its underwear. It burns away, taunting us in our helplessness, an entire movie crew and cast not knowing what to do but watch the fake castle at the center of the story they were filming burn to the ground courtesy of the American Air Force.

There is the rustling of people getting out of the trenches, a few stifled tears playing treble to the bass of grunting under the weight of bodies that have gotten too old for the kind of acrobatics that physical preservation demands now.

"Well, that's that," a voice says.

"There's nothing else to do," another voice says. It's the actor, using his vocal training to loft his voice above the murmurs. "This film cannot continue," he says. Several murmurs agree.

"*Yetttssshhhh!*" comes a hissing rattle that freezes everyone.

It is what would have been *Yes!* coming from a normal mouth, But it comes from the mangled young SS officer who lurches out of a cloud of dust. Because of his grotesque appearance I can only focus on one part of him, which leaves the rest of him like a moving picture that is mostly out of focus. I have concentrated on the good side of his face, the side that had not been hollowed out. "Over!" he rasps. He is having difficulty moving and stumbles on debris, grabbing an overturned wheelbarrow to steady himself. "*The film essss done. Finizzz.*" He coughs like something has come loose under his uniform which he clutches with the one hand he has left.

Everyone waits for him to finish coughing, frozen in varying degrees of comprehension of what is coming next.

"*Aaaaarrrrrggg!*" It is a sound like someone permanently clearing his throat. Finally he spits out something that lands close to me. It is a tooth. No one but me looks at it and for an instant the mangled young SS officer's one good eye fixes itself on me in fury, as if I alone can see his decrepit state and he hates me for it. If the last decade has taught us anything it is that they do not need an excuse to kill. The SS kills the way an engine runs; it is routine, expected, all just a part of the machinery.

I look away and the hatred veers off into the blue.

"*Because the film essss done, I will tell Auurrheeeeyennnberrr*—he means Oranienburg, the local SS headquarters—*that you harrrr all to bee sent to the frauunnt.*"—he means front, the front where old men and boys are being thrown into the final futile battle against the vast meat grinder that is the Russian army which is making steaming carcasses out of them all. Old men, boys—and now film crews.

Sobbing breaks loose amid muffled cries of panic from the crew members.

"*Untersturmführer,*" calls out the director.

"*Yesssss?*" That single eye sweeps past me again like a searchlight in search of a kill.

"I am the director here." Said quietly as a simple statement. But nothing is simple now; no one talks that way to the SS.

"*Director? Director? You! Are zuhh firpahgoa!*"—he means: first to go. To the front obviously. Joining the other men hopelessly unprepared for combat, dying in droves.

The director does not back down. Quietly, patiently, he talks to the mangled young SS officer as the rest of us watch hardly daring to breathe. "*Untersturmführer* please. I understand that you have sacrificed your youth, your beauty for the Fatherland and the glories of the Reich. But it is over. Lost."

This mangled young SS officer, once a fearsome figure, is now a flailing scarecrow lurching in all directions with the fires in the wreckage playing light off the cavities of his face, casting shadows where smooth flesh should be flowering.

"*Lost?*" Spit out like a poison. "*Du bist ein verräter! Ich werrrrrrrrr...*" He probably means I will have you shot; hanged, tortured and all the rest of it. The mind numbs and the memory of a film director who was recently executed for disobeying orders is a spectre hanging over everything.

The mangled young SS officer stares at whomever his wavering gaze can fix upon. It is a stare of pure fury, perhaps even hatred. The one good hand grips a metal pole for balance and the other hand no longer exists. In its place the folded and empty sleeve flaps, pinned up under all those medals. The sleeve then vibrates like a piano key making no sound. And then "*Queile Kitler! Queile Kitler! Queile Kitler!*"

Then he falls face forward. A blossoming red patch of blood staining the back of his otherwise immaculate uniform. The spreading stain is the only movement in that moment of stunned silence.

Someone says what seems like the obvious: "He's dead. He has to be."

But he's not. With crab-like movements he crawls a few feet, feels his back and says what sounds like, "Not again." He motions toward the studio medic, an older woman who looks like she's being asked to tend to a tarantula.

The director says quietly "Find the writer. Hurry! We need to rewrite this piece of shit."

There is an awkward silence, the kind where everyone wants someone else to say something first.

The writer of the movie script cannot be found so the director asks for anyone who can type. When an older man from the accounting department reluctantly raises his hand, a desk, chair and typewriter are brought out and set down on the rubble. He sits in the chair and waits as the director, the actor, the cameraman and a producer argue about how to keep the movie going when the movie-set Bavarian castle that was central to the story has just been bombed to fluttering shreds by the American air force.

The producer announces the problem can be solved by writing a line for the actor where he says The Saracens have invaded and burned the castle!

"There were no Saracens in Bavaria, you idiot," says the director.

"Do you want to do the movie or not?"

"I'm not putting Saracens in my movie. We'd be laughed out of the theater."

"There are no theaters left for anyone to be laughing at us. They've all been bombed to bits."

"Then what are we doing here?"

"Making a movie."

"If there's no theaters for a film to be shown who cares if the film has some Saracens?"

"Oh come on!" says the accountant.

The producer sinks onto a piece of a wall that had been destroyed. "A disaster. We're finished."

I blurt out something. I don't know where it comes from but I say it anyway: "Make it about madness." They turn to look at me wondering who I am. "Madness," I press on, "Make it about a woman who is going mad and sometimes the castle vanishes in her mind."

"Madness," Karin says as if awakening. "Of course. Brilliant!"

For now *Brilliant!* wins the day. Madness is what will be filmed. About an hour later, the film crew is setting up for a scene where Karin has to go into a state of delusion and imagine that the castle has vanished.

Minutes later the entire Babelsberg film crew is transfixed by what is being filmed. Karin is portraying a woman who suddenly sees the Bavarian castle vanish before her eyes, almost a definition of madness come to life.

But in the middle of her scene, the camera operator suddenly mutters a whispered curse, takes his eye away from the viewfinder and sits up above the still-rolling camera like one of those meercats in the Berlin Zoo. Something is barely visible in the background, something that should not be there. The director sees it too. He yells "Cut!" and is about to unleash his usual verbal barrage when he realizes it is the twisted young SS man scraping himself toward us again, his damaged legs and one remaining arm spidering toward us in tangled anarchy.

His caved-in face is covered with soot, smeared into a sweat stained collage of jagged contours. His black eye patch is missing and that hole where his eye once was is an abyss pulling in whatever light it once saw.

"Stop!" he shouts several times, lurching like his whole body was made up of rubber bands breaking one after another in quick succession.

Then something like *Zuh rieschnunsta shed ee wants cokady* came out of his mouth. No one knew what he was saying.

Zuh rieschnunsta shed ee wants a cokady he screamed again, furious in his mangled impotence. For a moment I could imagine the way he must have been before he was disfigured by whatever explosive force had rendered him physically hideous. I could see him as handsome, maybe charming but more likely fearsome and zealous, a warrior for the Reich imbued with the terrifying beauty that some of them possess.

Only the accountant understood *cakady*, "He means comedy. What he said was 'The Reichminister said he wants a comedy!'"

Comedy? The word lands in our midst like an unexploded bomb.

"I know what he said," the director snaps.

We all know. We have known since the defeat at Stalingrad over a year ago. The decree came almost secretly from Goebbels, from his Ministry of Public Enlightenment and Propaganda, ordering the movie studios, UFA, Tobis and the rest to make people laugh. Anything to take our minds off the obvious: that the war had become a disaster, not the glorious triumph they had been telling us about. If a film was not to be stirringly heroic then it was definitely to be light-hearted, or better yet, funny.

"Ah yes, comedy," says the director. Just how do you propose we continue with a comedy when the Americans blew our castle to bits?"

But suddenly none of it matters anymore.

Because from just over the little rise in the road leading to the sound stage, the barrel of a tank appears like a swollen arrow that could obliterate us all.

The director doesn't understand. He waves his arms in a sideways motion. "Get out of the shot!" he yells indignantly. The tank in the distance just snorts exhaust fumes and then settles like a dozy beast sunning itself.

"We are filming here! Clear the shot. Move!"

Doann. The loud whisper comes from the young SS man.

"He says 'Don't'" the accountant whispers.

"What does he know about filmmaking?" the director snaps. Then someone says what suddenly no one needs to be told: "Russians". In mid movement and word a contagion of fear freezes everyone.

The director takes a single step forward, squinting. "What? They're not our tanks?"

He barely gets the last word out before he is hurled backward by the force of the bullet that rips open his chest.

And this is when the circus begins.

Yes, a circus, the part where the clowns come running in all at once, falling all over one another. Even with the director lying dead in front of us, that is all I can think of because what is happening up there around the tank is an eerie clown show. Wildly dressed figures stumble and run in bizarre circles like overgrown children. They are Russian soldiers. Dozens of them, maybe more, who have torn the costume department to pieces.

Some are trying on women's wigs and gowns and one is wearing a brassiere over a cowboy outfit with others dressed as Napoleon or Caesar or the Kaiser, circling and falling from bicycles or running into each other.

No one understands what is happening until there is a shriek and a large woman bursts from the side door of the big sound stage, yelling at the clown show, barging in among them and tearing at Napoleon's coat. It is Frau Haller, the famous head of the UFA costume department. Even from a distance you can hear her yelling, "These clothes do not belong to you!"

Ee udd not do tat. The mangled young SS man is shaking.

"She should not do that," translates the accountant.

Ust ey ill com or me. Chorchor zuh essis iz zeh avoti schpor...Hen ey come for huh woam.

"First they will come for me. Torturing the SS is their favorite sport... Then they will come for the women."

More Russian soldiers tumble out of the studio doors. Many of them appear to be from the Asian republics of the Soviet Union. The Mongols and the Asiatic Hordes that Goebbels had been warning about for months in his radio broadcasts.

And here they are: The Hordes, The Ivans. The conquerors.

Some of them are now dressed as gladiators, others as ballerinas, Prussian kings and even one in a clown costume. Frau Haller is almost hysterical, pawing and tugging at the costumes. "I have created these! You are defiling the costumes!" she screams. "Stop! You are pigs!"

Caesar grows tired of it all and smacks Frau Haller with such force that she topples backwards. Then Caesar and the clown fall onto her ripping and tugging as she shrieks and slaps at them, trying to cover herself as her clothes are being torn off. From where we are, it looks like a feeding frenzy.

She is pulled by one arm, enormous in her mud-smeared, jiggling nakedness into the grass where the Kaiser takes down his pants and falls on top of her while Caesar and Napoleon laugh and wait their turn.

The young SS Untersturmführer is the only one of the men, the only one of any of us, who even moves. He walks out into the center of the little road.

U wan cokady?

"You want comedy?"

He forces his face into a rictus smile, stretching its remnants into a contortion that make the abyss of his eyehole turn from round to oval. He is holding something close to his chest, something he pulls apart with a barely audible click, heard between the shrieks of Frau Haller.

Ey ull ow ra allzuh woam

"They will now—." Before the accountant finishes translating, there is an explosion. It is from the grenade the young SS man held against his body. Its force knocks some of the film crew to the ground as pieces of him are sent flying in all directions, splattering through a fine red mist. What is left of him is only the lower half—two legs stand attached to nothing but held up by the stiff black boots that go almost to the knees.

For a moment, the remnants of two legs encased in gleaming jackboots stand like wavering columns in a wasteland, supporting nothing.

Behind them in the distance, the Kaiser gets up off of a moaning Frau Haller and hurries to join the circus coming toward us.

The two legs topple over.

The accountant staggers to his feet. "What he said before he blew himself up was, 'They will now rape all the women.'"

3

WHAT IS NOW KNOWN:

A few kilometers away it is almost time for it to happen. Only the oldest daughter, twelve-year-old Helga, has a sense that nothing is as they are being told. Those who have been close to the Goebbels family over the years have sensed that Helga long ago began to wonder about it all. She alone turned away from "Uncle Führer" when he came near. There is a seriousness about Helga that now veers to something between sadness and panic. She is asking her mother if they are going to die, a question to which Magda Goebbels always lets her daughter know how silly it is.

But Helga knows what her mother does not want any of them to know— that they are in terrible danger. What she cannot know is that she and her brother and her sisters will soon be murdered. And the murderer will be her own mother who is now soothing her fears.

But Helga's fears are based on more than she will ever understand. What she cannot know, only sense as she hears the terrible noises of the Soviet guns drawing closer is that two fierce Russian army commanders want her dead. There is nothing personal in it. It will merely be what is later to be called collateral damage of an ego-drenched contest between these two fierce men. Because right now, out there beyond where all that noise is coming from, Marshall Georgy Zhukov and Marshall Ivan Konev are in a vicious competition, each wanting to claim the glory of being the first Russian commander to get to Berlin. Neither man knows fear nor has any patience with it. Both are short, crude, brilliant and ruthless. Their troops are there to die by the thousands if needed. Blood and flesh are flung across the paths to Berlin as they each push on for glory. And no matter which one gets to the heart of Berlin first, the fate of Josef and Magda and their children, Helga, Hilde, Helmut, Holde, Hedda, and Heide has already been written,

Magda would agree. Fear is a wasted emotion now. After a bitter decade of glamor and humiliation as the wife of the priapic Josef Goebbels, she has erected walls within her mind to block out whatever she does not want to think about. It has become simpler for her in the past few weeks and days.

She has become a believer. In Buddhism.

Why, it makes everything so clear, so easy! These Buddhist principles that tell Magda the children are innocents; they have not been part of all this mass butchery. So if they were to die now they would be guaranteed rebirth, with their souls, their sweet, innocent souls intact in a new life. Why of course! In Buddhism, Magda is giving her children life, reborn into a new blessed life in a world none can yet know.

But of course first they have to die.

And this is what 12-year-old Helga senses. No one has told her but she knows in that way that a child knows when the words all around her are the same as she has heard before but none of them sound the same. Now when they come out of the mouths of the adults these same words are rushed, tense, stricken. So she asks her mother why they have to die, and why they can't leave—questions that will never penetrate those walls within Magda's mind. Again and again twelve-year-old Helga asks her mother and always the words are soothing but the sounds they make are not.

It is night and the children are all in their immaculate, white night clothes, all lying in one room of the bunker. Magda enters with a man they do not know. He is Dr. Kunz, Magda's dentist who informs the children that it is time for their vaccinations. Terrible diseases are out there he says. And everyone is getting vaccinations their mother adds. The words sound like falling metal to Helga.

The injection Dr. Kunz gives each of them is not a vaccine; it is morphine which soon renders the children unconscious.

But then Dr. Kunz will go no further; even in the midst of slaughter, he has a fit of moral obstinacy; he refuses to help Magda murder these six, beautiful children. They are sleeping as you wanted. Leave them. But Magda will not leave them. How else can they be reborn in their Buddhist purity? They must die. So she hurries into the newer part of the Führerbunker to find Hitler's physician, Dr. Ludwig Stumpfegger who returns to the children's room with Magda and helps her crush the cyanide tablets and then pour the poison powder into each comatose child.

At least, that is one of the versions.

Another version of how the Goebbels' children were murdered has them dying of whatever Dr. Kunz injected them with.

Still another version has Magda finding a complete stranger, a doctor who had taken shelter from the bombardment in the Führerbunker, and enlisting him to help her kill the children.

But for what happened after the murder of her children there is only one version: Magda comes down the stairs from the children's room crying. She sits at a table, playing solitaire and saying nothing. Josef Goebbels joins her at the table. The Russian artillery outside provides the only sound. At 9 p.m., they get up and calmly walk up steps leading to an exit. Outside in the cool night, cans of gasoline have been readied for the burning of their bodies. They stand silently. Magda bites down on a cyanide capsule and collapses. Then with the pistol he has had ready, Goebbels fires a bullet into his head.

One of the two officers who had been ordered to be present follows another order and fires a bullet into each body to make sure they are dead. And then the two officers begin soaking the bodies of Magda and Josef Goebbels with gasoline.

But it does not end there.

The next morning, Marshall Georgy Zhukov is triumphant. His troops have snuffed out the last of the German defenses in Berlin. A few of his soldiers discover the entrance to the Führerbunker and force their way inside. It is eerie, silent in there. They enter a room and find six beautiful children, sleeping, serene. Or so it appears. They are all in immaculate white dressing gowns and the five girls have white bows in their hair. They look peaceful, most of them.

But one of them does not look peaceful at all. The oldest girl has terrible bruises on her face as if she had struggled, as if force had been used to get the terrible white powder into her mouth.

Helga knew.

You learn that chaos can save you.

It is the lesson you do not want to learn. But there are times you have no choice. Survival is mostly luck but sometimes it is also the blessing bestowed by chaos. Chaos is fickle. It can immobilize warriors yet fill clerks with cunning.

And that second wave of the American bombers, those shiny birds of death spewing out their bombs, created the kind of chaos I have learned to cherish whenever I knew I was close to death. Watching the Russian soldiers racing across the movie studio picking out women to rape, death was strewn around like so much human rubble.

The bombs fell in places that made no sense. But then almost nothing in this war has really made any sense. They fell just beyond the tattered movie sets, the grand facades that exploded in spectacular funnels of flame that instantly evaporated whatever lust was driving the Russians, sending them racing back, some with their pants still down around their knees, stubby little men suddenly rendered ridiculous.

We fled.

Bicycling into the leafy strangeness of the Grunewald, the forest that years ago had a suburb implanted into it. A nature reserve for the affluent, the comfortable, who in better days before the war were resplendent in all their usual obliviousness. War? No one would dare fight us. Don't be silly.

The American and British bombing has spared large areas of the Grunewald but still the roads are mostly empty. We pass coniferous trees towering over houses that once promised design, reason and civilization. And none of it prevailed. We cycle past houses I remember. Houses inhabited by the good, the solid, the sensible who assured me that all would be well. Because: Hitler has assured us.

But I don't think about that now, frantically bicycling up this leafy hillside street and flapping through the Grunewald, wondering if I am smothering the bicycle seat, making it disappear and hoping no one else sees me from behind. And how can I be thinking of such things in the midst of all this? Good god. Vanity still has its place even now—now of all times!

Karin is unusually quiet as she pedals. It is the silence that overcomes her whenever events wipe out what had been her certainties about how the world should work. For all her emotional flamboyance, she has always been certain the world is a rational place. A place where movie people are left alone by smiling Russian soldiers. When the world does not work as she had been certain it would, the silences arrive as she tries to make it rational again. The silences never last. She always finds a way to make her world work the way she just knows it will.

Further to the west on a hillside street we come across a woman, tall, with silver-blonde hair swept back behind her in an elegant roll.

Ah yes... Frau...? Meier? Möller? I don't remember the name. But I remember the gown she wore that night. How could I not forget the gown? At the elegant Italian embassy reception where I wrote that Frau whatever-her name-was *was dressed in a sweeping Chanel creation that was much admired by the ambassador Count Ciano who—*

Which of course was that code. Always code! My entire gossip column in those last years existed in code! Writing the truth would get you killed.

And so what did all this *sweeping Chanel creation…much admired by the ambassador…* etc.…mean? Simply that amid all the diplomatic propriety and formality this elegant silver-blonde Berlin matron was being eyed by Count Ciano the sex-crazed Italian ambassador as the one he would honor later that night with a royally diplomatic fuck (when all the tedious guests had departed of course). While meanwhile Count Ciano's wife, who just happened to be Mussolini's daughter was selecting which Nazi jack booted personification of her erotic fantasies was going to drill her to the bedposts while her husband was in some other room lunging into what lay beneath that Chanel creation.

Sex. And variations of sex not spoken of in proper places. Really. People don't understand that it was all about sex. Or the lack of it. That was it—all of what happened. Sex was inversely tied in to the slaughter our people unleashed. Oh don't get me started.

But the language. Ah yes, the language. Please excuse me. We never used to talk like that. Fuck, fuck, fuck. This gutter language. We do now. After all this, what could possibly have the power to shock? Words? But words got us into all this. I hold words responsible too. They got us into all this but they were never strong enough to get us out of it.

We see this Frau whatever-her-name-is by the side of the road ahead. But she is no longer elegant. No longer lithe, merely emaciated. And no longer wearing that sweeping Chanel creation. Or anything else except what looks like the remnants of a man's dressing gown, torn and smeared in blood. Actually it's her who's smeared in more blood than what she wears. Up to her elbows. And streaked across her face like war paint of the tribe of the vanquished, the starving, the mad. Where once her eyes would glide serenely across the salon now she snaps out a mad stare like tracer bullets as she shrieks into leafy stillness.

I am thankful that Karin has seen none of this. Even before Frau whatever-her-name-is had appeared, Karin was more interested in whatever was happening in the nearby woods. A deer had raced through the underbrush, followed quickly by a second one, just as startled. Karin put down her bicycle and hurried into the woods. An animal in distress could always be counted on to draw Karin to it, certain that she could solve whatever the problem was.

In the road near her house an emaciated horse has died in its traces, collapsing and turning over the cart it was pulling while its owner, a ragged little man in a sailor hat screamed curses at it. And then turning his shouting at Frau-whatever-her name-was as she bustled, huffing and hysterical out of her house flashing a large kitchen knife like a weapon of war.

"Stay away from my horse!"

"Your horse is dead!"

"Frau, he is my horse!"

"He's not a horse."

"He is so a horse!"

"Not any more! Now he's food! Do you understand? Food!"

As the little man keeps yelling and jumping up and down in the road Frau-whatever-her name-is is already slicing off a slab of the horse's flank, the blood pulsing across her. The little man is running after his possessions that had scattered when the cart overturned.

But his yelling is already attracting another scavenger, and him I also knew.

Oh did I know him.

More precisely, I knew what this new scavenger used to be. In a word: terrifying. It is Sturmbannführer Geisler. Or what is left of him. A fleshy man with a rubbery face that could be read on a scale from blank to chilling. At his worst, at his most lethal, he was a case of mediocrity boiled down to a vengeful husk. In any other world, one without all this murderous strutting and pageantry Willi as he was once known, poor bumbling Willi Geisler, would have been lucky to be a clerk. Or maybe a perfectly fine plumber or a ditch digger. But here in these past dozen years with his gleaming boots, his black Nazi uniform with its deaths-head insignia, Sturmbannführer Geisler shone with the sleek savagery of the SS. Feared by the prisoners in the camp at Oranienburg just to the north of here. On his random inspections none dared lock eyes with him lest those watery eyes congealed into the terror of the SS. To do so could be a beating if you were lucky. And if not, if Sturmbannführer Geisler was having a bad day: maybe the terrible dogs. Or a bullet. Or hanging or the ovens or whatever else was being done that day.

But now? Now, strangely Sturmbannführer Willi is naked without all that leather and gleaming metal, all the belts and medals and runes and boots. He is just a bumbling and ordinary man. A tremulous clerk hurrying down from his family's house in the woods, flabby mounds of him swaying like pudding, rolling in different directions under the straining cloth of a shirt from another life. No longer are there the gleaming jackboots and all that. Not now. Not when there are all these stories of what happens to any SS man captured by the Ivans. No, now there can be no jackboots, no deaths-head. Only the billowing softness of an ordinary man.

As he too stumbles toward the dead horse with his knife.

There is something almost primordial about it, like wild beasts snarling around the carcass of their prey. Mere months ago Sturmbannführer Geisler would have been the largest jackal at the carcass. But now he is just Willi. Whining, indignant pouty Willi as he is pushed aside in all this bloodiness. Willi is no match for Frau-whatever-her name-is who, those same months ago would have trembled before his cinched and belted savagery.

You see, the men are having the most difficulty with what has happened. Where once they were fortified by all that pageantry, all the gleam and banners, now they are naked just like Willi. All his power is gone and he is no longer sure who or what he is. He cannot even handle this shrill former sweeping Chanel creation woman whose mad cries and slashing blade has already carved off the choicest cuts of the dead horse.

Willi can only wait, jabbering and whining like the weakest jackal waiting for his turn. Which comes when the woman staggers off toward her home, slabs of raw horsemeat on either shoulder, leaving their bloody trails behind them. But Willi, poor Willi the former Sturmbannführer Geisler is made even more ridiculous by a low rumble that sounds just as he is heaving mightily at the carcass, trying to turn this dead horse over to get at the other flank.

The rumble grows louder. So loud that in the midst of his grunting, gasping attempts to turn the dead horse over he stops. Willi listens. Looks puzzled. And sees nothing but a moment of the damp green stillness of a coniferous spring in the last days of a hideous war.

Which is when the Russian tank appears.

In a roar and a cloud of smoke it announces itself on the distant forest road and then, framed in the dead horse's legs, sits there rumbling and shuddering on the hillside. It is a beast all its own, a dirty brown monster with a turret that swivels, stops, and then swivels again as if it is looking for something. There are no insignias, no pageantry flowing from it. No leather, no death heads, no gleaming. It is a pure, dirty, functional object of workmanlike brutality. The only connection to any shred of humanity is a huge number: **60** in white paint on the side of the turret.

Willi whimpers in its sight. He lets go of the horse's legs, backing up and now that Russian tanks have just breached the boundaries of Berlin, trying to make himself the opposite of what he made himself at Oranienburg. As the Reich is in its final death throes, crumbling under the tracks of monsters like this.

Gelatinous Willi scuttles back into the shrubbery and vanishes as if he never existed. The tank rolls closer, down the hill with others of its kind following, an undulating line of unthinking monsters coming straight toward me and the ragged little man with what's left of his dead horse.

I do not even have time to search for Karin. My first impulse is to run. It is a justifiable reaction. But foolish. One exploding huff from that massive barrel sticking out of the turret and I would be nothing but a fine spray, vaporized by the kind of shell that could obliterate a house. I stand there and for some reason it doesn't immediately occur to me to remember that I have stopped my bicycle in the middle of the road. Right in the path of all this thundering steel.

I've never been any good at this bluster kind of thing. So now it's me, armed with what?—indignation? Staring down a few thousand kilos of Russian fury roaring straight at me. So I do what any sensible person would under these circumstances: I prepare to die. It may sound silly but I don't know what else to do.

Me and my bicycle, the last defense against the ravenous armaments hurtling toward me.

I am nothing before it. I await my Judgment.

But **60** stops—actually it shudders to a skidding halt. Filling all I can see with the clanking menace of steel and iron. Snorting fumes and noisy rage.

A noise sounds from above. A clanking noise of the hatch opening on the turret. A skinny little head pokes up from the steel monster. Wide eyes and looking more scared than I am. A funny looking little Slavic face.

Narrow and with a large nose. He blurts out something I do not understand.

I shake my head. He looks confused and then:

"We are lost," he says in perfect German. He is young, oddly naïve for someone controlling such a beast.

"So are we," I say.

"Where is Berlin?"

"There," I say pointing behind me.

"Thank you," he says.

"How do you speak German?" I ask.

"My parents."

And then an awkward moment as I stay in the middle of the road.

"Please move," he says.

"No."

"Please."

"Are you going to hurt us?"

"Yes," he says. "If you don't move I will have to kill you. I'm sorry." And he seems to mean it. "Behind me," he says. Behind him, in a tank that had 104 painted on its turret, another face comes up, this one older, stern and jagged as if chiseled out of anger. "He is my superior." The little Slav waves an *okay* sign to the man behind.

"Why isn't he in front of you then?"

"Because the lead tanks always gets hit. They put peasants like me in it. So I can be killed instead of him."

"I hope you don't get killed,"

I move my bicycle to the side of the road. I am starting to like this Ivan. He looked so distraught over maybe having had to kill me.

"Where are you going?" he asks.

"Over there," I say pointing toward the west. "To Berlin."

"Don't. There are troops behind us. Our troops," he says pointing in the direction of Babelsberg. "Heading to Berlin too. But they are not nice like us. Not at all. You do not want to be near them"

I do not want him to know Karin is now watching from the bushes. "I have to go there to protect my sister," is all I can think of to say.

"Is she pretty?"

"Why?"

"Because if she is, it will be bad," he says. "Very bad."

TWO

4

Sixteen years earlier

FOR A LONG TIME I have wanted to talk about gossip.

Or perhaps more accurately, the raw power of gossip. When I was hired at *Vosstiche Zeitung*, I was indignant when I was told I would be a junior gossip columnist. *This* is what I had studied so hard for? *This* is what I took all those history courses for? To end up reporting on old ladies at tea parties? Of the eight newly hired reporters I was the only female and the others could not understand my irritation.

Did I think a woman was going to be given "normal" reporting assignments? And did I not understand how fortunate I was even to have gotten one of the rare female positions?

Yes I did and No I did not.

Which was exactly what I told myself I would convey in forceful terms to the editor who had been assigned to be my boss. So I marched through that buzz of activity in the huge newsroom where hundreds of men always seemed to be in controlled panic to put out the next day's edition. I rehearsed exactly what I was going to say. But by the time I was approaching the closed office door of Herr Langen the editor who I had never met, I was wondering if my timing might be a little off.

I no longer wondered the instant I opened his door after knocking.

"*What?*" he snapped even before I had fully opened the door. It was a word shot out like musket-fire from somewhere under a green visor he wore as he kept marking up an article with a slashing red pencil. It looked like the paper was bleeding from all the red slashes.

All I could see of him was the top of his head, his dark, closely cropped hair encircled by that green visor. I wished I could close the door and creep out backwards.

Another musket shot: "*What?*"

"I would like to talk to you," I said trying to steady my voice.

"That much is obvious," his words clattering out at me.

The visor lifted. I found myself staring into a chiseled face, almost as if Herr Langen had been lifted from one of those Roman statues in the Pergamon museum. It was a face that was holding firm against the arrival of features from an older self. And when the shadows of the green visor had lifted even more, I found myself immobilized by startlingly blue eyes blazing impatience.

"Why are you here?"

"I'm the new gossip columnist."

"And?"

"And I don't really like gossip."

That imperious face softened into what I thought was bemusement. "You don't like gossip?"

"No sir."

"Good. Neither do I."

I was confused. "I thought I might cover politics or—"

"We don't care what you thought," he said. "And here's what is going to happen: You are going to grow to love gossip. Do you understand me?

"No."

He almost smiled. "Ah. I see. Well let me suggest that you find something in it that you can love. Otherwise go to work in a store selling dresses. Do you understand?"

I was too intimidated to say anything.

"Find something in gossip that will rise above anything that has ever been done before. Now do you understand?"

"I think so," I said untruthfully.

"Good. Because if you can't, we'll probably have to fire you." He went back to the pages in front of him, the visor tilting down as the blue eyes vanished under it. "Now then: I'm busy. Please leave."

I returned to the newsroom unsure of what to do until I saw several of the young men who had been hired with me. They had been watching my uncertain foray into the intimidating terrain of the editors' offices. Some of them were smirking, and one of them said "So! Did he offer you the job of political reporter?"

"Yes," I said as grandly as I could. "And I turned it down."

"Oh really?" Said through a barrage of smirks.

"Why would I want a demotion?" I said sweeping past them to my desk in the midst of a sea of other desks, piles of paper, clattering machines and people hurrying because that was what people here did.

Two of the young men followed me, determined to make me understand that being the gossip columnist was the lowest rung of the journalistic ladder. I turned around and confronted them. "You obviously have no understanding of the power of gossip," I said hoping I sounded as if I believed what I was saying.

"The power of gossip?" one of them said, laughing.

I turned on a pfennig so quickly they almost ran into me. I shoved a finger under the nose of my lead attacker. "You! And your type! You could have prevented the war if you'd paid attention to gossip."

That stopped them in their tracks. "What?"

"While you fools are writing about politics, you'd do more good writing about who's seducing who. And who couldn't seduce who. And who was jealous of who. And who was still an involuntary virgin. *That* is the real politics!"

"Don't you think that's a little rich?" came the reply said with wilting conviction.

"No! I do not. If you political types had been reporting on Kaiser Willi's desperate and unrequited need to be loved by his grandmother, the British Queen, you might have stopped him taking Germany to war against Britain! But what do you ponderous political types do? You report on treaties and conferences. And you miss it all! Do you not understand? Gossip is the real news!"

I turned and stormed off. Hoping no one saw me smiling.

Because suddenly I loved gossip.

I couldn't wait to be the gossip columnist.

In those days, walking into that newsroom which seemed to go on forever, I had no idea that the law of inverse scarcity was at work. In other words I never truly appreciated what I saw every day—and had quickly taken for granted. The House of Ullstein was one of the world's great news operations. Even the Americans with their TIME and LIFE, or the British with their big newspaper chains could not compete with the vast power and influence of the Ullstein empire. From the elegance of the doormen's uniforms to the noisy vacuum tubes sucking containers of rolled up articles out of reporters' hands and blasting them to editors a football field away, everything about the House of Ullstein was unique.

In Berlin alone it put out two daily editions of *Vossiche Zeitung*, one mid-day *BZ* newspaper; the mammoth *Morgenpost* newspaper, and the feisty *Tempo*.

And on top of that it churned out more weekly magazines than anyone I knew could keep track of. So it was easy to feel anonymous in that onrush of people with deadlines. Everything about the newsroom induced a level of raw excitement. At first it almost overwhelmed me. But then I calmed down, ignored all the chatter around me, and simply went about doing what I was hired to do.

And over the months that followed, something strange, maybe even unique happened:

People began paying attention to my gossip column.

In the *Vossiche Zeitung's* darkened newsroom on the night of the Peruvian legation reception, Herr Langen my editor was quietly furious when he looked at what I'd turned in. I had to sit mutely in his office, listening to him curse as he slashed his red pencil across whole sections of what I had written.

Tonight was one of those nights when Herr Langen must have felt under pressure, because a cigarette hung precariously from the side of his mouth, barely visible under the green eye visor that collected smoke. "*Fat SA thugs?*" he blurted at me. "You can't say that."

"Well they were."

"Yes, of course they were." Accompanied by another slash of the red pencil accompanied by scrawls from his pen. Herr Langen looked up through the green-visored miasma of cigarette smoke. More red slashes and scrawls. Then he handed the page back to me. What was left was about ten lines—*a splendid night of Latin hors d'oevres... and...with fine Andean wine flowing...and...with witty antipodean conversation...*

"None of this is what I wrote."

"Exactly."

"But it's not even what happened."

"How old are you?"

"Twenty two."

"Of course. Are you a communist?"

"No."

"A Nazi?"

"*No*! Why are you asking me these questions?"

"To see if you have any idea of what is going on. And you don't."

At which point I did the only thing that seemed natural. I threw down the sheet of paper and willed myself to stay calm. He rubbed his eyes like he'd seen it all a hundred times before and just had to wait it out.

"I'm sorry." I was embarrassed over being so emotional.

"Do you know who owns this newspaper?"

"The Ullsteins."

"That is not the answer the Nazis—your *fat thugs* would give."

"I don't understand."

"Jews. That is the answer your *fat thugs* would give. They are just looking for an excuse to attack. To drive out the Ullsteins. And the rest of us. So anytime those drunken barbarians appear in your column they now will be *exuberant authority figures*. Do you understand? Jews own this newspaper! And so you are never to write anything that will give those men an excuse to close us down. Is that clear?"

5

A FEW MONTHS AFTER I had begun my job as a trainee at *Vossiche Zeitung,* our father returned home from the bank at the usual time. He had always been sort of invisible. Before, if you were walking along a busy street, father was the person you would miss. He was one of the grey, invisible men who worked in offices where they had no power.

But now nothing about father was invisible.

From across the street we barely recognized him. He moved differently, more like someone who knew exactly where he was going. And was sure he would get there. But it wasn't just the difference in the way he walked.

But the most obvious difference was what he was wearing. The grey suit was gone. Instead he was wearing dark pants with a brown suit coat that had two large pockets at his hips and two smaller breast pockets, all of them with buttoned flaps. Around his waist was a brown leather belt. On his head was a brown military hat, the kind with a shiny black visor. But all that was a blur compared to what I could not take my eyes off: Around the left sleeve of his coat was a red armband.

In the center of the armband was a white circle and in that circle was a black swastika.

"Wow," said Karin. "Father's wearing a Nazi uniform. Mother's going to have an absolute fit."

That evening I had to accompany one of the more experienced reporters who watched over me as I covered a reception at the Panamanian legation. As the junior society columnist, I was sort of apprenticing at the parties of the minor countries where none of the real luminaries of the Berlin diplomatic world showed up. But tonight something unusual happened. Several Nazi thugs arrived, pushing their way past the liveried servants and headed straight for the champagne tray which they emptied in minutes. One of the Peruvian legation officials muttered to me that the shorter of the two invaders had been a local plumber who had been fired six months earlier.

No one dared stop them because they were dressed in the ominously brown uniforms of the SA, their bulging forms camouflaged behind billowing brown shirts strapped down by diagonal and horizontal leather belts that held britches in place. But none of that mattered to me, not the belts nor the jackboots, nor the boorish bullying—none of that.

All I saw was what was on the left sleeve of these Nazis—a red armband. In the center of the armband was a white circle and in that circle was a swastika.

Just like father's.

I got home late that night. Even before I opened the front door I could hear Karin yelling.

Father was sitting in a pool of light at the end of the long dining room table. Immaculate in his new uniform and as still as a statue, only his eyes moved following me until words broke out: "Sit. Please." I did. And then endured one of his silences that seemed to go on forever.

"How was your evening?" he said working hard to sound interested.

"Fine," I said allowing him to escape the obligation of feigning interest,

"Good," he said.

"What is this uniform you've been wearing?"

"I am a *Haupstellenleiter*."

"What is that?"

"I am in charge of the local office of the party."

"The Nazi party."

He didn't answer, looking straight at me, with just the side of his forehead twitching in tiny spasms.

"I just wrote a column for my newspaper. Describing the Nazis I met tonight. The word I wanted to use to describe them was *thugs*."

"What has got to do with me?"

"They are Nazis. You are...."

"I deal in paper. And gold. That is my job."

"What about the bank?"

"The bank and the party are joining together."

"Sometimes on my way to work now, I see people getting beaten up on the street."

"These are emotional times we live in."

"But you are joining them."

"You might infer that. And as such, those who do not show respect can expect to pay a price. Do you understand?"

I didn't understand at all.

"Respect," he said again.

6

WHAT IS NOW KNOWN:

In the 1920s and on into the early 1930s, Berlin had become a sexual circus. Nothing like it had occurred in modern human history. A few years after World War I what had been condemned as filth and debauchery was suddenly celebrated as entertainment. And what had once been perversion now became artistry, all of it gaining centrifugal social force until Berlin joyously proclaimed itself to be "Sodom on the Spree." With the old Prussian restraints no longer able to hold back the collective libido of a society that pronounced itself freed from shackles of sexual restraint. What started as a kind of emancipation quickly became a frenzied orgy that swept through Berlin.

By the mid 1920s it was almost impossible to find a sexual act that was worth declaring illegal. Or even shameful. Or that should not be performed onstage in front of thrill-seeking audiences, many of whom would soon be imitating whatever sexual acts they had just paid to see.

Mere prostitution became as prevalent and variegated as wine with its own appellations and vintages—The Half-Silks being the office girls who sold sex after work for extra money; the Nuttes being the teenage girls who did everything they could to look like boys in order to please the pedophiles; and the Munzis and the Boot-whores and the Grasshoppers; the Minettes and the...

The categories went on and on in sexual metastasis until they ate through the outer limits of imagination, leaving only whatever abyss had already tormented those who were staring into it.

And these were just for the women, the tens of thousands of women whose numbers grew every year. And then there were those who were neither adult not female: the boys, the girls, the men and those in between, all selling what they had to offer in a city that had become a sexual bazaar with parents selling daughters; mothers enlisting teenage daughters to sell themselves as a team; and boys earning pocket money by finding men in clubs across the city.

It was the clubs, the cabarets, the lachnotals and the rough bars that brought sexual tourists from around the world. Lesbian, homosexual, transvestite or simply old-fashioned male-female, the names of the clubs still evoke the era: Café Dorian Gray; Kakadu Bar; Adonis lounge; Noster's Cottage, and the others spread all across the city drawing in everyone from movie stars to English poets. Some clubs became the settings for movies about the era. While others became simply legendary.

Like the most famous club of them all, The Eldorado, the transvestite club that became so successful its owner had to open a second location.

It was famous in so many ways—for Marlene Dietrich's frequent visits; for the club's motto hanging above the front door ('Here it is right!'); or just for the supremely gorgeous women who were not women when they removed their flamboyant costumes.

But the real significance of The Eldorado was only recognized when the Nazis came to power and everything came to a quick, jarring end. It was The Eldorado, more than any of the other sex clubs, for which the Nazi's reserved their most vehemently hostile yet conflicted treatment,

It was closed within weeks of Hitler taking power and soon after, any trace of its existence was obliterated as its exterior was covered by Nazi banners and signs befitting its new role as local headquarters of the SA, the brownshirt Storm Troopers.

Many wondered if it was because so many employees and patrons of The Eldorado were also SA Storm Troopers in their other life.

The *Ursel IV* was not a huge boat, only about as long as the average house, but when docked, it revealed the elegance of its teak paneling, gleaming brass fittings and a small chandelier in the main enclosed section below deck.

Most of it was now strewn with broken champagne glasses and torn pieces of women's underwear draped on what looked like a low altar held up at each end by sculptures shaped like penises.

A large painting of Hindu pornography lay in a corner and scattered around it were several discarded turbans. Only the white life preservers revealed a clue to what had happened; on them was written *HANUSSEN*.

When I got close to the boat a caretaker, an old man with an eye patch under pure white hair, sat on an overturned pail holding a mop and smoking a curved pipe.

"This time? Disgusting! Far worse than usual," he said without ever looking at me. He was talking as if I was someone he knew.

"What was?"

At first he didn't answer. "We are in trouble," he said.

"Who is?"

"All of us." He puffed on his pipe. "On this boat I clean up what can be cleaned, what you can see. But what you cannot see is the depraved filth that can never be cleaned."

"And that is your job?"

"Yes. After seeing what I have seen on this perverted man's boat I am considering becoming a communist. This job offends decency."

"Why do you do it then?"

"If you have to ask that question you would not understand the answer." The answer was more obvious than he thought; his clothes were patched and one sleeve of his shirt was frayed at the cuff.

A low faint noise came from the boat. At first I thought it was just the groaning noise that wooden planks sometimes make around water. But looking closer into that room inside the boat I saw that a young, dark-haired woman had rolled into view on the floor. She was naked.

"I've been waiting," he said. "Until she is decent. Please, can you get this naked whore dressed so I can do my work."

Her name was either Inga or Ingrid, it changed back and forth as I looked for something for her to wear and she decided she was probably Inga. For several minutes after she first rolled into view she could not even stand up.

As I found what was left of her clothes something caught my attention. "Is this blood?" There were red flecks spattered like tracks across the teak.

"They whipped him," she mumbled. "*He* did, *He* whipped him." she corrected herself. "Helldorff." Then she passed out again, dark haired, lithe nearly naked and unconscious amid the broken bottles. I found men's trousers and shirt that I put on her so the old man with the eye patch could start cleaning up.

"One eye and it has to see twice the filth," he muttered.

"I need to talk to you about this filth."

"Are you a plumber? Peering into other people's excrement?"

I write for *Vossiche Zeitung*,"

It was as if something had jolted him into a more intense level of awareness. "I have nothing to say," he snapped.

"But—"

"Do you not understand? Nothing! I saw nothing."

Which was when I realized that the girl on the floor had fluttered back into consciousness. "Fuck you grandpa. We watched you last night. Out there in the shadows past the dock wanking yourself off while you were watching the orgasm girl."

At the age of nineteen Karin had become the orgasm girl.

Inga's florid description spared nothing about the night before. And embellished everything. It had got started when the *Ursel IV* returned to the dock in the mid afternoon, a boatload of partially clad men, women and a few teenage boys. All of who had been served champagne and various drugs no one had ever heard of, by young Indian waiters dressed exactly as Hanussen had ordered, in only turbans and white pantaloons.

The boat's captain had been ordered to scan the coast with binoculars, looking for a big Mercedes, one probably flying the Nazi flags from its stanchions. "Nazis starboard," came the cry that was met with cheers. The *Ursel IV* immediately changed course, heading toward the dock.

On the dock Count Wolf Heinrich von Helldorff was waiting impatiently, his big chauffeur-driven Mercedes looming behind him like some mobile fortress.

Helldorff had the kind of face that is seen differently by different people: young-exhausted; or handsome-devious; or charming-distracted.

Or simply, brutal.

To me it was the face of a weak king.

With fading blonde hair combed back and parted in the middle, he projected a gaze that never landed on someone long enough to leave a mark of either emotion or conviction. Even when smiling he conveyed a weightless joy that vanished into the air leaving emptiness in his wake. But what gave him presence in whatever room he entered, was a subdued air of superiority that attracted both men and women in different ways. Often he seemed to have a more important conversation going on in his head which, in the insecure, would create a perverse gratitude for having been granted time in his presence.

Rising quickly through the ranks of the SA, Helldorff had begun attending the embassy parties I wrote about. I had seen him at several of the recent French and Italian receptions and the difference between him and the other SA men fascinated me. Where they exuded brutality, Helldorff masked it. He glided rather than marched, the residue of a patrician child grown into a man not completely free of a spoiled and willful past.

Nor was he free of the rumours that trailed him like invisible tendrils. Slanderous whispers of a previous life, a wreckage of failed businesses and debt back in the Prussian countryside near Leipzig. These had been given weight by allegations in Berlin of unpaid bills to tailors, Mercedes Benz and the trainers of his racehorses.

But even the gamblers he owed money to—normally ruthless in their collection methods, approached him cautiously.

Count Helldorff and his selective approach to financial obligations were not to be confronted casually. Not when, he was becoming, with Goebbels, one of the two most powerful Nazis in Berlin. And not when it was somewhere between rumour and fact that Helldorff would be appointed the Chief of Police when the Nazis took power. As everyone could tell he would. In the same way they could tell when a storm would arrive by watching it roll in across the countryside.

On the *Ursel IV,* Hanussen had put on one of the turbans and climbed to the bow, waving like a schoolboy to the imperious figure on the dock. Even as the *Ursel IV* was racing toward the dock under full power, urged on by Hanussen, Helldorff had the look of someone irritated because it was all taking so long. He stood in front of his Mercedes, wearing riding boots polished to such a sheen that the late afternoon sun reflected off them.

In so many ways Hanussen was the opposite of Helldorff. Eager and craving attention, he was a brilliant showman for whom the spotlight was more powerful than the drugs he had handed out on the *Ursel IV.*

Hanussen had become famous, wealthy and surrounded by those of the powerful and adoring rich who craved answers to the unanswerable. And who better to provide answers than Hanussen—the the most urgently self-promoting spiritualist, psychic, hypnotist and clairvoyant in a city filled with them?

With combed-back black hair, a fleshy face and bushy eyebrows above eyes that seemed to drill holes into the minds of whoever they chose to fix on, Erik Jan Hanussen had positioned himself skillfully between fame and notoriety.

He had just prophesized that Hitler would soon rule Germany. It was a prophecy that electrified Berlin's fashionable society, And with it came the rumour that the Nazi leader himself had secretly summoned Hanussen to his temporary suite in the Kaiserhof hotel. Fascinated by Hanussen's ability to capture the minds of those who flocked to see him, Hitler stood in front of a mirror, rehearsing his next speech and allowing himself to be guided by Hanussen in cadence, tempo and gestures.

At a crucial moment in history, Hanussen had become the link between mysticism and raw power. And both elements were there on the *Ursel IV* when Helldorff came aboard.

But to Karin and Inga, Helldorff was just another man coming on board to paw at the young women that Hanussen had brought to the boat. She and Inga were below deck, giggling and whispering to one another about what would happen if either was chosen by Hanussen for what was to come. Neither knew exactly what was expected of them until Helldorff and Hanussen came below deck to talk in private.

It took Hanussen several minutes of animated conversation to realize that Helldorff had heard nothing. His attention was totally fixed on the young blonde talking to her friend.

He knew her. But how? Where?

And then she turned, her eyes scanning the guests—and he knew. That night at the *Himmel u Hölle* during the whipping scene. Where Helldorff had been transfixed. And not merely by each flick of the lash in the hands of the naked young beauty who could not stop giggling as she pretended to flay the naked men who crawled around the stage like rodents.

There was a kind of insolence, almost derision that she directed to the men in the audience. And even from a distance it thrilled Helldorff.

When she pranced off the stage Helldorff had maneuvered close enough to it to see her eyes—those blue-green eyes that to him were those of a wolf. He would never forget those eyes.

In the chaos of the crowds at *Himmel u Hölle* he had not gotten past the fool guarding the stage door until the SA men he called in had beaten the man senseless. By that time, the SA troops had surrounded the *club,* checking the identity of anyone trying to leave. Helldorff was determined to find her. That girl!

Every one of the nude dancers was called out and a flashlight shone in their face until Helldorff could wave them on.

She was not there.

He went back inside and grabbed the owner of *Himmel u Hölle* by the throat and threatened physical violence unless he found out the name and address of the naked young beauty with the whip.

The owner had no idea who she was. The naked young beauty had always refused to give her name.

On the *Ursel IV*, Karin was brought out from below-deck wearing nothing but a veil-like covering that hung from her shoulders down across her body. She was led to a profane altar draped with a white fur rug by an almost naked woman with a boy's body. Karin was already in a near trance when the boy-like woman laid her back across the altar in her diaphanous covering and then turned back to the assembled throng crowding the upper deck and said, "Master, she awaits you."

With a theatrical flourish, Indian servants in turbans and pantaloons pushed the crowd back, clearing a path for Hanussen to emerge, his eyes unblinking and fixed as if he too was in a trance. He stood over the altar where Karin lay, her eyes closed and rustling beneath the full-length veil. He stared down at her, moving his hands back and forth just above her body for several silent minutes and then whispered what the hushed crowd could barely hear: "Your lover is here…your lover."

Karin began moaning softly.

"Your lover. He is here. With you." His voice was silky, quiet, insistent. *"About to go in* you. You can feel him. *In* you."

It went on and on, his words flowing together in undulating rhythms like some force that lifted Karin in slow writhing that was coming now in waves, sending some of the onlookers into the farthest reaches of the *Ursel IV* driven by their own fornicating imperatives. But the others stayed and watched, drawn to the sight of a young woman, a girl, writhing in ecstasy.

Your lover. In you. In you. In you.

Karin was writhing faster now, sending the veil fluttering and settling.

Fluttering and settling. *In you in you.*

With a swooping motion a conductor would envy, Hanussen swept the veil from Karin's body leaving her naked and writhing on the altar, her eyes fiercely closed in a slow and orgasmic frenzy that was still building until it reached a cry that serrated the cheers and shouts obliterating the twilight silence of the lake.

An hour later, Karin sat demurely in the stern seating area of the *Ursel IV* as unapproachable as a newly discovered deity. Hanussen had let it be known that 'his women', the ones he had just hypnotized, were to be left to themselves after whatever state they had emerged from. Only Inga sat with her, at first seemingly to soothe her after what had happened. But it was noticed that they were given to strange bursts of giggling.

Giggling? After an orgasm for the ages?

Hanussen was too busy, accepting congratulations from lower-deck connoisseurs of such matters to notice any giggling. But Helldorff was not. Helldorff missed nothing. Or almost nothing.

What he could not have known was that Inga was giggling over Karin's description of faking everything she had done on that profane altar. She had simply been imitating everything she had heard through the thin walls of the dingy tenement room they shared in Neukölln. Their landlady, who they called *Mutter*, proudly ran a communist brothel on a capital-ist payment system—*sex is free until it's not*—and the groans, moans and shrieks that came through the walls were research for an actress—which Karin now insisted she was.

At the other end of the boat, Helldorff endured several conversations, staring over other peoples' shoulders at Karin instead of listening to who-ever was droning on in front of him.

This girl! Hanussen's rules meant nothing to Helldorff—even though Hanussen was secretly saving him from financial ruin. In mid-sentence Helldorff pushed past the man who was talking to him and walked back to the stern of the *Ursel IV.*

It was the high polished boots that Karin noticed first. She looked in mild irritation at this man with who was suddenly looming over her and Inga.

"Excuse me?" she said hoping her irritation was conveyed. "I am talking to my friend," the words leaving her like darts.

"I think perhaps *we* might talk," said Helldorff suddenly showing unease.

"I think perhaps not."

"You are being rude."

"So are you."

"Do you know who I am?"

"Why would I care?"

Helldorff barely remembered the last time he felt this quivering that would overtake him in moments when he suddenly had no power. For the past year or maybe more—ever since he had become an important Nazi, women had responded to his approach with what Helldorff deemed to be awe and deference. And he had grown bored with it.

"You might care one day soon," was the best he could now come up with.

"Really? Well then I'll wait."

"Maybe by then time will have run out."

Karin looked him up and down. He was just some man, older than thirty—any man older than thirty was just *old*, and besides he was standing there wrapped in tweed and leather as if that was supposed to impress her. "It's already run out," she said. "You're old."

"Thirty-four is old?"

"Ancient. Now leave us alone."

"No." Helldorff's reputation overtook the quivering that he hoped was not showing. Because this was becoming too public; people were watching. And displays of insolence could not be tolerated. Not now that people knew he was an important Nazi.

"*Yes!*" Karin's reaction was so sharp that Helldorff took a step backward.

He was even more aware that others were watching him, the next Nazi regent of Berlin being spurned by some orgasmic little trollop. "Bad things can happen," he said.

Karin looked him up and down. "They already are."

For a moment he faltered. And then he swiveled in Teutonic ferocity, his eyes alighting on a young Indian waiter hurrying past with a tray of champagne. He bellowed, "You. What's your name?"

"Vihaan," said the boy with eyes suddenly clouding with unease.

With a sweep of his hand, Helldorff sent the champagne glasses on Vihaan's tray flying. They shattered in various locations across the deck. Helldorff's hand was bleeding from the blow. "Look what you've done." Helldorff held his bleeding hand in front of him as if it was some alien appendage.

The young Indian waiter took a step backward, not fast enough to miss the blow from Helldorff's other hand that sent him tumbling into the broken glass. "I am truly sorry sir," he said in a quavering voice, lying on the floor and picking a large piece of glass out of his arm. The other Indian waiters quickly gathered around Vihaan each outdoing the others in obsequious ministrations intended to defuse Helldorff's fury.

"Get up," he said to the boy in a voice more threatening because of its seething quietness. He reached down to the top of one of his gleaming riding boots and from a built-in vertical sheath, withdrew a riding whip. He slashed the whip in front of him, scattering the other waiters. Then he brought it down across the chest of the stumbling Vihaan, sending him reeling back onto a floor of broken glass.

A cascade of gasps came from those who hurried onto the deck. Hanussen pushed his way through several barely clothed women but was stopped by Helldorff's outstretched hand. Needing to save face, Hanussen assured the women around him, "I encourage spontaneity."

Helldorff circled the deck methodically swinging the whip, cutting through the air with a slicing hiss as he circled the crying boy who was edging backwards through the glass. The centrifugal force of his fury had created a silence interrupted only by the slicing sound of the whip as it lashed the boy.

"Stop it!"

Karin's fierce words came softly but cut through the moment with the same sharp force as the whip-crack. She stood up and placed herself between the terrified boy and Helldorff. Nothing else needed to be said; it was her stare that stopped him. Ever since she was a little girl, Karin could stare with an intensity that was almost impaling. Cold and searing, her wolf's blue-green eyes were the outer edge of a soul that no force could reach. And then when whatever had disturbed her was over with, her face resumed the angelic innocence.

I never knew which was the mask and which was Karin.

Shorn of its seething indignation, Helldorff's watery gaze was no match for Karin's. No one else on the *Ursel IV* would have been capable of understanding that Helldorff's response—the cracking of the whip and the posturing fury were just a façade covering irreversible weakness.

"A woman of spirit. I like that." Helldorff said straining to keep control. Then he turned to Hanussen and snapped "Get me to the shore."

Before the *Ursel IV* reached the shore, Inga saw something on the lower deck. Later she realized that merely having observed what happened could have gotten her killed. She saw Hanussen urgently fumbling through a briefcase until he came up with an envelope that spilled money in two big envelopes. They were quickly transferred to a leather pouch and handed to Helldorff who acknowledged the offering with a constricted smile. He stepped onto the dock without looking back and then vanished into the big Mercedes.

Clutching the envelopes stuffed with money.

7

I DROVE INGA BACK TO Neukölln. Twice I had to stop the car while she got out and threw up. "The fish," she kept saying over and over. Inga was one of those people diminished by daylight. In everything from complexion to bone structure, night would be her ally. By the cruelty of the noonday sun, her collarbones and ribs cast shadows. She was uncommonly aware of realities of her situation. As we drove through the affluence of Dahlem and Wilmersdorf she looked at what we were passing and said, "I sometimes feel like an ornament on the tree. And unless some rich man is blind enough to be attracted by what glitters, I'm finished in a couple of years. Or maybe a bit more if my breasts hold up."

I turned east toward Neukölln and the streets became more ragged and crowded, filled with more horse-drawn carts than cars. The clanking and faded yellow streetcars had a tattered, dented quality, like exhausted mechanical beasts labouring in their traces. The air filled with the smells of rot, smoke and non-existent plumbing. There were fewer fedoras and more workers' caps on the streets. Clothes were often marked by patches or grease and dirt. From the windows of the apartments, clothes and banners flew, most with the hammer and sickle or communist slogans. The whole effect was that of a drab canyon of greys and browns with walls of soot that gave the illusion of closing in as the teeming jumble of humanity pressed around us.

Then I realized what was even more different about it: everyone was walking in the same direction. Not just walking—hurrying, surging around my car so that it felt as if we were being carried along on a tide. When Inga told me to turn right at the next intersection, I had to edge the car into a slow curving motion in order not to collide with the people pressed around it.

I was so focused on avoiding a collision that I could not respond to Inga's cry of amazement: "Oh look, look, look!"

A roiling crowd had gathered in front of a dull grey slab of an old tenement building in front of us at the bottom of a dead-end street. A single red banner with no images or slogans on it fluttered from the roof, all the way to the ground. In front of it was an enormous Mercedes. And one SA driver in full brown-shirt uniform, looking nervous as he stood beside the car and tried to act calm as the crowd circled the car, yelling insults at him.

"Helldorff's Mercedes," said Inga before I could ask.

I parked my car and we walked the remaining hundred meters. At some point the riptide of humanity was pulling us in different directions Inga grabbed my hand and yelled, "In here."

I found myself tugged into a basement door of a tenement and then following Inga, running along a long, darkened corridor with crudely boarded doors over tiny windowless rooms where people lived in a space no bigger than a closet. Voices swirled around us as we ran as far as a door that opened onto a flight of dirty stairs. "The back entrance," Inga yelled before vanishing through a doorway that led to another corridor, this one with a window at the end that blared sunlight shining past the silhouette of an unclothed girl or maybe a woman, it was hard to tell.

"Erma?"

The girl turned toward us, covering herself with a towel that only partly hid her nakedness. She was pretty, about eighteen, with perfectly brushed blonde hair and refined features, the kind that looked out of place in the dingy corridor. Beside her was another door opening into a room where a large camera had been set up in front of a couch. "Erma poses for dirty pictures," said Inga trying to sound helpful.

"We have to eat you know," Erma said sounding defensive.

"Where are your clothes?"

"They're in the front room. But I can't get back to it because Karin is there arguing with some Nazi. Mother doesn't want me to be around Nazis. She says they're bad for business."

I walked forward toward the sound of voices. Erma followed clutching the towel that did not go down to her waist. "Why do you bother having a towel?" asked Inga. "Since when are you afraid to be naked?"

"Mother doesn't want Nazis getting free looks," Erma said, acting as if everything was getting to be a nuisance. "Honestly."

The door to the front room was open. Karin was standing beside the balcony window that opened onto the street and Helldorff was pacing in the room behind her. The noise and angry chanting from the gathering crowd on the street below made it hard to hear.

Whenever Karin was challenged, she had the unnerving ability to shut down any unneeded emotions. The males in her life always found this disconcerting, starting years ago with little boys and year by year, edging up to men. Men like Helldorff who paced with anger and confusion, not sure how to respond to her cool, belittling silence.

"That's all?" he rasped

Karin finally replied. "Why should there be anything else? I don't even know you. And besides, this is all rather boring you know," Karin said in that uninterested voice that was almost like a mirror held up to whoever she was talking to.

You could tell that Helldorff was having trouble with the idea that someone found him boring. "Do you have any idea who I am?"

"Oh god not this again. And by the way, whoever you are, you're a terrible person."

For an instant Helldorff looked almost relieved. At least not *boring.* Some men became Nazis in order to escape being boring. Helldorff could have been one; it was hard to tell. "You'll change your opinion."

"I won't."

"You have no reason to hate me."

"You whipped that poor boy."

"That was for show."

"Take your show and leave."

"May I remind you—you are in a brothel and I am giving you a chance to know other things"

"Oh, so you do think I'm a whore is that it?" she said angrily.

"Did I say that?"

"For your information I am *not* a whore; I am merely staying here with a friend."

Helldorff's smirk found its mark. Karin was almost never infuriated. It was simply not part of her repertoire. But for a moment that cool façade of hers faltered. "You couldn't possibly know whether or not a woman is a whore. To men like you we all look like whores."

Helldorff looked down at the street scene, menacing and roiling as communists poured onto the street where his car was parked. "My apologies," he said. "I have obviously offended you. Please accept my regrets. I shall leave now."

Apologies and politeness often incapacitated Karin, disarming her cool resolve. She looked down at the street and suddenly showed concern. "Wait!" she called to him. "You should go out the back entrance."

"I do not go out back entrances." Now it was Helldorff who was cool.

"This is a communist area. Have you seen what's going on down there?"

"Yes."

"It's not safe."

And here was the moment—the exact moment I saw the flicker that passed between them and igniting something in Karin. The instant of capitulation and her invisible defenses vanishing as Helldorff showed a version of cool courage. He smiled politely, turned and strode out past me, past Inga and Erma into the hallway that was leading toward the savagery of the mob.

It was a mob that now had cornered his SA driver—*finally* one of the bastard Nazis! And now another one, an important one would soon be in their grasp to rip to shreds.

As two floors above, Karin raced to the window in guilt and concern over what she was sure was about to happen.

I knew at that moment that as much as she hated him, he had captured her. There was something that repulsed her and attracted her at the same time.

"It's not safe," she called out again, "Don't!" Her words vanishing into the rage of the crowd as it edged closer when Helldorff stepped out onto the sidewalk below. With his driver was urging him to get in the car, it was Helldorff's turn for a withering response. He cast a quick look up at Karin.

It was the look of someone who was almost bored.

Bored? Karin was confused. This was not the reaction other men in her life would have shown. In the face of physical danger, with a mob about to attack him, Helldorff's moment of nonchalance was etching deeply into wherever Karin's most unknown needs were kept.

There was nothing about him that showed he knew what would happen next in that moment before the drums sounded.

Drums?

Karin let out something between a gasp and "*Oh!*" and pointed toward the end of the block. It was as if a parade was approaching. The street was filling up with men in brown uniforms, swiveling sharply at right angles at the intersection and then marching toward Helldorff. There was row after row of brown-shirts pounding on the pavement with every synchronized step, all of them encased in leather from the boots, belts and straps. They were marching with slow and studied ferocity, driven on by two huge marching drums at the rear of the column that now looked like a single beast moving, a human battering ram, shoving, forcing aside whoever, whatever was in its path—until until the tallest of the drummers was hit by the wine bottle that shattered behind his left ear. It slammed him flat onto the pavement with a yodel-like cry of pain.

Then the giant marching beast exploded into its component parts, each of them flailing a club or a pistol. The street echoed with cries and the sharp crack of bone being broken again and again. It blossomed blood, pain and crumpled men.

As Helldorff stood quietly behind the car.

Like a sudden storm passing through, the violence suddenly ceased. Almost none of the brown-shirts had fallen. Most of those lying on the street, moaning in pain were wearing crude clothing and worker's caps, some now leaking redness.

Helldorff waited, surveying what had become a battlefield like a victorious general. He called over a young, blonde SA leader and motioned to where Karin stood watching. Then he got in the back of the big Mercedes without looking up at her. As the Mercedes threaded its way through the crawling wounded, Karin barely saw the young SA leader looking up.

When he got to the door of the apartment, the young SA leader blurted "I have been sent by Count Helldorff. My name is Karl,"

There was no response from Karin.

"Karl Ernst," he said shifting irritably like someone who was used to having his temper snuff out uncertainties. Without it he was awkward. "Count Helldorff has asked me to be available to assist you in contacting him whenever you wish."

"He said that?"

"Yes."

"Then I have a message for you to deliver to Count Helldorff."

"I'm listening"

"Tell him he does not make the rules," Karin said sweetly.

"You are putting me in an embarrassing situation."

"Do Nazis have embarrassing situations?" Karin was still looking out the window. In the distance Helldorff's Mercedes turned left at the intersection and vanished.

"Tell Count Helldorff that I have informed you to assist him when *he* wishes to contact *me*. I will *not* be contacting him"

Karl Ernst's already thin mouth became a slit across his face. "People do not talk that way to us. Not now."

"Well I just did."

Karl Ernst began to walk slowly back and forth staring at the floor as if he was thinking of how to exit a conversation he could not contain. He walked directly in front of Karin, "You know we *do* know each other."

"I have never seen you before."

"You have. "

She shook her head.

"The nightclub. Where I worked. *The Eldorado*. But you were only about fourteen years old," he said.

Karin's eyes narrowed in confusion. And then Karl Ernst removed his rounded SA hat with its leather chinstrap.

"Oh!" as if some cinch fell from her expression.

Without the hat, Karl Ernst looked younger, less severe. "You came with your uncle."

"The naughty club? Where the men dressed as women? Oh yes—you were the man who uncle Rudi talked to. At the entrance. You didn't want to let me in."

"It was not a place for a fourteen-year-old."

"I liked it."

"Yes. You met a movie star."

"Marlene! She was so nice. She said she was there to borrow clothes from the prettiest man there." Karin giggled. "She needed them for her movie."

"Blue Angel."

"Uncle Rudi said he bribed you to let me in."

He put the SA hat back on his head and stuck out his jaw as the chinstrap slid under it. "Things were different then."

Not long afterward as I was leaving the tenement, I heard yelling on the stairs behind me. When I reached the entrance and the street in front of that grey slab of a building, a dignified but disheveled-looking man hurried out behind me. He was being chased by the enormous woman Karin had introduced me to minutes earlier. She was Erma's mother— known as *Mutter*, imposing with grey hair pulled back behind her head in a bun and whose wide face shifted easily from a lacerating scowl to a smile that made you wonder what favorite relative she reminded you of. Now, with a cigarette dangling from the corner of her mouth, she obviously intimidated the man she was yelling at. He was much better dressed than anyone else on the street and was trying to flee from *Mutter* who was quickly counting money and running after him. "My girls do not work for what you just paid. Especially with the likes of you. Pay what you owe and take your capitalist exploitation elsewhere."

"Frau you will not talk to me like that."

"You cheap bastard, I'll talk to you however I like."

"I am used to better quality women."

"Really? Well my girls are used to better quality too. The smaller the dick, the harder they have to work. So pay up."

When people on the sidewalk began laughing the man took out several banknotes and flung them into the air before they landed at my feet as he hurried away.

I picked up the money and handed it to *Mutter* who smiled for the first time since she'd left the building. "You must be my good luck charm," she said in a voice that sounded like laughter being sandpapered.

8

TO BE UNCOMFORTABLY HONEST: AS a gossip columnist you're kind of a word whore.

Anyone in that job has to be. You are writing about manufactured glamour: sleek, glittering, overfed, and corrupt. And also, usually tedious. A banquet here. An afternoon reception there. An embassy dinner. A society ball. And what do you do? You manipulate and polish descriptions of these mendacious events, your aim being to get your readers aching with envy because they were not invited. That is one measure of success. And all the rest of it, it is false.

The strange part is that everyone involved knows it. It just reeks of Pirandello, plays within plays with everyone knowing their lines. From the Rumanian countess I might be writing about to the impoverished reader in Kreuzberg, everyone knew these chic events were, on the surface, nonsense.

Especially when Nazis routinely started showing up at embassy receptions—even before they officially took over the country. Their black or brown uniforms would be wedged in among the tuxedos and evening dresses like stains that could not be scrubbed out. And what was my role as Gossip Columnist? To write prose that made some fat *Standartenfuhrer* seem sleek. To transform tedious SA Group Leaders, thugs in any other world, into paragons of wit.

Everybody was in on the game. So what could be wrong?

Do I even have to answer?

It is why I reverted to code in my columns. Once the Nazis were on the verge of gaining power, I had no choice. It was a code that relied on varying levels of irony. For instance:

Unfortunate events meant a bloody rampage by Nazi thugs.

Ebullient officers meant drunken Nazis.

Detained on other business meant *a* guest who did not show up at the embassy reception because he or she was now in a concentration camp.

Celebrating future events meant that the Nazis at the reception knew that of some other country—Austria, Czechoslovakia, whatever, was about to be wiped out but news of its impending demise was not yet public.

Spirited exchange of views meant a fistfight, usually in the Men's bathroom.

The code grew and evolved every week.

For instance I concocted *behind closed doors diplomacy* instead of reporting that another *Standartenfuhrer* had left the reception and taken the wife of a Bulgarian diplomat up to an embassy bedroom from which their amorous howls could be heard two floors below.

Code was a way I could keep sanity, the tiniest claim to decency, and a chance not to be arrested. Or so I told myself. Friends of mine at the newspaper who went astray by even an adjective that displeased Goebbels ended up in the holding cells at the Prinz-Abrechtstrasse before the next morning edition came out. And many never came out alive.

Fear was the ultimate editor.

The ultimate headmaster.

Which is why Karin was unique. Unlike anyone else I have known in these terrible years she remained unchanged through it all.

So many others made deals with deeply denied devils even before that awful day in 1933 when the Nazis took over. All of them twisted and squirmed themselves into poses and postures, ignoring the rushing rivers of blood lust and the ceremonial trumpets of the grand death march.

Because for once in their lives they were being forced to do what they had never really had to do before—*choose*. Not just choose jobs or spouses or places to live. No; as the Nazis got closer to power, ordinary people were forced to make extraordinary, often terrifying moral choices—bravery or cowardice; compassion or cruel indifference; resistance or self-preservation. They were choices that were so often between life or death.

Among all those I knew, only Karin did not choose.

It never occurred to her. She simply remained herself while others like her had their heads roll into the bloody basket under the Nazi guillotine at Plötzensee prison. Which maybe is why I have always strived to save Karin.

Telling myself that a certain kind of innocence must be protected. Even my own.

Herr Langen glared at me. "Sex and hypnosis? And you want us to print this? This is more than just gossip. This is trash."

"But it all starts with gossip. It could become more than that." I was trying not to sound too eager. "But for now it is still gossip. Which is part of the world you have asked me to cover"

"It is not a story for Auntie Voss"—the century-old nickname for the *Vossiche Zeitung,* used mostly by the newspaper's employees like Herr Langen.

"But it involves a senior Nazi."

"You are a society columnist. Your specialty is gossip." He said it as a challenge. He had the look of a chess master facing an irritating child who'd just said 'Checkmate' Then he looked down, and again I was left looking at the end of a cigarette hanging from the side of his mouth sending tiny wisps of smoke up under the green visor.

"Everything is sex now. Our entire culture. We're drowning in it," he said veering away from the question. "We've had too many stories about it."

"But not with hypnosis." I said. "This makes it different."

"A hypnotist who is enthralling a Nazi?"

"Helldorff."

"One of the worst, most disgusting Nazis of them all." Whenever he was mulling over a response all you saw from across the desk was that visor and the top of his head. His words always seemed to come from somewhere else in his office with all its shadows and dark furniture.

"Tell me something, is this because of your sister?"

"I haven't seen my sister in over a week."

"That tells me nothing." His normal sharpness had long ago given him an enduring reputation, trailing newsroom stories of a fierce reporter, grilling those he thought were covering up the truth. "What have Helldorff and the hypnotist got to do with her?"

"I think they were training her."

"For what?"

"To be one of their girls."

"Their whores."

I would not answer.

"I'm sorry," he said. "That was not polite." The visor lifted again and I was looking into those blue eyes that could go from sad to fierce and back again in the space of a single sentence. "Count Helldorff is rumored to be the next Police Chief if the Nazis take over. He already is at the top of the SA here."

"I know."

"You are aware what happens when the SA disapprove of someone?"

"Yes." Savage beatings. Sometimes worse.

The quickness of my answer seemed to jar him. He sat back, looking everywhere but at me. "I told you last week that they want drive out the Ullsteins. This week they created a new word to do it—*Aryanize*—They want to *Aryanize* Auntie Voss. Fascinating isn't it? How language, the mere words that they use can be just as brutal as their clubs. Clever, devious bastards that they are.".

He leaned back into his chair, the way he always did when he deemed a debate or argument to be over.

After my first anxious encounters with him I had gradually come to like Herr Langen, and I began staying for a few extra minutes in his office to talk about things other than my news stories. He was a difficult man to know, always reserved in the way of someone with secrets. He could be warm, funny and intimidating, sometimes all at once.

But once, a few months earlier he had shown a moment of vulnerability, his Roman-statue features collapsing when he talked of losing his only child three years ago, a daughter who died of tuberculosis when she was very young.

Sometimes you could almost hear him thinking of her. As he was now.

"I no longer understand Berlin."

"You're the editor. Aren't you supposed to understand it?"

"No one can. Not now. Not when we have sent all that genius out into the world—Bach, Beethoven and Hegel and Kant. And now? Now we boast about Luna Park."

Luna Park was big amusement fairground at the far end of the Ku'damm.

He took off the visor and threw it aside. "Not long ago, when money could lose half its value overnight, my neighbors' daughter had two close friends—Madeline and Ruby. They were thirteen years old. And once a week, each was dressed in bathing costumes by their parents and taken to the *tart aquarium* at Luna Park."

The *tart aquarium* was the water chute where women in varying degrees of swimming suits would slide down, into view of the men sitting on the rim of the chute.

"Everyone pretended it was such good fun. If you know what I mean."

I knew what he meant.

"Their parents would hand out cards with their addresses on it to the men who clustered around Ruby and Madeline after they slid down the chute. And then the following night, with only those men who had paid a substantial entrance fee to enter the apartments of Madeline's and Ruby's parents, they would gather in the living rooms, perhaps six, eight or maybe ten men per living room, almost panting for these thirteen year olds to be brought out by their mothers and stripped totally naked as their fathers took bids from the men to see who got to spend the night with his daughter.

"And when the bidding was over and the winner of each of the girls had handed over the cash, he was allowed to escort the naked girl into a nearby room and spend hours doing whatever he wanted to her.

"And then in the morning, in each of the two homes, when the man had gone, the family would have breakfast as if nothing has happened. These were people I knew. So-called respectable people. Do you know how corroded, how degraded we all have to be for something like that to…."

He never finished what he was saying. He was cleaning his glasses as he sometimes did when something was upsetting him.

"How old is your sister now?"

"Karin? She's seventeen. She'll be eighteen in three months. But that's not what happened to her." I said. "Her case was different."

The glasses were cleaned. Again. And again. "Do you think I care if these people you write about in your gossip column want to fornicate their lives away? Or want to celebrate every new bestial perversion they dream up? No, it is the pendulum of history I care about. And the further it swings one way, the further it comes back the other way. Slicing toward the rest of us like a blade. And the Nazis are at the farthest, darkest edges of where the pendulum is swinging to. So don't tell me you're just writing gossip. When gossip becomes history, people get killed."

"So what do I do?"

"You leave out the history."

He kept cleaning his glasses long after they were clean. Finally he looked over at me.

"Okay. Go and do your story on Helldorff."

My column about the *Ursel IV*, when it ran, was buried in the back pages of *Vossiche Zeitung,* was barely recognizable. Compared to what I had first written it was a fairy tale about some quirky hypnotist who had entranced some rising political figures.

Herr Langen might as well have taken a meat cleaver to the typewritten pages I had turned in. They were more savagely edited than anything I had ever written. I never saw him while he was doing the editing and the resulting story fueled me with enough indignation to barge past his startled secretary, in through his office door that had been closed since I got back to the strangely tense and silent newsroom.

"This is terrible," I said opening the door, "A complete distortion. Where was all the debauchery? And the part about the orgasms? And the whippings on that boat? The bribery? The Nazis?"

I was talking into the silence of the top of his head shrouded by the green visor as smoke spewed up from around its edges. It was the first time I had seen him smoke in weeks.

"Well?" I took nothing for granted in the way I was talking to him. Any other editor would have thrown me out. And probably fired me. I pressed on: "Where are the journalistic standards?"

Smoke poured from under that visor. Then: a seething, hissing barrage as forceful as it was quiet, each word spit out like a knife being flung at me. "Don't-you-ever-lecture-me-again!"

The visor lifted. I couldn't stifle the gasp.

What confronted me was something like a ravaged death mask, his swollen and hideously bruised face with one of his eyes closed and leaking a mixture of blood and something else.

In shock and confusion I sputtered, "What happened?"

"*What happened*?" He roared through his shattered face, "And you claim to work for a newspaper?"

"I am so sorry," I said. I meant it. He was almost disfigured, fighting through whatever was the legacy of pain—and I was complaining about my story?

"Do you not know what happened?" A simple sentence spat out and loaded with derision.

"I'm sorry. I've been out at Lake Scharmützelee looking for Hanussen's boat and—"

"*Get out!*"

I was too confused to say anything. I backed out and was closing the door as the green visor lowered and his voice came from somewhere far away.

"Do you not understand? What you turned in as a story? If it was printed they would have done the same thing to you."

I found out later that Herr Langen had been felled with one punch and then kicked until he lost consciousness.

What happened to him was what was now going on all over Berlin. Herr Langen had just happened to be leaving the building and was on our street, Kochstrasse, right in front of the place where you would have thought such a thing was impossible—the legendary House of Ullstein newspapers. The barbarism was intentionally symbolic. Several brown-uniformed men from the *Sturmabteilungen*, the SA, were outside proclaiming that there were too many Jews in positions of power at *Vossiche Zeitung*.

Across Berlin the SA were beating up people on the street simply because they "looked Jewish" and if mistakes were occasionally made—like the time a Lutheran was beaten to death because he looked Jewish, well that was just the cost of the occasional lapse. To the SA, such a mistake was just part of the process of spreading terror.

I realized I had been in a different kind of unconsciousness, that of someone who had been chasing mere facts while something far larger was swallowing us all.

9

I FOUND THAT WITHOUT EVEN realizing it that I had made a decision.

Or, one of my decisions.

The first one had been made when mother finally died after all those terrible years of barely living. Standing by the graveside as her coffin was about to be lowered into the frozen ground, we found ourselves waiting for father. He had left the church service and sped away alone in his car without even waiting for the doorway consolations from the minister. Almost an hour later at the cemetery, the freezing wind whipped around us as we waited for him. No one quite knew what to do. The minister, wrapped in blankets, twice asked where father was, and the sullen gravediggers, blew into their rope-scarred hands and stamped their feet in futile attempts to stay warm.

The minister began shooting glances at me, part plea, part fury, expecting instructions that would absolve him of beginning without father. I had no idea what to do. In my devastated state, standing over mother's coffin, I was about to nod *Proceed* when I saw a car approaching. Father's car.

He stepped out of it and for an awful moment the bitter cold vanished as tiny wildfires of inner fury flared invisibly around the open grave. Father had gone home, changed out of his banker's suit and returned to stand over his wife's grave dressed in his Nazi uniform. So he could loom over her in the grave, in one final moment of victory.

There was never any return after that.

That same day I packed up my belongings and prepared to move out of the house in which I had grown up.

With tension and fear floating around everyone like a mist, you learned that some of the smallest actions could have enormous consequences. You just never knew which ones until afterwards.

Nothing else was ever as fateful as when Erma's mother, *Mutter*, gave me a small room to stay in while I was waiting for the right time to move my few possessions out of father's home and into an apartment. It was to be for a couple of weeks, a month at most. Or so I thought.

But lying there at night on that small bed in a room with remnants of distant light coming through a dirty window no larger than a magazine, I realized that I was not going to look for an apartment in Mitte, Charlottenburg or any of the other 'proper' sections of Berlin.

Living on my own was not what I wanted now, not when these fears seeped into the crevasses of my thoughts like fog coming in under a locked door. I needed the sounds and the security of others nearby as I fought for sleep in those long nights wondering what I was afraid of.

And I wondered what it was that made me feel safe merely being around *Mutter*. And why I was somehow comforted by the presence of this enormous woman with her coarse honesty and blistering opinions that were rendered casually, devoid of malice but loaded with the devastating insight of the street. They were usually dispensed from a battered kitchen table in front of a wheezing wood stove. From the dilapidated apartment *Mutter* ruled her little kingdom, telling Erma they were not *arm*—poor. Instead they were *ärmlich*—occasionally challenged in a financial way.

And also that it was not prostitution or pornography going on in those other rooms—it was social healing.

Mutter, was going through her own crisis. The "girls" she had employed for varying kinds of pornography were leaving her. Several had been nude dancers in the nightclubs that were being closed all over Berlin as the Nazis either threatened the owners or sometimes just marched in, broke everything in sight and beat up anyone who was there.

Already the photographic studio that *Mutter* used for pornographic pictures has been closed. Most of her "girls" had drifted away to the small towns they came from. And one of those who had stayed was a 47-year-old Swabian who could be heard at night raging against someone named Jürgen and then singing filthy Bavarian songs about rape and incest. *Mutter* had decided that the Swabian was heavy enough that if the Nazi came barging in she could always say she was the cleaning lady and not a prostitute.

Like most people who passed through her kitchen, I never knew her real name, only *Mutter*, the formidable presence in a faded housedress that bulged out in odd ways. Nothing about her prodigious breasts seemed quite right, straining under that house dress that was always stained from forays too close to her days-old pot of soup from which anyone was welcome to eat. The kitchen reeked from years of cooking that had left layers of grease on the wall behind the stove. Whenever *Mutter* got angry or drunk enough, she found whatever piece of cloth was nearby and flung it against the wall. A few of the projectiles would stick to the grease coating the wall and gradually become covered over like long buried artifacts. But most of the hurled rags or towels would stick for a moment and then slowly slide down. The result was vaguely artistic. If enough paprika was being cooked on the stove, the grease had a distinctly reddish hue. The overall effect of the wall was that it could have been displayed in one of the modern art galleries that the Nazis were closing all over Berlin.

When I first went into the kitchen, *Mutter* was busy trying to get drunk. Because of her capacity for cheap wine, she really had to work at it and already an unlabeled bottle was nearly consumed. "Erma. My daughter," she said several times. "My poor daughter." She beckoned for me to sit, craving an audience the way she always did when she drank too much. "Right at her prime she will be thrown into a terrible world. These fucking Nazis are demanding that sex be normal. This is suicidal. This country needs its perversions. Everyone knows that. The men here are as fucked up as any place on the planet."

"And this Hitler is smart. He knows this. Just look at him *jah*? He knows what he's doing. He takes away all their perversions and it all turns into rage that he can use. Hitler, that little eunuch is a genius".

"Shh" I said. Overheard remarks were now increasingly being reported to the local Nazis who kept records of those they intended to destroy once they took power.

"What? They're coming for an old cow like me? Not likely. Why would they pick on me? I have been saving the nation. I was draining the rage away, one fuck at a time. I should be given a medal. Now what are these twisted types going to do? I know these types, gagging on their own sperm until they want to declare war. *Der Fuehrer* knows this too. If humanitarians like me aren't providing those perverts with women to fuck they're going storm around looking for other countries to bash."

She got up walking uncertainly toward the wall and stood swaying as if invisible gusts of wind were momentarily blowing her backwards.

She reached up and with her first finger drew a horizontal line through the grease, announcing: "They draw a line through our lives." She pointed above the oozing line. "And everything above the line they say is legal." She lurched and pointed downward. "But everything else below the line is illegal.

"But the stupid fuckers keep moving the goddamn line. Before the Nazis came in everything I did was legal—the whores, the whack-job photographs and all that, they were all legal. You could have fucked a goat in front of the audience at the Opera and all the proper people would have just giggled. Why? Because it was above the line.

"But suddenly the Nazis come along and *poof!* they move the line way up here! And so now all this goat fucking at the Opera is suddenly illegal. And you can no longer look at dirty pictures or crawl around with a woman in leather whipping you. Explain *that* to me."

"I wouldn't even try."

"Good." She landed back on the kitchen chair with a thud and opened the newspaper—*Berlin am Morgen,* that was lying on the table.

"A communist rag," she said. "No offense, but it's easier to read than your rag."

But I was barely hearing what she said. I was leaning toward her, reading the headline above the big story on the front page: *A Charlatan Takes Over Berlin*! Under the headline was a photo of Hanussen. *Mutter* was holding the paper up in front of her, unaware that I was peering at the other side, reading such phrases as *clairvoyant to the Nazis... Hitler's swami... fabulist scum...*

It all vanished when *Mutter* suddenly put the paper down and found nothing unusual with me leaning toward her.

"My poor daughter is too good. Erma is pure. She is embarrassed by me and all my whores. She'll do well in Mecklenburg with that blockhead she's marrying. But understand, I take care of my whores, I look out for them." She looked at me, suddenly squinting through some haze only she could see.

"In your own way you're attractive but not beautiful," she said, "but you'll do okay. You'll get a man."

10

A WEEK LATER WHEN I fumbled through an explanation of why I wanted to stay, *Mutter* said "Of course you need to be here,"

"Being safe starts in the mind," she added. "Believe me, I know. After the men I've been with."

Mutter never made even the faintest attempt at softening brutal truths. She was relentless with her blunt comments. "You're sure there's no man involved?"

"No," I insisted as she drilled me with her piercing stare.

"Ach, yes. I believe you. You're the type who lies badly, I can tell. No wonder you need protection. Like a dog with no teeth."

It was always the nights.

I would lay there listening to noises in the night and *Mutter* became part of my symphonies. After our talk, I would sometimes hear her humming and it took me a while to realize that what I was listening to were lullabies. Sweet gentle little melodies that she hummed and giggled until they were shredded in a collision with one of her coughing fits.

I would sometimes hear one of the other women who tiptoed up to our floor and then down the hall to sit whispering with *Mutter*. She had become a kind of substitute mother for most of them. Maybe most of us. *Mutter* could have booked appointments for therapy sessions. Merely her presence somehow made the women feel comfortable enough to talk in ways they never did with others. It was as if there was no longer a need to keep up pretenses or hide from what *Mutter* could no doubt discover anyway.

Most of *Mutter's* late-night sessions were about personal topics that sooner or later broke free of whispers and could be heard through the thin walls. The first time I heard the Swabian and the whore from Cologne in the kitchen I could only catch a few words: *Nazis …dickless … unemployed...*

When the whispers grew so intense that it sounded like a lot of hissing coming from the kitchen, curiosity got the better of me. I got out of bed and went to join them. *Mutter* quickly became a kind of peacemaker telling the whore from Cologne that I was not there to write newspaper stories about her. The whore from Cologne was always suspecting people of doing bad things to her and would only look at me sideways never facing me or making eye contact. She had a large round face with eyebrows that looked painted on and reached sharp peaks over her eyes.

The Swabian was friendly, offering me a drink from the bottle they were sharing. "So what are we going to do about them?" she asked. When she saw that I didn't understand who she was talking about she explained, "The men."

"Poor bastards," agreed *Mutter*. Men were *Mutter's* favourite topic. She could talk about them endlessly. And not always charitably.

"I can think of at least half a dozen of my favourite perverts who will be in anguish," said the Swabian.

"In anguish?" I didn't understand what she was talking about. "How?"

"Well just look. The Nazis are depriving them of their perversions. They've made them all illegal now."

"How awful," said *Mutter*.

"Inhuman," agreed the Swabian. "And the stories about Hitler and all those—"

"*Shh*, " said the whore from Cologne looking around.

"—well? It's probably true. That lot is either too busy poking their things into each other or—"

"—or closing down brothels. And even the clubs: The *Hackepeter*, the *Braun*, the *Auluka* and all the other good sex clubs. Where is one to get old fashioned, weird perversions now?"

"An awful problem. My perverts—some of them will have terrible trouble acting normal. Especially if even the whorehouses are closed down for good," the Swabian said.

"Yes. Terrible things will happen now. These men are German after all."

"I have a businessman who cannot function unless he has a prostitute like me do unspeakable things to him three times a week. You don't want to know what I've stuck up his ass."

"As long as some of it didn't go into my soup afterwards," said *Mutter*.

"You should see the lawyer I get every Tuesday and Friday. I have to be waiting for him in the French maid's outfit he bought for me to wear."

"Do you whip him?'

"Him? No. That's the police inspector. Who I scolded for being part of the puritanicals the last time I whipped him. He said they had no choice. He almost cried. That was the night when thousands of the police had to take orders from the SA at the Bülowplatz."

"*Ach.* They killed people from around here that night. Beat them. Shot them. Communists. Some good ones too."

"My police inspector says either he has to be a Nazi now or be fired. Or worse. So now he can't even do his pervert things anymore."

"Seriously?" *Mutter* said indignantly. Don't they know that we provide a service? The whole country will be drowning in its own fantasies."

"Or in its own sperm that is backed up like a bad toilet."

Mutter agreed. "We are like the Red Cross for sex."

The two whores thought about it for a moment and then nodded. "We should get a medal," said the Swabian.

The only time I heard or saw *Mutter* act differently in her kitchen therapy sessions was with her daughter Erma who was getting ready to leave for Mecklenburg. She even sounded overly maternal, talking in a low voice urging Erma to seize the chance. Again and again it was whispered through the walls—*seize the chance.* Which in this case was the man, this Klaus, who had suddenly become attracted to Erma. Several times I heard them talking about him as *Herr B* and usually Erma was being instructed in what not to tell him about her former life here: her brothel; the dirty-photos studio on the ground floor; and posing naked. "Never, ever, ever!"

"What do I do?" *Mutter* asked me the next day. "My child has a chance to escape all this. To go to Mecklenburg. She's not like your sister you know."

"What has Karin got to do with all this?"

"Ach, your sister! I wish my Erma had what Karin has."

"What does Karin have?"

"Your sister is not like any of the others. She can be whoever you want her to be without ever losing herself. And then in the end you realize you don't know who she is. That is amazing." She thought for a moment and then added, "And terrifying."

THREE

11

MOTHER ALWAYS SAID THE LEAST when she was angriest at father.

When I was thirteen, she stayed silent for a week. It was right after father had organized a trip to Motzener See, the lake south of Tempelhof. We were going swimming he said. Sunshine and health. What could be better than that?

When we got there, walking down the path from where father had parked the car, I heard mother say his name like the crack of a whip: "*Erich*!" She had stopped and stood very still, staring fiercely toward the lake.

"Why don't those people have any clothes papa?" asked Karin who was then six years old. For several minutes mother and father battled through one of their low-voice seething arguments designed to inflict maximum fury while appearing perfectly calm to any onlookers. Father was accusing mother of being hopelessly old fashioned, a prude and even boring.

Her response was strange to me back then even at that age: "I know you Erich! I *know* you."

She kept repeating it until she realized we were surrounded by naked people, including families, on their way to the beach. When Karin wanted to know why the boys had those things between their legs, mother reached out to drag her back to the car. But father was there first, taking Karin by the hand and leading her toward the beach.

On the beach, father put a towel across the small strand of sand. All around us hordes of naked Germans ran into the water and splashed one another. Father looked better when he was dressed for work. Here he was wearing what looked like flimsy short pants that bulged out over his little potbelly. With his narrow shoulders it was like watching a pear on legs.

Naked men and boys raced into the water all around us.

"Is there somewhere I'm not supposed to look?" Karin asked.

"You can look anywhere," father said quickly.

"*They-are-children!*" mother said biting off each word as it left her mouth. It was practically a declaration of war.

"Precisely," said father in his own declaration. He stood up. "And children must learn how to appreciate what is natural and beautiful. Just look around you! Everyone here is naked."

"I don't care."

"All over Germany. Naked is normal now."

"Yes. But the problem is that *you* are not normal."

He glared at her, unbuttoned the short pants he wore and let them fall to his ankles.

Father was now nude like everyone else but mother and me, "Are you coming with me?"

"Me?" I asked, flustered.

"Not you," he snapped. "*Karin.*"

I was to remember the scorn of his answer and my humiliation for years. Or maybe it was what I did immediately afterwards that stayed with me for so long. Of all the possible choices of how I could react I chose oblivion.

Nothing. I showed nothing.

It was the only way I could fight back. Letting him know he could not get to me. Wound me. For being so foolish as to think it was *me* he wanted to come with him. In the face of what was father's almost lip-curling disdain for my innocent confusion—and yes, hopeful confusion, I wanted to wound back.

And match disdain with disdain. To make it seem as if his remark had just bounced off me. Instead of driving right through some inner sanctuary where everything fragile had taken refuge.

"Come," he beckoned to Karin.

Was I jealous? Of my little sister? Did I need so much to be the chosen one? Even like this? Instead of Karin who always got the approval, the looks, the praise. Maybe it was an awful secret within my soul: did I want to be her? Or what she would become?

The questions detonated silently within me. In a jumble that took me years to sort out.

"Why are you standing there?" father said in a sly voice to Karin. Then he picked her up and tossed her into waist deep water. She laughed and splashed back.

"Ah-ah-ah," he said playfully, pretending to scold her.

Karin giggled and fell into a gentle wave, coming up to the surface with her little blouse in her hand.

"My, my! Only taking off your blouse?" said father getting to his feet stumbling on what must have been an uneven surface under the water.

"I should keep my pants on," Karin giggled, but this time differently. It was the giggle of a confused child.

"Do *they* have pants on?" father said pointing to all the other naked people splashing through the lake. "Don't be a sissy."

Father never saw what hit him. To this day I'm not sure if it was the umbrella mother used to shade herself from the sun. Or maybe it was just a big stick she had picked up. Whatever it was, he never saw mother barging into the water, fully clothed and winding up like a lumberjack about to split a log. She delivered a thrashing blow that sent father pinwheeling into the waves. Then she scooped up Karin, putting her under one arm and grabbing her little blouse before storming back to the shore.

With a dazed and gasping Karin under her arm, mother turned back to face the suddenly silent, puzzled and naked hordes. Father resurfaced and staggered to his feet, his potbelly pumping in and out like the bellows we used to fan the embers of a fire.

Mother was already into the grove of trees by the shore with a squirming Karin under her arm. She turned back to see the horde of naked people staring at her. "*He is not normal!*" she yelled before turning and storming away.

Looking out at all those naked people, I realized they had no idea what she was talking about.

I had always wanted to be like mother.

Mother was the strongest person I knew.

But as a girl I never really understood how angry she was. Mostly at herself.

"Remember," she said to me several times, "No one ever really lets you down. You simply misjudge them." It was what she said whenever she and father had one of their seething silent periods. And she always said it as if she was talking to me, but really she was talking to herself.

It all went back to when mother was eighteen—that was the age when she and all her friends had to make the most fateful choice of their lives.

They had to choose a husband, to commit to a young man, a boy really, or risk being an "old maid".

It was a world where so often a girl became a woman while watching the boy who she found herself tied to, become a man she did not recognize.

Or love.

And a decade or two later, the results of their choice would become evident. Some of the not very popular girls had chosen awkward young men who went on to become fabulously successful. And these not-very-popular-girls found themselves becoming women of substance and wealth, desperately sought after by those formerly popular girls who had barely noticed them years earlier.

Because some of those once-popular girls had been less astute or lucky sometimes leading lives that were tragic.

Like mother.

She had chosen a young and witty man. In other words: father. And only later did she learn that that his wit was really just a corrosive cynicism. And the family into which she was marrying was ruled by his father, a fierce but sometimes jovial old patriarch in whose shadow her new husband wilted. And who had fled to a job in a bank where he could look imposing while being nothing more than an embittered clerk.

It took several years for mother to understand where all this bitterness—or maybe weakness, came from. Grandfather Helmut, father's father, could stride into a room and effortlessly fill it with a sense of raw excitement. But he was really only exciting to be around when father was there too. That was when grandfather performed with his odd mixture of boisterous humor and willfulness that made him the kind of man every other man in the room wanted to be.

But when it was just grandfather on his own, he was usually subdued, often sitting silently, letting those fierce eyes of his speak for him.

Father's eyes never stayed still long enough to be fierce. Which was strange because almost everything else about him was so rigid; or at least it was until you looked more closely and saw him quiver whenever something upset him. Which happened every time he and grandfather were together.

It was not just grandfather. Sometimes when I was a girl, I would hide outside father's library door listening to him rehearse what he was going to say the next day to his bosses at the bank in the monthly meeting. It was strange how much he was trying to sound like grandfather. And always, the following day he would return quivering, the way he got when he had no control over whatever was happening around him.

If there was an event that severed the first part of our lives from what came after, it came as a quiet moment that could so easily have gone unnoticed.

On an early evening when Karin was about twelve, she was playing in front of our house running back and forth in some game with friends. It was during the first warm evening of spring and Karin and her friends had tossed their coats to the ground as they chased one another back and forth. I had barely paid attention to them until I saw father standing as still as a statue behind the trees near the road. Returning from his office in his perfectly pressed grey suit, he was the endlessly immaculate image that he tended so precisely. With his darting brown eyes behind little glasses, dull blonde hair and the thin mustache that he thought would make him more acceptable as an official of the bank, he was not a man who attracted attention. Which I thought sometimes upset him.

But now there was something different about father as he watched Karin.

While she was playing with her friends, he stood peering through the budding shrubs, as still and tense as a cat watching something small. He was aware of nothing else.

Not even mother watching him from an upstairs window.

Mother missed almost nothing. About me, or Karin and especially about father. Later when mother got sick, I thought it would have been better if she had missed more. She *knew*. She knew more than anyone that the man she had been married to for years, should not be confused with the dignified specter in the gray suit returning every night from the bank.

And that evening she knew that what had so entranced father were the shadows falling across Karin's blouse as she ran and laughed with her friends. Small rippling contours of lightness and dark were falling across the billowing white silk of her blouse.

Father was seeing for the first time what mother and I had wordlessly acknowledged weeks ago, what he had missed under the heavy winter woolens hiding those shadows and contours on Karin, the prettiest child of them all.

His youngest daughter was developing breasts.

He stood watching her. Only his eyes moved in urgent sweeps, following Karin as she ran back and forth. And once a tiny noise, an involuntary squeak escaped him.

"*Karin!*" It was mother's voice. Calling out from above. Sharp and angry with the effect of a lightning bolt.

To father it might as well have been a lightning strike, the kind that jolts people right out of their shoes. He dropped the banking documents he was carrying, then frantically picked them up and reverted to the tight, precise way he had of greeting Karin and me, walking toward the front door as if he was thinking of bank loans.

Over the next few days, loud voices filled our house. The noisiest outbursts came from Karin. Mother had prepared for this day and Karin wanted no part of it. Which in this case were girdles. Not just any girdles, but the American kind from a Sears catalogue that she had a friend in New York order months ago. Mother was adamant that the Americans had more experience with what she called *men gone silly*, and therefore their women's girdles would be more like rubber fortresses than the flimsy German undergarments.

When Karin saw the girdle she reacted like something wild that was being forcibly tamed. Yelling and tears filled the house all day until father came home and we sat at the dinner table, with Karin looking, from the waist up, as smooth as the autobahn. There was not a shadow or contour to be seen. Which lasted until breakfast when the house was filled with the smell of burning girdles and Karin burst defiantly out of her room with her full array of contours and shadows.

Father complimented her on how much better she looked, and she beamed with pride. Mother said nothing.

A few days later, mother got sick for the first time. Before she got in the taxi and went to the hospital on her own, she told me that if anything happened to her it was me who should look after Karin, the "beautiful child," she called her.

Karin, who didn't quite understand what was happening, ran up to us, laughing until mother told her she'd be gone for several days. As she got into the taxi, Karin burst into tears in what was something between a tantrum and a plea.

"Tell your father I went to the hospital," mother said to me. "And take care of your sister."

Even today I hear her saying what she said.

And there have been times when I tried not to.

A month after she came back from the hospital, mother had the first of her strokes. It began as a headache that made her slump onto a garden chair. I was inside the house when I heard Karin yelling for me to come outside. When I got to the front door Karin was crying and screaming for me to help. She was holding mother up, keeping her from falling off the garden chair. The neighbor, Dr. Boese, got to them before I did, and lay mother gently on the stone path that wound through the garden. He yelled at me to get cold towels and ice cubes as mother said things that sounded like she was chewing on wool.

That night in the hospital even though mother was able to talk more clearly than a few hours earlier, she still struggled to find words. While her mind was functioning as always, she had lost so much of her ability to speak. Words, when they came, were forced and barely understandable.

Something changed again between her and father. I saw it in the way they looked at each other. Everything father did was correct, appropriate. He said all the right things in front of the nurses and me. He spoke of his *concern*, his *determination* to help her. But always it was *my wife*, never *Friëde* he was talking about. Or to. And when the nurses left and it was just the three of us, a look passed between father and mother that left acid all around. It was looks of victory and defeat.

Father framed the moment with the faintest trace of a smile.

Mother responded with an expression of her own, one that signaled both defiance and futility. Tears were streaming down her face. In some unspoken way I understood that in the endless undeclared war between them, father had won.

That night I sat in her bedroom and listened to that new, low voice of hers, now slower after the stroke. "Listen," she rasped. "That day... at the lake... everyone was naked... If something happens to me...." She hesitated as if words were like jigsaw pieces from a different puzzle. "...Your father. Nothing can change what he is." The puzzle became more impenetrable. There was only the sound of her coarse breathing.

"You have to protect your sister," she whispered. "Until she understands where danger comes from."

Until she understands... I have never stopped hearing her words. And among the many reasons I would like to be able to talk to mother now is to ask: *What do I do if she never understands?*

There was a second stroke a month later, this one more severe and leaving her barely able to stand.

One side of her face was frozen in a contorted tangle of confusion and words now came out like vowels and grunts being pulled through your ears. I became her translator. For some reason I was able to understand the twisted words she made.

So on that afternoon, I listened carefully as she made what sounded to father like noises.

"What's she saying?" father asked.

"She wants to know where you're taking Karin."

"To the doctor."

Another guttural tangle of sounds from mother.

"She wants to know what doctor."

Father was already leaving the room where mother lay across the couch, struggling to get up. "A doctor. What does it matter?"

Mother made a noise.

"She says it does matter."

Father turned irritably as if he should not have to explain himself. "Dr. Hirschfeld," he said

Mother bellowed sounds even I could not understand. Father paid no attention and left.

Later that morning Karin left the house with father. She departed as a young girl and came back hours later as something else.

There was much that was unusual about what happened that day, even as they were leaving the house when father took Karin by the hand, guiding her out the door. This was not normal. Father never held our hands.

At the window I looked down to the street at father and Karin. All that uncomplicated sunniness of hers in full flower, her blonde hair sailing across her smile whenever she turned back to wave.

I ran after them. But a taxi had already taken them away. And to this day I can still hear mother's mangled words.

The Karin who left the house that morning would not have understood the strands of innocence and childhood had been invisibly woven around her. And that on that morning she was still a girl, uncomplicated and sunny, her hair swirling whenever she turned her head, like a veil covering happy secrets

But hours later when they came back, her smile was gone, replaced by crinkled, confused looks. She wouldn't say a word to anyone, sitting on the swing in the garden moving aimlessly back and forth. When I went out and sat on the other swing, waiting for her to say something it was as if I was invisible. "Do you want to talk?" I asked. She just kept twirling slowly on the swing with that cascade of blonde hair swirling gracefully,

As I was leaving she called out, "I don't understand."

"What don't you understand?"

"Why would famous army officers wear women's underwear under their uniforms?"

Late that night I went to mother's room as I did whenever she made one of the sounds that now passed for the words she could not form. For almost a day she had been calling out something that sounded like *Thhhanngrrecchhh*! Even I could not understand what she was trying to say. "Thanks?" I tried. "Dreck?" Tears rolled down her cheeks. "A wreck?"

In the near darkness she thrashed and cried on the bed as I held her hand until she lay still, exhausted and defeated. After a while I kissed her forehead and got up to leave.

Thheeeechhhh! She whispered. And suddenly I knew.

"Sex?" I said. That's what you're trying to say?

She nodded. And made the same *Thheeeechhhh*! noise over and over but now it came in sobbing waves as if her mind had frozen. When father came upstairs and asked irritably why she was making all that noise I told him I didn't know. But he had moved on anyway, no longer viewing mother as even an obstacle to what he wanted.

Now it was me. I was the obstacle. I stood between him and Karin.

What is now known:

No one had done as much for sexual research as Dr. Magnus Hirschfeld. In certain academic research quarters of Berlin, Vienna, Paris and London the bulky man with the walrus mustache and the large bow ties was a

revered figure. With his air of scholarly gravitas, the formidable founder of the renowned Institut fuer Sexual-Wissenschaft *was at Berlin's intellectual center of the transformation that would come to be recognized as one of the wildest decades in the history of the western world.*

Sex became a form of currency all its own in late 1920s Berlin, as inflation rendered paper money almost worthless. Suddenly, restrictions on sex were thrown aside; everything was permitted—joyously, proudly and most of all, openly. By the early 1930's the old-fashioned understanding of the word normal *ceased to have any meaning. Which is exactly as it should be, said Dr. Hirschfeld to those from around the world who came to him seeking advice and comfort at the Institute for Sexual Science.*

Sex in all its incarnations—from biology to sociology, was exalted and studied in the Institute's ornate mansion behind linden trees on the edge of the Tiergarten, the huge park in the center of Berlin. In the midst of what had been a fiercely militaristic society Magnus Hirschfeld celebrated homosexuality, transvestitism and sexual rejuvenation. Lectures on sex toys and pills for better performance were all part of his Institute's daily activities and for added research there was always the Institute's enormous library of pornography that was open to all.

Only the most distinguished guests were guided through the mansion by Hirschfeld himself, who proudly showed the antique, steam-driven dildo machines, the whips, chains and leather collars, the life-sized sex dolls, and the half-pant legs and overcoat outfits specially designed for men who wanted to flash women on the street. And among hundreds of other sexual delights were the living examples that could be exhibited: the hermaphrodites and the beautiful boys with perfect female breasts.

But the highlight of the tour was always the exhibit showing the lacy, feminine underwear taken off the bodies of fiercely Prussian army officers who had fallen in previous wars.

It was a way of saying what no longer needed to be put into words. Who else but the forceful, the compelling Dr. Hirschfeld would have the influence to validate, to legitimize, almost every form of sexuality that could be devised or imagined? Everything was permitted. Nothing was forbidden.

But there was another side to it all whenever Hirschfeld was not in public, when he was just Magnus. In the privacy he reserved for himself and those he trusted, he could be proudly ridiculous and childish. Then, it was all just tickling and giggling with his lover Karl. And dressing up in frumpy women's clothes that were deemed an embarrassment by all the cool, sleek transvestites in clubs like the Eldorado or the Monocle. Tante Magnesia they called him, sneeringly. Hirschfeld did not care.

But, in a very different way, others did. And because of them it ended in a flash, all of it when Hitler came to power.

Within months of the Nazis taking over, one of their first and most urgent acts was to burn "un-German" books. The first book burning, in May 1933, was presided over by Josef Goebbels watching from the balcony at State Opera Square; it was the burning of tens of thousands of books and documents.

What was never mentioned in the attack on all this "un-German" material as it went up in flames was that much of it was from Magnus Hirschfeld's Institute for Sexual Science. And the pyre contained the sexual records of thousands of high-ranking Nazis who no longer could afford to be known as having once been among the clientele and admirers of Magnus Hirschfeld.

Karin had changed in ways so subtle that most people we knew might not even have noticed. Where once she was laughing and carefree, now all of that was overlaid with a willful carelessness. And that sunny charm occasionally still flickered to life but now it could be cut through by bouts of impatience and anger.

I waited for an entire day and then as casually as I could I asked: "What did the doctor say?"

"*Doctor*?" Karin replied, using that one word coming back at me like a razor-edged echo.

"The one you saw with father."

A twelve-year old's confusion overcame her; she looked as if she had thoughts that were struggling to break free. Finally: "He said it's okay to look everywhere."

"Look where everywhere?"

"Father wants me to go to beach with him again. The Doctor said it was okay to look everywhere."

"Everywhere?"

"At all the things men have between their legs."

"I don't think you should go back to that beach."

"Doctor Hirschfeld said it was okay. He said everything is okay."

"Everything?"

"Father kept asking him. Like he wanted him to say it was okay."

"What was okay?"

"I don't want to talk about it."

"Tell me."

"Things."

"What things?"

She started yelling. "Things he did! *Things!*"

"I want to know what things."

She suddenly erupted in a crying rage. "No! No! You're stupid, Go away!"

Then she ran out of the house. Hours later, I found her sitting by the back door, sullen and silent. She would neither look at me nor respond to my questions about how she felt. So I sat beside her in silence as the sun went down. Then she looked at me and said, "You don't understand."

"What don't I understand?"

"That I want him to hurt."

For an entire year, whenever father came up to the bedroom that I now insisted on sharing with Karin, she would sit against the wall on the farthest edge of her bed and answer him in a monotone voice while staring at the floor. And as months passed, he found excuses to show up at the door to our bedroom more often. There was always some question about school tomorrow. Or homework. Or exams.

But that was not it. Not remotely.

He was there because he had a thirteen-year-old daughter with the body of a woman.

"Good night papa. We need to go to sleep." I would say with my best smile and get up and close the door firmly, in his face. There was no other way.

And some nights I would lie in bed and hear him downstairs. At first, I could not make out what the sounds were that I was hearing. When I crept down the stairs and sat in the darkness I could see him alone in his library. He was pacing back and forth, drinking out of a bottle and raging at someone who existed only in his mind.

"I am! Do you not understand? *I am!*" he raged to his ghosts. "You need to admit it." And then more yelling that I couldn't understand until: "You cannot cope with what I am! The true me!" And then he slipped on the rug that shot out from under him. He landed on the floor of the library, lying flat on his back sobbing as the liquor flowed slowly out of the bottle he still clutched, staining his shirt a deep red.

On the stairs, I silently got up and went back to our room.

It went on like this for months. On some nights it was obvious who the invisible person was. Sometimes it was his superiors at the bank. Other times it was grandpapa. But mostly it was mother.

I think she could hear him, lying there in the terrible stillness one floor above his library.

During the worst of his library rages I would go into mother's room and sit beside her on the bed, stroking her hand. She had long ago given up trying to fight through her affliction to make sounds. But in the faint light, her eyes were more eloquent than the ranting that came from below.

Sometimes with one of the nurses who had been hired to care for her, mother would venture outside in her wheelchair. Once, on one of her late afternoon forays into the outside world, she came face to face with father who had come home early from work. So separate were their lives now that it was the first time that had seen each other in months. The nurse had stopped pushing the wheelchair; mother and father stared at each other through the charred debris of what had once joined them together. In that moment of stillness now, one looked down, the other looked up. And then father nodded politely and walked around the wheelchair where mother remained staring into air.

Sometime in that next spring, father stopped coming home until very late at night. It was not long afterwards that Karin threw a vase of flowers that shattered on the dining room wall near his head. "Pig!" she yelled and raced up the stairs.

That night in the darkness she did something she almost never did: she talked openly. For weeks she had been a tangle of unreleased thoughts but on this night she sat up in the shadows and said, "He *is* a swine you know." The times when Karin needed you to believe her was when she would talk the most.

"That is not polite," I said. "It is a terrible thing to say about your own father."

The silence went on forever. And then she said simply: "Berta."

"Berta?"

"A girl at my school. She's fourteen. She laughs at me."

"Why does she laugh at you?"

"Because I'm his daughter. Berta's a *nutte*. They go out afterward and are paid to do things with men. She and two other girls from my class do it."

"What things?"

"Sex things."

"What has this got to do with father?"

"He is one of the men."

"One of…?" I couldn't finish the question.

"The men!" She was irritated at having to fill in the blank for me. Then a long angry silence. "You should hear the way she makes fun of him for the way he shakes all over when she holds up her skirt. And then they laugh at me."

These were the days when Karin said almost nothing to father. And I hardly saw him because I was just starting my job at the newspaper and evenings were when I was training to report on the endless diplomatic parties that the *Vossiche Zeitung* editors prided themselves on covering. Many nights when I returned, father was not home and Karin was asleep. Sometimes she would be suspended between sleep and vigilance, snapping awake when I entered our room, indignantly pouring out tales from the *nuttes* about father. They had become Karin's tormenters, purveyors of malicious gossip about our father's nightly activities around the Freidrichstrasse and the most debauched of its clubs.

If I lay awake long enough at night, I would sometimes hear him come in, often stumbling toward the ground floor library where he now slept.

On most mornings he would sit alone eating the breakfast prepared by the maid who had been hired when mother became sick. Silent, still and immaculate in his grey suit, clutching one of his morning newspapers, he looked like he was sculpted out of tin. A raised eyebrow or a quiet *Good morning*, was as much as I ever got from him. And then at exactly twelve minutes after eight—not eleven or thirteen minutes, always twelve minutes, he would get up and walk the eight paces to where his briefcase waited beside the door. He would make one final inspection of his gleaming shoes, polished to a high shine by the maid who lived in fear of his wrath.

It was a rhythm that changed only once in those years before mother died.

And who better to change it than Uncle Rudi? We always knew that anything he changed would be totally turned upside down. Which is what happened to our lives on that Saturday night when his beautiful Mercedes convertible careened in through the gates, dented, steaming, and with a shattered windshield. It lurched to a screeching halt on our driveway and he stumbled out of it barely conscious and bleeding. It was the first time we had seen Uncle Rudi in years.

"I'm here for a rest," he announced grandly before collapsing on the cobblestones.

"I think this is trouble," said Karin and I didn't even ask her what kind of trouble she was thinking of. There were just too many when it came to Uncle Rudi. For one, we knew that father hated his brother. Half-brother actually; they shared Grandpa Helmut as their father although you'd never know it. Uncle Rudi was three years younger than father but on the few times we saw them together it was hard to believe they were related at all.

Uncle Rudi was movie star handsome, almost oddly beautiful with those dark searching eyes set in a slender face with a wide, thin mouth that was always fixed somewhere between a smile and a sneer. But what truly made that face of his almost magnetic were the two long thin scars that ran along his left cheek.

When both Karin and I were much younger and unfettered by tactfulness we would ask uncle Rudi how he got those scars. He would smile and make up some story about hunting Abyssinian lions or wrestling Tasmanian crocodiles and we would laugh and shriek at his outlandish tales of invented valor, each one growing more ridiculous until we were all laughing.

Finally when I was about fourteen years old I got up the courage to ask him if they were Prussian dueling scars. The kind of honour-drenched wounds young men had once sought to prove their bravery. And when I asked him, he fell silent for a moment and then worked that beautiful mouth into a faint smile.

And began talking of hunting Sumatran tigers with his bare hands.

Uncle Rudi was never invited to our home but occasionally he would show up unannounced and act as if he was not aware of father's corrosive silence. You didn't have to be a genius to figure our why father loathed him. Uncle Rudi was everything father wanted to be. And wasn't.

And more than that, grandfather Helmut only came to our home when Uncle Rudi was there. Which is another way of saying that grandpapa almost never came to see his oldest son.

But now on this night, Uncle Rudi was lying on the hallway floor which was as far as we had been able to drag him. Even worse, he was bleeding into the Persian rug.

"Not good," I said.

"The rug?"

"Uncle Rudi."

"The rug too," she said. Karin got down on her hands and knees and peered at Uncle Rudi's beautiful but battered face. "Father will have a fit."

Neither of us knew what to do—much less how to turn off the engine of his Mercedes that was still running in front of our house.

It stayed there with the engine running until Uncle Rudi was revived by the ice that the housekeeper put on his head. He lurched back outside, grappled with something beside the steering wheel that turned off the engine and then collapsed again, half inside the now-silent car.

Again we didn't know what to do. The only thing I could think of was phoning Grandpa Helmut. He was already in bed when I got up the courage to make the call and his voice was ragged with irritation until I said the words *Uncle Rudi.* Even though he was coming from Wilmersdorf, grandfather was there in less than an hour hurrying over to Uncle Rudi, muttering loving curses as he hauled him upright beside the Mercedes. With me and Karin helping, he dragged him back into the house, insisting that he must be put onto the small downstairs bed.

"Uh-oh," said Karin, "Grandpa that's where father sleeps."

"Too bad," grandfather wheezed. "He'll have to sleep somewhere else."

Karin and I looked at each other.

"Your Uncle Rudi has a problem," grandfather pronounced. "He has been beaten up." Grandfather Helmut sounded proud as he delivered his assessment.

That night my newfound newspaperwoman's instincts prevailed. I waited from the shadows of the stairs for father to return. I was sure there was a story about to happen.

It did. Father came in well past midnight as he usually did on Saturday nights. I heard his car arrive and saw him stand in front of Uncle Rudi's Mercedes and then lurch toward the front door, falling once before elbowing it open. The main entrance was dark; a faint light from the library revealed Uncle Rudi sprawled across father's bed. Stumbling toward the room, father began yelling insults so slurred that it was impossible to know what he was saying.

From the darkness came a quiet voice: "Stop it." It was grandfather. He was always most scary when he was quiet. And now he was both quiet and invisible, sitting in the depths of the hall shadows where father had not noticed him.

"What is happening?" father asked. "I do not understand what…" said with shock as if he was listening to his own words being cracked in half.

"You have never understood anything." Grandfather's words snapped out like a lash.

Father looked around, confused. "This is my house."

"You have this house mainly because you inherited our family's name."

Father sagged as if had been punched. He slumped into a chair and said in a weak voice, "He is in *my* bed."

"Rudi is wounded." Grandfather's terrible soft voice was a stiletto being used in darkness. "One son felled in battle, the other felled from his whoring."

"You don't understand."

"I understand. I understand that one son is fighting for the fatherland. And the other is the reason he has to fight."

Nothing but noises came from father until: "…what fighting? For the fatherland?"

"In Neukölln. Rudi went in with the SA and fought the communists. He was obviously one of the heroes."

"I fight." Whiny, indignant.

"Where? In the bank with clerks who cannot defend themselves? With your Friedrichstrasse whores? In the whip and leather clubs? Where? Tell me!"

"That is not fair."

"Fairness is not the issue. Honour is."

I had never heard father, our strict, fierce father cry. Little convulsions shook him as he struggled for words.

Grandfather emerged from the shadows, slowly, serenely. He looked down at father. Then he left. And when the door closed behind him it was as if the tiny flicker of remaining light was sucked out of the house. Father was slumped over, silent. Uncle Rudi was lying across the bed. The only movement was the faint rustling on the stairs behind me. It was Karin. She had seen everything.

"Communists?" she whispered. "Fighting?"

I had only heard stories that different groups of people were coming together and yelling at each other.

Karin whispered again, almost giggling, "Uncle Rudi is so exciting,"

What is now known:

In the desolation of the years after the First World War unemployed, embittered or merely disillusioned men in Berlin band together and fight one another with the viciousness of predators bringing down prey. Without warning, bloody street battles can erupt anywhere—busy intersections, cinemas, restaurants, anywhere where knives, razors, broken bottles, jagged beer mugs and chair legs can be used to maim or kill. Men walking along the wrong street can suddenly be swarmed by a pack, savagely beaten, stripped naked and left on the sidewalk as bloody, comatose rubble.

The outer districts of Berlin are forming behind the two fiercest banners of the epoch: in districts like Neukölln in the east or Wedding in the north the red banner of communism flies, attracting hundreds of thousands to its promise of a better life once Moscow rules all. But in other districts like Spandau in the west, a smaller group is gathering strength behind the swastika, attracting equally disaffected men by the sense of purpose they find from listening to the messianic oratory of Adolf Hitler. Dressed in the brown uniform of the Sturmabteilungen, *they become known to the world as the SA, the Storm Troopers who metastasize from dingy beer halls across all of Germany, whipping, punching, beating their way into control of, first the streets, and then the halls of power.*

The man who has been chosen to lead the Nazi party in Berlin is a deformed and limping young narcissist, a failed playwright, who had grown up pale and thin, enduring such devastating failures that he contemplates suicide and meticulously writes his will, leaving his clothes and his books to his brothers.

But then Josef Goebbels changes his mind about killing himself and decides to go back to school.

At the age of twenty-nine Goebbels arrives in Berlin having just been appointed by Hitler as Gauleiter, the Nazi party boss of operations in the city. With only six hundred members, not even enough to fill a meeting hall, Goebbels makes a simple decision: Attack. Always attack. After watching some of his Nazis beaten up, Goebbels announces, "Whoever can conquer the streets can conquer the masses."

He organizes provocative Nazi street marches close to communist areas and limping deep among lines of his burly SA Storm Troopers, Goebbels is relentlessly self-conscious about his club foot as he yells "Even those of us who suffered wounds in the war have come to march."

But Goebbels doesn't just want a showdown. He wants martyrs. Nazi martyrs. He privately calculates that if he can get his own people to bleed and even better, die, he can attract fierce new members vowing revenge against the Red Menace.

He will get his martyrs.

He rents a meeting hall deep in the northern working-class district of Wedding, the very heart of communism in Berlin. Goebbels knows exactly what will happen when the Nazi swastika banners are draped over the building and by the time he gets there, the hall is packed and seething with menace as the communist Red Front street gangs fill so many of the seats that the police decide to block others from entering, fearing a bloodbath. It is so perfect—exactly what Goebbels wants.

When he makes his way up to the front of the hall he is cursed and screamed at by the communists—just as he had hoped. And with rage sifting through the fetid hall like something combustible it is impossible to establish order. Again: so perfect! So what else can Goebbels do? What else? …except look for some ignition for all that sifting rage. So—reluctantly of course, because what else could he do?—he gives the signal for the SA Storm Troopers to march into the crowd unleashing fists, knives, (To save the Nazi Fatherland of course!) shards of glass, clubs, iron bars and whatever else can be used.

Which of course are returned in the name of the communist Motherland by a roughly equal number of fists, knives, clubs and the like.

When it is over and the communists have been driven out of the hall, maimed and bloody Nazi Storm Troopers lay across the floor, some in agony from serious wounds. Goebbels has them loaded onto the stretchers that had been ordered days earlier and carried up to the front of the hall—where the camera angles will be better. And when not all the stretchers are occupied, he orders unscathed Nazis to be heavily bandaged and lie groaning like the others. It is brilliant. The next day, the photographs and headlines emblazon the Berlin newspapers. By the thousands, would-be Nazis rally to the cause. The streets are soon filled with Storm Troopers vowing revenge for their injured brethren.

But still Goebbels wants more. He wants what transcends mere politics; he wants to enter the realm of the holy. To make Nazism almost spiritual. He wants a martyr who can be—in Nazi terms, beatified. He wants Nazism to be dripping with sacraments just like the Christian church that he has come to hate so much.

But good martyrs are hard to find.

Several prospects turn out to be garden variety drunks who are found to have died by combat with the bottle, or tawdry suicides who float inconveniently in Berlin's canals.

But then Goebbels gets his wish: the holy grail of martyrs! A twenty two year old Storm Trooper, Horst Wessel is murdered.

Wonderful!

Better still are the specifics: he is shot dead at close range in a cowardly attack. And best of all, he was shot by a communist!

It was as if all the boxes checked in the invisible checklist in Goebbels' mind.

*But it gets even more perfect. Before he was shot dead, the young Storm Trooper had the convenient habit of writing stirring songs. One of those songs—*Raise The Flag—*was later adapted to become known as* The Horst Wessel Song.

> Raise the flag! The ranks tightly closed!
> The Storm Troopers march with calm, firm step
> And | Comrades, shot by the Red Front reactionaries
> March in spirit within our ranks

With a massive Nazi funeral arranged by Goebbels who fills the streets with banners and chanting Storm Troopers, Horst Wessel becomes the martyr he has been looking for. With emotional speeches Goebbels elevates the dead Nazi to sainted martyrdom and declared The Horst Wessel Song *to be the national anthem of Nazi Germany.*

And from that day on, no one dares talk of what was openly whispered— that Horst Wessel had really been a thug and a pimp, murdered in his prostitute's apartment by another pimp who just happened to be a communist.

And by the time the Nazis take control, anyone uttering such blasphemy could be arrested by the Gestapo and taken to Plötzensee prison to be beheaded for "insulting the Reich".

Karin was fascinated by Uncle Rudi.

At least part of his allure was the way he so easily displaced father from the library that had been his domain for months. During the five days Uncle Rudi stayed with us Karin regularly skipped into the library, bringing him tea or merely listening to his playfully embellished stories of courage under fire during the wild night of battling communists at this place called Wedding.

Neither Karin nor I had ever been to Wedding. All we knew was that it was where Uncle Rudi and his friends had been fighting all *the bad people.*

Or so Karin insisted. She believed everything he told her.

She made sure that father was aware that Uncle Rudi had obviously been *so* heroic. Fighting to protect the fatherland against bad men, these communists, who were trying to attack his friend just because he wanted to make a speech.

During those five days Uncle Rudi stayed with us, the years of anger between him and father were peeled back like something overripe and dripping poison from its core. Father was seething, precise, clipped while Uncle Rudi was charming, and spontaneous in a way that our household had never before seen. Both of them seemed to fill their roles more fully with each day that passed.

Father returned temporarily to sleeping in "mother's room" on a small cot he had set up near the window. From the doorway I watched mother's eyes flash in mute confusion as he set himself up in the room in which they had once shared their nights. He turned to see her watching him and as if he felt impaled by her gaze, he allowed a tight little smile to escape, saying it would only be for a few nights. *Until that bastard Rudi leaves.*

She had recently regained some movement in her right hand and had been able to scrawl words on the paper that lay beside her. But now her hand just moved back and forth on the paper, holding the pencil like it was a spike and leaving jagged marks on the page that father did not notice.

On the second night I was awoken by creaking on the wooden stairs, Karin's bed was empty. A moment later was when the yelling started. It started with the bellowing from father: "In your nightgown?" that was followed by confusion from Karin that quickly became indignation as Uncle Rudi joined in.

"Oh Erich come on. She was just standing in the doorway talking to me."

"In her nightgown?"

"Yes in her nightgown Erich. The same one that could pass for a winter coat. And why are you going on about this?"

"Yes, why papa?" Karin yelled storming back toward the stairs.

Upstairs, Karin settled back in to her bed. The suffocating silence in our house resumed. After a while Karin whispered, "Uncle Rudi is much more interesting than father."

"You shouldn't talk like that," I whispered back.

"Why?"

"Things are difficult enough here."

"You know something else? Father knows it. That is why he doesn't like Uncle Rudi being here."

The next afternoon the Mercedes was missing from the parking area beside our house and Karin had not returned from school. Father came home, looked around, and then packed up Uncle Rudi's belongings, dumping them outside the front door. With his face tighter than usual he sat down for dinner until the sound of the approaching Mercedes. Seeing Karin jump out of it laughing was the fuse that lit what came next. Which was a screech. Father never, in his life as we knew him, had screeched. But he did here. It was the sound like a cornered animal makes. Shrill. Terrified. Unintelligible. Until a single word formed.

Lipstick?

Hours later when exhaustion had settled over our house posing as peace, Karin got up from her bed and whispered across the darkness: "Watch."

She lit a candle. And then she took out the tube of lipstick that father had not been able to find. She placed it on the little table between our beds. It stood upright between us.

Then she went to what she called her purse, which was really just a big bag for carrying schoolbooks and clothes for her gymnasium. From it she pulled female underwear—not the girl underwear she had always worn. And then a flimsy blouse. And a tight skirt. And stockings that were meant to be fastened to garters.

"Uncle Rudi bought all this for me. As a joke."

"A joke?'

"He said it would make father go crazy."

She put it on, one piece of clothing at a time. And when she was finished, she leaned into a little jeweled case looking into its mirror and applied lipstick to what became in that half-light, lush full lips that no one could imagine being those of a girl.

I had just watched that girl become—in her own mind, a woman. And somehow it terrified me. "And what happened after he bought you all these clothes?"

"He didn't do anything if that's what you're asking."

"Okay then, what did he do?"

"He took me to see his friend."

"What friend?"

"Herr Heck. At the zoo. I loved the zoo. Herr Heck is important in the zoo. The director."

"Did you wear these clothes at the zoo?"

"Oh don't be silly. I got to see the elephants and the baboons and the monkeys. And the lions, I loved the lions! I'm going back next week to see them again. Uncle Rudi knows so many important people. But don't worry. He's different than father."

"How is he different?"

"He's normal. And nice."

I barely heard her. I was looking at the tube of lipstick that stood upright on the little table between us.

In silhouette, it had the shape of a bullet.

I lay there. Waiting. "Father became a Nazi because he was jealous of Uncle Rudi. You know that don't you?"

"Go to sleep."

"It's true, it is. He looks silly in that Nazi uniform. But he just wants to be like Uncle Rudi," she whispered.

"Shh."

"He was furious when I told him he looked silly in that Nazi uniform."

"Good night."

I waited until I heard the soft rasping she made when she was in the deepest part of her sleep. Then I got up and with a lantern, I silently went upstairs to where mother lay trapped within her own body. I nodded to her nurse who understood enough to depart to another room down the hall. Mother was awake. Night and day meant nothing to her anymore.

Recently I was becoming less certain that she was always lucid. There were nights when she would scrawl words on the paper that made no sense. Sometimes she was as mentally alert as ever, but other times she seemed to confuse dates and people from years ago.

Her eyes followed me as I approached the bed. I had never come to her room so late. Her right hand scrawled on the paper.

OK? it said.

"Oh we're fine," I said maybe too quickly and then told her about the better parts of my evening at the legation reception, leaving out both the two thugs and also returning home to the uniform that father was wearing. But I didn't finish what I had planned to say because like some out-of-control Morse code machine, the smallest finger on her right hand was tapping furiously against the pad of paper. Only when I stopped talking did that finger fall silent and still.

"What?" I asked.

WHAT? she scrawled back on the paper. Almost as if we were dueling.

"Father," I said.

She took what for her was a deep breath and held the pad out toward me with that same word on it: *WHAT?*

"Do you remember? Six years ago." I said.

WHAT?

"When I turned sixteen you said you wanted to say something to me. But you didn't."

She shook her head: *NO.* Then: LATER.

"Later is now."

WHY?

I told her the truth about what I had seen at the Peruvian legation, about the two SA thugs. And about what I had seen happening on the streets. And then finally about father coming home tonight in a Nazi uniform.

Stillness. Her eyes never wavered. Her finger never tapped. Then: *HIM? NAZI?*

"Yes," I nodded. "Father."

Whatever the inner force was that had sustained her seemed to leave like air rushing from a puncture in something precious. She shook her head and became smaller in that bed. It took her a long time to write what came to fill a page with her large, erratic scrawl: GRANDMOTHER NO.

It was obvious to her that I didn't understand.

NOT GRANDMOTHER.

Then: BIRGIT.

"Birgit?" Not until I looked into mother's stare that was urging me down a corridor of memory did I understand who she was talking about. Birgit was the woman who had been the servant at grandfather's house since she was young. My memories were of her with silver hair pulled back from an unlined face, an ageless quality that went on well past her middle years. She was taller than most women and I remembered whispers when we were young that maybe Birgit had never married because most of the men would never want to be shorter than their wife. Yet Birgit was one of those women with Nordic features and cheekbones that cast shadows, so in other words she was the kind of woman that a lot of German men fantasized about no matter how tall they were.

Something about Birgit's life never made sense to me when I was growing up.

I also remembered her because mother had been so close to Birgit when I was younger.

Years ago whenever mother had one of those bitter fights with father, she would go to grandfather's home and spend hours with Birgit which was unusual because servants did not usually enter into lives of people in the social classes above theirs. Birgit had a serenity that attracted people like mother. And years earlier, after grandfather's wife died, Birgit stayed on as the servant in charge of that large house.

She suddenly became ill and died one December when it was so cold that the gravediggers had trouble digging through the hardened ground. It was as if Birgit was fighting to stay with us.

What I remember from that awful day was that there was only mother, Karin, me and grandfather at Birgit's funeral. And that grandfather could not stand to see the casket going into the ground. With some strange noise, he turned and leaned into the bitter wind, fighting his way to the car where he sat alone for the rest of the service.

Not wanting anyone to see that he had been crying.

And now: Again: BIRGIT mother scrawled on the pad of paper.

"Yes," I said not understanding. "Birgit?"

She wrote again: GRANDMOTHER. That stare again. YOU.

She was pointing at me.

"Birgit?" A gale force of memories twisted, turned inside out and then shattered. "…is father's mother? *And she is my grandmother?*"

Mother nodded. And then looked at me as if we'd already moved past all that. And that I should have known it long ago.

Then when she thought I'd understood what she had said she turned the pad of paper toward me. On it were two words:

BIRGIT JEW.

FOUR

12

1933

I AM FINE. EVERYTHING IS fine.

I am fine. Everything is fine.

Hitler and the Nazis were days away from taking over the entire country.

I am fine. Everything is fine.

And then I wasn't. And *it* wasn't.

I lay there in the darkness seized by fears I could not even identify. It had never happened to me before, being a fearful person without knowing why I was afraid. But so many others were feeling what I felt.

It was probably another reason why I had come to belong here at *Mutters*. Truly belong in a way I had never felt anywhere else. The fetid air, the smells, the cries in the night piercing the thin walls, they had somehow all become part of my world now. Those cries and noises were my own form of symphony, played on instruments of confusion, pain and exhaustion. I envied those who cried out in the night. At least they knew what made them afraid. Or even angry.

The Swabian prostitute had Jürgen. Inga had her fear of losing her looks before she found the man she knew was out there somewhere waiting to meet her.

And the whore from Cologne who was constantly returning after another doomed love affair was afraid of losing whatever clothes she had.

And Hildegard, the new tenant down the hall in the small room beside the bathroom, a dark-haired attractive woman in her fifties who had once been married and wealthy was afraid of what she called 'another breakdown' and could sometimes be heard sobbing quietly.

And *Mutter* had her fear of not being able to feed us all. When she was drinking in the kitchen late at night it became the percussion section. She would thrash the wall with whatever cloths she could find, some of which would be found in the morning sticking to its greasy surface.

Only Karin seemed fearless in the way she had always been. And for that, I wondered, and I envied her.

Sometimes I would sit and wait out the random hammer blows of *Mutter's* bluntness. She was always brutal but never malicious except for the Nazis about whom she was as cutting as she could be: "Such geniuses those Nazis are. They give all these little men a tiny bit of power, just enough power to make them feel big for the first time in their lives." she would say as Erma was making *Shh* sounds that *Mutter* disregarded. And "Look at all those enormous flags and banners and loudspeakers they have. Probably smart. How else can they create aggression in people with inferiority complexes?" she said waving Erma aside before she could utter a sound.

Sooner or later *Mutter* would come up with something to take her mind off whatever she had been telling you. Usually she would be standing at the stove in her stained housecoat, occasionally blending fallen ash from her cigarette in with the stew she was making for the rest of us. Or later in the day she would settle back with whatever cheap liquor she could find, revealing her sympathetic nature in direct proportion to the amount of alcohol she consumed.

On this night, she rummaged through a corrugated pile of personal papers until she found what she was looking for.

It was a photograph of a beautiful young woman taken decades ago.

"Look at this woman," she said holding the photograph in front of me. The young woman in the photograph was beautiful with almond shaped eyes set in a face that Marlene Dietrich would envy. She was dressed in a full-length evening gown that even with the styles of that era revealed a slender figure draped in elegance.

I almost gasped. Because looking from the photo to *Mutter* I was stunned to find myself looking at the same woman. Those almond eyes were still there but they were buried in what looked like entrances to caves of flesh, and the wide, full lips had settled, grown and fallen like the rest of her.

"I should be proclaimed a famous scientist," *Mutter* insisted through lips partly immobilized by the cigarette dangling between them at the side of her mouth. "Forget this Einstein character. If you want to know about the effects of gravity I'm better than that fuzzy haired academic. Just look at me—I'm my own experiment on gravity," she said with her raspy laugh that could have ejected the remaining buttons of her stained housecoat from the force of the jellied mass shaking beneath them. Different parts of her shook at different times

"And you want to know the secret of it all?" she said, her voice turning phlegmy after gagging on an errant swallow of smoke. "I was never happy back then when I was beautiful. I kept telling myself I was but I wasn't. You know what got me out of there?"

She didn't wait for a question to propel her into what came next.

"What got me out of that life was the worst type of man you could ever meet: A stiff-dicked bastard who should have been fucking the mirror and not me. But I still owe him for some things. He was a communist you know."

Another attempt to drain the bottle fortified her for the memories that came while she was still wiping her chin. "Because you know how I ended up here? With a brothel? Instead of in some mansion out in Wannsee? Or the Grunewald? I could have had been one of those women fucking for luxury, complete with maids and servants wiping snot or worse from the noses and asses of perfect children while I drank martinis all afternoon and compared affairs with the other elegant ladies as we waited for our pudgy banker-husbands to come home.

"I had offers you know. Two bankers and one Krupp. God I could have been so pampered. And look where I am now. One of them was actually attractive and I had every reason to marry him."

"Why didn't you?"

"I didn't have the un-reason. With the fucking communist I had a million un-reasons. And maybe that was what I was all about in those days. I craved the shock, the outrage, the pain and the fury he gave me. Sometimes I miss it even now. But I don't miss all that communist shit. And all his other women. The last time I saw him I had to listen to him lecture me about how bourgeois I was for being jealous. But just to show there were no hard feelings he said he would fuck me one last time. When he approached me, my knee got him right between the legs.

"So his act of charity was called off on account of equipment failure." She laughed at the memory of it and until other memories pulled her down. "A week later he was dead. Police bullet. In that May 1st riot. I wasn't surprised."

She upended the bottle, partially missing her mouth. Wine ran down the rivulets forming the border between her cheek and her chin and then dripped onto her housedress like something from a slow leaking faucet.

"But I tell you what. I got a gift from him. The gift of sex like I could never have dreamed of. Before the communist—"

"Did the communist have a name?"

"*Ach.* If I have to say his name then I start thinking about him again. Really thinking about him. And if I do that then...." She sat staring blankly into the greasy wall behind the stove, drinking occasionally until in one quick, violent motion she flung a dishtowel at the wall. It embedded itself into the bubbling grease with a loud slapping motion and then edged its way down the wall like something dying in slow motion.

"Stupid bastard." *Mutter* watched it like a vanquished foe, expiring on some field of battle. "Yes. Sex. There is always that. *Was* always. But it was a gift, make no mistake. The bankers and all the rest, they do it like they were mechanical clocks. You almost expected to hear '*cuckoo-cuckoo*' when they finished. But from that communist I learned gifts. After the great way he fucked why do you think I opened a whorehouse when it ended between him and me?"

"I'm not sure I understand," I said. "One doesn't necessarily lead to the other does it?"

"Ach. So rational, so rational." She was lost in thought until she said, "Please. Just leave me alone."

It was long after midnight when all else was still and silent. I got up and went to my door of my room that was closest to the kitchen.

There was muffled sobbing. And arguing, the kind of lowered voice furies that thrash silence.

Peering out I saw *Mutter* sitting alone, a bottle in one hand, a Bible in the other. She was arguing with someone who did not exist, waving the wine bottle and pointing it at the greasy wall behind the stove, which apparently was where her invisible tormentor resided.

I didn't want her to be embarrassed so I closed the door and coughed loud enough that she would hear it. Then I opened the door and went toward the kitchen. What I had not seen before were the tears that had been running down her face and that in wiping them away, she left only moist smears. She attempted a look of defiance that she could not sustain.

She turned away from me, trying to hide the Bible she had been holding.

"Can I ask you something?"

"Why is it that when people want to irritate you, they always ask if they can ask you something?"

"You never seemed really religious to me."

"That's not a question."

"Sorry," I said. "Are you really religious? Or is it just to keep up appearances?"

"Well you insufferable shit," she said and then took a long drink out of the bottle. Then she coughed and said, "Both."

She opened the Bible and read, "For God is not a God of disorder." She looked up over her glasses. "First Corinthians. Now do you see?"

"No."

"For a while I loved communism. At first I thought it was because of the sex. But that ended and then I realized it was because it provided all the answers, all the rules. I didn't have to think; decide or worry. Everything was all laid out.

"But then when my bastard communist got himself killed, I realized I didn't really believe in it anymore. But I needed something—anything to fight off all that freedom I couldn't go back to. It scared the hell out of me—all those choices, decisions, responsibilities. I needed something to replace communism. So what else is there but this?"

She held up the Bible. "It's like a bannister when you're at the top of the stairs. It's there so you never have to think about how close you are to plunging over the edge."

"And so you really believe all this?"

"If I say I do, then I do," she said slamming the Bible shut.

13

KARL ERNST STOOD AT THE door of *The Eldorado* waiting for Karin.

It was almost a month after he had climbed the stairs of *Mutter's* tenement to deliver Helldorff's message to Karin. As a young, and rising Nazi, he knew that *The Eldorado* was only days away from being forcibly shut down by his own SA. But that was for tomorrow, whenever it came. For now it was just one of the quickly vanishing contradictions of life as the old order was being crushed.

Tonight, dressed in his high leather SA boots but wearing a white shirt open at the neck, he scanned the throngs that lined Nollendorfplatz. All of them straining to get his attention, the beautiful boys, the boys who were not quite the women they wanted to be (only the beauties could get Karl's attention) and the annoying tourists, all of them insisting they were not, *definitely not* inclined toward this homo thing. Just looking.

And then there were the movie stars: Marlene, who just could not stay away, and Rudolph Valentino and Greta Garbo.

And tonight for third time this week, there was Karin and Inga and Erma; each had her own reasons for being there. For Inga it was the frenzied glamour, a world that enthralled her. For Erma it was the adulation of the transvestites who wanted her cool beauty for their own.

But for Karin the only reason she even bothered to accompany them was because Karl, the young SA leader had asked her to be there.

On weekday evenings Karl would wait impatiently for Mugette the transvestite showgirl to finish her performance onstage. Sometime Mugette could be interminable, soaking up all the applause with her porcelain face and doll-like features beneath the huge floral hat, her slender body swirling endlessly across the stage in her rose-encrusted chiffon dress.

When Mugette's act was over—*finally!* and the club was emptying out was when he could talk to Karin.

In theory, Karl was supposed to be the conduit to Count Helldorff who was too busy, simply too *important* to be seen chasing after this willful girl. So he ordered Karl Ernst to keep contact with her.

But Karl Ernst did more than that; he became oddly dependent on Karin. And often when she did not want to see Helldorff, he made excuses for her: she was sick; it was that time of the month; he couldn't find her, anything that would keep her with him for another hour or so. Just to talk.

She possessed what Karl Ernst needed most. The ability to understand him.

He needed her for absolution in so many ways he could never admit. Even though it irritated him, this need to have someone hear *his* side of the terrible things he has done, leading SA troops raging along the Ku'damm or on forays into Kreuzberg, beating up communists and Jews. Despite his unreflective nature he just needed to make confessions to someone who would just *listen.*

But they were not exactly confessions; it was more like ordering someone to agree with him.

And Karin listened. Endlessly. It was this strange power that she possessed, one that made others who she barely knew wonder why they were explaining so much to her. And needing her to understand.

What Karl Ernst, up to his soul in bloody beatings, most needed was just a word, a gesture from her.

But what he could not know was that Karin was the ultimate believer in goodness. She was convinced it was lodged in the soul of everyone who interested her. Redemption was possible, she was sure of it. Even though the stories of those battered workers and Jews almost made her cry. It was horrible what was happening. And why was this Karl being so *mean*? But she never lost faith in her ability to see that someone like Karl Ernst was doing terrible things simply because he did not understand how decent he really could be.

If only he tried.

Some day he would. Karin was sure of it. She *saw* it. That decency. It *had* to be there. Surely. He simply had to give it a chance.

But there was something else Karl tried to make sure she understood—that he really *was* masculine. No matter what it might look like here in *The Eldorado.*

In the nearly empty club, he would try to make Karin understand that he was only involved with other men sexually because Ernst Röhm had insisted on it. And because he owed everything to Röhm, *of course* she would understand.

Karin had no idea who Ernst Röhm was.

She had heard the name somewhere but did not know that the bulging, almost piggy-like Ernst Röhm was then the violent force at the center of the Nazis, the leader of the SA. With his round angry face, little eyes and tiny toothbrush mustache, Röhm was the leader whose raw brutality had been backing the still shaky efforts of Adolf Hitler to consolidate power.

Of course Karin had heard of Adolph Hitler. He was some noisy little man from Munich. But this other person—this Röhm?

Ernst Röhm was defiantly, proudly, homosexual. And expected the most attractive of those he groomed for power—young, handsome men like Karl to be "open to understanding".

"But it was not what you probably think it is," Karl told Karin again and again.

Karin had no idea what she thought it was. It was all too puzzling to her at first, the idea of men being with men—really *being* with them? In bed for instance. How did *that* work?

And this *Wandervogel*, she had heard of it but getting boys to go out into the wilderness, whole troops of boys who were encouraged to love other boys? *That* was what *Wandervogel* was?

All the boys she knew were—

"Are you listening to me?" Karl was suddenly right in front of her talking in a voice that was between urgent and irritated.

"Yes. Yes."

"You understand? The ancient Greeks?"

"No." *Ancient Greeks? What do they have to with anything?*"

"The fiercest warriors, the Spartans and all the rest were men, beautiful men, brave men, who loved one another. And they fought to the death, feared by their enemies as *we* are feared. Not like those old queens like Magnus Hirschfeld and—"

"It's late."

"What does that have to do with anything?"

"I have to go."

She knew instantly that she had said wrong thing. The ring of scar tissue under his right eye always turned red whenever he was angry and now it was crimson.

"You are laughing at what I say."

"No. Don't be ridiculous."

It was as if the word was spring-loaded, flinging Karl Ernst into another terrifying part of himself. Enraged, Karl Ernst the young, soon-to-be supreme *Sturmabteilung* leader of Berlin ripped most of the dress right off Karin In those shadows of the empty backstage at *The Eldorado*, he screamed *"Ridiculous?"*

"Why are you doing this?" Karin half-cried, half-fought as she pounded on his chest while his hands tore at remnants of her flimsy dress and then reached round to what was left of her underwear and ripped it away.

"Why? You have to ask?" He was grappling with his belt. "When you say I am ridiculous?"

"That's not what I meant. It's just that no man I know has—Don't!"

"You say I am not a man?"

"*What*? That's crazy!"

"Crazy?" He was almost hysterical with rage.

"I didn't mean—"

Quickly and coarsely it happened. He pinned her onto a bench, pulled down his pants and forced himself inside her as she fought and cried. She felt him pulsing within her, gasping and thrusting.

And then suddenly it was over,

He lessened his grip and pulled out of her, suddenly almost apologetic. She pushed him as hard as she could so that he fell backwards with his britches down around his gleaming boots. She grabbed whatever covering she could find as he wrestled his pants upward and staggered to his feet.

From out of the shadows came a silky voice.

"The Mercedes is waiting outside." It was Mugette. Looking out from behind a curtain, her porcelain face a mask.

"Helldorff," gasped Karl. "I was supposed to make sure you were delivered to him tonight."

"Delivered?"

"Yes!" Karl Ernst was suspended between self-righteousness and some kind of nervous collapse. "The Count wants you."

"Delivered?" she said again, looking down at the shreds of her clothing scattered across the floor. "I need a dress," she said to the face peering through the bunched up curtains. Mugette nodded and hurried back to her dressing room.

Slowly, and staring right at Karl Ernst, she picked up his SA hat that lay on the floor, the pill box cap with the Nazi eagle and swastika emblem on the front. She crumpled it up, not taking her eyes off him.

Then she slowly wiped the space between her legs. Over and over again until the crown of the hat was stained, viscous and dripping.

"Here's your hat." She dropped it at his feet.

I had come to believe that what Karin possesses is a selective goodness overlaid on a sense of willful innocence. Combined, they can allow terrible things to happen.

After all this, I have come to fear that certain kind of goodness as much as I fear evil. It is the kind of willful goodness that exists in a state of deep inner certainty, utterly convinced that the world could never support evil if only good people were given a chance to explain goodness to evildoers.

It is all so decent, so sensible. And so stripped bare of the imagination and the honesty needed to admit that goodness fertilizes the kind of evil that I see it all around me.

14

ON THAT NIGHT WHEN KARIN stumbled out of *The Eldorado* in the makeshift dress, the SA driver who was waiting outside in Helldorff's Mercedes gave no hint that he saw anything unusual.

The man's entire livelihood depended on never seeing anything unusual. Not even in what he was seeing now—the obvious absence of any underwear on the young lady, or even a petticoat. And at first, the bare feet.

It was only when he saw her heading toward a broken bottle on the sidewalk that the driver hurried toward her, picking her up in a sideways swooping motion, disregarding her yells to be put down.

Only Mugette was there to hear her protesting and trilled, "Oh how romantic!" as she ran after them with Karin's shoes. The driver tossed them into the back seat of the Mercedes where he had dumped Karin and then quickly got in and roared away. As the Mercedes drove down Tauentzienstrasse and slowed to make an abrupt right turn, Karin gabbed the door handle and yanked it upward. Nothing happened. In the rear-view mirror she saw the driver's eyes yielding nothing.

Through the windows she watched Berlin pass by, parts of it she had never seen. Charlottenburg she knew but by the time the houses yielded to a kind of forest in the city she realized it must the Grunewald. And then beyond that came the sign for Dahlem and she realized she had no idea where she was. With her bare feet on the luxurious leather seat and her knees pulled up to her chin she yelled at the SA driver: "I want to go home."

The driver's eyes never flickered to the rear-view mirror until they passed another sign, this one saying Zehlendorf. The rain was coming down.

Then he said sharply, "Take your feet off the seats."

She had never seen a boulevard with so many beautiful houses set back on park-like settings and illuminated by discreetly hidden lights. The

Mercedes slowed down, turned sharply and stopped. As if by magic, huge wrought iron gates opened and it cruised along a cobble stone path, past the grand main entrance and around to a side door.

"I'm going to scream," she said hoping she sounded threatening as the SA driver opened the rear door. The driver, an older man with an angry square face just stood there looking more menacing than she remembered.

From somewhere in the shadows came a silky voice: "It's all right. You're safe. No one's going to hurt you."

When the driver stepped aside, she saw Helldorff holding an umbrella. "Please," he said.

She got out of the car and went inside.

In a high ceilinged, baronial living room, with wooden beams and a huge stone fireplace with flames that gave the only illumination, Helldorff walked to a high-backed leather chair and watched Karin. She was moving through the vastness of the room like a cat in an unfamiliar place.

"Am I kidnapped?" she asked.

"You can leave any time you want."

"Then why am I here?"

"So I can apologize."

"You? Apologize?"

In the flickering light, Helldorff allowed himself the faintest of smiles and over the watery gaze of blue eyes that seemed to Karin somehow haunted.

"For what happened on that boat. I never really had the chance to apologize."

"*Now* you want to apologize? That was a long time ago,"

"Not really."

She walked in front of the huge fireplace as its light sculpted the silhouette of her body in the strange and flimsy dress she was wearing. She had never seen such a room before. It was ornate in a way that seemed to come out of some fairy tale book. And with burnished wood inlays on the walls and the chairs that looked like something from a palace. Everything fascinated her including the leaded glass windows that threw crisscross shadows on the gleaming floors.

The glint of something shiny caught her eye. Protruding from under a table was a pile of elegant picture frames. One of them was an ornate silver frame that reflected the dancing light of the fire. She turned it over and found herself staring at a photograph of about a dozen people arranged around a solemn looking older couple. It looked like a family with younger women and men as well as children arrayed around the couple.

"Who are they?" She held the photo up for Helldorff to see.

"What is that?" he said, startled as if she had said something wrong. The patrician look of his face suddenly fell away leaving only the impatient irritation she had seen before.

"Are these people your family?"

"What people?"

"The ones in the photograph." She held it up.

"Put those down," he said sharply from across the darkened room.

"Is this your family?" she persisted.

"No," he yelled back.

"Then who are they?"

"People who used to live here."

"Why did they leave?"

"They decided it was time to go."

"Go where?"

"Some other country. Put that back where you found it."

He had escorted her up the wide and graceful curving staircase leading to the second floor, opened the bedroom door and told this was her bedroom.

"*My* bedroom?"

She had never seen a bedroom like this one. It was many times as big as any bedroom she had ever slept in. Lit by candlelight that cast quavering shadows and with quilted covers as thick as a snowfall on a big four-poster bed under its own canopy, the room seemed almost magical to Karin. More so because Helldorff behaved with almost fawning rectitude.

He watched her walk slowly through the shadows inspecting everything. "I once had a room like this. When I was younger."

"Where?"

"Near Merseburg. In Prussia. We used to have a lot of things there."

"What happened to it?"

"I lost it."

"How do you lose a room?"

"My mother. She took it back."

When she turned around to ask how his mother took a room back, he was gone.

Later, when she was under the billowing covers wondering what was happening to her, the creak of hinges signaled the opening of the door. Helldorff stood in a silk evening coat that looked to have been made for a much bigger man. "Don't be afraid," he said.

"It never occurred to me to be afraid." She was aware, as she was before, that defiance excited him in some bizarre way.

He sat in one of the throne-like chairs near the bed. "I am sorry."

He waited for Karin to ask him what he was sorry for. But Karin already possessed an understanding of power played out at its lowest level, the level of two people, of a man and a woman, the kind of understanding that can never be taught or learned. And those who possess it have no idea how it came into their possession. It is far more instinct than reason or intellect.

And in that moment Karin knew that Helldorff's craving of a response from her stripped him of all his strutting power for at least that instant of unease flooding through him.

As he waited for her to say something—*anything.*

So she chose the cruelest response:

Silence.

It sent the gaze of those watery blue eyes darting around the room seeking a place safe enough to settle on. "Did you hear what I said?"

She nodded.

"For what happened on that yacht. I am truly sorry. I don't know what happened to me."

Silence.

"I have never done that before."

"You whipped a boy."

"Yes. But that is not what I do. That is not who I am."

"Then who are you?"

In slow deliberate motions he rocked back and forth in the chair and then got up and went to the door. Before he closed it he said "I am better than who you think I am."

And then waited for her response.

Again she gave none. And then for a moment, she understood that as he waited, she had a strange kind of control.

She turned away, lying on her side until she heard the door close,

Karin fell asleep under the billowing covers and dreamed dreams she had never had before. They were dreams of crowds waving to her, people trying to get her attention and calling her name.

She awoke in complete darkness when the covers were raised and Helldorff eased himself under the covers beside her. "It will be all right," he whispered.

She kept her back to him and said nothing, waiting to see what would happen. He pressed against her. She felt him momentarily aroused and then murmuring *It will be all right* over and over again he held her tightly against him. She could smell the alcohol that came on his breath in sweet and sickly little bursts. She lay awake until his breathing against the back of her neck became soft and rasping.

Then she gently loosened his grip, quietly got out of the bed, leaving the bedroom and walking toward the big room downstairs, the one with the fireplace. But there were so many other doors on the way, all of them closed. She opened one. The room was empty. So was the next one. But the third door yielded a strange silhouette, like a miniature hill in the middle of the room. It yielded to the touch and when she turned on a light, she found herself looking at a mound of clothes piled almost up to her shoulders. There were men's suits and heavy winter coats mixed in with dresses and gowns in several different sizes. And dozens of pairs of shoes mixed in among all the clothes.

What fascinated Karin was how different the clothes were from the ones she and her family had worn. There was just something better about them, the way they felt, the way they were styled and the sweet hint of floral fragrance that came from everywhere in the pile. They were beautiful to hold, to smell, to look at.

She had never thought of clothes as being like flowers or works of art. She was putting down a beautiful black gown when a patch of vibrant green caught her eye. Tugging at it, she pulled out a summer dress. She held it up in the faint light. Clothes had never interested her before, but something about this green dress made her feel strangely better about herself, better than what she felt walking into the room. She held it in front of her, searching for a mirror, a reflection, and finding none she decided to try it on.

The dress fit. Perfectly. Or almost. Only when she raised her arms was there a slight tightening around her breasts. But that was nothing compared to the way she felt walking around in that new green dress. She just knew it!—she was more beautiful, more assured, more—

She felt the shaking on her arm and opened her eyes, squinting into the shards of morning sun coming through the leaded glass windows of the room that seemed bigger in the daylight. He was standing over her. She heard him ask, "Where did you find the dress?" before she rolled over and went back to sleep without answering him.

She stayed through one day and into the next, fascinated but not understanding what she was seeing.

Helldorff was different here. When he was involved in whatever it was that he did, his sense of command was imposing, almost intimidating. From a distance she watched his easy confidence and sense of control as other big cars flying small Nazi flags came through the gates, bringing grey, intense men to meetings at the large house. His cool assurance never faltered among all the jackboots and the swastikas and Mercedes, not even when she saw that odd-looking man arrive. She only recognized Josef Goebbels because of the newspaper photograph that Uncle Rudi had proudly shown her after the brawl with the communists in Wedding. It was a photograph of an angry Goebbels making a speech as Nazis and communists were fighting below him.

She decided Goebbels looked just as angry here, the kind of person who is irritated because he can't remember what he was supposed to be irritated about.

Karin watched from over near the hedges where she sat on a wooden bench pretending to read a book becoming even more fascinated by the difference between the Helldorff in the bedroom last night and what she saw here—how smoothly among men he played power as if was an instrument.

From the car behind Goebbels several *Schutzstaffel* Nazis in their black SS uniforms and gleaming boots hurried out with pistols in their hands. Two of them followed Goebbels inside and the others remained by his car. When they saw Karin, one of them came over to her. He was young, massive and intense.

"Who are you and why are you here?"

"I live here," she said sweetly even though the SS Nazi was not friendly.

"Do not move from here. Stay where we can see you." He turned with almost a snap of his boots.

When she called out in that same innocent voice: "Why?" it looked to her like he'd touched something hot. He jerked around in one motion that left her facing raw indignation.

"Did you say 'Why'?"

"Yes," she said cheerfully.

"No one ever asks us 'Why?' Do you understand?"

She thought about keeping it going but deciding that the face in front of her had never seen a smile, she nodded sweetly.

An hour later as most of the big cars and jackboots were leaving, Goebbels emerged from the house, smiling at Helldorff and then hurrying to his car, looking straight ahead as if he saw nothing but his own thoughts.

Later that day a totally different kind of visitor showed up. Two of them, rough looking men in rumpled suits, came in an older car and she heard yelling about money that Helldorff owed. When they left, Helldorff could be heard giving orders into the phone. Someone had to get over here! Now!

An hour later another car came through the gates, this one a large yellow Maybach convertible with a shiny black spare tire covering embedded into the driver's side front fender. Behind the wheel was Hanussen, the man she recognized from the *Ursel IV*, his fleshy face flickering with irritation as he got out holding a package. Before he reached the entrance he saw Karin.

"I know you from somewhere," he said squinting like an appraiser who had just found his glasses. "Aha! You're the orgasm girl. On the boat."

Karin smiled and said nothing. Hanussen retreated a couple of steps. "So *you're* here?"

"Yes. *I'm* here. Why are you here?"

The puzzlement on Hanussen's face gave way to a sly smile as he looked up and down her body. "Such an impudent girl. Well, well, well. You rascal you Wolf. Well done!" He was backing up, clutching a bulky package as he went toward the entrance.

Later after Hanussen had left and Helldorff was in an adjoining hall-way talking in low tones on the phone, Karin walked into the vast room and found Hanussen's package lying on the long dark table to the right of the fireplace. She opened it and bricks of money fell out, bundled Reichsmarks spilling out onto the table. It was more money than she had ever imagined could exist in one place.

"You are entering into my business," said the voice coming from behind her. Helldorff stood in the doorway trying to look angry.

For a moment she wavered between the eighteen-year-old she was and the woman Helldorff needed to see. Something in her sensed that his was an anger that was trying to imitate power, the flimsy kind that could be stripped bare by whatever posturing he craved to have torn away from him.

"Your business?" she snapped at him, "Did it ever occur to you that you entered into *my* business by dragging me here?" She was curious where this sharp tone came from. It didn't sound like the voice she always thought was hers.

"I needed to explain."

"You said that. Did I ask you to?"

"Why are you acting like this?"

"I'm not acting like anything." She stared and waited, having no idea what he would say. And wondering if she had gone too far.

"Okay," he said not looking at her as if he couldn't. It reminded her of some of the boys in the playground at her school.

"Why is all this money here?"

He didn't answer.

She shook her head and walked out of the room.

That night in the same bedroom, he again sat next to the bed she was in and just wanted to talk. She found it strange in so many ways. And the more assured and cool she was, the more eager he was just to talk. And she sensed, to please her. When she asked again about the bundles of money on the table and he mumbled something about an arrangement he had, she interrupted: "I can't understand a thing you're saying."

"We have an arrangement," he said speaking precisely. "Me and Hanussen."

"What arrangement?"

"I protect him."

"And so he brings you money?"

"Protecting him is difficult. He's a fool. He's always going too far."

"Too far how?"

"I can't talk about it."

"I want to know."

"It involves Hitler."

And with that, she realized she had reached a line that could not be crossed. All she knew about Hitler was that he was this man who was now very important. And who made everyone else either exhilarated or afraid.

"I'm tired," she said turning away from him. "I'm going to sleep."

"Yes."

She was aware of him not moving. Sitting there, waiting for her to turn back toward him. She was also vaguely aware of the force such a simple gesture would have—a girl from next to nowhere turning her back on a man who shed his vast power when he was with her, A powerful man waiting—longing, for her to turn back toward him as a woman, one who would fill the sudden emptiness her mere presence created within him.

He remained sitting in that chair

She did not move, lying in the huge bed under the billowing covers, staring out through the window at the faint image of trees.

"Of course," he said quietly. And got up and quietly and left, a knight having left his armour in some other room.

Karin lay there in the faint light.

She understood something else: whatever was happening, it could all end in a flash of rediscovered rage. That vast emptiness of Helldorff's could be filled in an instant with scalding poison. And her strings to the marionette could snap and she would never know it until it was too late.

When he came back to her bed, as she knew he would, she did not resist or pull away. Instead she spun around and sat up. In the faint light coming through the window she saw the flicker of his uncertainty. She had already made up her mind what she would do, pulling him onto the bed beside her and rolling him onto his back.

"Take everything off." She said it like she remembered being told to take off her snow boots when she was little. He obeyed and was soon naked, covering himself as he sat up. She startled him ripping the covers out of his hands. "Lie on your back."

He obeyed.

She looked down at him knowing he felt uncomfortable. "Prepare yourself," she ordered.

"Prepare...?

"Of course. How do you expect me to mount you? When you're like that?" She glanced sideways.

"Yes, of course, of course." He began tugging at himself.

She got off the bed and walked to the door. "Where are you going?" he called out.

"I'll be back. When you're ready." She closed the door behind her.

She had no idea why she left the room or where she was going. She walked through the darkened hallway to where a window was framed around a small seating area. She sat, her chin against her knees looking out at the grounds of this imposing and silent house. Outside, she saw headlights suddenly shining through the wrought iron gates that opened and a car drove through and stopped. A group of men in brown uniforms, high boots and carrying guns got out and took up positions by the gate. The night guards were here. Armed and full of menace.

Protecting the man lying on the bed tugging at himself.

When she went back into the bedroom, he was making noises that were somewhere between grunting and a cry for help. She took over, knowing exactly what she must do but not understanding how she knew it.

"Shh," she said several times. "I'll do it." She reached down, stroking him as she said, "Oh look at you. Look at you. That's it." And then she got on top of him, putting him inside her and rocking back and forth, wondering if she would see any of the armed men through the bedroom window as he shuddered and groaned beneath her.

The next morning there were more big cars transporting lumpy looking men, some of them wearing uniforms. Except for the photos uncle Rudi had showed her, the most imposing images of Nazis were the posters which all showed young, blonde haired men with wonderful cheekbones and glowing blue eyes.

But these men outside confused her. They looked as if they had been made from leftover spare parts that didn't fit properly. They were dumpy or chinless or sagging in unfortunate places. The most ridiculous were the bulging ones looking like poorly made sausages in their straining uniforms that seemed to be held together by the brown leather strap that came over the shoulder diagonally and fastened on the belt holding up the britches. One of them—Röhm she heard him called, the one with the little piggy face, was the sausage most likely to split out of its casing.

But it was the boots!—she was fascinated by the boots on the shrimpy ones who were walking around like they were suddenly giants. You could tell that when they were wearing those boots and looked in the mirror they saw the posters. And in those mirrors they were probably taller than the perfect men in the posters.

But even with the boots and the big cars and the Nazi flags flying from the front fenders none of them looked anything like the posters.

Inside the house, she heard the meeting going on in the big dining room that was guarded by more lesser men who had mastered the ability to look unpleasant.

She walked through the large room and again that same low glint caught her eye. Under the table the picture frames were still scattered as she had left them. The photo with an entire family posed stared up at her. She picked it up. And found all of them staring—*glaring*? right out of the photograph, starting with the older man seated among children and two younger women seated beside him in front of young men she took to be their husbands. Or maybe their brothers.

And she was sure they were all looking at her. Accusing her.

But in the second row there was another face staring out of the photo, smiling at her in a way that Karin just knew meant they could be friends. She too was young, somewhere between being a girl and a woman. She was pretty and probably almost shy behind that impish little smile she beamed out from that grey fog of solemnity.

Karin knelt in front of the pile of framed photos and began shuffling them, looking for more images of this young woman. There were several of the older man and his wife; and two of each of the younger men and their families.

And then in a small silver frame, there she was!

Smiling with a sly joy that burst out right out of the photograph! Karin instantly knew she had found a kindred spirit in this grey world. She turned it over and saw a handwritten inscription: *Annemarie at 17*. She shuffled though more of the photos looking for Annemarie. She just knew that she and Annemarie could talk and laugh for hours.

There were more formal photos; and one with the young men playing badminton; and picnics.

And one where the men all wore those little round hats that she remembered hearing called Jewish hats,

Annemarie was almost always in the background, never attracting attention, yet always the most magnetic of the faces. Karin kept shuffling through the framed photos until a small wooden frame encircled an image that made her gasp. It was one of the few that were in colour, a photo of Annemarie playfully curtsying as she laughed, holding the hem of her dress.

It was the dress that froze Karin in momentary shock. A beautiful summer dress. A *green* summer dress! The same one that Karin had taken from that pile of clothing. The same one she was now wearing.

The dining room door opened and there was the sudden sound of the bulging men talking. The collision of those voices and the image in her hands sent words, half-formed and tumbling from her:

Oh no, no, no.... Annemarie I am so sorry... Please... this dress... I did not know it is yours...

She wanted to rip the dress off and stand naked in front of the bulging men who were now looking at her from across the room as they bunched together in little circles of muttered remarks that ended abruptly as Helldorff strode from the dining room. He saw the men looking at Karin kneeling on the floor and tried to defuse the whispers, "Yes, the cleaning ladies are definitely getting younger," and then skillfully herded them toward the door.

When the last of the big cars had driven away, he came back into the big room, avoiding her stare. He went upstairs and returned in a different coat.

"Why are you sitting on the floor?"

"Where are you going?"

"I have to oversee some business.'

"Where?"

"On the Ku'damm."

"I'm going too."

"This is official business that—"

"I said: *I-am-going-too!*" Her words came out quietly but with each one hiding a blade. She was beginning to be able to predict what his reaction would be when she was stern and demanding. He looked away, nodded and then adjusted his cufflinks.

Berlin was so different from the back seat of this big Mercedes

She had never before seen it this way. People scurried out of the way when they saw the small Nazi flags flying from the front fenders. Officious traffic policemen, some still wearing the old style uniforms with the shiny tub-like hats, hastily whistled opposing traffic to a halt, waving them through.

And some saluted.

With its sliding glass partition between them and the driver, Helldorff watched the waves of humanity parting before him. "Very soon, when our power is totally consolidated, they'll clear the roads from one side to the other." When she said nothing, he added, "Wait till you see it."

She decided he was working hard to appear at ease. Which for him was futile.

The Mercedes drove in a circular route into Charlottenburg where the traffic intensified, and Karin stared out at streets clogged with double decker buses and yellow streetcars closely following one another like mechanical sled dog teams. Horse drawn carts and bicyclists wove among the clutter of cars and the blur of colours became part of the kaleidoscope of her thoughts, interrupted when she saw that they were passing the Ka De We department store—and at that moment she knew what the next hour of her life would be like.

She remembered the Ka De We from watching two of her classmates make their first attempts at prostitution by standing idly outside on Tauentzienstrasse and seeing if men would approach them. They had been dared by older, fourteen-year-old girls and not wanting to be cast out of their group they took up the challenge. With several classmates, Karin had watched from across Tauentzienstrasse, fascinated as the two girls began to walk slowly in front of the massive grey stone building with its arched street-level showcase windows on either side of the central vertical turrets that framed the vaulted entrance. By their second pass in front of the building, men were following them.

"Some of my best friends became prostitutes right there," she said casually.

"Really?" Helldorff said suddenly sounding alert.

"A few years ago," she said trying to act bored.

"How old were they?"

"About twelve,"

Helldorff opened the glass partition between them and the driver, "Slow down," he said. The Mercedes settled back into the clutter instead of pushing through it. "Were you ever one of them?"

"Don't be stupid."

"I just was wondering. I mean so many girls are doing it."

"I want to go to the zoo."

"What?"

"The zoo. It's right over there," she said pointing to the west.

"I don't have time for this."

"Fine. Then let me out right here."

Helldorff sat back in the seat, his lips tightening. "To the zoo," he said to the driver and then slid the glass partition closed. The Mercedes made a sharp turn into the traffic as a policeman ran out into the street, blowing a whistle and clearing a path as oncoming traffic screeched to a halt.

She held something out in front of his face. "I don't think *she* ever did it, do you? Become a prostitute I mean." It was a photograph of a smiling young woman. A colour photograph. "This is Annemarie."

"Who is Annemarie?"

"Look closely."

"Is this a game?"

"Not at all. Her name, written on the back of the photograph is Annemarie. She was seventeen when it was taken."

"Look can we play this game some other time because I—"

"Do you see anything strange about this photograph?"

Irritably he looked at it again. "No."

"Look again."

He looked from the photo to Karin and then back again as a flicker of comprehension dampened the anger.

"I am wearing *her* dress! How is that possible?" It was a question and an accusation wrapped tightly together.

"How would I know?"

"Well you should know! This dress was lying in a pile of clothes in your mansion." She held the photograph up again. "I needed something to wear. I found this. But it's hers."

"So?"

"So why isn't she there? Living in the house? Instead of you?"

"Do I really need to explain it to you?"

"Yes."

"She's a Jew."

"That's it?"

"Of course."

"Where is she now?"

"How would I know? Perhaps some place near Tempelhof."

"What is near Tempelhof?"

"A place where they take Jews. She'll be fine. What are you doing?"

"Taking off her dress. What does it look like? I'm going to fly her dress like a flag."

"Don't! Not here! Keep your dress on!"

"Annemarie deserves a flag."

The car had turned right at the U-Bahn station and cruised to a halt in front of the zoo entrance. Helldorff was looking around, panic stricken that someone might notice the commotion going on inside the big car with the Nazi flags flying from the fenders. "Stop! I am ordering you."

She was yelling now. And almost in tears. "Ordering me to do what? Wear what you robbed from Annemarie?"

"What are you taking about—*robbed*? For God sakes they were Jews."

"Let's go to this Tempelhof place and give her her dress back, okay?"

"Stop this nonsense. Right now. Stop."

"You stop!"

He slapped her so hard thoughts exploded in her head. For a moment she lay back against the side window, stunned and disheveled, the dress unbuttoned and hanging around her neck.

"You are in your underwear. That is not appropriate!"

Through the ache in her face she laughed, a tiny, gurgling laugh as she whispered "Yes it is."

She was vaguely aware of his hand coming back toward her face when she lashed out with her own hand, fingers and nails outstretched, raking his cheek and drawing enough blood that he instantly grappled for a handkerchief.

She threw open the car door and bolted as Helldorff yelled for the driver to catch her.

But the driver was no match for Karin, racing into the zoo in her underwear, holding the green dress aloft like a banner that flew behind her.

I know Karin as well as anyone could know her. Which is to say that to me she was mostly a mystery. But something I did know: fleeing that car and Helldorff was probably the most political act of her life. Usually her view of humanity blocked any kind of political understanding or awareness. Politics was for other people. At that point in her life everything was personal; it was just who she was.

If she believed it, she saw it. And the world around her had to conform.

Until the world around her couldn't. And some unknown line got crossed. Annemarie's green dress was such a line.

15

I AM SUPPOSED TO BE writing what is just gossip. But when a Nazi shows up at a garden party hosted by someone his men have just clubbed almost to death what do you do?

I mean *really* do?

I cannot help myself. If I was smart, I should stick to what is purely gossip. But these days it all becomes one big mess where frivolity and brutality smile at one another and pretend that nothing means anything.

All these diplomatic receptions—the Rumanian, the Paraguayan, the Italian and all the rest are like a distorted mirror held up to what is really happening. I'm creating problems for myself merely by going to them. They're making me impatient with all the small talk and champagne when I've just come from the streets where another reality is going on.

This other reality is forcing me to refine my coded language even more—drunken Nazis have gone through so many code-words that they have now become *enthusiastic officials*. And SS men beating a professor outside the Belgian embassy becoming *a typical flamboyant expression of political dialogue*. More readers are learning to decipher what I write. Which is good news, but also makes me wonder if *they—the enthusiastic officials* are also deciphering my words.

Yet I am starting to feel it is not enough. I am more and more restless within my profession, looking for ways to wrap history into a tissue of gossip.

But so often I fail.

For instance, yesterday I joined in the gushing over the *foie gras* at the elegant pearl-infested reception in the home of Countess von der Groeben. I hated hearing myself talk. Because only an hour earlier I had walked past the hideous work of the Painting Squads, the thugs who deface buildings and advertisements with crudely painted swastikas and Nazi slogans.

My problem is that more than ever, I am now in two different worlds—the streets and the elegant receptions. There is no way to keep them apart.

Nor do I really want to. But faced with Herr Langen's slashing read pencil I have to at least try. When I sit down at my typewriter the two worlds collide and too often merge.

In a purely professional sense I know that Herr Langen and his red pencil are right, even though I defend my writing and argue with him in a way I suspect he would not tolerate from others.

On this last column he was hunched over the two typewritten pages I had written about the piano recital that had been held at the Tiergarten mansion of Hitler's most devoted fan, Helene Bechstein the owner of the Bechstein piano factory.

As he read what I wrote a strand of smoke and then a cloud of it poured out from under the visor. "Frau Bechstein," he snorted. "Disgusting old woman. The Nazi's den mother."

I barely heard what he was saying. I was so focused on his hand—his left hand, that everything else drifted out of my thoughts.

"Well?"

"I'm sorry. What did you say?"

"*Wölfchen*?" he snorted. You wrote "*Wölfchen—my little wolf*?"

"That's what Frau Bechstein calls Hitler."

"Is that important?"

"I think it shows something. How she feels about him."

"Do you have any idea how many old, rich women are trying to play mother to Hitler? Not just Bechstein—Frau Bruckmann is buying him the proper suits and ties. And teaching him how to eat in polite company. And her family is the best publisher of literature we have!"

He scanned my pages, reading quickly. "And for god sake—Helldorff? What was *he* doing at a piano recital?"

"All the big Nazis want Frau Bechstein to notice them. They know she tells Hitler who she likes. And he listens to her."

"Helldorff and culture!" he almost laughed. "The mind reels. What did they play on one of Frau Bechstein's illustrious pianos? Beethoven Number 5? Tchaikovsky's Concerto Number 1? Or would a boor like Helldorff even know what he was listening to?"

But it was still his hand that was absorbing all my attention. I had heard stories. Finally I blurted out, "Where is your wedding ring?"

His left hand slammed down on the desk. "My private life is not anyone else's concern."

"None of our lives are private anymore. Not with what is happening."

He raised his head and glared at me.

"I'm sorry if I'm intruding. Two years ago I would have agreed with you. But not now" I added.

Silence and smoke. Then the visor came off. He sat back, the furrows on his face deeper than I remembered. "You are aware of Count Helldorff's idea of his own personal Jewish extradition program?"

"No."

"He has now been appointed Chief of Police here in Berlin. And he is giving—*selling* us exit visas to get out of Germany before the slaughter starts. As long as we can meet his price?"

I sat in complete silence not even nodding.

"Do you understand? He knows people are desperate to get the exit visa. So he strips us of everything. Anything that can be ripped away or sold off. And all of it goes to Helldorff. From jewelry to houses to automobiles to gold coins. Everything must be sold off to pay for the exit visas that only he can grant.

"Emma—my wife is in France now. She's safe. Only because the wedding ring brought the total of what we could pay to the bare minimum for one person."

"I am so sorry."

"Don't be. I am at peace now. She is safe."

I don't know how long it was that we sat in silence until he picked up another newspaper from his desk. It was one of the smaller papers printed in Kreuzberg. "You want to know what gossip can do now? This is what I was afraid you'd bring me."

He held up a page for me to read: *Political bigshot takes drive to zoo with half-naked club beauty.*

"Why are you showing me this?"

"Because a few hours after they published this story the newspaper was firebombed."

"I knew about this. And I know about Helldorff in the big Mercedes driving down the Ku'damm," I said.

"I half-suspected you'd be tempted to write about this."

"No."

"Why not?"

"Because of the *half-naked club beauty* they talk about." I somehow couldn't finish what I wanted to say.

"What about this half-naked beauty?"

"That was my sister."

It had been late afternoon when I had gotten a phone call at my desk at *Vossiche Zeitung*. The newspaper switchboard operator said there was "a call from the baboon cage." For a moment I thought it was some kind of silly joke. But then it dawned on me that whatever it was, somehow Karin had to be involved. No one else knew the zoo in the way that she did.

Sometime around her fourteenth birthday, Karin began spending hours after school roaming the vast labyrinth of caged artificial hills, caves and forests, befriending the zookeepers and asking to help whenever she could. And when Uncle Rudi introduced her to Dr. Heck, the zoo's director, she begged him to let her help feed the baby tigers.

But it was the monkeys she loved the most and Katherina the zookeeper in charge of the apes soon allowed her to help feed them even though it was against the rules of the zoo. Katherina was a quiet dark-haired woman who recognized nothing about herself in Karin except for a fierce devotion to the animals.

She taught Karin the differences between the apes: the gorillas, the baboons, the monkeys and the orangutans. And how to recognize that the baboons were about to enter into bloody battle with one another because the matriarch had just died, and the other females would rip each other to pieces until one of them was recognized as the new leader. Karin spent hours beside the baboon cage convinced she could soothe them away from warfare. And when one of her favorites, a female she had named Esmeralda was suddenly missing from the cage, she was told that the baboon had died of old age. Even though blood was still pooled near the artificial stone cliff at the back of the cage Karin decided that Esmeralda had led a good life and had died peacefully.

But now with all the buzzing chaos of the *Vossiche Zeitung* newsroom around me it was jarring to hear Katherina on the phone, saying that I needed to get there quickly. It was too complicated to explain she said. And could I bring something to wear? A dress perhaps?

I raced out down to the Markgrafenstrasse entrance of the Ullstein building where Burmester the enormous doorman in his grey overcoat with its corporate crest already had a taxi waiting for me. Burmester was the lord of his little domain of sidewalk and taxi drivers competed for his attention. The driver he had summoned for me promptly announced a shortcut and turned onto Kochstrasse which was so jammed with cars and buses and horse drawn carts that he might as well have driven into wet concrete.

Almost an hour later, I had the taxi stop at the Ka De We where I ran in and bought a summer dress in Karin's size.

My next stop was father's house, where much of my belongings were still piled in a suitcase. Mercifully he was not there and the keys to the old car that he almost never used were hanging in the hallway.

In his car I drove up to the big *ZOOLOG. GARTEN* sign at the front gate of the zoo it was late afternoon and Gustav the keeper of the lion cages was waiting for me. He hurried me through the waning crowds to where Katherina was waiting. She was a woman of warmth, someone who you knew could handle anything human after mediating the various battles of the apes. But on this day the lines around her big almond-coloured eyes were deeper than usual.

"Your sister," she said.

"Of course," I said.

There was a sense of urgency to her, one that shut off questions. She led me to a cage where small monkeys were bouncing all over like they had springs in their feet. And in the middle of them, laughing, was Karin.

Actually when I looked more closely she wasn't laughing. Tears were rolling down her cheeks.

"Why are you crying?"

"Am I?"

I drove her past Tempelhof airport. She wanted to go out to *where the laundry is*— which is another way of saying the working-class sections of Berlin where the laundry was hung on apartment balconies like banners and the streets were filled more with horse-drawn carts than with cars. She was dressed in the new summer dress I'd bought at Ka De We and clutched a rolled-up paper bag. For the entire journey she talked with a forced cheerfulness, with rapid bursts of joy about the apes and how playful they were and why can't we all just be like those cute little monkeys who-

I pulled over to the curb, shut off the engine and put my arm on her shoulder It released a barrage of impatient indignation. "Why are you stopping the car?" she said. "Let's go! "

"What happened to you?"

"No, no, no, no!" she shook her head and reached for the door handle. I reached out and grabbed her arm, which was like finding a detonator you didn't know about. She shook fiercely and rocked back and forth. "*Don't, don't, don't....*"

"It's okay, "was all I could say.

"We have to go somewhere."

"Where?"

"I need to help Annemarie."

"Who's Annemarie?"

"Helldorff is living in her home. He said she was now somewhere near Tempelhof. Does that mean anything?"

Oh yes, it meant something. I tried not to react.

"What?" she said looking uncertain. "Why did you get that look?"

"I don't think you want to go there."

"There? What is *there*?"

"Columbia House."

She looked blank. She had no idea what I was talking about—the most terrifying of all the newly created Nazi prisons in Berlin, only a kilometer or two from where we were. On the edges of Tempelhof airport, it had been an abandoned military prison, but its new incarnation was still so recent that only a few people were aware of the horror going on inside.

"I have to give Annemarie her dress," she said quickly opening the paper bag and taking out a beautiful green dress. And with it came tumbling the stories of her night with Helldorff and the pile of clothes and the big cars driving up to Helldorff's mansion. And when she finished she blurted out, "It's not good is it? For Annemarie?"

"No. It's not," I said. And wondered how she so often formed the closest attachments to those who were usually most distant from her. Or to animals. Maybe it was because neither could get close to her. Disappoint her. Hurt her.

I started the car, driving north-east until we were passing barricades and barbed wire in the streets that were cordoned off around Columbia House. Armed Nazi guards, some with fierce dogs, were everywhere. She stared through the windows of the car until she slumped back in the seat and closed her eyes.

We drove the rest of the way in silence past drab grey and brown soot-covered tenements until we turned onto the street where *Mutter's* tenement loomed at the end.

"I want Annemarie to feel good," Karin said. "I owe it to her."

Inside, in *Mutter's* kitchen, she held out the paper bag. "I have something for you." Erma looked inside the bag, her eyes widening and then running along the corridor to her room.

"I hope Annemarie would approve," Karin said. "Her dress is giving someone else joy." Erma returned, suddenly chic in her vibrantly green new summer dress.

Erma embraced and thanked Karin who turned away from me.

"How do you know if you're pregnant?" Karin whispered obviously not wanting me to hear.

Darkness.

I lay on the bed, my thoughts drowning out the sounds and voices coming through the tenement walls.

Back then, years ago, it seemed like a badge of honour, having insights that those so much older than you did not. I was always the mature one. Or so they said. Even when I was just a girl. It was flattering to have the adults comment on how poised, how mature you were. I was the one looking out for adults who could not look out for themselves, either because of illness or the kind of weakness that no child could understand.

But: Was I ever really young?

Only much later do you realize that all this maturity that was forced upon you has robbed you of something precious.

Your youth.

So I lay there in the darkness projecting images of my childhood and longing to find some silliness, something so foolish or reckless that only a child could do it. I craved childishness because I wanted to know that somehow I actually had a childhood.

But I could find only fleeting moments and it threw me into a silent frenzy of wanting to explode into sheer, joyous irresponsibility.

Anything to reclaim this part of my life that I missed.

But I can't.

It would be like going back to the deserted scene of a party I forgot to go to.

16

June 1934

WHAT IS NOW KNOWN:

With his Eldorado Club days behind him, and not yet 30 years old, Karl Ernst is at the height of his power. It is just over a year after the Nazis have seized control of the nation and Ernst has just been appointed supreme SA leader of Berlin.

But there is a problem. There are rumours from his old days at the Eldorado: Transvestites. Wild sex. Bisexuality.

And all that.

So Karl Ernst urgently needs a bride to dispel those rumours. So he takes as his bride, Minnes Wolf, a dark-haired, more definitively female version of Mugette, and on June 29, 1934 in a spectacular Nazi-themed ceremony they walk down an aisle flanked on both sides by Nazi Storm Troopers in full steel helmeted dress uniforms, followed by Reichsmarschall Herman Göring— only Hitler is more powerful—and beside him, is the porcine, scowling leader of the SA, Ernst Röhm. And behind Göring and Röhm are the elite of the Nazi party, all in full uniform.

It is as close to a royal wedding as the Nazis can stage.

And one day later the newlyweds are being driven in the back of a limousine, heading for the port of Bremen where they will sail in connubial bliss to a honeymoon in Madeira.

But a car is seen approaching behind them.

It is driving at high-speed. There is not one but two cars speeding behind them. Two cars of the Schutzstaffel. In other words: the SS. They were the blackshirts to Ernst's and Röhm's brownshirts. But why? Why are they speeding toward the bride and groom? Intolerable! Ernst is furious. There will be an enquiry into this outrage—

The SS gunmen in the lead vehicle open fire.

They are careful to kill only the bride and the driver. Karl Ernst is dragged screaming from the car, beaten, tied up and flown back to Berlin.

What Karl Ernst cannot have known was that he is just one of thousands of devoted Nazis about to perish in what becomes known as The Night of the Long Knives. And that his SA leader, seducer, mentor, Ernst Röhm had gone from that spectacular wedding one day earlier, to a spa resort near Munich where he and hundreds of other SA leaders were to meet.

And Karl Ernst could not have known that Hitler had grown suspicious of Röhm, deciding to wipe out the entire SA hierarchy as they slept at the spa, some with male lovers and with women's underwear in the dresser drawers.

In the middle of the night, holding a whip and followed by SS killers, Hitler himself barged in on a sleeping Röhm and ordered him to kill himself. When Röhm refused, Hitler had him shot.

And almost six hundred kilometers away the firing squad lined up as Karl Ernst was dragged before it. No one knows what he thought or the confusion that exploded within him as the firing squad was given its orders to fire.

I was called into Herr Langen's office, not knowing why I was there. He ignored me when I entered, sitting there as if he was tangled up in his own thoughts. The silence was awkward and I wondered if I had misunderstood the summons to his office.

Something so simple that it seemed strange happened: Herr Langen stood up. I was so used to seeing him sitting behind his desk as if he had grown roots that I did not remember how tall he was. He walked to his open office door and closed it. "Do not feel you have to stay here and listen to me."

I was confused. "Are you all right?"

It was as if he hadn't heard me as he walked slowly around the office. "I just had the most awful thought." He kept walking slowly in circles. "If my daughter had lived I may not have been able to afford to get her out of the country. So God forgive me, maybe in some awful way it was better for her. Dying, I mean."

I was shocked. "Why do you say that?"

"Because of what is coming. Not many people can see the full frenzy of what lies ahead. But I suspect you can see it. I'm sure you can. Can't you?"

"Of course. Every day I see more high-ranking thugs—"

He stopped me. "It's not those thugs who I fear the most. They are only the usual three percent, five percent, whatever, of sadists and killers. Right now I most fear the great mass who really don't care one way or another. They are the empty ones. They all need to be given meaning and belonging. Religion and sports can only do so much. They are the real danger."

He was searching through the piles of material on his desk until he found a small newspaper. "I saved this," he announced, holding up one of the more obscure daily newspapers from Kreuzberg, an area of Berlin known for its irreverent attitudes to authority.

"Another of those little newspapers. The kind that loves trashy headlines" He held it up so I could not miss: "*Political bigshot loses half-dressed beauty to the zoo!*"

"Why are we're talking about this again?"

"This is gossip, wouldn't you say? With a headline like that?"

"So?"

"The gossip reporter who wrote this story died yesterday. He had been in a coma for two hours after this was on the newsstands. And in the official police report it says that he died of 'injuries from a fall.'"

He fell silent again until he sat back in that old oak chair and talked to the ceiling.

"But our crime reporters say that the poor gossip writer... "he held up the Kreuzberg newspaper again, "...was beaten with canes. Flailed until the muscles and tendons were dangling loose in places because he had no skin left to contain their remnants."

"Why are you telling me this?"

"Because I want you to leave gossip and do something else."

"No."

"I'm going to move you to covering transportation. Or gardening."

"You can't."

"Oh really? Why can't I?"

"Because I'll quit first." There was strained silence. "You're forcing me to quit."

"Don't you understand?"

I said nothing. He got up and walked over to a battered but elegant old bookcase. "What do you see?"

"A bookcase."

"That's all?"

"An elegant bookcase." I was getting confused. "Made of some kind of beautiful wood. Like some kind of burl walnut."

"Precisely. And you've got used to looking at all its beauty? Its elegance? Its permanence? Solid. Eternal."

Then he reached up and with his fingers, pried the top edge of the elegant bookcase. It peeled off the surface, a sheet of wood, as thin as a piece of paper, uncovering the ugliness below it.

"That beautiful walnut that you thought was the whole bookcase is nothing more than a sheet as flimsy veneer masking the crude wood beneath it. So look out on the streets. The cafes. The theaters. The concerts. The libraries—a veneer. All of it. Covering what lies beneath."

He went back to his desk, standing behind it, looking at me, almost through me. "The veneer is coming off."

I nodded.

"I'm trying to protect you."

"Thank you. But I am the gossip columnist."

He looked at me for a moment. Then he sat down and the red pencil went back to work.

17

KARIN HAD HURRIED FROM THE farthest end of the paint-peeled corridor when she overheard the whore from Cologne screaming at me. She was telling me not to try to borrow any of her clothes for the English reception I was going to.

I was in the kitchen with *Mutter* when Karin barged in."What English reception?" she wanted to know. Then she answered her own question. "The afternoon reception for the British Military Attaché, right?" she almost demanded. "I want to go too."

Karin had never taken much interest in what I did for *Vossiche Zeitung,* and protocol made little sense to her.

"How do you know whose party it is?"

"I just know," she said.

Two days later, approaching the British embassy Karin was excited in ways I had not seen for years. At first I thought she might be feeling intimidated by the almost operatic cast of characters, the military officers from dozens of nations, many of them peacocks strutting their medals that caught the afternoon light.

Being the hosts, the British had to rise above their drab understated uniforms so they resorted to bagpipes, sending out a couple of Scotsmen in kilts to provide an unanswerable show.

Entering the grand ballroom Karin acted as if it was just another evening with a group of people who barely interested her. She scanned the assembled throng until she found what she was looking for. On the far side of the room there were fleeting glimpses of bright red, the swastika armbands on the uniforms of the Nazi officers.

And looking at the center of that group of officers I suddenly understood why she had wanted to come to this reception.

Helldorff.

He was being introduced to an officer from the Italian military but the instant he saw Karin across the length of the ballroom it was as if something jolted him and he immediately maneuvered the Italian so that he could look over the man's shoulder right at Karin.

"Was this why you wanted to come here?" I asked her, trying not to let my indignation show.

"So? He's got it coming to him."

"Got *what* coming to him?"

"He deserves to suffer."

"Karin, he's a Nazi. He makes others suffer."

"Just watch."

"You ran away from him. At the zoo. Remember?"

She ignored my question. She had that smile of hers, the one where her lips smiled but not her eyes. "Don't you think he's everything father wants to be?"

What? "What did you just say?"

Nothing about Helldorff—Count Wolf-Heinrich Julius Otto Bernhard Fritz Herman Graf von Helldorff, the powerful newly appointed SS leader for Berlin, member of the Reichstag and Police Chief of Berlin reminded me even slightly of father. *Father*? Our scrawny, bank-clerk father?

"Do you have any idea what you're saying? There's nothing remotely similar to father."

"Except one thing."

"What?"

"They're both Nazis so they can be more important than they ever were before. And father would love to be him. But he's more powerful than father could ever be."

And then she was gone. Vanishing serenely into all that gold braid, all those medals, all that din.

She headed straight toward a startled junior civilian official in the British embassy who suddenly found himself the fierce focus of Karin's attentions. There seemed to be nothing special about this pale young man until it occurred to me that he was the kind of lesser aristocracy that would probably populate their countryside, inherit vast swaths of land, go to Oxford or Cambridge, and hunt foxes.

And above all, wear tweed.

In other words this young British official was the kind of country squire Helldorff always wanted to be.

Karin knew exactly what she was doing.

She calibrated her attention to the young Englishman to get the reactions she wanted from Helldorff who was watching as if he was going to catapult out of the conversational clutches of some droning Italian military man.

Moments after extricating himself, Helldorff found his exit route blocked by a flotilla of old British worthies, the kind who were then telling each other what a splendid chap this Hitler fellow was. One of them grasped Helldorff's hand, shaking it theatrically and then introducing him to the tedious looking man with a sweeping-brush mustache standing beside him.

It was at the moment that this sweeping-brush mustache man became the center of attention as a British Major General took the microphone and began introducing him to the assembled dignitaries.

*...my distinct pleasure to introduce you to our special guest....*The British Major General stumbled through proclamations of how excited they were to be joined by Lord Rothermere ...*one of the true titans of the British daily newspapers!*

This true titan turned out to be the sweeping-brush mustache man who lumbered toward the microphone looking as if he had just eaten something bad.

This was Lord Rothermere? *The* Lord Rothermere?

Our Berlin newsroom had reverberated to the mention of this Englishman's name for months. We had been first confused, and then astounded by his declarations of love for the Nazis. We simply could not believe what we were hearing.

Once he got to the microphone he lived up to his reputation, a dumpy Englishman singing the praises of the Nazis. An English Lord! Telling *us* what a wonderful example of humanity the SS represented.

And what a great man Hitler was.

And this from an *Englishman*?

What is now known:

In the 1930's the British upper classes, as personified by Lord Rothermere, could, in hindsight, be considered traitors.

Starting with Rothermere—actually it's just Harold, because if you take away all that Lordship and Viscount business Rothermere is just plain Harold. Plain old Harold Harmsworth to be precise.

And yes, Harold does own some of the biggest newspapers in England, the Daily Mirror, the Daily Mail and others, seventeen in all, with the Daily Mirror alone selling over 3,000,000 copies a day, and yes, Harold is supposed to be the third richest man in Britain. But really Harold—Lord Rothermere, is just another unhappy man who at this point in his life would rather be away from his wife and spend his time gambling. In the gloom of London winters he longs to be at his villa in the south of France only a short drive away from the Monte Carlo Sporting Club where he spends endless hours gambling away large sums of money when he is not indulging one of his mistresses.

But what stands in the way of this state of contentment are those beastly Bolsheviks, the same awful communists who have taken over Russia and now are metastasizing through the body politic of Europe. Harold is just like so many others in the British upper classes. Because communism has become their greatest fear. It is a mortal threat not only to their wealth, their titles and their estates but also to their very lives.

All because of what happened just sixteen years ago to one of their very own: Nicky as his sister called him, dear Nicky—Russia's Czar Nicholas II and his entire family were gunned down in a filthy basement in as savage an execution as the Bolsheviks could carry out. And then Nicky, his wife, his son, his daughters, were stripped naked—all of them, before their mutilated bodies were dumped down a mineshaft.

It is a nightmare that keeps the British aristocracy up at night wishing their ancestors had not filled in the moats and gotten rid of the drawbridges. Like other royals across Europe they are in crisis over what happened.

Because what happened to poor Nicky, they can all imagine happening to them.

But these Nazi chaps are looking rather promising—beating on the heads of any communists they can find. Splendid!

So now in Berlin, at the English Military Attaché's reception as Lord Rothermere drones on...

...While Helldorff cares for none of this English nonsense. He hears nothing, cares for nothing because suddenly he cannot see her. She was here, right here! But she has vanished!

But Helldorff is certain he will find her.

18

EVEN BEFORE WE LEFT THE British embassy, I had decided that going right back to *Mutter's* was not an option. Not when Helldorff could show up there again in his big Mercedes and wait for Karin. So I stalled, pretending that I needed my car that was again parked behind father's house.

"As long as we don't have to talk to father," she said. "Or even see him."

For most of the ride in a taxi Karin stared out the window and smiled as if she had a secret. "There's something quite delicious about watching him suffer."

Him was Helldorff but I did not want to talk about it in the taxi. It was just not safe. Some of the drivers were making themselves heroes by reporting conversations to the Nazis,

We walked the last few blocks to father's house. "What makes you think he's suffering?"

"Because he can't get what he wants," she said in a voice that became tighter as we got close to the gate. "Spoiled little boys grow up to be spoiled big boys and—"

She stopped in mid-sentence the moment we walked past the gate.

A big Mercedes was parked in the courtyard. It wasn't so much parked as it was hidden in the darkest part of the cobblestone parking area, partly behind the tall hedge. It was the kind of car now driven by the highest ranking Nazis but the stanchions sticking up from its fenders that should have held Nazi banners were bare. For a moment I was confused, wondering if perhaps I had led us into a trap.

But Karin figured it out immediately: "Uncle Rudi," she said in a whisper.

Inside, we felt like burglars, creeping in silently afraid that father might be there.

"Aha!" said Uncle Rudi quietly. He sat in the shadows at the far end of the largest room of the house, his beautiful, scarred face mysterious as always. "Are you alone?" When we said we were he stood up and smiled.

"Wonderful. I was preparing for a confrontation with your father. Who is never pleased to see me here."

"Where is father?"

"The housekeeper says he is away. On business."

Father? Away? He never travels anywhere.

But Karin was already laughing as she almost ran to him, throwing herself at him as he gave her a hug.

"Hello Uncle Rudi," I said trying not to feel awkward by comparison.

"Now Bella, don't be your solemn newspaper-lady self," he said beckoning to me. Some unwanted thunderbolt of self-awareness suddenly struck me. Compared to Karin's unfettered display of emotions I felt awkward and hopelessly foolish. Was I to leap into his arms too?—and look even more foolish? And all the while, Karin was scattering emotional exuberance all over, simply because that was just what she did naturally.

"Uncle Rudi?"

"Yes Bella?" With a raised eyebrow as his signal that he knew the solemn newspaper-lady was talking now."

"Why are you here?"

He looked me right in the eye, never lessening that terrifying smile of his. "I am in hiding."

"Who are you hiding from?"

"Why my fellow Nazis of course."

It took me a while to understand it all: Uncle Rudi hiding from his own people? From the SA and this newer force known as the SS? And tonight, they both wanted to kill him?

"Why?" I asked when Karin had gone looking for father's liquor supply.

"Because I am overruling them on certain matters."

"And for that they want to kill you?"

"Yes. The jungle is filling up with carnivores. And each wants to be king of that same jungle."

"What 'certain matters' have you overruled them on?"

"It's not important."

"It is."

That beautiful face shed whatever familial gentleness it had been able to sustain. He almost scared me. "Bella. No more questions. Okay?"

"I am not Karin."

"I know that."

I persisted. "Why?"

His eyes became almost wolf-like. "I have a new job."

"What?"

"Formally it is called Chief of the Prussian Secret State Police."

For a moment I just returned the stare. "Oh no." was all I thought of to say.

"It's not what it looks like," he said.

"Oh why are you doing this?" I almost groaned at him. He did not answer, just stared at me. "I am so disappointed in you."

"I am sorry to hear that," he said, "but not surprised."

"I always wanted you to be just another wealthy wastrel. Scary sometimes but generally harmless."

"I am sorry to have disappointed you." He smiled.

"The Prussian State Police," I said almost filling in a silence because I didn't know what else to say.

"The Prussian State Police are being given a new name," he said.

"What?"

"The Gestapo."

"Oh Uncle Rudi!" I got up and walked out. At almost the exact moment that Karin rushed in with several bottles of fathers' liquor. All I heard was giggling and laughter as I left the room.

Sleep can be a cruel thief. It can rob and mock at the same time. Some of the most graceful among us can be shorn of their dignity lying there with mouths open like drooling corpses or snoring in clattering volleys. It would horrify them were they able to see themselves.

None was ever stripped barer than Karin. Particularly after even one drink. She would lay sprawled wherever she sank, head back and bugling out snores that could rattle a cavalry. Even from father's library to which I had retreated, I could hear her snoring evolve until it sounded like a woodpecker being strangled inside your thoughts. There was no way you could ignore it.

For a while I thought about going upstairs to my old room that was still preserved in the state that I left it. But some instinct told me to remain close enough to the front entrance door. Father's small bed lay in the corner of the library, immaculately made up, the white goose feather cover pulled tightly under the pillow with geometric precision. I lay down on the carpeted floor outside his room and tried to sleep.

I lay there trying to ignore the volley of snores until a faint shadow loomed and Uncle Rudi spoke softly to me in a name I hadn't heard since I was a girl: "*Bellachen.*"

"Please," I said.

"I want you to understand."

"What is there to understand? You're one of *them.*"

"So it would appear." His voice was scary and silky at the same time. The shadow over me moved. He had closed the door and was sitting in a chair. "I am going to leave soon. I will find another place for tonight. But I want you to listen to me."

"Is that it? You came here to make me listen to you?"

"I came here because last night I released two men from prison. From Prinz Albrechtstrasse. One was Weiss, the former Berlin deputy police chief who the SS were going to send to Columbia House to kill. And also a writer flogged almost to death in a basement cell by the brownshirts. The same murderous thugs who went crazy when they found out that I let those men go and in their drunken rage set out to find me."

"Why did you let those men go?"

"They didn't deserve to be there."

"Who does?'

"You are asking an irrelevant question *Bellachen*. Guilt and innocence are quaint and irrelevant concepts now. When we are all fleeing for our lives."

"You? Fleeing? In your position?"

"Both of the SS and the SA would kill me in a flash if they could find me tonight. And they have tried. Nothing is as it seems. The SS hates the SA. The SA hates a police force like mine. And Göring hates Himmler. And Goebbels hates Göring. And Heydrich is more twisted into hatred than any of them. So tonight it is dangerous for me. I need to hide some-where until it dies down. By tomorrow the powerful men who are my protectors will have informed the powerful men who want me dead that I am not to be killed. And all will be—what's the word? *normal?*"

For a long time he sat there in silence. "I joined a movement that is no longer what I believed it would be. But make no mistake—I believed in it. And parts of it, like stopping the communists I still believe in. But terrible things are becoming normal. Things none of us believed would ever happen."

"Then why are you still even a part of it?"

"Because there still might be a chance to stop the worst of what is happening.

"And you really believe that?"

"I have to believe it. I have no choice."

He waited for me to respond. I said nothing. "The other thing I wanted to tell you is that if you are in trouble—"

"Why would I be in trouble?"

"No one is immune to what is happening. I will do what I can to help you. When, and if, the time comes." He got up and left.

Karin was not there when I woke up the next morning.

Nor was she at *Mutter's* the following night. It wasn't all that unusual for Karin to be away for a day or two, often staying with friends in Babelsberg or Wilmersdorf. But on the third day, I was in my room listening to *Mutter's* side of a strange telephone conversation about Karin. Whoever she was talking to was in the movie business. And when she hung up, *Mutter* called out to me.

"Bongers," she said when I got to the kitchen.

I didn't know who, or what, she was talking about.

"It doesn't matter. Just understand that Bongers is important. And that she's one of us."

I still didn't understand.

"Your sister," *Mutter* said. "Bongers had set up an audition with one of the biggest shithead movie producers at UFA. And she never even showed up."

Mutter bellowed for Inga and Erma who traipsed into the kitchen. When *Mutter* asked them if they knew what happened to Karin, they looked at each other as if it was the most obvious thing in the world:

"The big car," said Erma.

"What big car?"

"The car that the creepy hypnotist sent over. Three days ago. The man with the orgies on his boat."

After two more days when no one had heard from Karin, I decided I had to do something. But what? And where? The only place I could think of was the opulent new Palace Of The Occult, an old mansion that Hanussen the clairvoyant had converted into his idea of a pagan shrine.

Hanussen's fame had been enormously increased after he predicted the Reichstag fire that gave Hitler the excuse to seize control of the country. It was when Hanussen began openly bragging of his influence with the Nazis. So I was aware that his Palace of The Occult might be crowded now that the elites of Berlin society were flocking to fawn over this egomaniacal new darling of theirs.

I arrived just after dark, at first trying not to be conspicuous as a single woman and then being vaguely amused at being in the midst of a crush of well-dressed women hurrying toward the massive doors. Just inside the front entrance peculiar music curled in the darkness around you as you moved deeper through artfully placed lights hidden in ceilings.

Looming shadows from ornate pillars were like omens falling across mystical signs and symbols on the floors.

In a large, crowded room, a tingling state of static agitation rippled among the fashionable and the powerful of Berlin, basking in their own sophistication. I recognized a Prussian prince, several film stars, and Count Fässbender and his wife. And dappled among them were black and brown swatches of SA and SS officers, Nazis who were trying hard not to show an eagerness matching that of the breathlessly chic society types.

But like everyone else there, they quivered in urgent anticipation.

A sudden drum roll preceded a rumble from under a cordoned-off part of the floor. Behind velvet ropes, the floor in front of us opened up and a cloud of mist rose from the chasm as something like a flying carpet emerged from the depths.

Sitting cross-legged on this flying carpet was Hanussen, opening his arms grandly to the accompaniment of ecstatic squeals and cheers from the assembled devotees. Even the SA officers in their Storm Trooper uniforms could not sustain their intimidating presence, giving in to the rapturous applause and cheers surging around them.

Hanussen looked over to a group of elegant women. "You!" His deep voice boomed out like distant thunder. "Come here!"

He was beckoning to one of the women, dark haired, attractive but with an uncertain air that intensified as he fixed his piercing stare on her.

"Give me something from your purse."

She blushed and teetered toward him, fumbling in her purse for a set of keys which she gave to Hanussen who cupped them in his hands as his eyes rolled back. He pressed his hands to the side of his head as if trying to squeeze out the answers he was seeking.

"Is it Emma? No, wait: Ilse? Am I close?"

"Irmgard," said the dark-haired woman. "How did you know?"

Hanussen disregarded her; he held one hand levitating above her keys and then intoned, "Why do I see problems? Are you married?" The change in Irmgard was immediate, as if something had jolted her in a way she tried to hide. "Yes, I am," she said as the smile vanished from her face.

"Yes, yes of course you are," said Hanussen his thick eyebrows riding the fleshiness of his face. "But it is not going well, is it?"

Irmgard bit her bottom lip and said shook her head.

"Not well at all."

More head shaking.

Hanussen was almost in a trance of his own making. "No, no wait.... I can see you want a divorce—" She froze. "Do I see another woman here?"

Amid gasps and applause, Irmgard burst into tears. One of her elegant friends hurried into the pool of light, put her arm around her and gently led her back to the shadows as a young assistant in flowing black robes appeared with trays of champagne.

Another woman was called up into the lights, a wispy young blonde who told of sleeping with her mother's lover when she was thirteen. Gasps, applause, tears. In soft, incessant waves, Hanussen gave her a glass of champagne, talking to her in slow rhythmic tones until, amid more gasps, she slumped and fell to the floor.

Hanussen's assistants hurried out from the darkness, lifting her up onto a low cot with wheels. Hanussen pointed to a door made of frosted glass announcing that on other side of it was the *Room of Healing*—where souls went to heal, he said. Looking as if she was in a deep sleep, the woman was wheeled through the door that swung shut behind her.

"Can you hear me talking as your soul heals?" Hanussen called out to her.

At first, silence. Then: "*Yess!* I hear you," came in a murmur from beyond the door.

Hanussen called out again, telling her she needed to relive what it was like when she slept with her mother's lover. Over and over he told her, ordered her, to relive what had happened and at one point he stopped her: "Did you say *she*? Your mother's lover was a *she*?"

From beyond that frosted glass door came a muffled and slowly building aria of sobs, unintelligible curses and then—the rhythmical moans of an orgasm. *Another orgasm*? I said to myself. The man is obsessed with them.

I began edging my way out of the big room when something—*someone*, caught my eye over near what looked like a hidden entrance.

Helldorff.

He had quietly entered and was so intent on being unnoticed that he somehow became conspicuous.

I strained to keep him in my sight as he wove through the edges of the lights as moans and gasps swirled around the room. I forced my way through the packed crowd while he quietly edged along the outer wall.

He almost reached the edge when I intercepted him. "Where's my sister?"

For a moment he struggled to remember where he had seen me. And who this sister might be. "Karin," I added sharply.

Irritated recognition flickered through his eyes. That was his first reaction. Followed instantly by the fury of weakness in power as it was being challenged. "For your own good I suggest you show some manners."

"My manners are not the issue. My sister is. Where is she?"

There was that one instant when I knew his natural response would have been to slap me. But instantly the moment was obliterated by a barrage of blinding light that swung onto Helldorff. *He's here!* Hanussen's voice boomed out: *My great honour to present to you! Count Wolf-Heinrich Julius Otto Bernhard Fritz Hermann Ferdinand Graf von Helldorff…"*

It was an aria of Hanussen's hero worship, almost embarrassing in its cloying adulation

"…emblematic of the courageous members of the Sturmabteilungen…"

Helldorff had been trying to remain in the shadows and now stood impaled by the blinding light, his face fixed into a seething smile that blazed contempt. Hanussen had no idea what was really happening as he rushed toward him. Helldorff gripped his arm, leaned in with a seething whisper; and then quickly turned and departed.

It was only later that I realized Helldorff's slight motion of his head had been in my direction.

19

TO THIS DAY IT IS a blur. All of it. I remember watching Helldorff depart, and then hearing Hanussen's voice bellowing *Aha! Apparently we have another guest! Please! Come right up!* I turned to see that it was me he was beckoning to, smiling crookedly with that jumble of teeth and lips that looked like fat worms writhing around scattered Chiclets.

Don't be shy. A reporter who's shy! Imagine that!

A reporter? How did he know? My instinct was to run but hands had locked around me, easing me, skillfully forcing me, toward the stage as if I was gliding just above the floor borne by his incessantly jubilant assistants and the cheers of the assembled. Someone thrust a tall slender glass into my hands. It was something amber and fizzy and before I knew what was really happening. I was being urged to drink a toast

To the Fatherland! and so of course I drank. There was no choice. Champagne! they said and in all the toasts and lights it just seemed too strange, the way the colours flowed together.

Hanussen's voice seemed to bend around me, getting louder and then far away *And now my dear, am I correct in thinking that you know you were not invited tonight?* I didn't know what he meant. I no longer knew what anything meant. *You are one of the lying classes now aren't you? Otherwise known as reporters.* Laughter came in hard blocks of sound banging against something and falling out of those contorted faces.

But now it was my own words: "You are being rude. I am with *Vossiche Zeitung.*"

"Aha! At least you are not communist! Almost as bad though." I heard more laughter clattering all around me.

"Your act is preposterous," I said. My voice sounded like it was just sort of tumbling out of me like fat verbal sausages.

"Preposterous?" he was trying hard to make it sound as if he was laughing at me. But he wasn't.

"And probably a fraud." Why was I saying these things? My mouth suddenly had a mind of its own.

Hanussen's eyebrows shot up. He was the kind of person who could tolerate only adulation. Anything else enraged him. "Well we'll see about that!... "He was dangling something in front of my eyes.

"See about what?" My voice seemed like it was being spoken from across the room and was working its way back to me. Everything was starting to change shapes and colours.

"Preposterous?" I heard him say again. This time he said it like the word was slapping something. He was trying to act as if he didn't care about being challenged. But even through the haze I felt the ferocity of the eternally insecure.

That was the last complete thought I remembered being able to form. After that I was frozen into myself, terrified as numbness swept through me. Something had happened to me and I was unable to move my arms and legs. I had lost all control. That rubbery face of his was moving in and out now like a doughy wrecking ball smashing my barely formed thoughts. And then I was being moved—on what? It felt like I was on wheels, and where were they moving me?

And dreams? Was I dreaming? Terrible dreams of faces, mostly Hanussen's, but there were others. But which others? Cubist Storm Troopers being rearranged into noses and eyes and mouths that tumbled across one another. Looming over me.

Hurting me.

And then blackness. Utter, total blackness that after a while faded into mere darkness as I struggled back up to the surface of consciousness. Tiny fragments of light were being driven into my eyes while I struggled to throw off whatever cloak lay across my mind.

I gasped and struggled to sit up.

A frosted glass door that let in the fragments of light that revealed wreckage all around. Outlines of empty bottles and debris were barely visible before the small room started to spin around and I fell back on some kind of hard bed, maybe just a wide plank that oozed a stickiness when my hand fell across it. That stickiness was also on me as I realized my other hand was on bare skin—my own, in places where my clothes should have been.

I was naked.

All that was covering me were rags that once had been my blouse. And one stocking.

And there was a pain that was making itself known, coming up through the depths within me and a jagged tearing of something *down there* where I reached with my hand until something warm and fluid stopped me just before the pain deep within exploded and the blackness, the beautiful blackness returned.

And as it was pulling me in, I wondered if this was what death was like.

I awoke.

I think it was the Swabian prostitute's filthy Bavarian songs that snapped me back into consciousness. Again it was dark but not like the absolute obliteration of light that had come before. This was a normal darkness with fringes of light and other sensory accompaniments like the smells of the soup on the stove, the sounds of Jürgen being cursed and *Mutter*'s snoring as she lay sprawled in a large chair, a burned-out cigarette between her fingers and her faded housedress barely covering her large knees.

Whatever I had been laying on creaked under my weight as I turned and put one foot on the floor. *Mutter's* eyes snapped open. "Aha," was all she said.

For what seemed like a minute I couldn't get my mouth to work. She just sat there watching, examining, me. "How did I get here?"

She thought before answering: "The Gestapo."

At first I thought she was making a silly joke. "I'm being serious."

"So am I. You were brought here by two Gestapo men who carried you upstairs wrapped in a blanket. And don't think that didn't get the neighbours talking."

I was still pulling thoughts and words out of whatever fog filled my mind. I looked down at myself and thought perhaps there was some mistake. Maybe what I was looking at wasn't me—in a garish pink dress that was cut so low that for a moment I was embarrassed.

"This dress? Pink? What...?"

Mutter found something to relight her cigarette and waited for my thoughts to settle. "The whore from Cologne is the same size as you. Once again she left her clothes behind when she departed to wherever she went this time," she explained. "You should look through her things and take what you want. It's about time we made one of her paranoid fantasies come true. Your own clothes have always looked rather boring if you don't mind me saying."

"Where are my clothes?"

"When you came in wrapped in that blanket you were wearing only one stocking."

"That's impossible."

"I should know. I had to clean you up."

"Clean me?"

She thought for a moment. "You don't understand, do you?"

"Understand what?"

"You were raped."

I sank back onto whatever I had been lying on. The darkness yielded more. Light crept in. The sounds of a day being started came from beyond the walls. When it had beaten back the night I felt the need to say something, anything. "I have to go to work."

"It's Sunday."

"No it's not. Yesterday was Tuesday."

"Tuesday was five days ago. "

That night, lying in bed I heard Karin arrive. She was as cheerful and bubbly as a schoolgirl until *Mutter* bombarded her with questions.

With difficulty I got up and went out to the kitchen in time to be confronted by Karin's indignation. "What do you mean where did I go? That's *my* business."

"Unfortunately it became your sister's business."

"What are you talking about now?"

"Eight days ago. In the middle of the night when you got in Hanussen's big car. You vanished."

She burst out laughing. "Really? *That's* what the fuss is all about? What a bunch of busybodies."

In one stunningly quick swipe, *Mutter* slapped her face. Karin rocked backward in disbelief, her mouth moving but no sound coming out. Mutter pushed her back onto the chair. "Your sister had to go looking for you. And because of that—because of you, she was raped you stupid little fool."

Karin erupted in tears. I had not seen her cry like this since she was a child. It was not just crying; it was a deluge of sobs. Some inner reflex took over and I went to comfort her—which was when *Mutter* held her hand out, stopping me. "Let her snivel and snot herself out," she said.

From the corner of her eye Karin flashed another flicker of indignation that she managed to subdue with more sobs.

Minutes later when all was quiet and the three of us were sitting silently around the wood stove, *Mutter* regurgitated something phlegmy enough to hold together as it arced from her lips to a sizzling extinction on the searing top surface of the stove. Then she turned to Karin: "So? Out with it."

Karin took a deep breath and spilled out a tale about wanting Helldorff to suffer more. So by getting into the car that Hanussen had sent for her and then when it stopped, fleeing into an S Bahn station Helldorff would go into a frenzy. Or so she thought.

There was more, much more, about spending a night at an actor's apartment—"We didn't do anything"—and then two days up near Schwerin on the Baltic Sea and then...

I could not absorb any of it. Maybe because I knew that a few hours from now she would barely remember this night. Or the week that came before it.

The next morning for the first time in a week, I left *Mutter's*. It hurt to walk so I got on the first yellow double decker bus that came along, sitting upstairs as it headed through the heart of Berlin on Unter den Linden surrounded by flowers and trees blooming on the edges of the boulevard and in the center between the lanes of traffic.

It somehow felt safe to be up there above the swirl of traffic and the white uniformed traffic policemen in the intersections waving their arms at cars and people like demented marionettes.

Merely being above the people on the streets felt comforting as if you could pass through them without being part of them. I needed that feeling. Looking down on it all somehow made me feel like a tourist, as if I was *in* Berlin but not *of* Berlin. It was a feeling I liked, maybe needed.

But then from the opposite sidewalk I heard singing. It was a group of boys who, except for the short pants, were dressed like young Storm Troopers. They were striding, arms swinging in unison, their brown shirts and ties synchronized like parts of a single being. And in that one voice wound from many young throats came a falsetto version of the *Horst Wessel Song.*

I got off the bus and found a taxi.

When I got to the House of Ullstein and went inside the first thing I noticed were so many new faces. In the *Vossiche Zeitung* newsroom there were several men I didn't know, sitting around in a circle just talking, drinking coffee, smoking and reading other newspapers as if they had nothing else to do. This would never have been allowed even a couple of months ago. But no editors were around to say anything.

When I knocked on Herr Langen's office door it was a different voice that said, "Come in." I entered and was momentarily too surprised even to speak. A second desk had been brought in to Herr Langen's office and behind it sat a bulky, florid man who looked to be plummeting quickly out of youthfulness. Unlike Herr Langen, he was immaculately dressed in a suit that looked as if it had never been unbuttoned.

"This is Brecht," said Herr Langen, never looking up above his green visor. "He's the new official Nazi editor."

"The advisor," corrected Brecht with an oddly prim little smile. "I'm here to help."

"The Nazi's very own editor," said Herr Langen. His surly responses were making me nervous. Everyone had heard stories of men being badly beaten for even their tone of voice when talking to Nazis.

But Brecht seemed oblivious to either nuance or insult. "To be helpful. And make sure you avoid any unpleasantness." He came across as a man who had spent a lifetime trying to please others. And now, could not adjust to others having to please him.

"He's a friend of Goebbels."

Brecht missed the intonation and took it as a compliment. "Those of us close to him call him Joop," he said proudly.

Goebbels? The cadaverous clubfoot? *Joop?* The feared Minister of Public Enlightenment and Propaganda? The imagery fell in on itself.

Herr Langen's green visor no longer shielded most of his face. He was looking at me and maybe it was my imagination or some kind of guilt but I suddenly felt like a student explaining why I hadn't shown up for class. Part of Herr Langen's genius was that he would know things about you before you did.

"We need some privacy," he said to Brecht.

"Really?" said Brecht, looking hurt as if he was being expelled from a clubhouse. "I'm here to help you know." Silence made him nervous. "Okay, okay," he said getting up and going to the door. "I'm still the boss here though."

"Of course you are."

Herr Langen watched him leave, listening for the *click* of the door as it closed and then he did something unusual for him; he took off his visor and flung it onto the desk.

"This place is now crawling with informers, turncoats and thugs. And of all the Nazis out there, I have to get this slathering lap dog who keeps wanting to be my friend. Which is terrifying. Weak people wanting to be both Nazis and your friend are the most lethal of all."

I was wondering how to tell him why I hadn't been at the office for six days. And whether he would even believe what I was about to tell him.

But then what he said left my anxieties in a heap around me. "I know all about it. What happened to you."

"All?" I was flustered.

He shrugged. "Most of it. Hanussen. Helldorff. And being drugged."

"I was hypnotized."

"Never drink a toast with a charlatan like Hanussen. The champagne will be spiked."

"What else do you know?"

"Everything, " he said looking away as if to spare me. And why was I feeling embarrassed? Ashamed even? And furious with myself because I felt like that? What had *I* done? *Me*? Feeling as if whatever had happened—that awful thing, was *my* fault? How does shame even—

The pencil I was holding snapped in half. Only then did I realize how fast I was breathing.

"Do you want to take some time away from work?"

"No." I felt as if I was sitting outside myself listening to my voice as it came out, solemn, certain and confidant. Everything I was not. "I want to work. I want to be busy—"

I was suddenly aware that was he holding a handkerchief in front of me. "Why are giving me this?"

"Because you're weeping."

I felt my face. It was streaked with tears. "I am so sorry."

"There's no need to be." Before he returned to his desk he touched my shoulder in a gentle motion, which in that moment meant more to me than any human gesture I had experienced in years.

And it was when he took his hand away that I realized how much I craved human touch. "How do you know all this?"

"That slathering lap dog. Brecht."

"Him? How would he know?"

"He doesn't. But last week he told me that he had been instructed to make sure I was in this office Thursday night. I waited. For a long time. There was no knock at the door. It just opened and a man came in and sat down where you are now. He was one of those men who look like they always need to shave. He never introduced himself, never even looked at me. He just took out a notepad and read from it. All the details."

All?

"Starting with the time you arrived at Hanussen's so-called Palace of The Occult last Tuesday and ending when you were found in a disheveled state thirteen hours later. It took him probably about ten minutes to read it all. And when he finished, he simply folded the notepad, got up and walked out the door."

"Who was he?"

"He was dressed in a long leather coat." And then waited for me to say the obvious.

"The Gestapo."

Herr Langen nodded. "I've asked myself why. Why would they do that?" With his elbow on the desk and one hand under his chin he just sat there staring at me. It made me intensely uncomfortable that he didn't say anything.

"Why are you looking at me like that?"

"I'm not sure I understand why this man from the Gestapo came to see me," he said.

The compartment where I stored the secrets was crumbling inside me. "My father's half-brother is the man who was chosen to run the Gestapo."

I thought he might jump up. Or yell. Or throw his visor. He just sat there for the longest time. "You mean Diehls?"

"We know him as Uncle Rudi."

"Diehls? *Uncle Rudi?*"

I nodded. Uncomfortably.

"Your Uncle Rudi is the least bad of an awful lot."

"I was afraid to tell you."

"You should be. Are you close to him?"

"No. I mean yes! When we were young we thought he was wonderful because he was everything our father was not. Funny. Warm."

"And now?"

"I have asked myself over and over how someone like Uncle Rudi could even be a Nazi. Let alone the Gestapo."

"Let me tell you something about your Uncle Rudi. No one in my synagogue is sure what to make of him. He is a fierce enemy of the communists. But he has quietly helped many of us. He has just gotten two Jews we know released from Columbia House. Including Weiss, the former deputy police chief. And that is making him enemies, powerful enemies. Big Nazis like Himmler who want his job. So you may not have to ask yourself that question for long."

"Why?"

"They will kill him." He shrugged as if I was naïve to be surprised. "It's how they do things now. Look what happened to Hanussen."

"Hanussen? What?" My look made him realize I had no idea what he was talking about.

"Two days ago. Don't you know?"

What is now known:

Jan Erik Hanussen has reached the pinnacle of every world he has been in. Across central Europe he has been famous for over a decade, known as the Danish clairvoyant who could fill theaters with rapturous audiences thrilling to his feats of magic, hypnosis and telepathic communication.

But by the time that Hitler seizes total control of Germany, Hanussen is not merely famous, he is powerful. Or so he thinks. In both Berlin's chic society and even in its brutal political world, Hanussen now inspires the awe he believes he deserves.

Even more amazing, Hanussen has reason to believe he has the adulation of the SA, the dreaded Storm Troopers who are strangely devoted to him, often showing up at his performances and cheering him on. Several of the most powerful Nazis in Berlin, among them Count Wolf Heinrich von Helldorff whose new position is that of High Police Commissioner of Berlin, are often seen in his presence.

Helldorff sometimes provides an honour guard for Hanussen, and nothing gets the society types talking quite as much as the sight of a clairvoyant given official protection by twenty-five Nazi Storm Troopers.

Adding to this aura of power and celebrity are stories that Hanussen never denies, stories that he has coached Hitler in the art of public speaking. And that he has guided the Fuehrer from an average speaker into a hypnotic orator, that he has trained him in the cadence and the gestures that create a spellbinding leader.

By almost any standard, Hanussen is obviously a shrewd showman and a powerful political Svengali.

But those standards are wrong. Completely.

He is none of that. Like his act, everything about him is an illusion at best, a fraud at worst.

Behind that act is a preening egotist who is obsessively obsequious, stupidly naïve about his own power and dangerously reckless in whom he trusts.

His access to power comes simply from having bought his way into the SA Stormtroopers. Long ago Hanussen figured out that men like Helldorff were secretly in ruinous debt. Helldorff alone has gambling debts of several hundred thousand Reichsmarks—debts from which Hanussen saves him again and again.

Bundles of cash are handed over to the indebted Storm Troopers and all Hanussen asks in return is that they sign a simple IOU. And as time passes, Hanussen acquires a stack of IOU's. Not only Helldorff, but also Ernst Röhm himself, commander of the entire SA has signed his name to several IOUs in exchange for piles of Hanussen's money.

At first the growing stack of IOU's sits on Hanussen's desk simply because he doesn't bother to throw them away. But then a use for these little papers begins to suggest itself. The more these dangerous, powerful men are indebted to him, the more they will do what he wants.

Or so he thinks.

There is one other area where his life is an illusion, the most dangerous one of them all. He is not Danish. And he is not a Christian. Nor is he even Jan Erik Hanussen.

And so when damning documents arrive at the offices of the local communist newspaper, Berlin am Morgen proving that Hanussen is not who he says he is, the news is soon plastered across its front pages:

Hitler Under The Spell of a Jew?
Fraudulent Nazi is Really A Jewish Clairvoyant!

And then Hitler hears about the matter. Enough! He is furious. Orders are given to Helldorff, coming in the form of a chilling ultimatum. Helldorff panics at what could be revealed about his own tawdry ties to Hanussen. He cannot let this happen. Helldorff becomes desperate to save himself.

But Hanussen cannot hear the headlines becoming muffled drumbeats. He still openly brags of how the Storm Troopers owe him money. So no one will dare do anything to him. Especially Helldorff. Obviously.

But early on a Friday evening in late March, Hanussen is in his luxurious apartment preparing for a performance at the Scala Theater. Several Storm Troopers show up, barging in and demanding the IOU's. When Hanussen refuses to turn them over he is told he is being charged with secretly conspiring with the communists.

Hanussen cannot believe what is happening to him. Where are his friends? Especially Helldorff! His "close friend"? Who owes him so much money? And those other SA types? The ones he has rescued from bankruptcy? Where are they to save him? Has he not bought them new uniforms; given them money when they needed it? Why are they acting this way?

Outrageous!

But the SA men have new orders. These orders are clear and brutal.

Hanussen is clubbed, thrown down a flight of stairs, beaten savagely and then shot three times at close range. His body is transported at night to a forest north of Berlin where it will be found two weeks later by a man cutting down trees.

For his final illusion, Hanussen, or what is left of him, is barely recognizable.

20

I WOULD HEAR THE PHONE calls come in to *Mutter* who would talk in worried and hushed tones. I would hear *Goebbels…* and… *Karin* uttered in the same sentence and then repeated an hour or two later.

"You need to talk to your sister," *Mutter* said to me after one of these phone volleys. "There is a problem. They have cast her in a big movie to be shot at Babelsberg. Not the leading role but close to it."

"So?"

"So Goebbels office phoned wanting to know who she is."

"And that's a problem?"

"Believe me, that's a big problem."

Karin was sleeping when I went into her room and tried to explain what I'd been told.

"Goebbels?" said Karin sounding bored, her eyes still closed. "And you think I don't know all that nonsense?"

"What are you talking about?"

"I could handle Goebbels."

"I beg your pardon?"

"Oh for godsakes. It would just be fucking."

Then she went to sleep, the faint light brushing away the darkness from that perfect face.

I could handle Goebbels.

No one else could have said such a thing. Reckless. Stupid. Oblivious, So why, in some strange way, do I envy that reckless side of her?

As I set out every evening into the false, glittering and increasingly fearful world of gossip. Since the Nazis took over, month by month it is getting deadlier.

And there is no way I or anyone else could *handle Goebbels.*

As the Minister of Public Enlightenment and Propaganda, if Goebbels disapproves of anything in any of my columns, I am in trouble. Every word I write is now like its own little bomb that could detonate because the Nazis are so easily enraged by whatever does not glorify them.

So as a gossip columnist, or as I am now officially called, a *Diplomatic Society columnist,* how do I handle, for example, one of the scariest dangers of them all—-the increasingly bizarre personal life of Magda Goebbels the new wife of Josef Goebbels?

Writing about them is like juggling barbed wire.

On one hand, I encounter Josef and Magda either together or separately at the obligatory diplomatic parties. *That* is the straightforward, ordinary, boring news—or at least the news I'm supposed to report.

But my problem is that I am practically gagging on what I know but cannot write. For instance, even though they were married not even two years ago in what was the most elaborate of the Nazi weddings—Hitler was Goebbels' best man! Their marriage is a wreck.

Which is where the gossip problem begins: because Magda had once said that the first time she saw this odd-looking man with the twisted, frail body, she was so overwhelmed by his intensity and charisma, so awed by his magnetism that she thought she would "burst into flames."

At so many big events, it is obvious that fire has been put out. Their marriage is starting to resemble the smoldering ruins of connubial arson.

Why? Because Goebbels is cheating on Magda so spectacularly that the din of whispers about his affairs is deafening within the minds of all who dare not mention the subject in public.

Now, Magda has started showing up at receptions on her own and looking frozen in defensive indignation behind that rigid smile, as if an argument was raging in her head. She has an odd but striking presence, attractive but not beautiful and suspended somewhere between blandly pleasant and aggressively blonde.

It becomes close to public knowledge that her husband is driven by what's between his legs—and he couldn't keep it in his pants if they were welded shut.

So try writing about *that!* Even in gossip columnist code. *High ranking Nazi does horizontal mambo with*—There's just no way.

Not even combining it with stories about the immense good luck of Magda's new husband who has just taken over the movie business in Berlin. Where his priapic tendencies with young actresses have secretly earned him the nickname: *The Goat of Babelsberg.*

Good luck with getting *that* into print!

Especially after what's been happening to people who offend him.

What is now known:

To Josef Goebbels, the Reich Minister of Public Enlightenment and Propaganda, there is nothing really unusual about the way he runs his movie studios. Mere months after the Nazis take power he has come to accept it as his destiny; it is almost normal that he should be the most powerful studio boss in the history of motion pictures.

To the envy of movie moguls in America and Britain, Goebbels has discovered the best way to get consistently good reviews for his films.

He has simply taken over all the newspapers.

He will soon have driven out the owners of the largest newspaper publishing chains like the House of Ullstein—for whom Bella works, and these owners will be lucky to escape with their lives.

Soon, every morning at 11 am in the Propaganda Ministry, Josef Goebbels convenes a meeting of newspaper editors and tells them what their newspapers will be writing today. Often he orders them to create news articles that will signal yet another attack on the Jews. And if reporters do not do exactly as he demands, he threatens to send in the Storm Troopers.

It proves to be an effective editing method.

For Goebbels all of it has one simple purpose: to shape and control the mood and thoughts of the German people. No matter what, they must believe in the Führer and in the march to war.

Goebbels' genius is in understanding what others have not yet grasped— that movies, and radio and newspapers are all simply propaganda. Collectively they are like an instrument that must be played with great skill. And no one plays it better than Goebbels who knows that the instrument is there to reinforce what the people already want to feel.

And to ignite passions that already exist.

Or to decide what the reviews to a movie will say before anyone has seen it.

Even more than Louis B. Mayer running MGM, or Jack Warner in his own Hollywood fiefdom at Warner Bros, Goebbels becomes obsessive with the films he oversees. No detail is too small, even the changes he demands in the costumes for Marika Rökk one of his biggest stars, and then after the costumes, he revises the choreography on her dance numbers.

But all this is a mere diversion. Deceptively so. Because in deciding on costumes or screenplays that are to be put into production, or selecting directors and writers and choosing actors and actresses his powers are not all that different from the Hollywood moguls he compares himself to. But unlike the Louis B. Mayers, the Warner Brothers and the Sam Goldwyns, Goebbels' power extends far beyond mere movies

Because when he is not reading movie screenplays he is working closely with Hitler and the rest of the Nazi hierarchy on preparations for the bloodiest war the world will ever know.

Which to Josef Goebbels, is as it should be.

"She's the respectable one."

I didn't understand.

"Bongers."

I still didn't know what *Mutter* was talking about.

"Both of us deal in girls. But the difference is that she can talk about what she does in polite society." *Mutter* acted as if she was making a joke until suddenly she threw a filthy dishtowel against the wall.

I sat there watching the dishtowel slowly edge its way down through the grease until it found its rightful position about knee-high behind the old wood stove.

"You will get a phone call. When she's ready."

"When who's going to be ready?"

"Bongers," said *Mutter* as if that would explain it. Then she laughed. "Bongers is the top film casting director in Berlin. She and I are best friends."

The next day, I was at my desk at the newspaper when I got a phone call from a woman who would not give her name, saying only that she was "a friend" and then said something about the need to protect my sister from "a certain prominent person."

I instantly understood that she was talking about Josef Goebbels.

I raced off to the address she gave me, which I recognized as the Berlin Film Office, taking the U-Bahn and getting out at the teeming Friederichstrasse station. I walked several blocks, past the street vendors and the newsstands, navigating the usual piles of horse manure as I crossed the street, reaching the linden trees and the heroic statues that look down on the wide Unter den Linden.

In the reception area of the Film Office a woman with a clipboard asked me what part I was there to audition for. "None," I replied and she looked confused, retreating behind the door with mottled glass. The reception area was filled with young men and women holding pieces of paper and moving their lips as they read.

"If you're not an actress, why are you here?" one of the young women said in an accusatory tone. As if I was taking up both space and concentration from those who were silently rehearsing scenes. Her attitude quickly changed when the door opened and an oddly imposing woman with close cropped red hair was smiling at me and calling my name. No one had to tell me it was Bongers.

"You know *Bongers*?" the young woman whispered, awestruck. "Put in a good word for me. Marta, remember my name—Marta!"

I smiled as I got up. "Maria, you said? Sure."

"*Marta*!" she hissed.

Else Bongers was distinctive in many ways, the least of which was perhaps being the most powerful casting director in the Berlin film business. With her piercing blue eyes framed by red hair on a head that looked a little too large for her body, she had a presence more memorable than most of those who were auditioning for her.

In her third-floor office overlooking the bustling Unter den Linden, all the noise of the street faded as she sat in a large chair asking me confusing questions. Questions that began in generalities quickly tightened into asking what I thought about what was happening *out there*, she said nodding toward the street.

I stopped her in mid-sentence. "Let's clarify this. You're asking me if I'm a Nazi."

She said nothing.

"Or if I approve of what's happening *out there*. Let me tell you—"

It was her turn to interrupt me.

"Yes, or no." Those blue eyes could stop a freight train.

I just shook my head slowly and mouthed *No*.

"Good" she said letting herself relax. "Ilse told me you were okay, but these days I check for myself."

"Ilse?"

"Ah yes. I forgot."

"Forgot what?"

"You know her as *Mutter*."

"Oh."

"Such a beauty she was. Such a tragedy."

"I don't usually think of *Mutter* as a tragedy."

"You didn't know her twenty-five years ago."

"I saw pictures of her."

"The photos only tell part of her story."

"She told me about her communist if that's what you mean."

"And about what he did to her?"

"He left her. Or she left him."

"That's the least of it. He had many women. It drove Ilse—*Mutter*, crazy but for some reason she felt protective toward the youngest of the other women he was sleeping with, a sweet girl from Munich. One night she heard that he had beaten this girl senseless. After she had found the girl and bandaged her, Ilse went looking for her communist. When she found him in a bar she broke a beer bottle over his head, knocking him to the floor. Everyone laughed at the communist and if there was one thing he could not stand it was being laughed at. Before she had even gotten a block away, he caught up to her and with a large pistol, fired sideways at her in a way that would get the most revenge. Do the most damage. In every way. Physically. Emotionally."

She looked at me expecting a reaction. For a moment I didn't know what she meant. But I remembered something—something I hadn't quite understood, about the faded housedress that bulged out in odd ways so that nothing about her breasts seemed quite right. I made a motion with my hands moving across my body in odd ways below my shoulders.

Bongers nodded. "The bullet went through her sideways. Destroying part of what she believed made her a woman. Made her desirable. Her breast were destroyed."

"After the weeks in hospital, she stayed with me for six months. I never saw anyone so devastated. And within a year she had gained 60 kilos, maybe more. She never wanted to be with a man again. Because she couldn't. Or so she said. 'With a deformity like I have now?' she asked me."

"But what changed everything was when the young girl from Munich found her. And asked her to be her protector. Against the different men she was with, the men who paid her every night. And that was when Ilse became *Mutter*."

"A Madam."

"No. Madams take a percentage of what their girls earn. *Mutter* never did that. The only thing she asked of this young girl from Munich was that she tell her what is was like. If ever she felt, really *felt* something with one of these men in her body. Did it touch her emotions? And her soul if ever such a thing happened."

The imagery hung in the air between us.

"Later that changed. She became more businesslike. She had to."

Silence.

"So!" Bongers suddenly said, the word cutting through my thoughts like a blade. "Your sister."

"Yes," I said. "Karin."

"You've heard of the black swan? The white tiger? Those creatures that are as rare as they are beautiful? That is your sister. Once in a very long time I get someone like her. Do you have any idea of the gift she has?"

"No. I'm not sure I do." The idea of Karin having such gifts never occurred to me. You just don't think of your little sister in that way until suddenly you look back at everything through a different turn of the kaleidoscope.

"It can't be taught. It can't even be learned. I have actors who work like dogs for years trying to master their craft and they never come close to what your sister can do. She is an actress for the ages."

"But that's not what you wanted to talk to me about."

"Actually it is. You see I have a seen a few other gifted souls in my time. And for one reason or another at least half of them ended up on the rubbish heap. But in the case of Karin—" she looked around and lowered her voice, "—she has the misfortune of having been seen by Goebbels. And not just seen—*desired*."

"Meaning what?"

"Meaning that Goebbels has just sent us a message from the Ministry. It said that he—and I quote: "wants to get to know her better.""

"Decode that for me please."

"If his previous attempts "to get to know" young actresses can be used as a means of predicting events, here is what the Minister of Public Enlightenment and Propaganda will do with Karin if she is foolish enough to accept his invitation: First comes the dinner at the Ministry in his private dining room. Over dinner Goebbels will make an initial assessment:

Is she just a pretty idiot...?" Bongers expected me to finish the thought left unspoken.

"And if she *is* just a pretty idiot? What then?"

"Then by the time the schnapps has been served the pretty idiot will be naked on her back with Goebbels pounding various protuberances into her."

"And if she is *not* just a pretty idiot?"

"Ah. Then it gets more interesting. There is witty talk. Flattery. Charm. Yes charm, coming from that twisted monster. And other meetings will be quickly arranged. All very innocent. But unseen, unspoken calculations are being made: Starting with where his wife Magda happens to be on any particular night. Is she at home in Berlin? Or out at Schwanenwerder, their house on the lake? You see Goebbels is actually scared of Magda in some strange way. He lies to her constantly but lives in fear of his lies being found out."

"How do you know this?"

"My dear, the actresses looking to be cast in films actually crave my approval more than his. And so when I pump them for information, they tell me everything. So then, on one of these charming, innocent evenings when Magda is at the Berlin home, Goebbels will suggest a drive in the country. To show his young prey his new secret villa at Bogensee. And an hour later they will arrive at this sprawling fornication hut in the forest. Where no one can hear her cry out if she is so inclined to cry out. And some of them do cry out. Do you need more?"

"Why am I here?"

"I need your help. For your sister." I must have made some reaction that caused her to say, "Forgive me for putting it this way but your sister is as clueless as she is talented."

I found myself nodding.

The plan Bongers had worked out to help Karin was complicated and risky. She had already sent a message to the Ministry of Public Enlightenment and Propaganda saying that unfortunately the young lady whose presence was requested had already left for the Torbis studios in the Grunewald.

And then when Torbis studios got the same request it would be intercepted by a woman who had been waiting by the phone. She would answer the call saying the young actress had just been sent to an audition out at UFA in Babelsberg.

And then next, another one of Bongers' group would be at UFA, answering the call and saying that the young actress had phoned from the Terra studios where she had been delayed. And then another woman at the Terra studio in Woltersdorf would answer that phone and say she would look to see if this young actress was on the premises.

And on and on.

Until this little network of women, all of them close friends of Bongers, had worn down the Goat of Babelsberg and he got tired of hearing his anxious assistants deliver the confusing news.

And then in a sullen fury, he would probably order flowers to be delivered to Magda.

"How can I help?" I said.

"Our efforts have so far been good for two, maybe three, days. After that Goebbels has usually forgotten about whoever it is he's chasing. That has been our experience with other actresses. But that is changing. Goebbels is beginning to suspect something. So he has assigned SS men to investigate. We think that at most we have one full day now to protect an actress in this way. After that, other ways have to be found to keep them hidden.

"Which is where...

She finished the sentence for me: "...you come in."

Late that afternoon I drove out to Woltersdorf and the small Terra film studio where an irritated Karin was waiting with Frau Voigt, a cheery older woman

"Quite a handful your sister," she whispered. "Hurry. Bongers just phoned. Goebbels has sent several of his men on their way here to investigate. I would suggest you leave quickly."

On the way out of the studio Karin was lying back in the seat beside me and closing her eyes as I drove. "A complete waste of time," she said. "I come all the way out here for an audition in a film that doesn't exist."

She never saw a car flying small Nazi flags as it roared into the parking area we had just left.

What is now known:

Babelsberg, the legendary movie studio just outside Berlin? The one that was envied by all the old Hollywood moguls?

It became so different.

After what happened to The Hedgehog.

But no one dares talk about him. Or even mention his name. Flamboyant. Opinionated. Confident. Herbert Selpin got the nickname The Hedgehog for the most obvious reason. Selpin is called The Hedgehog by those who found themselves removing invisible barbs after confrontations with him.

*In the early 1930's Selpin is one of Germany's most charismatic film directors, A former boxer with a quick and biting wit, Selpin is stylish and often wears tinted glasses. When the Nazis take over the movie business, he is at the height of his fame and artistic power. When the call comes from Josef Goebbels, Selpin is told that the most prestigious film of the year—*Titanic *will be his to direct.*

It is to be a masterpiece Goebbels insists, with a story that he has had the screenwriters busy creating.

It will be a film about the sinking of the famous ocean liner but really Goebbels sees it as a story of the greedy British industrialists. The same British industrialists who might soon be leading a war effort against Germany.

To make the film, Goebbels arranges for Selpin to be given hundreds of Kreigsmarine sailors for scenes where the Titanic is at sea. But after a week working with these sailors, Selpin decides they are useless; worse than useless because they are either too drunk to do what they are told or else spending their time chasing the female extras in the film. In a fury, Selpin curses the sailors, curses the officers in charge of them—and most dangerous of all, curses the entire German military.

Which is where The Hedgehog's barbs are turned in on himself.

Friends tell him he is putting a gun to his head. It is known that Goebbels now personally signs death warrants that lead to the execution of those in the movie business who he believes have committed the crime of "utterances hostile to the state."

But the Hedgehog cannot help himself. Not even when he is called into the office of a furious Goebbels who cannot believe what he has heard about his director. On such moments in the world of Josef Goebbels, do lives either continue or be snuffed out. Selpin's fate is sealed in the one moment when he admits to what he has said about the German military—and then announces that he would say it again.

Josef Goebbels, movie studio boss instantly becomes Josef Goebbels, Reich Minister of Public Enlightenment and Propaganda. He orders that the Hedgehog be arrested. The two SS men who escorted Selpin into Goebbels' office grab him and drag him away.

Less than a day later Herbert Selpin, the Hedgehog is found dead in his cell. Goebbels orders that the death be ruled a suicide.

Because after all: he committed the crime of "utterances hostile to the state."

What can be clearer?

21

THE WHORE FROM COLOGNE WAS having some kind of a fit. She had become hysterically convinced that I was stealing her clothes. Because most of my clothes were still packed in a suitcase that had been left at home —father's home now, she was sure that I would soon run out of dresses and plunder her closet. At first I thought she was joking, but her outbursts quickly changed my mind.

"Don't argue with madness," *Mutter* said to me late at night. "I learned that long ago. Just get your suitcase. Fill the closet here with your own clothes. That will calm her down."

That suitcase, filled with every dress I could cram into it, had sat for months in my old room at father's house waiting for me to retrieve it. I had stalled for as long as I could, not wanting another of the acidic confrontations with father whose was now blaming me and Karin for most of the problems in his life.

I waited until a weekday afternoon when I was sure father would not be there. Approaching the house through the little wooded area where berries grew at this time of year, I heard the sound of a car approaching. Then another and then a third one.

I kept walking through the wooded area, circling back to the house after reaching the road. Through the trees I could see three cars outside; two were new Fords that were not as imposing as Uncle Rudi's car but still exuding the official power of the Nazis merely by the black-uniformed chauffeurs standing beside them with all the charm of attack dogs. The other car was more subdued, an Adler I think, one that lesser bureaucrats might drive on official business.

Lesser bureaucrats like father.

Going in through the back door. I could hear voices coming from the library. Whenever father spoke, he sounded so eager to please, so fawning that I suddenly had to overcome the urge to close the door and wait outside.

The words I could identify—*"Switzerland... Geneva... Reichsbank..."*—were swallowed up by talk of gold and arguments over carats. And indignation over *"the lower classes and their pathetic 18 karats."* To which I heard father agree with the kind of fervour I had seen him express years ago when he wanted grandfather's approval.

For half an hour I sat unnoticed in the shadows of the dining room until bulging men in Nazi uniforms left the library in a small swarm and went outside to the waiting Fords. Father followed them dressed in his light brown military style suit coat with the red and white swastika armband.

I heard him say things that did not sound like what father would ever say: *My next trip to Switzerland...* and, *...maximizing the return to the Reich.*

Then he assured them that all would be done with the usual efficiency.

...the usual efficiency?

I had almost forgotten. It was something he used to say so often when we were children. I always wondered if it was why neither Karin nor I were remotely efficient at anything.

Car doors slammed, and engines were started as father returned quickly to his library. There was an odd clanking noise that sounded. I'd never heard a noise like this before. It came again from his office, a dull metallic thud followed by a higher pitched and fainter clinking noise like something fragile was settling.

I walked through the corridor and stood in the doorway watching him writing in a ledger. In front of him on the desk were three identical, strange objects. They were cloth bags made out of grey felt-like material, each with a cinch-cord drawn tight at the top. Each bag had the imprint of a swastika and was about the size of a very large melon.

He suddenly saw me and it was as if he'd been electrocuted. "Good god!" He rasped, "Don't scare me like that. And what exactly are you doing here?"

"What did I hear about Switzerland?"

He looked startled, bristling with the odd combination of defiance and defensiveness that he showed whenever he felt he had been confronted. "I am at a senior level—a very senior middle level."

"Congratulations," I said only because it sounded like the correct thing to say.

"At the Reichsbank. So I am going to Switzerland every month."

"You never liked to travel."

"But this travel is an honour. I have been entrusted in dealing with the Swiss banks concerning the property of the Reich. And by the way, that Adler that is parked outside? The Reichsbank has provided it for my use."

"You must be important." As I asked myself *Why am I saying this?*

"Well I am."

"Obviously."

He looked pleased. "I am an official," he said with finality. He adjusted the light over his desk and put on his glasses.

Something struck me as curious. When he adjusted the light on his desk a shiny object in the top of one of those bags had reflected a glint that caught my eye. "What is in those bags?"

"The property of Reich," he said rising up without ever leaving his chair. He reached around the three felt bags with the swastikas on them, pulling them protectively toward him. And as he did, something strange happened. A little gold object fell out onto the desk.

A ring. A gold wedding ring.

"The property of the Reich?" I knew my voice sounded screechy. I couldn't help it. "A ring?"

"This cannot be seen by unauthorized personnel."

"A *wedding* ring?" Images I did not want to see tumbled through my thoughts. Almost by reflex, I hit the bag. Dozens of gold rings flew from it.

"Stop! Stay back." He was in a panic, his arms waving all over.

I hit the bag again. Dozens, hundreds, of wedding rings flew from it, scattering across his desk. "You can be arrested for this!" he screeched.

"Switzerland?" Now it was me who was yelling. "That's what you do?"

He looked terrified, a feckless mix of quivering and fury. "I will call, the SS," he shouted picking up the telephone. I ripped the phone out of his hand and pulled on the cord so hard it came out of the wall.

"These are wedding rings! From people who loved each other!" Now it was me who was yelling. "How dare you!"

He shrieked and somehow it pleased me for that moment before I lost all control, flinging myself *with the usual efficiency* at those bags sending the rings flying all over. And as emotional as I was, I could hear a thousand voices coming from those rings, a deafening chorus of cherished vows and psalms of love and lives joined together, all of them now ripped apart.

"I'm sorry, I'm sorry!" I yelled to the rings, scattering them, kicking them in some sad hope that one of them would escape the Swiss smelter that awaited them.

Father was shrieking and jumping all over, grabbing at the rings, yelling at me to stop, and then threatening me with the SS as he fell to the floor, slapping at rolling rings careening all over, little fugitives making a break for it. There were so many that the library floor sizzled with them, rings rolling in mad patterns until they spun onto the wooden tiles and lay there in the hundreds, waiting to be kicked back to life by my shoes. Anything—*anything* not to go back into those black Nazi bags of murdered dreams and destroyed lives.

And then be taken by him to Switzerland. To be melted into gold bars. *As property of the Reich*!

Hysterically, father grabbed a metal ruler on his desk and swung it, edge first toward me. It acted like a dull knife leaving an instant welt that seeped a fine slit of blood. For a moment it stunned me. I looked down at the blood that was dripping down onto his desk and onto one of the rings that lay there. I picked up the ring, looked at it, trying to read the inscription on the inner circumference. Before I could, he raised the metal ruler again and I did something I could never have imagined.

Ever.

I lashed out. Physically. On pure instinct I folded the hand holding the ring into a fist and swung it sideways as hard as I could.

The force of the blow caught him on the side of his face, on his jaw and sent him reeling backwards, crashing over a wastebasket and catapulting into the lower part of the back wall. He lay on the floor making gagging noises between groans and crying out about the Reich and what it would do to me. When he finally spoke it was a gurgling version of "You can be sent away for this."

But I was already leaving the library, heading for the front door with the one bloody wedding ring still in my hand.

It was not until almost twelve years later that I would see him again, when the carnage was at its worst and he would do the only thing that ever really gave his life any meaning.

After leaving father's home I willed myself to go to the reception at the Honduran legation partly out of duty. I knew Herr Langen was expecting a column from me especially since those South American reception usually ended up as absurd cultural collisions. Something amusing could usually be found to write about.

I liked them most for the chance that the Cubans might show up and start dancing to their own music which meant that some overstuffed Nazi would blunder into buffoonery without knowing it. Buried under jackboots, medals, belts, buckles, holsters and britches, and fortified by the courage of too much alcohol, he would become the Nazi who made the mistake of deciding that the honour of the Reich was at stake on the dance floor.

Which is what exactly happened at the Honduran legation as some bulging *Ortsgruppenleiter*, florid, wheezing and swiveling furiously was beginning to be aware of his own ridiculousness, swiveling his hips and moving his feet. He began to look like a disintegrating robot as medals and buckles shimmered in all directions, clinking, clanking and bouncing. While his ceremonial sword was smacking other guests and swinging around, spectacularly clearing tables of well-filled wine glasses.

Fury and panic were setting in—which was usually the part I enjoyed the most. But not on this night.

Rings. Everywhere.

Why was I the only one who knew what was really happening, seeing what no one else there saw. Right there! Hundreds, thousands, millions of them rolling all over floor.

Suddenly, I desperately had to leave.

Hours later I sat at my desk. Every time I tried to write even a sentence all I could see were those rings. Suddenly my ability to form words had left me.

I sat staring across the almost empty newsroom. It was quiet in that way that something fierce is quiet when it sleeps. There was always a sense that frenzy and action were only an eye blink away,

No one seemed to notice I was even there until Lutz—or Lutzi as he was known, saw me. Tall, nervous and always brushing his limp blonde hair away from his forehead, Lutzi hurried over from the other side of the newsroom. With his awkward way of approaching people he always appeared to be inwardly rehearsing what to say in order to make a good impression.

"Oh Bella I'm so glad you're here; Herr Langen is having one of those times"

"One of those times?"

"You know. Difficult. He sent me to try and find you."

"I'll go there soon Lutzi. I just want a moment on my own."

"Please. Don't make him upset with me." Lutzi had the amazing ability to turn other people's problems—real or potential, into something about himself.

"Why would you think he'd be upset with you?"

"I don't want him to be, that's all."

"I'm sure you're absolutely fine."

"Oh. Okay." He stood there brushing his blonde hair back off his forehead in that repetitive motion he made whenever he got nervous.

I didn't want to keep the conversation going. There was a cloying neediness to him that most times clung list a mist. His presence just seemed to suck oxygen away from my thoughts.

"I think he must be pleased with the work I'm doing don't you?" Lutzi asked.

"Yes Lutzi. He must be." Then I turned my back on him.

When I knocked on the door to Herr Langen's office I half-expected to hear Brecht's voice. But it was the irritated *"Yes?"* that oddly gave me comfort as I opened the door. Herr Langen was alone at the small desk he now worked at, next to his old desk, the one that Brecht sat behind when he was there.

Herr Langen's green visor snapped up as if his head was attached to a spring. "Your column? Where is it?" His eyes were as challenging as I had ever seen them. "Nothing?" It was somewhere between an angry statement and a question. "Right now we have *nothing*!—an empty space where your column should be. Where is the column on the Honduran embassy reception?" He waited for me to say something. I couldn't.

"I tried." It was as much as I could say. And it was true.

Herr Langen's anger had not subsided. "Oh so you tried?" There was no attempt to hide the sarcasm. "You are not paid merely to try."

I nodded dumbly. He expected a response. "Instead of your column I had to insert a filler article about gardening." All I could do was nod again. "Do you know the calls I've been dodging? From upstairs?"

I did the only thing I was capable of. I took out the one blood smeared wedding ring I had salvaged from the bundles on father's desk. I put it on the desk in front of him. And then I did something that infuriated me; something I had never done since I was six years old.

I burst into tears.

I sat there holding up the ring with tears running down my face and making wheezy, snotty noises that embarrassed me. I was appalled at my weak outburst, *This is not who I am!* But it *was* me. And whatever that image of me looked like, it caused Herr Langen's tough-minded rectitude to totally unravel. In a flash he went from stern taskmaster to a fussing protector.

Merely the sight of the ring jolted him in a way he would not admit to. But my tears were what really left him defenseless. Which made me feel so manipulative. But I couldn't help it. The tears just kept coming until Herr Langen had run out of handkerchiefs pulled from a supply in his desk drawer,

"I am so sorry," I said when I could finally form words.

"It's all right," he insisted over and over again. I thought he was about to start weeping too. Not because of me; because of the ring that he was looking at as if it had some power over him. And it did.

"Where is this from?"

I started to form words and couldn't. All he heard was...*father...my father...* But the thought of what I was about to reveal choked me up all over again. Herr Langen sat back and waited.

Finally, when I had no more tears left I said, "I must ask you two things. First, I must ask you not to hate me for what I am about to tell you. And secondly, I am praying you will not tell anyone here."

He remained as still as a sphinx. I kept going. And told him about father. And the bags of gold wedding rings. When I finished, he sat there staring into space.

"My father has never really done anything important in his life."

"Precisely. Which is why he is so terrifying. He is like the millions of others who are as ordinary as water. They have never been anything special. But put them in one of those uniforms with all the braid and swastikas and runes and death's heads and suddenly they look in the mirror and for the first time in their little lives they see a warrior looking back at them. Hitler's no fool. He knows this. Why do you think the Nazis spend so much on uniforms?"

I just nodded wiping away smudges around my eyes and nervously picking up the gold ring that lay on his desk. "It has writing inside."

I handed it to him. He brought it close to his face. "Hebrew."

He adjusted his glasses and moved the ring into the light and read: "*I love you.*" He slumped back in his chair. "Oh God...." He never finished what he was going to say. I don't think he was aware of wrapping his left hand into his right in a slow twisting motion.

"What should I do with the ring?" I asked.

"Wear it. You are the one who saved it from the smelter."

I hesitated.

"Wear it! " he said. "In the name of the love with which it was given."

Slowly I put the ring on the third finger of my right hand. I had expected it would feel very wrong to be wearing it. Herr Langen sensed this.

"You were expecting it to feel just a bit obscene weren't you?" he said. I nodded. "And somehow it doesn't,"

"Because I'm just the trustee. It's not mine; Someone has to keep alive the—"

I was interrupted by a sharp knocking on his office door and without waiting for a response, Lutzi hurried in, holding out a sheaf of teletype pages. "I think you might want to read these sir."

I expected one of Herr Langen's sharp little outbursts for which he was known whenever some unsuspecting employee interrupted him in his office. I couldn't believe it when he simply looked up with a wry smile and said, "Thank you Herr Lutz."

Lutzi beamed, almost panting like a dog whose master had rubbed its ears.

I was seeing a different side of Herr Langen. He had a softer side that was now coming out with certain people. One of them was Lutzi. Against the advice of other senior editors he had hired the 21-year-old Lutz as an apprentice reporter. The other editors found him too awkward to be a reporter. With his eagerness to please, Lutzi could be irritating in a clinging kind of way. He was almost out of place in a newsroom of edgy personalities, many of whom called him *Rabbit* because of his slightly protruding front teeth

He stood brushing the shank of blonde hair to the side of his forehead as he did dozens of times a day. It was almost his trademark, a nervous tic that always lessened whenever he talked to Herr Langen who was one of the few who did not make him nervous.

Lutzi backed out of the office, smiling.

When he was gone, Herr Langen said, "I had Lutz assigned to the Alexanderplatz. If he can handle those clowns in the Polizeipräsidium, nothing will ever make him nervous again."

22

I WAS WITNESSING THE ULTIMATE humbling.

While their entire way of life was crumbling before their eyes, the old Prussian aristocrats dressed in tuxedoes and evening gowns could muster only nervous smiles as they were ignored or mocked by barely literate men in swastika armbands and high leather boots.

All that elegance that once reeked of permanent power was disintegrating. Pillars and chandeliers were crashing invisibly all around them while this insolent former corporal entered the grand ballroom behind a menacing chevron of massive black-clad SS guards.

And so I wrote:

To the excitement of the other guests, the new chancellor
Adolph Hitler also attended. He looked relaxed and
chatted amiably with several dignitaries who were
charmed by his presence. Many of the elderly generals
from the War lined up to talk to him and later said
how much they looked forward to offering him advice.

Herr Langen was amazed.

He put down the red pencil without having made a single mark on the pages I had turned in. "You're learning. Finally."

"Learning? Learning what? To write drivel?" I had never used that tone of voice with him before. I didn't mean to; it just came out that way.

He looked right at me with that steely blue-eyed gaze of his. "So what exactly would you have wanted to write?"

"I would have written that before Hitler showed up, von Papen and all the ridiculous nobles were sneering at the mere mention of his name. But then, as Hitler was about to enter, von Papen ran around like a pathetic and excited schoolboy announcing, "He is here!". And also that all the Grand Dukes and Duchesses were falling over each other for a place close to the entrance just to have Hitler acknowledge them. Just minutes after they had all mocked him! And the comical sight of von Papen turning into a fawning waiter, bringing food to Hitler who took the plate without a word. And that...." I stopped and thought.

"Are you finished?"

"For the moment. No wait—there was a very rich princess who swooned when Hitler kissed her hand. There. That's it."

"Hitler kissed a woman's hand?"

"Several. He looked ridiculous when he did it. I should have put that in too."

"So why didn't you?"

The question irritated me. "Do you think I like sitting here watching you take your red pencil to what I write? Over and over again? And-"

"Oh really?" He interrupted me. "Is it that? Or is it because now you've fallen into line? In your mind you're the one taking the red pencil to what you want to say before you even write it. You don't need me to do it for you now."

"That's ridiculous!"

"And you're angry about it?"

"The mind is captured...," he said "...to save the body. Dohndorf could have used that lesson."

"Dohndorf? The funny guy in sports? What about him?"

"Two days ago he wrote an article praising a Jewish football player. The printers found what was left of him this morning. His face was unrecognizable."

Fear was like a mist on the streets that you walked through. Everywhere there were murmurs of people disappearing into new concentration camps that were rumoured to have been created. Informers were everywhere and one overheard remark could lead to a denunciation. People had simply disappeared for what they said too loudly. Everyone had seen the SS or the Gestapo dragging men—and sometimes women, out of their apartments.

We were all falling into *der Deutsche blick—the German look*, which had us looking around in all directions before talking to anyone on the streets. Checking that no one else was listening to us.

So much was changing now. Walking beside Karin on the street outside *Mutter's* apartment I asked her if she noticed what was different on the grim streets of Neukölln. "The weather?" she asked not really interested.

"The communists," I said. "No one is a communist now." Which on the outside at least was true. Gone were the massive rallies and the huge red banners hanging from balconies. Now shorn of all the banners, there were just drab and soot covered buildings exhaling ancient odors. Even the headquarters of the German Communist Party, Karl Liebknecht Haus, had been stripped bare of its massive *Soviet Germany* signs and its address had changed overnight. No longer was it on Bülowplatz; suddenly the Nazis had changed the street name to Horst-Wessel-Platz.

In just months the communists had gone from almost winning the election to being hunted down by the Nazis. Suddenly there was no one who would admit having ever been a communist. It was as if they had vanished.

"Oh who knows where they are." said Karin. "Maybe they just got tired of all that marching and yelling."

Someone on the street in front of us was waving.

It took me a moment to see it was Erma. "Guess where I'm going?" she said and then answered her own question: "Mecklenburg." She had none of Karin's breezy certainties and was eager to please in a way that Karin was not.

"What are you going to do in Mecklenburg?" said Karin. Making it sound like Erma would living in a coal mine.

"A man," she giggled. "Klaus thinks it will be safer to be there in the war."

"What war?"

"The war." Erma said as if we should have understood. She giggled at the thought for a moment and then looked defensive. "Well? Don't you feel it? Everyone I know is sure we're going to have a war."

That night I lay on the bed in the little room listening to the Swabian prostitute rant in her sleep about that bastard Jürgen who had apparently married someone else years ago. I drifted through my own dreams, all of them involving Hitler and the fawning aristocrats I had seen. In every dream I had a tiny revolver in my purse and when I got close enough to take it out and fire at him point-blank, I could not get the purse to open. The dream came back every time I fell asleep and by morning I was exhausted and depressed that I had not been able to change history.

I awoke when *Mutter* called me from the kitchen. There had been a call for me on the communal phone, a man who left neither his name nor a message.

The only person who knew the number here was Herr Langen.

Berlin was seething.

Everywhere I turned there was violence. Storm Troopers were chasing anyone who looked Jewish across sidewalks of shattered glass, beating them with clubs when they stumbled.

Every road I drove on while leaving Neukölln had marching or yelling Nazis smashing windows of stores owned by Jews. Further up on the Ku'damm at Degginger's Fabric store where I had often gone to buy cloth for our clothes, Storm Troopers stood in the doorway laughing while others pasted *Do Not Buy From Jews* signs on the windows and a crowd cheered them on.

When I finally got to Kochstrasse, the House of Ullstein was so different from its usual bustling center of street life. The exterior of the building seemed strangely quiet and just as unusual was the absence of Burmester, the enormous doorman who always stood guard on the sidewalk in his grey overcoat with the Ullstein crest.

Inside in the newsroom, there was a kind of disconnected tension. Everyone moved with strangled haste, as if invisible elastic bands were pulling at them. No one made eye contact and greetings were brushed aside tersely.

I knocked on Herr Langen's door and entered. Again he was alone; Brecht was nowhere to be seen. "Have you been living in a cave?"

"What's going on here?"

"The Nazis are calling it The Boycott. I didn't want you here today."

"Why?"

"That column you wrote about Hitler and the fawning old aristocrats—Goebbels read it and was furious. He thought Hitler should have been portrayed as being more virile, more heroic."

"*What?* It just was a boring society reception. That's ridiculous."

"If Goebbels says it, it stops being ridiculous. You're one of their targets now."

As he was talking, a strange noise came from outside, at first faint and then aggressive. *Thwap. Thwap. Thwap. Thwap.*

It was the first time I ever saw him open the shutters on his office windows. Daylight seemed like an intruder, and he blinked irritably in its presence. "Aha," was all he said peering out onto the street below. The street had filled with goose-stepping SA Storm Troopers, their feet pounding the pavement in unison as if there was something on it to be exterminated. *Thwap. Thwap. Thwap.*

He closed the shutters and took his place behind the desk in the gloom of his office as calmly as if he was posing for a portrait. *Thwap. Thwap.* Noise exploded into the hallways and newsroom out beyond his door but growing closer. We sat in his office like two people knowing that a terrible storm was approaching our flimsy shelter and there was nothing we could do but wait for it to hit us.

"Just stay calm," Herr Langen said in a quiet voice. "No matter what happens."

An instant later his office door was flung open and a seething young Storm Trooper stood glaring at us while others stomped through the newsroom behind him yelling "Jews out!" over and over again. The young Storm Trooper yelled over the din, "No Jews hiding in offices! Out!"

I looked closer, first in horror, then in amazement.

"*Lutzi?*"

"Obersturmmann Hentschel to you!" Lutzi snapped. In his brown cap, shirt and wide britches, crisscrossed with leather straps and belts he looked somewhere between menacing and ridiculous.

I didn't understand Herr Langen. He leaned back as relaxed as I'd ever seen him. "Lutzi, Lutzi, Lutzi. You too?" He had never called him *Lutzi* before, always *Lutz* or *Herr Lutz.*

For a moment Lutzi looked confused and the power of his uniform failed him. None of its leather and brass was enough to mask the awkward apprentice reporter who reappeared for the briefest of moments, his upper lip quivering over his protruding front teeth. He struggled to recover and looking over Herr Langen's head he snapped, "I have orders."

"Of course you do, Lutzi. Of course you do." Herr Langen's assured calmness was the last thing Lutzi expected to be facing when he kicked open the door to the office.

He seemed not to know what to do next. He tried to brush at his blonde hair in that motion he always made when he was uncertain. But his cap that covered his hair was knocked sideways making him look even more absurd. He stood immobilized, encased in a uniform that seemed to be all that was holding him up.

A savage shout came from behind him: "Obersturmmann Hentschel!"

"Yes *Scharführer*?" barked Lutzi.

The doorway almost filled with a huge and angry Storm Trooper. "Get them out of there." I knew him instantly and couldn't stop myself from blurting out, "Herr Burmester? Is *this* why you aren't out in front of the building?"

"Things are different now," said Burmester the doorman, apparently now a *Scharführer*.

Except for the ballooning britches of his SA uniform he looked smaller without that great grey doorman's overcoat, the one he always wore standing out in front of the building. "Everyone must go into the newsroom."

It was Burmester's same face confronting us—but where was that smiling, helpful person behind it? How had this scowling Storm Trooper taken over the face and body of our friendly doorman?

Almost dazed, I left Herr Langen's office and went into the huge newsroom where Storm Troopers were marching, singing the Horst Wessel song and chanting 'No more Jews!" over and over again. Several of the Ullstein brothers' offices were being torn apart.

As the floor filled with Nazis, some of the most recognized names, the most cantankerous personalities in the newspaper business stood immobilized like sheep in a pen.

After enough destruction was done, *Scharführer* Burmester barked orders at them, the Storm Troopers stamped their way out.

And then it was over.

An hour later reports from the streets were that the Nazi attacks there had also stopped as suddenly as they began. But in the newsroom, the staff of *Vossiche Zeitung* was struggling to act like nothing had happened. No one wanted to talk about it. Or maybe more accurately, they were afraid to talk about it because it was becoming obvious that some of the janitors and printers were ardent Nazis, relaying whatever happened in the newsroom directly to Goebbels' office.

Early that afternoon, before leaving for the reception at the Japanese embassy I went back to Herr Langen's office which still bore the results of the vandalism. A bookcase remained turned over and papers were strewn across one corner of his office. Herr Langen had made no effort to restore any semblance of order.

"Now it begins," he said when the door closed behind me. "The veneer is being ripped off."

He found a letter and held it up to the light. "My wife. She is in France now. Part of me is there with her." It was the first time in weeks I had seen him smile.

Back in the newsroom I was retrieving notes on my desk when I saw Lutzi from across the newsroom. He was back in his normal clothes now and was trying to look busy because he knew I was staring at him. And outside as I left the building, Burmester the doorman was once again there wearing that great grey overcoat with the Ullstein logo on it. He tipped his cap and motioned to a taxi that he already had waiting for me. I thanked him and got in as he held the door for me.

Burmester smiled and wished me a good day.

23

SOMEHOW THE NIGHTMARES CAME BACK. Fierce and in volleys that flung me in and out of exhausted, terrified sleep.

In them a man's face loomed over me. It was a different face this time, sharp featured with a strange gap between his two upper front teeth. In my nightmares that gap grew closer to my face as I tried to fight him off. In the middle of the night I woke up soaked in perspiration and gasping.

The door to my room was open and *Mutter* was standing holding a lantern. I started to apologize for making noise but she held out her hand. "Child, child, you're safe. I know it doesn't just go away " *Mutter* said. "You were raped. It will take time. A lot of time. You can't just turn off the hurt." And then she added, "I know."

I lay back on the bed, afraid that my heart would pound itself right out of my body.

"Several of my girls had the same reaction when they chose some miserable fucker who—"

I interrupted her. "I didn't choose anyone."

"I understand But It all comes down to the same thing—a dick where it doesn't belong." She took a long drink from a bottle of something homemade. "You think you could be pregnant?"

"Oh my god, don't even-"

"I got a guy who can take care of it. I sent one of my girls to Dr. Heller. A real doctor too. Did a good job. She was back here working a few weeks later. Six, seven customers a day."

The next night, fortified by cheap wine, *Mutter* sank into an ominous mood. When something was really irritating her, she would sometimes look for ways to get everyone so worked up and arguing that voices were raised and doors were slammed. It was her way of providing cover for whatever outrageous things she had decided needed to be said.

I watched the streets pass by from the upper deck of the bus where it felt safe, removed from it all. It had become a place of daily refuge. Moving through Kreuzberg, it was like watching robots moving through the streets in some theater production. For scenery there were massive Nazi banners, newly draped down the height of entire buildings like red scars emblazoned with black swastikas. Fluttering in places where only a year ago they would have been ripped down. But now the fear was so great on the streets that no one would dare even touch one of them.

The streets were like some Fritz Lang movie, with shuffling hordes moving stiffly through a collective invisible fog, not daring even to look at those banners in places like Kreuzberg, Moabit, Neükolln and Wedding and so many other areas of Berlin that had never come close to supporting the Nazis.

But that is not what scared me as I looked down. What scared me was that people were getting used to it all—to the banners, to the terror. And it was happening so quickly. What was considered normal was being redefined almost weekly.

But now something else caught my attention. A large car; it was driving beside the bus, not trying to pass it just staying along side for several blocks like an outrider of some kind. In the rear seat was a man looking up to the second deck of the bus I was on. He saw me looking down at him and yelled something to whoever else was in the car. It sped up and swerved in front of the bus that lurched to a stop in a clatter of horns. Loud voices came from the front of the bus below, and then abruptly ceased. A man in a leather coat climbed to the upper deck of the bus, looked around and then pointed at me.

"Come," was all he said.

No one around me moved or even looked up. It had become the way people reacted whenever someone near them was singled out by the Gestapo.

Seated in the back of the large car, I was driven through the crowded streets. It was as Karin has described it—feeling strangely removed from what was happening on the other side of the car windows. I kept seeing it as theater with other cars and people hurrying to get out of the way. Maybe theater was wrong; circus might be more accurate as the policemen scurried with almost clown-like motions, waving the big car onward.

Just being inside that big Gestapo car would test a wavering moral code, watching people jump back in fear as you roared past. Those people on the street, the ones who jumped aside, the *ordinary* people, they understood. They knew this was raw power slicing through their miserable traffic jams like a razor. They *knew,* even without all the banners and emblems. They had come to sense brutality when it raced toward them.

And these three unsmiling men in the large car? Who knows what they were a year ago? Milkmen? Clerks? Waiters? Whatever. Now they were the *men in the large car.* And after barging through traffic, blaring that unheard horn of raw entitlement, what sense of identity could exist with all their former milkmen colleagues? Fellow clerks? Waiters?

None. Absolutely none.

Of course. They were Gestapo. Now.

It would just *do* something to you.

The three unsmiling men looked at their watches as if they were timing something. When I asked if we were late, one of them pretended to smile and said, "Things have to be done properly." The big car circled up to Unter Den Linden and then headed back down Wilhelmstrasse, the street that always made my skin crawl, the street with all the Ministries hiding behind their bland facades, places where lives were now being planned out of existence.

"Where are we?" I asked when the car made a right turn on a street I thought I recognized.

"Prinz Albrechtstrasse," the driver said.

"Right on time," said the one beside me, looking pleased. He was a doughy man who seemed to have too many teeth for the size of his face, causing his lower jaw to jut out.

I knew where we were and what this building once was. I had been inside it when it was the School of Industrial Arts and Crafts. Now it was known simply as Prinz Albrechtstrasse, the epicenter of terror.

The address alone left mere citizens immobilized with fear.

This looming Gestapo headquarters stretched out in grey solemnity almost to the end of the block. It was literally around the corner from the centers of Nazi power—Hitler's Chancellery and Göring's and Goebbels' offices, It was five floors of façade-like decorative pillars surrounding thin, tall windows leading to a sloping mansard roof. Around the front entrance was a sculpted arch that supported a small stone balcony inhabited by two massive statues of artisans at work.

The large black car stopped not far from the building and the three Gestapo men in the car debated about which entrance to use, finally opening the car door and guiding me by the arm toward the front door. I shook my arm away from the doughy Gestapo man holding my elbow. He laughed in that way that made me think of a cat amusing itself with a cornered mouse.

Inside I was led through vast hallways smelling of fresh paint. I was told to sit on a long bench under Nazi banners over massive, curved windows blaring sunlight onto parquet floors as earnest looking men hurried back and forth or clustered in small groups beside sculpted marble busts of Hitler.

"Wait," was all the Gestapo man said before he walked away.

I felt almost detached when I should have been raw with anxiety or even terror like everyone else brought in here. Instead I had actually summoned up a sense of irritation and did not want to dwell on where it came from.

I was seated beside a sharp-featured little woman with grey hair like steel wool and a face that looked as if it was chiseled out of rock. She sat on the bench rocking back and forth ever so slightly, her hands strangling one another.

"Are you okay?"

She didn't answer. She just kept staring straight ahead, rocking almost imperceptibly. I wondered if she was deaf.

SS men in their black uniforms congregated at the end of the long corridor like crows waiting for carrion.

A thin man in a rumpled suit approached and motioned to me. "Come," he said. When I got up the little woman clutched at my arm, looking at me for the first time. "My son," she said. "My son is in here. Somewhere."

The thin man walked closely behind me as if I might try to escape on the way to the big staircase curving into a basement at the southern part of the building.

I had the strangest sensation walking into that basement; I had been there before for the first story I ever wrote for *Vossiche Zeitung*, an article about the sculptors creating masterworks for a palace being built by one of the Krupp family. It was where huge slabs of marble and granite were being chiseled into heroic human forms by sculptors.

But now it was so different.

That same space was now a dark corridor with jail cells along one wall. Now all I heard was moaning coming through the small openings in the cell doors, about shoulder high and latticed with steel bars.

The thin man outdid himself with a voice that sounded like it came through a megaphone: "*At the doors! All of you swine! At the doors! Now!*"

In ragged succession, faces fell against the bars from inside the cells, some smearing blood or oozing other fluids. That dim light filled with a terrible irony in a place that once had transformed rock into human form. Now it was the human form reduced to rubble. What had once been faces was now flesh rearranged into pulp. Eyes closed and blackened, noses crushed, teeth missing.

The thin man said, "Walk. And look at the faces in the cells. Carefully."

"I can't do this," I said.

"For their sake you will do this," he said sounding vaguely bored. "They will suffer if you don't"

I looked to see if he meant what he said. I didn't need an answer. His eyes said it all.

I walked ahead, looking. First cell: a shattered boy, maybe eighteen years old, burbling absolution through bloody broken teeth. Second cell: an old man with dried blood in snow-white hair. Third cell: a tiny man, mouse-like and trying to peer over the opening by clinging to the bars with fingers stripped of fingernails.

And so it went. Fourth cell. Fifth cell. Sixth cell.

And then at the seventh cell my mind detonated. I couldn't help it. I just started screaming.

24

"I'M SORRY."

It was the figure of a man in silhouette.

He was walking casually toward me from the far end of the corridor.

"*Bellachen*," Uncle Rudi said softly, "By the time my man got to you in that Palace of The Occult or whatever Hanussen called it, the door was bolted shut. He had to fire a bullet through the bolt. You had been stripped naked and a partly dressed man was raping you."

Someone brought me water and I sat up trying to focus on what was in front of me. "But it's okay," he said. "You are safe. Because we have the man who was doing it to you. You just identified him."

Uncle Rudi nodded to the thin man who walked over to the ragged form moaning on the floor. He grabbed the man by the hair, jerking his head back.

It was the face from the seventh cell.

Which was when Uncle Rudi's hand grabbed my arm steadying me.

Because when the head was yanked back, I was looking into the exact same face of my nightmares—or was it more than nightmares? Those sharp features with a strange gap between his two upper front teeth. The same gap that in my nightmares grew closer to my face as I tried to fight him *off*—-

The man slithering on the prison floor, this man with the strange gap between his two upper front teeth was crying, sniveling, pleading. "*Please!* I didn't intend to do it. I didn't want to."

"You didn't want to what?" Uncle Rudi said soothingly

"Please," the man on the floor sobbed.

Uncle Rudi repeated the question, speaking so softly I could barely hear him. The man on the floor just sobbed.

"Answer the question," Uncle Rudi said and when the only response was "*Please, please,*" he nodded again to the thin man who stepped forward holding a whip that looked like a longer version of a leather riding crop. Instinctively I called out as Uncle Rudi patted my arm and the thin man slashed twice at the writhing heap of rags on the floor.

In the explosions of sobbing, words joined together. "I didn't want to."

"Didn't want to what?"

"Rape her.… *Please, please, please!*"

"Then why did you?"

"I had to."

"*Had to?*""

"Hanussen told me to!" He was almost screeching now.

"Do you always rape a woman just because someone *tells* you to?"

The sputtering bloody words came in gasps and cries. "No, no no!"

"Then why did you?"

"Because of Hanussen!"

Another nod. Another whip slash *Ssssssslaak* and the shrieks that came after. I stood up. I couldn't stand any of it: Not the beating, not the man himself, nor what Uncle Rudi was doing. "Stop it," I yelled.

No one paid any attention to me.

"Hanussen ordered me! I had no choice."

"Of course you did."

"No! You don't understand!" *Ssssssslaak.* The whip slashed again. *Please, please, please.*

"Tell me, did she say *please* that night at Hanussen's?" *Ssssssslaak* "Did she?"

"Yes, yes."

"And look what happened to her when she said *please.*"

"Sorry. *Sorry!*"

"Say please to her. Go on. Say please. And let's see what happens."

"No!" I yelled again, this time standing up and said, "Don't do this. I don't want this."

"Oh *please, please!*"

A nod from uncle Rudi to the thin man.

Ssssssslaak. Screams, Cries.

"Look at her when you say it," said Uncle Rudi who put his hand out in front of me, his smooth, calm voice riding the surface of the pain and fear, blossoming into strange colours in all the whiteness of that sculptor's studio.

But all I could see were iridescent lines gleaming in the cold light coming through the tiny windows. Such pretty lines they were, those scars across the left side of Uncle Rudi's beautiful face. Shiny, like bars across my mind because I saw but I did not see; I heard but I did not hear. The groveling, the shrieks and all the rest of it were so distant that they never intruded on the one thought that hung before my eyes:

What if I am pregnant? And this is the father of my child?

He was on the floor sobbing. "I was ordered to go inside you. You understand."

Understand? I suddenly had the most overpowering urge to grab the whip and flay this man senseless. My mind caught fire. I had to leave. In the quickest way possible. I could not stand being there, staring down at this groveling wretch in front of me, hearing him talk of what he had done to me, what I wanted to wipe from my memory. I jumped up and bolted toward the staircase.

"Wait," Uncle Rudi called out after me. "I told him that unless you decide otherwise, he is doomed. He will be shot unless you save him. You now have more power over him than he had over you."

"Don't do this to me." I yelled racing up the stairs.

And while I was running something else happened—so quickly that I thought it could not possibly be real. But it was. A man threw himself over a railing several floors above me and hurtled to his death on the cold marble below.

I was almost at the entrance of the building when one of the Gestapo stopped me.

Minutes later in his big office, Uncle Rudi was very different than he has been downstairs. He seemed to have shrunk within himself. The silky coolness had vanished and his hand shook when he lit a cigarette. "I can almost hear what you're thinking," he said.

I sat by the window as empty as I have ever been. The sun came through and warmed me in ways I had not known I needed.

"I feel filthy."

"Yes." He took several jagged puffs of the cigarette. "I understand."

"You were my hero when I was a little girl. You were opposite of father. And I loved you for it. But now—"

"Now?"

"I'm trying to fit that memory together with... this," I said waving my hand around the Gestapo headquarters I was in. "Ten minutes ago, leaving that terrible basement, while I was coming up the big, curved staircase to this floor, before your men caught up to me, I heard yelling from above. I looked up to see an SS man trying to stop a ragged prisoner from clawing his way over the banister on the top floor. But the prisoner was too determined. He kept screaming "*No more!*" and then he threw himself over the banister into the stairwell, hurtling five floors to his doom on the marble floor at the bottom. What would he have meant by "No more"?

Uncle Rudi looked at me, with an unblinking stare. "I have no control over the SS."

"What would that doomed man have meant?"

"Probably no more torture."

"That man was only a meter away from me as he plummeted. Maybe it was my imagination but I felt as if our eyes met for that fragment of an instant as he was flashing past me to his death. And then? Have you ever heard a body hitting a hard surface from a great height? Think of a hundred sticks being broken all at once in one chilling *crack*. Sticks inside a sack filled with soup slamming into rock. And then what would you expect? Silence?"

Uncle Rudi just stared at me with eyes grown old and said nothing.

"No. What came next was laughter. I looked up to where the SS men were both looking down at the bloody mess and laughing.

Uncle Rudi looked at me. Not once did he blink. Not once did he move.

And then he slammed his hand down on the desk. His eyes almost shone with fury. "You have always had the luxury of not knowing what was really happening. I have not had that luxury. I have had nothing but communist attacks on our entire way of life. And *that* is where I will always side with the greater good."

"And you're telling me *this* is the greater good?"

"If I lose out to Himmler, if he takes over the Gestapo, a lot worse will happen."

"You? Lose out?"

"Everything is changing. The most skilled of the killers—people like Himmler and Heydrich and others. They want me gone."

"Why do they want you gone?"

"They have told Hitler that I am not hard enough on the Jews."

That compelling face with its scars turned away toward the pale light of the window. "For me the communists were easy. I loathed them. You need to be able to do terrible things sometimes. But now what they are doing to the Jews…even the women and the children. I just cannot.…"

He sank back in his chair, slowly swiveling as if he was trying to force words out of himself. "You need to realize something."

"What?"

"I've told you. I may not always be here to protect you.

"The Gestapo? *Protecting* someone?" He ignored the irony.

"You need to understand," he said. "My father—your grandfather, led an unusual life in many ways. His wife, the woman who you knew as grandmother had to put up with a lot from him."

"'The woman *who I knew* as grandmother'?"

"Someone else is your real grandmother."

"Birgit."

It caused him to turn quickly back toward me. "What do you know about her?"

"Mother. Before she died. She told me."

"Birgit was a Jew. So if this is ever discovered, your father, the newfound Nazi, will be declared half Jewish and sent to a concentration camp. And you and Karin, who are one quarter Jewish will follow. You'd all be sent east."

Sent east. To the concentration camps.

"Himmler, Goebbels, Heydrich—they can't wait to have their people start going through the birth records, the official documents, looking for anyone with Jewish blood. Who will then be exterminated.

He held up an ornate piece of paper in front of me so I could read it. "This is your father's baptism certificate. I took it out of the files. Where all such files are kept. Look carefully where it says *MOTHER*. Beside it is a name written by hand."

The handwritten name was *Birgit Cohnsberg (Jüdisch)*

"Here." He handed me the baptism certificate. "This is the only copy. I recommend you destroy it."

"Where did this come from?"

"The official records are up in Stettin."

I didn't understand. Stettin was several hours drive from Berlin, up near Poland.

"I went there last week to get the documents that could condemn you. All of you. I had a perfect excuse to be there. The thugs in the SA there are out of control. They are a bunch of extortionists imprisoning whoever they want in a prison camp that they set up in an old shipyard. As Gestapo head, I went there to see what those idiots are doing and try to rein them in. And since I happened to be up there no one would think it unusual for someone in my position to drop in on the city hall. And take a tour of where they kept the records."

"And what about you? Was Birgit your mother too?"

He shook his head. "My father, your grandfather, was a man of great appetites."

I tried to remember grandfather as being attractive to women. It was a picture that just never came into focus.

"It's not over," he said. " There is one more document sitting up there in Stettin like a time bomb. Your father's birth certificate," he said. "It will condemn you all."

"Why couldn't you get it too?"

"Last month all the birth certificates in Stettin were packed into boxes and transported to a local warehouse waiting for their new records building to be finished.

"And when it is, those boxes will be reopened, and you will be hunted down like the rest of the Jews."

25

THAT NIGHT THE ARGENTINEAN RECEPTION was everything we heard it would be. A raucous melding of two regimes that understood each other perfectly. With all the canapés, champagne and murky red wine amid the SS leather and medals and jackboots. The trumpets sounded when necessary and Goebbels, Göring, and Himmler all made an appearance.

I did my best but it was not good enough.

I took notes on who was wearing Chanel and who was in Schiaparelli. I noted the emphasis on beef for the canapés and the tango-themed music played by the accordion-laced orchestra. And I duly noted the collective elegance of all those in attendance, the beautifully dressed, the stylish and above all, the powerful. The entire evening was a tribute to elegantly disguised brutality.

I sat there while others danced, ate, drank and made banal speeches. And what was I doing when I should have been creating the raw details of the column that would appear in tomorrow's *Auntie Voss*?

Until I got up and left, I had been doodling like a child on what had been a blank piece of paper.

I got back to the newspaper later than usual and it took me a while to realize that Herr Langen was still in his office. When I knocked there was no answer. I cautiously opened the door. The office was almost back to being the same as it was before all this started. There was only a single desk, not the two that had been crammed in there. The lone desk was still immaculate, not at all like when it had been Herr Langen's, a static jumble of papers and files and paper wrappers.

A gleaming brass nameplate had been screwed onto the front of the desk: *Herr G. S. Brecht.*

A little crackling sound came from behind the immaculate desk. Herr Langen was sitting on the floor. *Herr Langen? On the floor?* No one I knew possessed more innate force and dignity, the kind that would never be found on an office floor.

Herr Langen spoke quietly without looking up. "What is it you want?" He was peering intently at something he was holding in his hand.

"You. I came to see you."

"No. You came to see the editor of *Vossiche Zeitung*. Unfortunately Herr Brecht is not here."

"But you are."

"Have you not heard?"

"Heard what?"

"Goebbels' latest?"

I said nothing. He took a moment away from a piece of glass he was studying to look at me. "The Editors' Law as it is called. We are gone—all of us. No Jews are allowed to write for or edit newspapers."

"Then what will you do?"

"I know only that I have been ordered to pack up and leave."

I put the pages I had brought on the empty desk and sank to the floor not far from him. "What are you doing?"

"My wife, my dear wife, makes ornaments, hand painted scenes on little glass squares. They are scenes of our life. They are all over our house, moments of our life together, seventeen years of painted scenes on those little squares of glass." He was piecing together fragments of glass he took from an envelope, holding each one up to the light. "She sent me this one from Paris. She's safe there now you know."

"It's broken. What happened to it?"

"It was opened. They smashed it and then taped the envelope shut again before it was delivered to me. So it fell out in pieces onto the floor when I opened it."

He squinted as he looked through the shards of glass he was holding up to the light. "We're still only in the beginning stages of all this. It will get worse. You're aware of that. Aren't you?"

I nodded. "What are you going to do?"

"I'll be all right." He pieced together several fragments, frowned and searched through the envelope He found a larger piece of glass and laid it among other shards on the floor. "Aha. I think it's of the Eiffel Tower. That's her. Standing there alone."

I had never seen him smile the way he was then.

The next day when it happened, I got to the newspaper too late to do anything.

It was some time that morning when Herr Langen and three other editors were leaving the House of Ullstein for the last time. Each was carrying his personal possessions in cloth bags and small boxes. Outside, a large truck was parked on the other side of the street.

Several black-uniformed SS men had gotten down from the benches in the back of the truck and walked toward the four editors as a crowd gathered, knowing there would be a show of some kind. One of the SS men had stood in front of them and handed a pair of scissors to Herr Langen.

"Cut off the other Jew's beard," the SS man said.

When Herr Langen stood there saying nothing, the SS officer smashed a wooden club into the boxes Herr Langen was holding. Pieces of glass crackled onto the pavement covered by pages with handwriting on them. The SS man picked up several of the pages. "What is this?"

"A book," said Herr Langen.

"It doesn't look like a book."

"It is not finished. I am writing it."

The SS man looked around and pointed to something on the street. "Tell me what that is."

"What a dog has left."

"You mean dog shit," said the SS man.

He walked over and dropped the pages onto the steaming pile and then stepping on top of them "Shit to shit." A few people in the gathering crowd laughed and cheered.

Herr Langen stood perfectly still. But his eyes did not.

When I arrived, he and the other three editors were being marched through the center of the street with large cardboard placards hanging in front of them, fastened by ropes looped around their necks. Each placard had handwritten scrawls across it. The one on the editor with the beard read: *I Have Been Insulting the Reich.* Another read *Jew Editor.* A third one read *I spread filth about the Reich.*

But Herr Langen? Scrawled on the cardboard hanging from string around his neck was the most basic affront to the civilization he cherished—a spelling mistake:

I am a lier.

The crowd around him was jeering and laughing now as he and the other three were marched toward the truck. For a fleeting moment I thought he saw me and then quickly looked away.

I could barely watch: Nothing was possible. If any of those men had made the slightest protest, a savage beating or painful death or both would have come instantly. So all that was left, was fury and humiliation, each at war with the other draining pride from Herr Langen's face.

But others? Like me, just standing there? Were we to remain silent?

I was not far from the truck, weaving through the onlookers until I was close enough to the SS officer to do the most futile thing I could have done:

"You can't do this!" I blurted out.

Even before the SS man could turn to see who had dared challenge him I saw Herr Langen flash a fierce look at me. I knew instantly that I had done something bad and in that moment came the sickening crunch of the wooden club landing across Herr Langen's arm. He cried out and stumbled.

"Can't do what?" said the SS man turning to the crowd who fell silent.

26

I WAS DETERMINED TO FIND him.

Sachsenhausen was the new concentration camp just outside Berlin. The journey there took me through forests that encircled the northern edges of the city. It was an eerie drive into a moment perfectly balanced between past and future. Somewhere around the outskirts of Birkenwerder the roads became bad and I drove past more horse drawn carts than cars, and crudely dressed farmers worked in the nearby fields. I passed two horses hitched to a slow-moving plow with a woman steering it from behind. It was as if I was driving through what I remembered from my childhood.

Then the present intervened. And with it, the future: Black shapes appeared on the horizon, low and moving quickly.

There were about a dozen of them led by big open cars with tightly spaced headlights the size of shields. The closer they got, the more those headlights became like eyes. Behind the lead vehicles were trucks carrying uniformed Nazi troops on wooden-backed rails and seats. All of them wore black and they were coming from Oranienburg, the town I was headed for, where the SS was building the Sachsenhausen concentration camp.

In Oranienburg a strange energy seeped through what had once been a sleepy town. The recent arrival of the SS had been overlaid on a millennium of slowness. Quaint market scenes were suddenly sliced through by SS vehicles and quiet streets could clatter with SS jackboots. Oranienburg was a place at war with its own nature. There was something menacing in even the most innocent of moments.

I parked on a street that I knew led to the new concentration camp. I waited; and late in the afternoon I saw in the rear-view mirror what I was looking for. I got out of the car carrying shopping bags as if I was going to the local butcher or baker.

It was a line of ragged men wearing crude coats, each with a number written on the left side over the chest, They all wore what looked like badly made berets and were struggling with the trunk of a freshly cut tree that they were carrying on their shoulders. It looked to be as long as three cars and was held aloft by about twenty struggling prisoners as SS guards swung rifle butts into those who were stumbling.

The line got closer like some massive centipede, grotesque in its convulsive lurching. At the front were two large men grappling to hold onto the end of the trunk. Behind them were the others, all shapes, all sizes, laboring to hold the tree trunk on their shoulders. Fear filled their eyes whenever an SS guard drew near.

And in the middle was Herr Langen, one arm bandaged, stumbling and bowed under the weight of the tree.

I gave thanks that he never saw me.

At Prinz Albrechtstrasse 8 it was quiet, not like before. I heard no screams this time, only the whispered conversation of ordinary looking men on their way to do what I imagined were unspeakable things. Occasionally the sound of jackboots on marble floors added a fierce staccato from a distance and then faded.

I waited, seated on the bench between the bronze busts of Hitler and Göring, under the high vaulted ceiling and in front of massive curved window frames.

Several times a low-ranking Gestapo man came out asking each time what exactly it was I wanted. I could see he was not used to people coming in by their own choice. He seemed too anxious and looked altogether too pink to be a Gestapo officer, like a white mouse with little glasses. But behind that tight little voice there was a manic quality that you just knew would take him far in his chosen profession.

Each time I told him who I wanted to see he looked at me as if I was mad. "You realize that the Head of the Gestapo is a busy man. He wants you to know that."

"Please inform the Head of the Gestapo that his visitor is busy too."

The white mouse peered at me through watery eyes. Just then a terrible, lacerating scream echoed from somewhere above. The white mouse looked upwards for a moment. "That is not how things should be done. Doors should be closed."

When he returned about an hour later, all he said was "Come."

Uncle Rudi was a different man. He sat behind his desk, as calm and still as I had ever seen him. "You obviously forgot," he said. "The last time you were here you said you felt filthy just being here."

"I need something."

"Well of course you do." He lit a cigarette and tried to keep me from seeing that his hand was shaking. "What?"

I blurted out what had happened to Herr Langen.

"So?"

"Can you help?"

He sat forward, leaning out of the afternoon light. He fixed me with as piercing stare as I had ever seen from him. "You want me to help with some run-of-the-mill Jew when I have to cope with the great Tingel-Tangel emergency?"

Did I hear correctly? "What?"

"Tingel-Tangel," he repeated. "That is my life now."

"I don't understand."

"Neither do I." He picked up documents on his desk one at a time. "But the Berlin Police, the Ministry of Public Enlightenment and Propaganda, the Office of Racial Policy and the Prussian Minister-President are all having a fit." He threw up his hands. "Over Tingel-Tangel!"

"What is...?"

"Laughter!" he said. "The problem is laughter."

He swiveled in his big chair so that he had his back to me. "Those papers on my desk are memos from the biggest Nazis you can imagine. Outraged, hysterical almost. Over Tingel-Tangel—a nightclub. A cabaret. With singing and dancing and comedy acts created by Jews and lesbians— all of them laughing and making jokes about Nazis—can you imagine? "

"And you?"

"Me? No. To tell you the truth, I rather enjoyed their show. Brilliantly subversive." I thought he smiled ever so slightly. "The leader of Tingel-Tangel, is a man named Finck. He will be brought in here soon.

"For making people laugh? Arrested?"

"It is now called 'Protective Custody' Much more humanitarian sounding don't you think?"

"Are you going to torture Finck?"

Instantly he became irritated in an almost apologetic way. "Look, I am doing what I can. I am trying. I will find a way to release him. And because of that—as I told you, I will not be here long." The scars on his face sagged as he sat back and looked up into something only he could see.

"So then—this Jew you were talking about? Langen was it?"

A week later I was back at Prinz Albrechtstrasse 8. The white mouse peered at me through his little glasses and I could have sworn I saw something different in those watery eyes. Almost like smugness. He motioned for me to follow him but about half way to Uncle Rudi's office he made a sudden left turn and walked down a different, dimly lit corridor. When I hesitated he ordered, "Come." It was a dingy and narrow corridor. Only a few of the doors to the shabby small offices were open and none were occupied. We passed two SS guards and kept going.

Finally, at the end of the corridor the white mouse motioned to an open door. "Here," he said with a pleased look, and then turned and walked back through the darkened corridor, his footsteps echoing on the marble floor. I walked toward the door and saw Uncle Rudi sitting behind a tiny desk in an office with bare walls, a small window and a concrete floor. It was as small and as drab as a cell. He was reading a book.

"My my. Quite an event. The first visitor to my new office." He did not look up as I entered and kept skimming through pages in the book.

"What are you doing here? In a place like this?"

It was as if he had not heard me. "I know it's here somewhere," he said. "It's one of these. I'm sure." He flipped through more pages and then stopped and looked up for the first time. "The English really do have the best poets. Even the old saber-rattlers. Aha! Listen:

If you can meet with Triumph and Disaster.
And treat those two imposters both the same."

"Why are you here? In this tiny office. If you can even call it an office."

"Our poets cannot match the English."

"Tell me what's happening."

It was as if he got smaller and quieter. "Ah yes. What's happening?" he murmured. "That is the question."

"Are you all right?"

"No."

"Why?"

"Himmler. He staged his little coup. I have been…how to put it? Deposed? It sounds so much better than 'fired'. Or 'purged'"

"What happens now?"

"Listen to me—last week you came to me just in time. I got this Herr Langen of yours out of Sachsenhausen," he said and then to my uncertain look. "I had him brought here and then I issued orders for him to be set free. He was let out through the back gate less than two hours ago.

"Thank you."

He looked away as if he had not heard me.

"What will happen to you now?"

He tried to smile. "I thought it would be different. I really did."

FIVE

27

I WAS FIRED FROM *VOSSICHE Zeitung.*

It was on the same day that the House of Ullstein collapsed with its owners fleeing the country for their lives, and the Nazis taking over their vast publishing empire.

I had been called into Brecht's office. I had to sit there while he folded and unfolded his pudgy hands on his gleaming, empty desk as he told me how much he *truly* regretted that I had *never learned* to support the Reich in the way that *so many other journalists* had done, and that *how unfortunate* it was that Minister Goebbels had noticed my lack of support for—-

In mid-sentence I thanked him, got up and walked toward the door stopping when he called out to me. When I turned around, he looked genuinely flustered. "Be very careful Frau Bella," he said.

"You're firing me but you want me to be careful?"

"Please. It is not me. It is their new Treachery Law."

"Is this a joke?"

"I wish it was. But please understand that it's not me doing this." He was almost squirming behind his gleaming desk. "They have sections in this law for what they call 'malignant' remarks about the Reich.

"And I am malignant?"

"Not you. it's what you write. They say you have been weaving sarcasm into your columns. And you use remarks that can be taken two ways. That column last week where you wrote that the reception at the Foreign Ministry was as choreographed as a Hollywood musical; they view it as being...."

I finished the sentence that he could not. "Malignant?"

"Yes. Precisely. You need to leave as soon as possible."

"Am I going to be chased out of here with a stick?"

"I overheard them talking—the Gestapo, when they came here. Your name has gone on a list. They will be looking for you. But fortunately...." He did not finish what he was saying.

"*Fortunately*? What is fortunate about any of this?"

"Ah yes," he said, his hands pressing together so his fingers formed a tiny steeple. "It may seem strange but you are fortunate. For now at least. You see it will take them weeks to get to people of your level. First they have to round up people at Herr Langen's level."

I got to the door of his office and was about to leave when I was glad to remember what I'd wanted to say to him for a long time. "You know how you keep saying 'It's not me doing this'?"

He nodded as if he expected good news.

"Well, it is you. So stop hiding behind others." I gave what I hoped was a smile and shut the door.

I hurried into the newsroom and took one last look. I had been trained well there, learning how gossip can be used as a weapon in the way that acid can drip through whatever seems indestructible. Or once in a while, it can be lethal in the sense that a stiletto can stop a heart.

I had no choice really. I had to find how to use it in ways I could never have imagined before.

Gossip had become my weapon.

They *were* looking for me.

Goebbels or someone in his Ministry ordered that every newspaper column I had written in the last year was to be re-read, after which about a dozen of them were declared to be *malignant* or *inflammatory,* both now illegal under this new Treachery Act.

And so my name automatically went on the list along with thousands of political, religious and academic names who had been declared subversive and were to be hunted down and shipped off to concentration camps.

But when the Gestapo—it was now Himmler's Gestapo not Uncle Rudi's, went looking for me they descended on an apartment in Charlottenburg I had rented but never moved into. The neighbours there—so I heard later, told them I had last been seen leaving for Westphalia. To those neighbours I have probably owed what small freedoms I have had, because once the Gestapo heard I had moved far away they would have closed my case in Berlin and moved on to other matters.

And so began my life underground.

A strange, sometimes terrifying, occasionally fulfilling life as a non-person. And always haunted by the feeling of being just a few steps ahead of the Gestapo.

Another thing that saved me was that I was one of those women who could be physically transformed by makeup—or the lack of it. So often, the mirror at dawn had shown a different person than the one I had been at those glittering evening receptions the evening before.

And so the old photos of me used by the Gestapo showed a woman encased and lacquered into place by the powders, the rouges, the mascaras, the lotions and potions and coverings and dyes and things that made me thinner, taller, blonder and sometimes even sculpted. The me who took refuge at *Mutters* looked very different from what had been bolted together on those glittering, empty nights. Now I could have walked past any Gestapo agent who was holding an old society-page photo of me.

But what really saved me was being at *Mutter's*.

I had realized how perfect we were for each other. She gave me sanctuary, anonymity and protection. And without knowing it, I gave her what she most needed—someone who would listen to her.

She loved subversion, perversion and any other *versions* that could be affixed to her makeshift clan.

I had gotten used to the mildly chaotic melodramas of *Mutter's* little domain that, for all its shabbiness, had a warmth that drew me in. Drew *us* in. Even Karin, who was becoming a minor celebrity for her roles in the movies, and could live anywhere she wanted, would shed her fine clothes in order to return anonymously to *Mutter's* several nights a week. All of us had come to feel like part of a glued together little family with its feuds, its tiny joys and its shared pain. And with complicated, irritating and yet oddly caring moments that were a reflection of *Mutter herself*.

And all of our little world was women.

Except for one man.

On the same day that I was fired from *Vossiche Zeitung*, I hurried to Herr Langen's house. He stood at the door of his house after I knocked loudly, caught between vague appreciation for what I had done for him and his normal irritation at having his privacy disturbed. He did not want me inside, but I simply pushed past him into his house, almost pulling him in behind me, closing the door and then locking it.

Years of tiptoeing around the fearsome editor, entering his sanctum with a timid knock and waiting for him to speak—it all vanished beneath my onrushing set of instructions. I told him—no, *ordered*, him: keep the door locked. Stay away from the windows. No lights—and on and on until he held up his hand and said, "No."

"You need to leave here quickly."

"And go where?" he said from a big overstuffed armchair in a room filled with books. "I appreciate what you have done. Now please leave."

"I'm going to ask you what you once asked me: 'Have you been living in a cave?'"

"You know perfectly well where I have been living. "

"You're putting others at risk." I blurted out.

"Who exactly am I putting at risk?"

"Right now? Me."

"Well then the solution is simple," he said. "Leave."

As he spoke the sound of a car door slamming could be heard outside. Then a second car door slammed. Heavy footsteps sounded on the steps. Then loud knocking on the door.

In terrible times there is a kind of language, almost a semiotics, attached to the knocking on a door. The level, the intensity and the cadence of the knocking convey a power relationship between the knocker and the knockee:

There are soft uncertain knocks of the *didn't mean to disturb you* kind.

There are solitary knocks of the *not sure I'm in the right place* variety.

There is the woodpecker rapping of the *I'm in a real hurry* type.

And then there are the pounding *Open the goddamn door* knocks.

The last one is the kind that come from either a spurned lover or the Gestapo. It should never result in the door being opened. *Ever*. Bad things happen when it is.

In the stillness of that darkened room Herr Langen and I held our breath as the door-battering knocking continued. It happened once, twice and then two more times. Each knock was bristling with anger, entitlement and the full force of the Reich. We were as still as we could be, our silence a counterpoint to the pounding on the door. A voice yelled "*Langen! Open!*"

Silence.

More knocking. Another yell. More silence. Muttering. And then the sound of the same heavy footsteps retreating, two more car door slams followed by an engine starting and fading into the distance.

Silence.

And then Herr Langen whispered, "Thank you." He motioned to me to follow him into another room where slivers of light intruded through spaces between the heavy curtains. Bookcases lined the walls and on some of the shelves were more of those little glass squares with hand-painted scenes. "I don't want to leave these behind." he said. "My wife made them."

"Find something to wrap them in," I said, barely looking at them. "And a bag to carry them." He looked as if he did not understand. And for someone so decisive, he seemed for a moment, strangely helpless.

"Just do as I say."

He nodded.

Herr Langen had reluctantly become part of *Mutter's* domain, vowing to stay for only a day or two.

Three days after arriving at *Mutter's*, Herr Langen unpacked the little glass squares that his wife had made. Announcing again, that this was only temporary, he carefully arranged them on a shelf in the small room he was occupying at the end of the hall. "Of course," I said.

But I had already known before then that he would stay.

I knew from the second night when he made his tea in the kitchen while *Mutter* was sitting in front of the stove matching his surliness. In some ways they were mirrors of one another. Somehow they were arguing about Nietzsche who *Mutter* knew of only because one of her former prostitutes had a philosophy professor as a longtime client who regularly tried to educate her in Nietzsche's master-slave theories.

"Nietzsche is the philosophical basis for all these jackbooted Nazi thugs," said Herr Langen.

"Well then I have good news for you and all the other woolly-headed thinker-types."

"*Really*?" said Herr Langen the way he used to say the word to anxious young reporters telling him something he thought was idiotic. He would wield that simple two-syllable word like a knife. Or maybe like a scimitar because it curled around as it was inflicting the wound that it took them a while to find.

But *Mutter* was immune to nuance. "Look, this professor was stupid in the way that only a thinker can be stupid," she growled blowing out a projectile of phlegm in an elegant arc that died like all the others as a sizzle on the stove. Herr Langen jumped back, appalled and was about to say something when she waved him aside, talking over the first sound he uttered; "This weirdo tried to convince my whore that what they were doing was part of this Nietzsche's master-slave theories. That slaves were the weak and the pathetic who needed to be ruled by their warrior class masters, the good and the strong."

"Pure Nietzsche," said Herr Langen, not meaning it.

"Yes but here's where my girls are better philosophers," said *Mutter*.

"Really?" said Herr Langen again, this time without the embedded sarcasm.

"My whore was no dunce. She read up on all that Nietzsche stuff and the next time this professor shows up she was ready with the whips, the chains, the handcuffs and all the rest. I sat here—right here! listening to him yodeling in ecstasy and pain as she sat on his back and made him ride her around the room as her slave."

"You know Nietzsche never had a sexual relationship with a woman?"

"Well there you go! Make me Head of Philosophy and give me all your male virgins and your jackbooted thugs and I'll have my girls teach them philosophy."

"And what do you do with the *Übermensch*?" Herr Langen said into *Mutter's* blank stare. "Nietzsche's superior man?" he explained.

"Aaach! Superior my fat ass. Do you have any idea how many big shots my girls have turned into happy groveling pussy worshippers?"

"Really?"

"You keep saying that. Let me tell you something: I've seen a world-class blowjob turn a capitalist into a raving socialist. I've seen mind-frying fucks turn atheists into altar boys. My girls could wipe out the entire philosophy department of any university you can name."

"May I sit down?" asked Herr Langen politely.

"Of course you may," said *Mutter* looking quite pleased.

At *Mutter's* we settled into what was the last thing I wanted: a routine.

But there was no choice. It wasn't as if Herr Langen and I could just go out and get another job or even walk casually on the streets. Any expedition into the outside world had its perils. Arousing suspicion could be done by even a wrong look or word. Berlin was filled with police forces now, all of them competing for raw material, namely Jews, subversives, comedians and other assorted forms of humanity the Reich deemed undesirable.

And also what was equally dangerous: the network of informers that had burrowed into seams of ordinary life in Berlin.

This was part of *Mutter's* genius: she understood where the threats might come from, where the treachery of the informers might find weak spots. She moved the whores from Swabia and Cologne into a separate wing on the floor below us to prevent their clients from seeing anything that might require an explanation. Then she spent hours spinning an invisible web of intuition around the newest boarder, Ilona the woman whose husband had been killed by the police. Over the course of an evening *Mutter* talked to her, charmed her, and drained every secret out of her. Ilona was dark haired, intrinsically tragic and flying against the gale force of nature in her attempts to be pretty.

"A complete liar," was *Mutter's* verdict. "A sad one, not a dangerous one. But sad liars have a weakness that can attract bad people. We can't have her among us"

And before the night was over, Ilona found herself moved to the other wing, into a basement room one floor below the whore from Cologne.

I began the life of a long-term boarder, paying *Mutter* my monthly rent out of what I had hidden away in the good years. Herr Langen had enough gold coins to pay several years' worth of *Mutter's* minimal rent. Money was not a problem. What did become a problem was a restlessness and a feeling that something needed to change.

It did. What changed everything was just an innocent, offhand remark from Herr Langen.

"I don't believe it" Herr Langen said one day, He was reading what was left of the Berlin newspapers and muttering to himself as he turned the pages. "I actually miss the gossip column."

"Right there, that is your problem," said *Mutter* stirring her pot of stew on the stove. "Gossip is too important to be left to a newspaper."

"I beg your pardon. A newspaper has a serious duty to report important news. Gossip is basically entertainment."

"Welllll!" said *Mutter* stretching out the word as if was elastic. "I beg *your* pardon. You are being a typical thinking type."

"I take that as a compliment."

"It's not."

"I'm asking you not to spit on the stove in my presence."

"Gossip should not be left to amateurs. No offense but that's what you are when it comes to something as central to our society as gossip."

"*Really*," snapped Herr Langen the way he used to say it. "And what exactly is your solution?"

"*Mundfunk*," said *Mutter* as if she expected us to know what she was talking about

And then she arced another gob of something clammy onto the stove in front of Herr Langen.

28

WE HAVE TO FACE THE awful truth: Goebbels is a kind of genius.

But there is another truth. A better one: *Mutter,* in her own way, is just as much of a genius.

Each of them figured out what almost no one else had been close to understanding. What Goebbels figured out was that without the new technology there would be no Nazi party. This new technology was what we know now as radio.

He understood that radio is power. No other regime has ever understood the power of technology like the Nazis. While other political factions looked down on radio as a glorified toy that played music Goebbels saw only its raw power.

But when the Nazis took over, he discovered that not one in a hundred homes could afford a radio. So one of the first things he did was go to the radio manufacturers and order them to churn out millions of the things for a fraction of the previous price. The *Volksempfänger*—the people's radio. Cheap. Workable. Simple. And powerful.

Because through those millions of *Volksempfänger,* he now bombards the Nazi messages into the homes of the nation. Because of him, no people on earth are so connected to this new technology as we are.

He understood that radio is what will mold the public will. Radio is the new technology, the weapon for whoever controls it. With it, Goebbels has found the way to create news—the exact kind of news he wants while suffocating whatever news he does not approve of.

And Goebbels is the sound track to it all. You can't *not* hear him. He is all over the airwaves. And having seen him in person I cannot reconcile the image of that twisted and fiercely bug-eyed, angry, little man with the booming, hypnotic voice I hear everywhere.

But *Mutter* is a match for Goebbels. Sitting in front of the old stove, chopping or peeling dubious ingredients for her stew, she explained there is 'broadcast' and then there is 'mouthcast'

Or *mundfunk.*

Broadcast is what the Nazis do on the radio. Goebbels made sure that the news beamed out from Berlin's Broadcast House—*Haus des Rundfunks,* was exactly what the Nazis wanted us to hear.

But according to *Mutter,* in the ghettoes and working-class areas of the city, mouthcasting—*mundfunk,* provides the real news. Usually it came wrapped in gossip and was passed by word of mouth from one person to another.

Gossip, she said, looking at me through the haze of the cigarette smoke as ashes burn tiny holes in her straining housecoat.

On any given day a well-crafted piece of gossip could be whispered at dawn in Neukölln and then shoot through the city, ending up in Spandau or Zehlendorf before sundown. Some of it might be inaccurate or exaggerated but much of it had more truth than the Nazi propaganda that came over the airwaves.

It had become the way news spread through the poorer areas of Berlin where a lot of people didn't believe what the Nazis were telling them in the newspapers and radio. The only way they could find out what was really happening was *mundfunk.*

The entire city was ripe for *mundfunk.*

Mutter stopped her lecture and looked at me again. "Well?" she said.

"*Mundfunk,*" I said. "There will be a new gossip column."

"Oh really? And what are you planning on putting in it? Or are you just going to make up gossip?" Herr Langen said.

"Of course not. We have been given a gift."

Even *Mutter* looked dubious "Did I miss this gift?"

"Karin," I said.

"*That's* what you call a gift?"

" Movies and Nazi leaders all in one film studio? What could possibly generate more gossip?"

For a moment that stopped them. Both *Mutter* and Herr Langen sat there thinking.

My idea was simple: Karin was at the center of all gossip in the country: the UFA film studios at Babelsberg. And for us it could be like a checkmate move—Goebbels genius being checkmated by *Mutter's*. Because with the movie business being run by Goebbels, this unfaithful Nazi husband who had the power of life and death as well as final decisions on casting young actresses, where on the entire planet was there a more spectacular cesspool of gossip?

I wanted to find all the covered-up scandals about Goebbels that were being whispered around the UFA movie studios, relate them to what was going on in the streets and then somehow find a way to send them on their way across Berlin through *mundfunk*.

"Ah," said Herr Langen. He always said *Ah* when he was still thinking about something. But you could tell he liked the idea. "Chaos might spout from little seeds of scandal."

What I did not realize was that *Mutter* had to clear everything she did through the ultimate authority. The Bible.

The next day she looked strangely uncertain. She was shaking her head and when I asked her what was wrong all she could say was, "Explain this to me again."

And when I did explain it again she looked strangely uneasy. "I don't know, I just don't know. What is Karin doing except finding ways to keep that sex-crazed Goebbels from getting into her knickers?"

The next day she asked me to explain it a third time. And even when Herr Langen gave his first tentative nod to what I suggested, she remained silent. It was not like *Mutter* to remain silent about anything.

That night after everyone was asleep when I heard soft humming coming from the kitchen. I tiptoed down the hallway until I saw her, leaning back in her large chair, a cigarette in one hand, a bottle in the other, her reading glasses pulled low on her nose and a Bible in her lap.

She looked up at me through her own personal fog and smiled. "It's okay," she said drinking happily from the bottle. "It's all okay."

"What is?"

"This gossip business of yours."

"The Bible? You're basing our gossip project on the Bible? This was your idea."

"Not everything has to make sense you know."

"Obviously."

A tiny ball of cigarette ash exploded on contact with her dirty house-coat, leaving a smear as she brushed it away. "I get ideas for things. But then I have to make sure I'm not breaking His rules." Then she held up the Bible. "See?"

"No."

"Exodus," she said, opening the Bible to a bookmarked page. "Exodus 20. The Ten Commandments chapter," she said and then read, "'*Thou shalt not bear false witness against thy neighbour.*' *That* was my problem with this gossip business."

"Even though you suggested it?

"*Aach.* There you go again. Making sense." She looked up into my amazement and took another drink. Then she went back to the Bible. "I wasn't sure I could be part of this gossip business of yours," she said. "Not with Exodus 20."

"Can I have a drink?" I said sitting down opposite her.

"But I remembered something," *Mutter* was flipping through many pages at once and then stopping. "Proverbs 16. Listen here: '*A whisperer separates best friends.*' So I read that and thought Ha! Our whispers, our *mundfunk,* could separate Goebbels from Hitler. Himmler from Göring. And all those other evil bastards. So it's obvious. Isn't it?"

"Of course," I said when it was not at all obvious.

"The Bible is instructing us to use gossip to drive these terrible men apart. So *mundfunk* is not only allowed, it is required."

I sat there staring into the fire within the open door of the woodstove and wondering where to begin. "Can I ask you something?"

"Would it make a difference if I said 'No'?"

"How can you run a brothel full of whores and believe in the Bible?"

"*Aach*—I figured out where the Bible went wrong. She was flipping through pages again settling on something near the end. "Ah yes. Matthew 5: '*Everyone who looks at a woman with lustful intention, has already committed adultery with her in his heart.*' See?"

I just kept drinking.

"Every man on earth has looked at a woman with lust. And now the Bible tells them they have already committed adultery in their heart without ever having gotten the bonus of having done it for real! Do you know what that does to these men? It drives them right to Freud. So without me and my whores who else would save these poor men from being neurotic?"

She leaned back and spit onto the stove again. "We're going to get those bastards," she said, smiling with wine running into the wrinkles around her mouth.

Neither Herr Langen nor I had any illusion about our *mundfunk* gossip stopping the Nazis. At most it would be a pebble under the feet that were wearing the jackboots. Or better still, we hoped for a sharp pebble. One that could create biting little controversies that might slow down what we all felt was the inevitable march into war.

For this to happen we needed to have gossip that could leap from the poorer areas of Berlin to where the decision makers worked and lived, the Wilhelmstrasses and the Grunewalds.

If it all worked as we wanted it to, getting to the *Obergruppenführers* and all that crowd might at least buy us what?—weeks? months? of minor-key chaos that would delay the war.

Or so we hoped.

29

SO WHILE THE NAZIS HAD the *Haus des Rundfunks*—the Broadcast House, an enormous gleaming, ceramic tiled building from which they blared radio propaganda, we had what we called the *Haus des Mundfunks*— *Mutter's* shabby, slum tenement. She appointed herself the publisher even though we told her we didn't need a publisher in the traditional newspaper sense.

It didn't matter to her; *Mutter* announced she was publisher and that was that. We noticed an immediate change, beginning when she started brushing her hair. No one could remember seeing her even hold a hairbrush before. And a few days later she washed her housecoat after deciding that a publisher shouldn't be seen walking around with stains on what she wore. But she kept the little ankle socks with the holes in them and the tattered slippers. "Most people never look below the crotch," she announced, the cigarette hanging from the side of her mouth sending ash down onto her newly cleaned housecoat.

Even before *mundfunk* began, we each slid easily into a role. Our plan was that I was to bring back the stories told to me by Karin. This of course, presumed Karin was willing to be part of our *mundfunk* project. Then Herr Langen and I would embellish the gossip just enough so that the stories could not be traced back to her. When that was done, *Mutter* would carefully find ways to get the gossip to her remaining whores. This had to be done carefully because none of the whores could be completely counted on in the ways we needed. One temper tantrum, one bitter feud, could jeopardize everything.

But what made it easier was their own love of gossip. There was nothing the Swabian loved more than showing the whore from Cologne that she knew more about what was happening *out there*. Even as they were both letting Eva in the basement apartment know how much more they knew was about what was *really* happening. Sometimes *Mutter* would reel out the gossip in fragments, letting the whores on the ground floor and the basement put the whole story together in a way that could be difficult to trace back.

And once these bits and pieces of gossip had been told to individual clients, they would be whispered across all of Berlin, speeding from mouth to mouth through every social class and occupation until they had been reassembled by people filling in the blanks into one big juicy and untraceable scandal.

At which point the *mundfunk* pebble would be in the jackboots.

For myself, and I think for Herr Langen too, the new venture into gossip filled a vacuum, where the tedium of days with no work stretched time into dank blocks of boredom. Of course before anything else, we had sheer survival to think about and neither of us could risk looking for work when the Gestapo were everywhere.

Mundfunk soaked up the empty hours as we planned for how it could work. And even better, it gave us a feeling of contributing, of being a part of something. Even Karin felt it. Which was unusual for her. Much of the time she was so focused on whatever her own world happened to be that anything else never had a chance of intruding.

To my surprise when I first cautiously mentioned trying to find gossip for "a new project" Karin's seized on the idea as if it was her own.

Ever since she had returned from having the baby, even she could not ignore what the Nazis were doing. She had changed after Else Bongers got her a small role in *Der Herrscher*, a film starring Emil Jannings the only actor who was so famous that Josef Goebbels felt the need to impress him.

Emil Jannings had returned from Hollywood where he had won the first Academy Award ever given out for Best Actor. No other German actor had ever become that famous. So when *Der Herrscher* was filming, Goebbels arranged a trip to the UFA studios at Babelsberg and gave advance notice that the studio bosses should make arrangements for him to spend time with the great Jannings.

Arriving on the set, Goebbels prepared to settle into the chair that had been provided for him when he noticed the young blonde he had lusted after at least three or four actresses ago. The one who had disappeared, what?—a year? Two years ago? Karin something—he wasn't sure if he ever knew her last name. The embers of this obsession roared into the usual inferno that consumed him whenever he was in the presence of a woman who had escaped him.

And right when he was calling for his assistants to bring this Karin whatever-her-name over to him, the bulky spectre of Emil Jannings came lumbering through the big lights, straight toward him, to pay homage, to prattle and flatter in the presence of the *Reichsminister*. Suddenly Josef Goebbels was seething—at this fool Emil Jannings who was transformed into this fatuous sycophant, this fawning irritant, the bumptious impediment to sexual conquest.

What is now known:

What Josef Goebbels would never know, would never want to know, is that he has many things in common with a Hollywood mogul to whom Emil Jannings owes all his great international fame.

But, in public at least, Goebbels would vehemently deny any similarity. Because after all, Louie B. Mayer is a Jew.

Born in Russia, Mayer was raised in poverty in Canada and then became fabulously wealthy and powerful as founder of the legendary Hollywood studio, MGM—Metro, Goldwyn, Mayer.

Movies are a fine business, Mayer always tells people. But the problem is that it is teeming with actors, directors and other irritants always having to be dealt with. Add in the lesser types: producers, writers and technicians, and you have one massive pain. Mayer is always looking for ways to let these artistic types know that studio bosses like him are the ultimate immovable objects.

And one day Louie B. Mayer comes up with the solution: The Academy Awards.

"The best way to handle these film people was to plaster them with medals," he says later. "If I got them medals they'd kill to be part of what I wanted to produce. Why do you think I created the Academy Awards?"

So there at the Hollywood Roosevelt hotel, Louie B. Mayer watches as stars like Charlie Chaplin are plastered with medals in front of almost three hundred of Hollywood's most famous and most powerful. But this German actor with the heavy accent? Emil Jannings?

Winning Best Actor for his performance in The Last Command?

Who the hell is he?

But then Louie B. Mayer decides it's all just fine. Spread the medals around. Who cares?

Mayer long ago decided he knows how to handle actors. And actresses too but they are more complicated. He and Goebbels can agree on that, Mayer has long insisted on the need to control them. For instance: Dorothy? She of the Yellow Brick Road? Dorothy from the Wizard of Oz?

Groped? Molested? Even as a teenager?

Repeatedly. By Louie B Mayer who begins by putting his hands on her breasts. And not just Mayer, "Don't think they all didn't try," Judy Garland says years later talking about what she got from the studio bosses.

To the star of The Wizard Of Oz they're all the same, these moguls, supplied by what seems like a never-ending torrent of beautiful young women, desperate to be famous. And all of them know the one magic sentence that unlocks the shackles of chastity:

"I can make you a star."

And like Mayer, Josef Goebbels knows this too. He is on a sexual tour of all the actresses that catch his attention. And he doesn't care who knows it or what people think. Because who is there to stand in his way?

So now, on the set of Der Herrscher, *Goebbels is impatient to tell this beautiful young actress, this Karin, that he can make her a star. For certain favours in return of course. But for the moment he cannot because the insufferable Emil Jannings will just not take the hint and leave.*

Goebbels sits in his chair glaring up at him and listening to this fool's endless stories about Hollywood and someone named Louie B. Mayer.

Goebbels actions were exactly as Bongers had predicted. First came the flowers; and then with the flowers came the constant phone calls from Goebbels' assistants at the Ministry, trying to arrange 'meetings'. And then as Bongers also predicted, Goebbels began making the phone calls himself.

Else Bongers could no longer help as she had in the past because Goebbels' aggressive assistants had now become more skilled at delivering actresses to him. Like retriever dogs they were trained to understand that the hunt was always on and whenever their master gave the signal, actresses were what they were there to fetch.

It was Goebbels' rediscovery of Karin on the set of *Der Herrscher* that made our *Mundfunk*, our gossip, possible.

But at first, it was not obvious to us, because sitting around the stove in the flickering light at *Mutter's*, the dilemma of protecting Karin while creating our new form of gossip created only silences. Karin had told us how Bongers' advice was to find some way to leave Babelsberg as soon as possible and stay away for months, maybe years.

The silence that followed was broken by *Mutter* impatiently asking, "So? Are you? Going to stay away?" Karin shook her head. "Then girl, what are you going to do?"

"The opposite." Karin said with a smile she always used when she felt the fiercest.

Herr Langen came into the warmth of the kitchen. "Are you foolish enough to be nice to the wild beast and think it won't devour you?"

"I've changed how I think about all this. No matter what I do, that particular wild beast will outrun me," Karin said. "So I am going to do the opposite."

"There is no opposite." Herr Langen said.

"Yes there is. I am going to run straight *toward* him. I am going to get so close he cannot touch me."

"Girl," said Mutter putting down the bottle of wine, always a sign that she was concerned. "We don't need you getting yourself killed just to bring back some gossip."

"I'll be perfectly fine. I'm going to have a protector."

"Are you crazy? Who can protect you from Goebbels?" I tried not to yell at her.

She just looked at us with the sweet little smile stretched invisibly across that iron will she has had since she was a little girl.

"Magda," she said.

Give credit where credit is due — our *mundfunk* was made possible by Magda Goebbels. One afternoon, in a fit of fury and despair after being humiliated by yet another of her husband's outrageously public affairs with one of the young actresses at his disposal, Magda gathered a group of friends around her. Her closest friends.

Which was exactly what Karin had decided to become.

It was a delicate plan, somewhere between folly and ingenuity. As Goebbels' flowers kept coming, Karin spent hours talking about her plan with Else Bongers who rolled her eyes but then quietly called in favours from film people she knew at Babelsberg. She got just enough rescheduling of Karin's role in *Der Herrscher* to make sure that for the next four days she would be so busy with long hours of filming that any social activity would obviously be out of the question.

On the fifth day when she was finished filming, Karin phoned a number she had been given and told the Ministry assistant how thrilled she was to accept the invitation. And to please tell the Minister. When Goebbels 'confused assistant was asking what invitation she was talking about, Karin hung up.

Then she told the Babelsberg production manager that she needed a car to take her to Josef and Magda Goebbels' home on the lake at Schwanenwerder knowing that no one would dare refuse a car and driver for such a request. An hour later she arrived at the afternoon garden party Magda Goebbels was hosting.

And walked right in as if she'd been invited.

The role in which Karin cast herself had what actors love to call an arc, the progression of changes that their character goes through.

It began as a confused and apologetic party-crasher—after all, there had been some silly mistake; she'd been sent an invitation by the Minister's own assistants, at least that's who she thought it came from, so *obviously* she wanted to be polite and show up but—*oh never mind! Stay, yes stay and let me introduce you to—*

And hours later she was progressing from vivacious guest to new friend to sympathetic listener, and finally more hours later to confidante in Magda Goebbels' world of waiting endlessly for men.

Karin gave a brilliant performance.

In some ways it wasn't merely a performance because she came to feel almost sorry for Magda. Which in itself was an accomplishment because Magda was hard to feel sorry for. After leaving the pampered life of a marriage to an adoring industrialist, Magda moved on to the Nazi's equivalent of royalty by marrying Josef Goebbels. And as she endlessly pointed out, with Hitler as the best man.

Cinched and stiffened by formidable layers of clothing, makeup and indignation Magda was already well into her semi annual routine of lying back, spreading herself and producing babies, anesthetized by a mist of repressed hysteria that wafted in from the endless bouts of humiliation her husband was putting her through.

But now at Schwanenwerder, by the time the sun was moving behind the trees on the other side of the lake, Karin was sitting on the lawn with Magda and her friend Ello, weaving the deep bonds of confession. So soothing, so understanding was Karin that each told the others secrets they almost never shared—and then only with those they trusted. Yet Magda could never have known how there was nothing to trust here. Or how false it all was—that this pretty actress was just playing a role, writing her own lines as she went along. And those stories, those beautiful stories that this Karin was telling, sympathetic, understanding stories—Magda was so grateful to have someone like her to talk to.

Almost nothing Karin shared with Magda had ever happened. After all, she decided, it was merely a drama. So naturally these stories were not totally false, just invented. But how was Magda to know?

Because now, so overwhelming was this pretty young girl's understanding of what she was going through and oh, the shared pain—*her too?* And this girl's tales of infidelity by her man, so humiliating that Magda drew her further into her very own aching web of secrets. She *understands!* And so young!

Knowing the pain of infidelity—*at her age!* But then *they* were all the same, these men. Poor thing, this Karin. So refined and elegant. And having once lost a job because she had refused to be seduced by some shameless, philandering and powerful man. A married man at that! Cheating on his wonderful wife!

Yes indeed, where had this Karin been? Not at all like the connivers, schemers and sluts that Magda sometimes sees Josef bringing...

...Oh let's not go into that.

But then poor Josef is working so hard these days.

Yes, yes, yes Karin thinks.

And so, just after sunset when the big Mercedes roars through the gates at Schwanenwerder, spewing out the black-covered SS men who guard *Reichministers*, the twisted, hobbling Goebbels steps out into a scene so charming that the seething within him will send him to doctors for days afterwards. Nothing in his vast and lethal power protects him from the headaches, backaches and general rheuminess that seize him whenever he has a fight with Magda.

But this is not a fight. Not even close. Because how can this be? This actress—Karin? Is that it? The very prey in his hunt. The one he has lusted after—sitting there with Magda? Looking demure... sweet.... luscious!

How can that be? How can she be here? As Magda's new friend. *Close* friend? Too close for him to even attempt to...Goebbels buckles. There is some mix-up! Outrageous! Someone caused this Karin to think the invitation was to Magda's garden party. Instead of his private apartment at the Ministry.

Assistants wilt under the searing stare Goebbels directs their way.

Because now here is Magda of all people, gushing praise and even worse, friendship. As that insufferable secret-sharing sisterhood blossoms, the kind of female bonding he loathes, the kind that practically welds the emotions of women like these together. And here is this Karin sitting inside the invisible fortifications of feminine togetherness that leaves his deluge of floral bouquets wilting in the heat of all this revolting niceness.

Goebbels turns to his assistants demanding to know who was responsible for telling this Karin she had been invited to the garden party. The SS guards watch, ready to do whatever is necessary.

As always.

At first when Karin told us what Magda had said to her, we thought she was making it up. But she wasn't. Magda had been on the verge of hysteria, crying out "I have been a loyal wife too long." She wanted people to know what a monster she was married to—but a monster she still desperately clung to. She confided only in a few women, her closest friends and the few people she could trust.

"*I want people to gossip about me.*"

"Magda actually said that?" I couldn't believe it. Neither could Herr Langen or *Mutter* at our late-night session in the kitchen.

"She did," said Karin.

"Well then," said *Mutter*, "who are we to argue?"

"Precisely," said Herr Langen.

"Let the *mundfunk* begin."

30

FINDING THAT FIRST PERFECT PIECE of gossip was not as easy as we thought it would be.

The requirements were so different from what I had been writing at *Vossiche Zeitung*. At first it seemed that because there was just so much sleaze and infidelity surrounding Goebbels, it would be simple to find the perfect little tale that could be told in a few sentences and have eyebrows raising all over Berlin.

It wasn't.

In that first week of *mundfunk*, Karin would return so late that even *Mutter* would have gone to bed. She would wake me with an excited, giggling whisper and then we would creep through the chill into the warmth of the wood stove in the kitchen. With every anecdote the whispers grew louder as her astonishment circled mine in muffled exclamations. Several times our chatter awoke Herr Langen who would appear bleary and irritated, a worn overcoat covering his pajamas and his hair looking more chaotic than usual.

With *Mutter's* volleys of snores clattering in from the other room, Karin's stories built one upon another until they were like pigments on a palette creating an image of the Goebbels' marriage, so lacerating in its furies and betrayals that in the telling it sounded like a blood sport.

We looked at one another across the wood stove weighing the gossip value of Magda's stories. The latest ones were laments of Josef now bringing young women back to Schwanenwerder, introducing them to Magda—and then telling her he wanted to take them to the guest house down by the lake. To "play music".

The music, such *music*! Karin thought the word came out of Magda's mouth like a snake uncoiling, "Music in the key of fornication," was how she described it to Karin, music was played with just Josef and his young conquests alone for hours in that guesthouse while Magda seethed up in the main house—as instructed.

With the children of course.

And then when he tired of these trophies and conquests, the Minister of Public Enlightenment and Propaganda had devised a brilliant maneuver to cast the young women aside: he simply married them off to his underlings. He would call in some ambitious young officer and inform him that this now-tiresome trophy was his dinner date for that night. And would instruct the young officer to do everything necessary to impress this cast-off.

Everything.

Magda's stories of having to attend the weddings of an endless cycle of her husband's former mistresses were told with a mist of hysteria seeping from within the tightly nailed compartment in which her furies were kept.

Herr Langen listened but did not join in our enthusiastic chorus of approval.

"No," he said. "This is not good enough. All this is just one big ball of erotic candy floss. There is nothing to grab into. We need more. Something specific. One incident that is recent, scandalous and simple."

It took one more day for Karin to return and say simply, "The Argentinians."

It was to become our first piece of *mundfunk.*

It was Magda's friend Ello who had first heard about it from friends at the Argentinian legation. Four of their diplomats had been kept sitting in Goebbels' waiting room for over an hour after the time they were scheduled to meet with him. Impatience gave way to full-blown indignation and propelled by muttered Argentinian curses they were leaving as the Minister emerged in the doorway to his private apartment attached to the office. Behind him, giggling and blowing kisses was a young woman dressed only in a towel that fell to her feet.

Waiting for at least an apology, an explanation, *anything* that would make them feel less stupid for having waited for an hour, all the Argentinians got was another round of giggling. They muttered more curses, shook their heads and walked out as Goebbels merely shrugged and went back to the young woman who was still grappling with the towel.

Hearing the story, Herr Langen sat back and said nothing for a moment. I imagined the green visor. "Perfect," he said, and smiled. "Our first gossip."

I could not remember the last time he smiled.

One day later, in a procession of official cars, Josef Goebbels arrived at *Haus des Rundfunks* where he made another of his searing speeches that were broadcast across the nation. If Goebbels had one talent, it was his fiery eloquence and with it, his ability to rouse Germany again and again. This time in announcing the Nuremberg Laws forbidding marriage and sexual intercourse between Jews and Germans. There would be, he announced, new concentration camps set up just for those enemies of the Fatherland who disobeyed this latest set of new laws.

After making the speech, Goebbels left the elegant *Haus des Rundfunks* and got into the back of the big Mercedes where the young woman in the towel—now wearing an evening dress, had been waiting.

It was on that same day that *mundfunk* had been put into action.

The gossip about the Argentinian delegation traveled first from the whores' rooms on the ground floor of *Mutter's* building, borne aloft by their talkative clients: a salesman from Munich, a policeman from Wedding, a clerk from Charlottenburg and a dentist from Schöneberg. By the time Goebbels and the woman in the towel were in bed at her apartment, the *mundfunk* gossip of the Argentinians' walkout had burrowed into all of Berlin.

At the time, we had no idea how successful it had been. But within a day or two we heard endless whispers about Goebbels and what Berliners called the horizontal tango lesson that had infuriated a group of Argentinians.

Next to go out across Berlin was the story of the young secretary who Magda caught climbing through the windows of the guesthouse when Josef was there "working on his speeches."

That gossip went out through an engineer from Alexanderplatz, a pilot from Tempelhof, an insurance executive from Wilmersdorf and a city councilor from Prenzlauer. By midnight the story had taken on a life of its own and came back to us as there having been dozens of young women glamouring through Goebbels' window.

Which was absolutely fine with us. We set out to collect more gossip, revising Karin's stories just enough to make them untraceable when they went out through our *mundfunk*.

But Herr Langen was uneasy.

"For the same reason, I never felt comfortable editing your column at Auntie Voss," he admitted that night. "I get uneasy when we play with the truth. I understand that we need to do it here. But without the truth I have lost my compass."

"Ach!" snorted *Mutter*, "We are not inventing anything. We are just taking what is there and polishing it to make it shiny. With little lies. Like the seasoning that makes rotten food so tasty."

For a moment Herr Langen said nothing. "All right then. Little lies," he said staring into the floor. "I can't believe I just said that."

So there were to be more. We were sure the next little lies would come back wrapped around the gossip from an afternoon tea at the Adlon Hotel. We learned that Magda had asked her friend Ello to invite Karin—that "wonderfully understanding girl". It was not so much an invitation as it was a command performance. Magda was used to giving commands. To look at her on such occasions you could see only an imposing woman as stern and fixed as the carved prow of an ancient warship plowing through turbulent seas. Magda had long ago known that she was good at being obeyed. And also at discarding irrelevant people leaving them behind in those turbulent seas when they did not conform to the changes in her personal life: A stepfather and a former lover who were Jewish? Gone. Servants who did not please her? Gone. A rich industrialist husband who bored her? Gone.

But not everything can simply be cast aside. For instance the way people stare at her. It irritates her that she cannot tell if they are looks of admiration or maybe something else. Like pity. Or something worse. Today the only thing to do in places like the elegant Adlon is plow through those stares that have brought the big dining room to a sudden silence as she enters, lacquered, trussed and staring straight ahead.

And where is that delightful girl?

An hour before Karin was to leave for the Adlon she was almost immobilized. We found her in Inga's room sitting as silent and still as a statue. *Mutter* even waved her hand slowly in front of Karin's face.

"I don't understand," was all Karin said, still looking straight ahead.

"About what?"

"All of it."

"Girl, none of us understand, " said *Mutter* settling onto the edge of Inga's little bed. "That is the deal we make with life. It protects you from having to deal with the answers. The answers are awful."

A noise came from the darkness and a tiny hand shot up through the shadows.

"Ah so that's it," said *Mutter*. "The baby."

"Max," said Karin.

"Is that why you are here?"

"Most of the time he is at the nursery in Potsdam. I only see him once a week. And every time I do, I try to understand why I feel almost nothing that I am supposed to feel. I gave birth to him. I'm not supposed to say this I know—but he could almost be any other woman's baby?"

"But he's not any other woman's baby."

"I have tried and tried to feel what I'm supposed to feel."

"I've never heard you say that" For as long as I could remember, I had seldom known Karin to think about consequences of anything she did. The trail she left behind simply did not exist. Not out of meanness, just out of willful devotion to the moment she was in—and on into what lay immediately before her. For her, the past had no mirror.

"Maybe I just need the right moment to feel something."

"A moment? You need a moment to feel something for your own baby?"

"Why are you talking to me like that? It's like in acting. You need that moment. Then the emotions flow. All good actors will tell you that."

"So you need some moment to be able to feel something for the boy?"

"Maybe. It's all just acting you know." She thought about it for a moment, seeming to be pleased with this revelation. "It's not like my little son disgusts me you know," she added. And then looking blankly into the silence she added, "I mean it."

"I do," she added for emphasis. But she looked away as she said it.

The first few minutes of that afternoon tea at the Adlon were awkward. Karin had hurried in, not at all like the way she had been days earlier at the garden party. She was distracted and somber, not living up to the unspoken demands Magda had imposed for anyone in her presence at this afternoon tea. It only changed when Karin apologized for her mood and then confessed to them about the baby, her infant son Max, that she felt guilty because wasn't she supposed to feel at least *some* maternal feelings for him?—but did not. To her surprise Magda seemed to rise up in wayward maternal solidarity.

Karin's admission burst through the dam of Magda's propriety and brought out a flood of empathy and relief. So intense was Magda's need to connect that it became the moment when she admitted to herself, sitting at the Adlon, encased, sculpted and stared-at, that she felt a dreaded stirring within her.

Again. God, a*nother* child?

Magda had tried for days to ignore it but she *knew* in all the same ways she had tried to ignore the previous one. She had wanted to ignore it. But hearing the stories from this young—this Karin, about the feeling of doubled guilt, the kind that comes from not feeling as she was supposed to feel and also being angry because she was *expected* to feel it. *How does she know, this girl?* Magda felt even closer to her. How could she know?—at her age! How could she have understood that kind of angry emptiness?

And now more of it was to come. Another child! Weren't Helga, Hildegard and Helmut enough? Wasn't Josef satisfied? Was she just there for breeding? Or for sex when he couldn't find it anywhere else? He constantly wanted more sex. Even on those terrible nights when he came home late and left her wondering if he was entering her unwashed.

And the result was now this stirring within her. Another girl, she was sure of it. She could feel it. Another girl to be loved but only in that deficient way that was all she was capable of. And it would not be enough, Magda knew it. Leaving her with the anger at never having been the mother she was silently, constantly, told herself she must be.

And because of it Magda was so thankful that this Karin could understand, could share.

At last, *someone*!

That one afternoon tea at the Adlon yielded enough gossip to keep *mundfunk* in business for a week. But the problem was that most of it was unusable because it was so intensely personal about Magda. It could have been quickly traced back to Karin.

But even with just the untraceable scraps of gossip, three weeks later we decided that *mundfunk* was working as it was intended to. Probably better.

We knew this because cinemas all over the country had been ordered to play newsreels showing the happy family of Josef and Magda Goebbels. There was absolutely no reason to make theater audiences sit through scenes of these happy people: happy children, happy husband, happy wife—except to fight off the buzz of gossip that was now swirling around them.

Gossip that was being whispered across the land saying that maybe this happy family was not so happy after all.

The sexual attention span of Goebbels' lust for any given actress could usually be measured in weeks, sometimes merely days.

To Karin's indignation another young actress, this one a Czech, had attracted his attention. A married Czech actress. Karin was in another movie when she first noticed her on the set in Babelsberg. When this Czech actress finished the filming of her only scene, she walked outside and got into the back of Goebbels' big chauffeur-driven vehicle that had showed up without him in it. The big Mercedes drove away with Karin watching it leave.

"What a bastard," Karin hissed that night.

"Are you irritated that he is no longer trying to be a bastard with you?" asked *Mutter.*

Karin acted as if she had not heard *Mutter.*

Mundfunk was there to tell the story—but only after the little lies had been added to hide the source of the gossip. Herr Langen and I made the actress *thought to be eastern European,* and changed the studio to Torbis, another smaller film company taken over by the Nazis.

And then we had the gossip summed up in a single sentence, what Herr Langen called 'the lead'—*Reichminister Goebbels is taking conquest of Eastern Europe to a sexual level,* the sentence that would automatically make someone want to hear more. And then came the rest of our invented tale overlaid on the flimsiest of truth—*he ran after her through the streets of Wannsee pleading with her to spend the night with him*—again, it just sounded good. Who knew if it had actually happened? And the streets of Wannsee? Not likely. Or even remotely possible.

But *mundfunk* was not about what was possible. It was about what the people of Berlin could believe was possible.

When Herr Langen and I finished honing this latest piece of gossip we sat around the wood stove with *Mutter* strategizing how to send our handiwork on its way. She had begun washing her dressing gown on a regular basis and now took her duties as self-proclaimed publisher with great seriousness. "Anything to see that Austrian corporal take it in the ass with sandpaper," she said with that wine dribbling grin of hers.

She could never call Hitler by his name. To *Mutter* he would always be the Austrian corporal.

Over the years I had seen Karin's temperamental fits come and go.

But not like this.

Without warning, she began careening through sulfurous mood changes that left us wondering on a daily basis, what stranger would be inhabiting her body. The most intense was the night she came back from Babelsberg dripping invisible pools of venom. Seated around the wood stove we all felt the eruption that was coming.

She had twisted a thick sheaf of rolled-up paper as if it was something to be strangled. But it was her silence, the stillness that always came before her storm.

We waited and pretended to notice nothing out of the ordinary until she suddenly jumped up and began moving chairs around and pointed to *Mutter*. "You are the duchess," she said.

Duchess?

"I'm making stew," said *Mutter*.

Karin ignored her. Then turning to Herr Langen: "You are King William's rival to the throne." And to me: "You are the rival's sister, the Countess."

We had no idea what was happening.

She turned her back to us, took several deep breaths, and then spun around. It was startling. I almost didn't recognize her. She was a different person, an imposing stranger who launched into a fiery speech:

"If any of you think I will be content to continue being the King's mistress you have been blind. I have so much more power than that and make no mistake I shall use it when I am Queen...."

We had no idea who this person inhabiting Karin's body was, but whoever she was we could not take our eyes off her until suddenly it ended and she slumped into a chair, spent.

"That was my role. I was going to be cast to play that role!" she whispered bitterly, "They lied to me."

Mutter was going on instinct, not knowing what Karin was talking about: "They lie to us all sweetie."

"No!" She spat out the word.

We waited. "That was my role. *Mine!* They promised it to me. I was going to play Elisa. The director told me. The studio. UFA even had me fitted for costumes. And then this!"

"This?"

"Goebbels!" She flung the rolled-up paper toward the stove where it ricocheted and landed at my feet. I unrolled what was a movie screenplay entitled *A Prussian Love Story*.

"Goebbels! That shriveled piece of ugliness. What does he know about anything but fucking actresses and beating up Jews?"

"Shh," said *Mutter* and Herr Langen at the same time.

"That was *my* role!" Karin stood up as if she was going to launch into another soliloquy. But she just remained, frozen in the light from the fire playing across her features. "And he ordered the studio to give it to that slut Baarova."

Baarova? None of us had heard the name before.

"The Czech slut he's fucking now. She stole that role from me. I am going to bring that bitch back down into the shit she came from. She's thinks she's an actress. That fucking whore!"

"Dearie please. Remember you're in a brothel," said *Mutter.* "We have our standards."

31

THERE WERE ONLY THREE WAYS that people in Berlin could find out what was happening: obviously there were the Nazi news sources; then there was the BBC, which broadcast in German from London. And finally there was us—*mundfunk*, using human nature instead of printing presses or radio towers.

The problem with the newspapers, all now owned by the Nazis, and the *Volksemfänger*—the 'people's radio', better known as *Goebbels' snout*, was that the news was whatever Goebbels and the Nazis wanted it to be.

With the BBC, the problem was that anyone caught listening to it would be charged with treason. And probably executed for it.

But *mundfunk* also had its own perils—especially for us, the initiators of the gossip. It was as if we had been reaching out in the dark, catching the tiny tail of some fluffy pet that we expected to find was small and playful but when the lights came on we were holding onto a monster that could devour us all.

Ever since our *mundfunk* had first mentioned this Czech actress Lida Baarova, Goebbels had been in a state of rage, ordering the Nazi security police to find out where this gossip was coming from.

He only had to look across his bed.

His wife was seething, vengeful—and spectacularly indiscreet. At another of Magda's afternoon parties Karin learned how out-of-control her wrath could get. Like many parties at Goebbels' house, there was almost no food served, so many of the guests found excuses to depart early leaving only a few of Magda's closest confidantes to hear stories she told in rising tones of hysteria—stories of Goebbels bringing this actress, *this Lida woman* home to Schwanenwerder *right here!* and sitting at the table—*that table right there!* and telling Magda how much he and Lida were in love. And 'Thank you for raising the children.' *He actually said that to me!*

Magda was spitting the words out through teeth clenched so tightly that Karin thought she looked as if she was wearing a mask of her own face. Her own fury at this Czech interloper matched Magda's and continued on into the night, burning through every conversation we tried to have around *Mutter's* kitchen stove. At first I had trouble understanding what Karin was telling us. I thought it was just another of her tirades about how Lida Baarova had stolen the role that was hers. For hours she stormed back and forth from her room to the kitchen spewing fragments of fury.

Herr Langen watched her, growing more concerned with every outburst. "Anger like hers makes mistakes," he said.

"Actresses," *Mutter* murmured and went back to making the stew. She pointed to it bubbling on the stove, "One ingredient can make it all go bad. You know that, don't you."

Late that night Karin sat quietly, still seething but drained of the melodrama. The story was even more bizarre than we could have imagined: the Czech actress, Lida Baarova had a husband, an actor named Gustav Frölich, who found Goebbels and his wife together in a car, kissing. The husband punched her right in front of Goebbels who did nothing.

"Stop!" interrupted Herr Langen. He turned to *Mutter* and me: "No more little lies." But he was smiling. "This calls for big lies." And what he concocted was a fairly big lie. In our piece of *mundfunk* it became Goebbels, not Lida, who was dragged out of the car and punched in the face by the irate husband.

We smoothed out the two-sentence gossip line that would reel people in to want to hear the rest of the tale. We invented a more public place where the punching happened; and then we casually sent it on its way when *Mutter* used what she called a reverse-information technique by going downstairs to the whores and acting indignant, as if they would have already heard about it from their clients. Why hadn't they hadn't told her about this Goebbels-being-punched business. *Surely* they must have heard all about it?

Our *mundfunk* was all over Berlin before the end of the week.

On the following Monday, fiery front-page editorials appeared, written and signed: *Josef Goebbels, Minister of Public Enlightenment and Propaganda.* They appeared in Nazi newspapers, warning of the dangers of "loose talk" based on "idle chatter" and "gutter talk" that was designed only for "feeble minds".

Much to his own amazement, Herr Langen now regarded gossip as being more relevant and accurate than any political commentary in the newspapers. After the husband-punching gossip he spent an entire day puzzling over how we should package the next *mundfunk*. This one was even more amazing than the others. It was a *ménage á trois* story that Magda had blurted out after an afternoon tea that her friend Ello hosted in her home: *Me! He wanted me in bed with him and that slut of his!* telling of how Goebbels had proposed they all share a bed—*and this! after he's got me pregnant again!*

Herr Langen and I sat opposite one another listening in amazement as Karin told the story.

Then he said, "There are no little lies needed for this one."

Instead we just created the opening two-sentences in which we always tried to send out our *mundfunk*. This one was in the form of a riddle. Herr Langen rolled his eyes and shook his head. "I used to have standards," he said.

Then that afternoon, the riddle was sent on its way:

—*Why is Josef Goebbels like an Arab?*

—*Because he wants more than one wife at the same time.*

The whore from Cologne heard that by the following morning, our gossip had reached the dairy all the way over in Pankow where the local women met to get milk poured into the cans they carried. That was probably a record. We calculated that our *mundfunk* had a speed of about three-and-a-half kilometers per hour.

But there was something else: the more we molded and changed the actual event to make it into gossip, the faster it seemed travel. Bigger lies spread faster than little ones. At first we didn't understand why but then we heard reports that Goebbels would explode in fury at our big lies, sending the SS out in all directions and making scenes that too many people saw. And of course talked about.

His tantrums and his searches for perpetrators only seemed to add to the velocity of the gossip.

Which usually came from his own wife.

32

MUTTER WAS A BORN TACTICIAN.

She could always see beyond tomorrow and figure out complications and rewards before anyone else. She had the antennae to detect the shifts in Gestapo operations that sometimes veered close to us. When it came to protecting her building and those who were in it, she was ruthless. She could spot weakness or treachery like a bloodhound tracking fugitives. Once she was onto the trail, no one could escape her.

Not even the low-level Nazi officials, who *Mutter* described as The Two Fools, easily the biggest threats to our *mundfunk*. Also known as Dick and Doof, their real names were Dieter and Günter. They were, *blockleiters*, the men the Nazis assigned to every city block, making sure they were free of subversives, Jews, communists and prostitutes.

Mutter's building housed all four.

Dick and Doof got their nicknames because they reminded *Mutter* of Laurel and Hardy, the famous Hollywood comedians whose movies had made us all laugh for almost a decade. Not even Goebbels dared shut out their films that were loved from Munich to the Baltic. Laurel and Hardy became known as Dick and Doof but they were also named Fat and Stupid by adoring moviegoers. And that was exactly what *Mutter* thought of Dieter and Günter when they were appointed as *blockleiters*.

"Ach!" she would say, "Fat and Stupid are going to get a noseful of quills." *Mutter* frequently told the story of when she was young and living in Italy with a dog—"all muscle and no brain, just like the man I was with then. The dog chased a porcupine and returned whimpering with a nose full of quills."

Anyone *Mutter* deemed stupid was someone destined for a snout full of quills.

Mutter's quills were different. It took a while for them to be felt. Dick and Doof had been living near her in Neukölln for years and *Mutter* had long ago decided that Dick was a run-of-the-mill pompous fool—but

Doof? "He's in a class of idiot all his own," she said. And in so many unspoken ways she let him know it. While everyone else on the block became nervous in Doof's presence, *Mutter* just rolled her eyes and made sure he saw her doing it.

"Stop that," I told her, "He'll find a way to get us in trouble."

"Hah!" she snorted. "*Leave the presence of a fool.*" I didn't understand what she was telling me. "Proverbs 14," she said as if that would explain it.

"Do I go to hell if I don't understand what you're talking about?"

"Probably," she said.

Around the wood stove that afternoon, helping her cut up the carrots she had traded for a handful of beechnuts, Mutter said. "There is only one thing you need to know about how that fool Doof came to think of himself as an important person."

"What?"

"Syphilis," she said and then hurried away to the butcher's shop before it closed.

When everything was quiet that night I heard voices out on the street. I got up and went to one of the windows at the end of the hallway. On the street below, Dick and Doof were converging at a mid-point on the block, stopping an old man at the invisible boundary of their territories. They were like two dogs tugging at a piece of meat. Each time one of them would let the man go, the other would stop him and make him show his papers all over again

Something in the older man snapped and he grew agitated, shaking his head and pleading. This set Dick and Doof off like dogs who'd suddenly discovered the meat was still living. Now neither of them wanted to be the one to let the old man go on his way. Each acted as if the other would see it as a sign of weakness so they demanded his papers all over again. The old man sank to the sidewalk moaning. Which left them with a problem of what to do now. They stood over him looking perplexed and irritated.

The problem was solved when Doof put two fingers between his teeth and whistled. A car going past them made a quick U turn and came to a stop blocking the street. It was the same Gestapo car we'd seen earlier from the rooftop. This made the old man almost hysterical. Even from a distance I could hear him crying out about his wife who was very ill. And when he was put into the back of the Gestapo car, I could hear him crying out about pills he had for his wife.

Dick and Doof said nothing as the car drove away. The carcass had been devoured; it was time to rest. Dick lumbered off into the darkness, his bulk shimmying in ways that made little wave-like shadows across the coat that was at least a couple of sizes too small for him. Doof waited long enough to see him vanish and then went into the shabby tenement building where he lived.

The street fell silent except for an occasional car driving past. I stepped back and saw Herr Langen at another window.

"I saw it." he said.

Mutter always thought ahead. Years ago, on the day after Doof announced that he and Dick were joining the Nazi party, *Mutter* had set out to gather whatever blackmail material she could find on both Dick and Doof.

She distrusted fools; she thought fools were more dangerous than a wise man. So she concentrated her efforts on Doof who was the thinner and more stupid of the two who became our *blockleiters,*

Dick was assigned to the long block that began at the far end of our street and went almost two hundred meters away from *Mutters'* building. But Doof was assigned to our block and was soon strutting around, reveling in his new power and sometimes wearing both his Nazi armband and his medals from the last war.

Mutter had met Doof recently at the Syphilis Clinic in the famous hospital in Mitte. She had taken one of her whores to the clinic, something she used to do on a regular basis, just to be safe. In Berlin's wildest days, before the Nazis took over, the clinic had become a common destination.

"I used to love going to the Syphilis Clinic," she said. "For me it was a major social event. Part comedy, part tragedy, all farce."

Mutter loved talking about the different types she met at the Syphilis Clinic: the defiantly decadent, the embarrassed preachers, the street hustlers and especially the royalty pretending they were just there inspecting one of their charities.

Syphilis was the great leveler.

"But the worst thing about it for us was that fool Doof. You'd have thought he ran the whole clinic, calling himself the "ward manager" when all he was, was a petty tyrant, a clerk ordering people around, even lecturing my whores. He was worse than a priest with an erection.

"And he was constantly trying to impress one of my whores, Gisela. So he was always inventing ways to make sure we had to see him in his office. He had this little windowless office, but it was filled with photographs of him in some place like Mongolia. Horses and igloo-type houses everywhere. And he wanted to show off the signs in his office in both Russian and German, most of them with the words *Quiet please SYPHILIS WARD*—in Russian writing!

"Doof that imbecile was trying to impress Gisela because he had gone on this big syphilis expedition to Mongolia. Hah! Even Gisela could figure out he was just the baggage handler."

But whenever Gisela was around him, Doof could not stop bragging about his time in Mongolia. He always wanted her to see the signs in his office that he had brought back from the expedition. He would proudly translate from the Russian:

Syphilis Treatment Center.

No Guns Allowed During Syphilis Tests.

As she told us around the kitchen stove, it was watching Doof strut and boast in front of Gisela that gave *Mutter* an idea.

"What?" I wanted to know.

"*Ach!* you'll figure it out." she said.

What is now known:

In the late 1920s, during Berlin's most decadent years before everything crashes down, enterprising German doctors have recognized the research opportunity presented by the sexual frenzy all around them. So they promptly set out to become world-class experts in syphilis.

And while they are doing this, in Russia the Soviets have a huge problem: syphilis.

In the critical years right after the Revolution, the Bolsheviks in Moscow are frantically trying to consolidate their recent takeover of eleven time zones worth of territory. So they designate an obscure and distant Asian part of their new empire—Buryat-Mongolia, to be the outpost of socialism in the Buddhist Orient. Moscow is desperate to make this outpost "the model of successful social transformation." But to their horror, the Soviet commissars find Buryat-Mongolia is riddled with syphilis, so much so that it imperils the whole glorious transformation.

They use the usual Soviet enticements: terror, slogans and propaganda. But these have only limited effect because this is a problem none of the commissars have any idea how to fix: the centuries old sexual habits and lack of hygiene that have led 200,000 of the 500,000 Buryats to be infected.

But Moscow demands it be fixed. Which is always dangerous for Commissars in the new Russia. Not fixing what Stalin sees as a problem can be both career and life ending. So the Council of People's Commissars contacts the hated capitalists, in this case the German doctors who are the experts on syphilis. The same German doctors who are now swabbing the sexual apparatus of what seems like half of wildly decadent Berlin.

The doctors in Berlin agree to put together an expedition into distant Buryat-Mongolia to help cure these nomadic tribes 8000 kilometers to the east. Equipped with medical supplies, signs in both languages, translators and Doof as their baggage handler the Germans set off, on an expedition.

The Germans believe they are on a medical mission.

But Moscow sees it differently. The Kremlin sees these German doctors as being there to get what they call "unenlightened people" physically and mentally healthy enough to build the Soviet empire.

A Soviet empire that will, in a decade and a half, have Russian tanks and troops on the streets of Berlin, the city they have just conquered.

Hating the word *blockwart*, which was what most people called *blockleiters*, Doof now used the skills he had honed in the Syphilis Clinic to make people's lives a miserable thicket of petty bureaucratic indignities, not to mention bringing the Gestapo down on them if he suspected anything.

Doof was now what he had always wanted to be—a man to be feared.

"For the first time in his pathetic life that idiot gets to be the big man," *Mutter* said as she watched Doof on the day after he was appointed *blockleiter*, walking slowly along the sidewalk as people avoided eye contact with him. "The insect discovers its poison. Time to let it sting its own ass."

A few days later, she parked herself on the front steps peeling potatoes as Doof approached. The closer he got the more she let the peels fall onto the sidewalk around her feet.

"That is not the Nazi way of doing things," Doof announced. Mutter just kept peeling, creating a little pile of peels around her feet.

Doof looked as if he was trying to inflate himself to appear more imposing. "In case you haven't noticed *Mutter*, I am someone who can make your life difficult," he said.

Mutter just kept peeling. "Günter you stupid bastard, you've made my life difficult since the moment I met you. You're a pain in the ass."

"I can have you arrested if I—"

"I am saving your sorry hide, and you talk to me about potato peels?"

Doof expression swung from irritation to confusion. "What did you just say?"

"You heard me. I'm saving you."

"From what?"

"From being arrested by the Gestapo and thrown into a concentration camp." Mutter reached into her dirty housecoat and took out a small photograph. "And don't tell me you don't remember Gisela, the crazy whore."

Doof almost sputtered. "I will have you know that—"

Mutter interrupted. "Oh shove it up your ass Doof. You practically dribbled every time you saw her. And by the way you cheap bastard, you still owe her for the last fuck. And for this too." She held up the photo, the image facing away from him.

With a snapping sound she turned the photo around and Doof found himself looking at a photo of his younger self, grinning into the camera—and naked except for a Russian army hat and a communist banner falling from his shoulders. Kneeling at his feet was a naked woman, her back to the camera.

"And by the way that's Gisela playing with your penis. Or maybe trying to find it."

Doof looked as if parts of him were going to come loose under the pressure. "This photo was destroyed! She promised me!" he whispered.

"She lied? What a surprise. A whore lying! I am *so* shocked!" Potato peels flew all over. "And by the way she claims to have made three copies of this photo."

"Where is she? I want to know."

"And she sent this too." She took out another photo and handed it to him. "A photo of your old communist party card. Just imagine what the Gestapo would say if they saw this."

Doof's hands trembled as he looked at it for an instant before jamming it in his pocket. "That was years ago. I was barely out of school! Young and stupid and—"

"…and now you're older and still stupid."

"How did she get this?" Doof screeched out a whisper, struggling to keep his desperation from showing,

Mutter looked impatient with such a naïve question. "Stole it you idiot. How else would she get it? Probably you were fucking her and dressed up like Stalin."

He looked around in swivel-head motions to see if anyone was watching. "You have to help me," he rasped. "You *have* to."

"I already am you idiot."

"You are?"

"I've been mailing money to an address Gisela sent. In Stuttgart. Once a month since February."

"Mailing money? What for?"

"To save your sorry ass." Another explosion of peels, these landing on Doof's polished shoes. "*Fifty* marks a month. Blackmail money."

Doof's look of groveling gratitude was suddenly ripped away by a bolt of suspicion. "Why are you helping me? What's in it for you?"

"Are you really that stupid? If the Gestapo saw either of these photographs they'll drag you away. And when they torture you, you'd babble like a baby."

"Yes, yes. I would not do well under torture."

"That much I already figured out. Look Günter, you want the truth? You're basically a traitorous type."

"Do you realize who you're talking to?"

"Yes. A communist who switched over to the Nazis when they started winning."

"*Mutter*, I don't want this to get around, okay?"

"Then think it through. If the Gestapo got you, they'd torture you first and then turn you over to SS who would just shoot you. But before that you'd babble like a fool, telling them everything. Including where that photograph was taken. Then I'd be in the shit. They'd raid my place. So I'm saving my own skin too. As well as your sorry hide. Do you really think I *want* to pay fifty marks a month?"

"How can you afford it?"

"In theory I can't."

"Then...?"

"My whores."

"But whorehouses are no longer supposed to be operating."

"Oh really? Then how do you propose paying the blackmail?"

"But there are new laws against brothels."

"Fine, then I'll throw all my whores out and have no money to keep you and me out of the dungeons at Prinz Albrechtstrasse."

"No wait."

"I've even thought about raising the price my whores charge."

"Yes. Perhaps that's something to consider."

Doof became the uneasy protector of *Mutter's* building. But that was only part of what *Mutter* used him for.

She discovered that he could be valuable to us in another way: his insatiable need to gossip.

As a former communist, his dislike of 'the bosses' had never really left him and a juicy little scandal involving someone like Goebbels always threw him into inner conflict, having to choose between his newfound Nazi worship and his old communist class struggle. In the end the gossip always won and Doof could be relied on to show others that he knew something they did not. It became another source of the power he thought he wielded.

And with the gossip about this Czech actress, Doof might as well have been a megaphone. He unknowingly assisted our *mundfunk,* propelling the gossip through Neukölln faster than anything *Mutter* and her whores had ever done before.

We learned that he was smart enough—unusual for Doof, to disguise his gossiping as concern for the Nazi party. At a meeting of low-level Nazi officials he made a speech saying they needed to protect their beloved leaders like Goebbels from the threats posed by scheming Czechs and other Europeans. No one knew what he was talking about which gave Doof a chance to solemnly announce what he had heard 'from those who knew'. Before the meeting ended, our gossip about Goebbels sneaking around so Magda wouldn't find out his latest rendezvous with the Czech actress had been phoned across Berlin. It spread far faster than we could ever have imagined, getting as far as Spandau by sunset.

That night Herr Langen was suddenly no longer listening to what we were saying. He was holding his first two fingers to his lips in a *Shh* motion. We fell silent as a strange and distant roar like the distant cough of something deadly. The roar came through the walls and windows and then it faded. It came again, this time more forceful and angrier, building until the night shook.

Outside on the Herr Langen's rooftop area, nothing out of the ordinary could be seen but the roar grew until all of Berlin trembled like some distant beast was awakening in a rage.

"The new army tanks. Panzer II's. Waiting to move out."

What is now known:

The panzers are to be part of the drum-drenched ceremony welcoming the Italian fascist leader Mussolini to Berlin. It signals so many things. The most obvious is that war is coming. And perhaps the least obvious is the triumph of Josef Goebbels.

For two days of grandiosity and adulation, the vast display of Nazi military might sends another unmistakable message to the rest of Europe. Mussolini speaks in fractured German and proclaims Italy's allegiance to Hitler and announces to six hundred and fifty thousand wildly cheering spectators, "We will march together to the end." They all understand that 'We' means the Italian fascists and the German fascists.

And 'the end' is another way of saying the obliteration of Europe as it is now.

It is Goebbels' triumph. He has orchestrated not just the mandatory several hundred thousand cheering citizens to 'Seig Heil' themselves into the usual ecstasy. No, Josef Goebbels has driven his staff and technicians to deliver what no one thought would be possible: The World. Propelled by the genius of German technology Goebbels mounts the speakers podium and tells them the startling news: The World is here with us! German technical brilliance is broadcasting this spectacle of Nazi grandiosity around the world, across Europe, North America and South America. Goebbels has arranged to beam it all to the distant millions. As it is happening!

No one dreamed such a thing could be possible.

As the cheering floods over him, pride explodes in a million German minds! For us! For the Führer! And for this amazing Josef Goebbels then turns toward the Führer who nods his approval.

But in the midst of this drum drenched celebration what almost no one has noticed while Goebbels has been speaking is that in the middle of his speech he does something odd....

...he takes off his watch.

Out of six hundred and fifty thousand enraptured onlookers only two people pay attention to such a tiny gesture. Deep amid the throngs, the Czech actress, Lida Baarova sees her lover take off his watch. It is the signal Goebbels has prepared her for, telling her to be on the lookout for it—in the midst of this vast orgiastic militaristic bacchanal. It is the code that only they know! the code that, Goebbels tells Baarova, will show her that he loves her—simply by taking off his watch.

She sees it and thrills to one of history's great secret proclamations of love.

But someone else sees it: Hitler. And he wonders why his Minister of Public Enlightenment and Propaganda is taking off his watch in the middle of his speech. He has seen Goebbels make dozens of speeches, hundreds maybe. And never before has he taken off his watch.

At this point in his life, Hitler misses nothing.

33

THAT SKINNY BITCH.

That was how we knew her, what we called her, this woman doing so much damage on the street below us. And Herr Langen had become obsessed with her.

Not only obsessed, but he also talked of being left with invisible scars across cherished memories. Neither *Mutter* or I knew exactly what he meant.

"And she's Jewish!" he repeated many times. " And to her own people!" as he watched what was unfolding on the street below." Turning them over to those Nazis?"

I didn't know what he was talking about until *Mutter* and I went to see for ourselves. We stepped out onto what had become his rooftop patio that could not be seen from the surrounding buildings. He had placed old wooden crates holding down the edges of a large, ragged rug and found several chairs that looked like they were ready for the scrap dealer. It became a secret location that overlooked the streets below.

On that Saturday afternoon, we watched a woman on the street below. "I know that one," *Mutter* hissed, "*That skinny bitch,*" The woman loitered around the entrance of the shabby little cinema on the corner, talking to people as they went in to a matinee showing of *Der Herrscher*. She was thin, dark-haired and with sharp, unlined features on a face of indeterminate age; from a distance all you could make out was the fierceness.

"*That skinny bitch,*" *Mutter* said again because she seemed to like saying it. With her own inflated body, she used *skinny* as the ultimate insult. "Oh do I know that terrible woman!" she said. "Frau Traitor-Lady. Are you sure she's Jewish?"

"I knew her brother," said Herr Langen." She came into this world with a shriveled, ugly soul and she's spent her life making others pay for it."

"People here think she's Catholic."

"She's not."

On the street below Frau Traitor-Lady, *that skinny bitch*, had found an older woman she seemed to target, honing in on her with smiles that even from a distance were like a barrage of blades.

"Oh Lord, now it starts," said Herr Langen. "She's found a Jew to destroy."

"Jah, I know that older woman. The Jewish butcher's widow."

Herr Langen began praying softly in some language that I presumed was Hebrew. "I know what will happen now," he said, "and I should be cursed because I am not stopping it."

When the older woman went into the cinema, Frau Traitor-Lady hurried to the end of the block where Dick was intimidating everyone around him. Even from four stories above, you could feel an easily greased self-importance pumped full by the unease of people around him.

Frau Traitor-Lady pointed to the cinema and Dick nodded.

When the movie ended and people were leaving the cinema, Dick and two Gestapo agents were waiting for the older woman as she emerged. She was questioned on the street and we watched from what might as well have been a million kilometers away as she fainted and was picked up and dumped into a Gestapo car. "We will never see her again," said *Mutter*. "I want to feed *that skinny bitch* poison." She looked to Herr Langen for approval but something essential had been emptied out of him.

He clutched a railing unable to talk.

Maybe it was because I had known Herr Langen in the days when he ruled the *Vossische Zeitung* newsroom, with journalists trembling at his every glance. To me he was different in ways that I'm not sure *Mutter* or Karin or anyone else there understood. The others at *Mutter's* just knew him as this often-distracted man with the handsome Roman face. The man who spent hours reading and writing letters to his wife in France before asking Inga or *Mutter* to mail them for him

Several times a week he would emerge late at night and walk down the hall to talk with *Mutter* who sometimes brushed her hair when she knew she would see him.

One warm morning after we spent an hour weighing various rumours that Karin had brought back from the Babelsberg studios, he quietly asked if he could talk to me in private. It took me by surprise, and only later did

I realize how much I still saw him as the powerful editor who would have never asked for my presence; he would simply have ordered it.

Standing overlooking the street on his secret rooftop patio, he acted like a man with a problem he couldn't quite remember. "I need an honest answer," he said finally, looking away from me, "An opinion actually."

I waited. The distant traffic noise scraped and honked on the street below. "Okay."

"Do I look Jewish?"

"Excuse me?"

"I'm asking you a question."

I was too surprised and uneasy to know what to say. "I still feel very uncomfortable with what you've just asked me."

The fierceness in his face caught the overhead sunlight. He remained staring out across the other rooftops. He waited for me to say something else.

"You mean do you look like the men with the big round hats, the beards and the hair ringlets who—"

"No. Not that. This is a practical matter," he snapped.

"Talking about this makes me uncomfortable," I said.

"We've already established that."

"But Nazis in *Der Sturmer* write about 'looking Jewish' so I don't feel this is something that I should join in their—"

He interrupted sharply. "Okay, let me put it another way. Imagine that you fail to give me your honest assessment to what I have just asked, and because of that I have walked out onto that street down below us and *that woman* sees me. And then she and runs to those Gestapo agents who arrest me and fling me into another of their concentration camps. Like the butcher's widow. Would you feel '*uncomfortable*' because you had not given me an honest answer?"

In my mind I stumbled through different responses until finally I asked, "Is *the skinny bitch* down there?"

"Yes. She is there right now."

I hesitated and then said, "Turn around."

In a sense Herr Langen stood there emotionally naked and vulnerable as I studied his face. Something in me changed as I did—something in both of us.

An awkward silence. Then I said, "You've got blue eyes."

"That's it?"

"That's enough."

His next request was that I stay on his rooftop patio and watch him as he walked along the street for the first time since we had all moved in to *Mutters'* building.

He had asked it as a favour based on something I never expected to hear from him: fear. In years past, he seemed to have been without fear. But I was discovering that he had so many of them. The second greatest of his fears was just vanishing with no one knowing what had happened to him. So on that rooftop he asked if I would watch him as he walked along the street. It was important he said, for me to watch because he couldn't bear the thought that if something bad happened to him, no one would ever know.

But what he feared the most was not hearing from his wife—or her not hearing from him. Or about him, "If something bad happens."

It was because of his beloved Emma that he was now risking walking the Dick and Doof and *skinny bitch* gauntlet to get her letters from France that were being mailed to a family friend. From several days of rooftop observation Herr Langen had studied the dangers on the street, He decided that Doof would not be the problem; he missed most of what happening around him. But he noticed that Dick spent much of the day positioned at the end of the block, his massive body overflowing the chair he occupied as he observed everything and everyone that passed.

He decided that if he ever had problems on the street it would be because of either *the skinny bitch* or Dick, or both.

So setting off onto the street to get Emma's letters, Herr Langen did just as we had decided: no cigarette, no slouching, and simply walking as if he had to be somewhere and was a few minutes late. From high above I watched him striding among the crowds, checking his watch. He walked quickly, but not too quickly, past *the skinny bitch* who was patrolling her territory outside the shabby cinema. He walked within an arm's length of her and she never gave him a second look. And then further up the street past the corpulent Dick who was too busy harassing a junk collector whose horse-drawn cart had been pulled over to the curb.

From our rooftop I watched Herr Langen walk into the distance and then fade from view.

An hour later he was on Königstrasse at Danziger's, a decrepit restaurant that was where his once-wealthy cousin now ate watery meals. The cousin had grown up in a large Kaiserallee apartment filled with artwork and servants. That apartment had been taken over by the Nazis and given to an official in the Foreign Ministry, so Herr Langen's cousin now lived in the basement of the home of an Aryan friend. Usually a letter would arrive once a week from Emma in France, mailed to the Aryan friend so it would not arouse suspicion. The friend would pass it to the cousin who would then give it to Herr Langen in their weekly meeting at Danziger's.

While in that restaurant, having to listen to the grumbling of this cousin he had never liked, Herr Langen clutched the letter unopened and waited impatiently for the weekly mumbled tirade to end.

He would arrive back at *Mutters* in a state of exhilaration whenever a new letter from Emma had come. The letter was wonderful he would always say, always full of plans for their future once this Nazi business had run its course. Probably in a year or so, hopefully less.

But one evening he was different, almost uneasy. When he came out of his room later that night, he barely talked as he stared into the fire in the woodstove. We sat in silence.

"No," I said after a few minutes had passed.

"No what?"

"No I'm not going to sit in silence until you decide to talk."

"Sorry." He seemed to need someone to pull words out of him. "I have lived my life with language. I treasure it. It is like a barometer of the kind of civilization we find ourselves in. At Danziger's today I heard a new expression that still leaves me chilled. I was asking about my cousin's sister, the teacher who was arrested at school for being a Jew. He told me: 'She has been sent east.' *Sent east*—those words are now as terrifying as any I have ever heard. Everyone out there is suddenly so used to those words that they know exactly what they mean—all this in a few days."

"Yah," said *Mutter*, "I heard it on Saturday for the first time."

I said nothing about having heard the expression from Uncle Rudi. And I wondered if it was he who first said it.

"*Sent east*—dragged out of homes and stores and streets here in Berlin and packed into cattle cars that go east to these camps, KZ they call them, concentration camps, two or three hundred kilometers away, out near the Polish border. My cousin's sister: gentle, dignified, older, *her* in a cattle car?" I had never seen him as agitated. "*Sent east.* Two words—a little bucket of sound to hold all this terror that we may not be capable of keeping in our thoughts in case the barriers against madness are not strong enough,

He was looking at something only he could see. "I am so glad Emma is away from all this."

"How is she?"

For a moment he was silent. "She says that in Paris they expect war. But thank God the French have such a strong army."

A week later, Herr Langen returned from Danziger's with another letter from his wife. He went directly into his room, saying nothing to any of us. Later, at sunset, *Mutter* and I found him on the little roof space he had created, looking down at Dick on the street below waddling slowly in front of the stores calling people over and checking their papers. It was obvious that Herr Langen was enclosed by his own thoughts so we turned to leave, but were stopped when he whispered "Here she comes."

"Frau Traitor-Lady. *The skinny bitch,*" *Mutter* said it several times while we watched as the woman walked aimlessly looking for prey to feed to the Gestapo. She spotted a young man in a strange floppy hat, maybe a student. "Oh no," murmured Herr Langen. "I know his father. And I remember him as a child. A good boy."

"Jewish?" asked *Mutter.*

Herr Langen nodded.

On the street below us, *the skinny bitch* was smiling and acting friendly, talking to the young man before he went inside the cinema. Then she hurried up the street toward Dick who was seated in a chair scanning his domain.

"Hah, '*The one who ate our bread has lifted his heel against us,*'" said Mutter. "Psalms," she added as the woman talked excitedly to Dick and pointed to the cinema.

"I will be back," said Herr Langen. "But if I am not, please write to Emma. You will find the address on the letters in my room." He walked quickly toward the rooftop doorway leading back into the tenement. We saw him minutes later down on the street, casually walking toward the cinema which he entered as if he was just another moviegoer looking for a way to pass an afternoon.

"Now we wait to see whose heel gets lifted against who," said *Mutter.*

After about half an hour we spotted Herr Langen several hundred meters behind the cinema. He must have left through a rear exit door, He was walking past a nearby building and then disappeared down a side street.

A few minutes later, the boy hurried from the same exit door and vanished quickly on a different street.

Herr Langen arrived back on the roof. "The boy is safely on his way home. Now we see what happens."

When the movie ended, Dick and two Gestapo agents were on the sidewalk with the woman, scrutinizing people leaving the cinema. As more and more people filed past them and the young man did not appear the Gestapo agents' obvious irritation increased.

"Look, look!" *Mutter* was pointing, "They're furious. Hah! Gestapo men embarrassed in public. They're yelling at that shithead Dick." It was as if *Mutter* was doing radio commentary for a sporting event. "So now he's yelling at *the skinny bitch*. Look, look, they're all yelling at her! She's trying to run away. Oh look they're dragging her to the car."

That night, sitting around the wood stove it felt as if we should have been cause for at least a minor celebration. But Herr Langen turned away and seemed to be looking at something only he could see.

"There are no winners here." I couldn't tell if he was angry or sad.

34

"IT'S A MEASURING STICK FROM heaven," said *Mutter*. She was talking about Danziger's restaurant where Herr Langen met his cousin almost every week.

Danziger's became how we evaluated the impact of each individual piece of gossip. On the days that Herr Langen went to collect his wife's letters, he would listen to the conversations around him. Often, he would hear our gossip—or versions of it, being woven through the low voices and whispers.

On the night after his second trip to Danziger's, Herr Langen said almost as an afterthought "Did I tell you about one of my cousin's friends who whispered to me at Danziger's: 'Have you heard the crazy news? About Goebbels? And some Czech actress he's sleeping with? While Magda's throwing pots and pans at him?' And my cousin replied, 'Of course, everybody's talking about it.'"

"Hah!" said Mutter triumphantly. "We are a success. Which probably means something bad. But for now let's just enjoy it."

What was obvious was that the Lida Baarova and Goebbels affair was a pure gift to our little gossip venture. Herr Langen returned with stories of how her name could be heard rustling through the clinking of knives and forks at Danziger's. I'd never seen *Mutter* smile so much as she did listening to the news that *everybody was talking about it.*

Some of our gossip was so potent that it didn't need us to keep it going. Goebbels and Magda themselves saw to that. Goebbels had become so obsessed with Lida Baarova that his recklessness went further in giving life to our *mundfunk* than any lies—little or big, we could have invented. But then there was Magda who, by any standards the Nazis had ever devised or demanded, was totally out of control.

And what made Magda even more dangerous to them was that her entire life had been one of self-control, regimentation and discipline. She got out of bed every morning at exactly the same time no matter how late she had been out the night before. She brushed her teeth with the same number of strokes every morning and took the same nine minutes to brush her hair. Everywhere outside of her own bedroom she was always immaculately dressed and made up with her blonde hair perfectly lacquered in place.

But now, burned away by the rage and humiliation from what her husband was doing, this inwardly controlled Magda had been left in smoldering ruins at the feet of the new, reckless and very public Magda.

Even her closest friends could not calm her enough to stop what she was doing. Or saying. She had made it her business to get others on her side. And to do this she needed to spread the news of what she called *Josef's filthy details*. Her friends and Goebbels' assistants did everything they could to keep her stories from spreading.

But of course at *Mutter's* we quietly did exactly the opposite.

It became our nightly routine. When the fire in the old wood stove had died down and we had talked of other things, we settled in to sorting the *mundfunk* stories we had not yet sent on their way. There were so many:

There was Goebbels' secret house in the forests near Bogensee where he and Lida Baarova could now spend nights undisturbed by such nuisances as matrimonial indignation,

Then there was the cruise on the Havel last weekend on the *Baldur*, his yacht, where Goebbels was lying on the lower deck holding hands with Lida Baarova who wore a revealing two-piece bathing suit. On the top deck, seething and tearful, Magda sat, swaddled in figure-covering linens. Beside her, her friend Ello tried to keep her calm, listening to hissing vows of revenge and fury.

And when the fights at their home resumed again with Magda flinging dishes, Goebbels would retreat to his private apartment in the Ministry, summoning doctors to treat him for chest pains, stomach ailments and insomnia. He began using alcohol and drugs to help him sleep.

The symptoms would continue until he went back to Magda, who listened to his promises to make it all better. And then she would forgive him—until the cycle would start all over again.

This latest time it was at a very public event. Magda went to the big cabaret theater in Lehniner Platz with Ello and a few friends. Settling into the box seat, she was silently horrified to find herself only a few feet from Goebbels and Lida Baarova who were holding hands in the next box.

But for us gossip columnists, there was an even juicier story on the next night after the cabaret, when Goebbels crept home to a raging Magda, claiming he was only protecting Lida from the professional jealousy of the other actors out at Babelsberg. Even the usual massive bouquet of flowers he always brought to accompany his hand wringing did not work this time. The flowers flew everywhere as Magda's fury drove Goebbels out of the house, with shouting so loud that it was heard in the servants' house.

When the front door opened, Magda could be heard yelling, "And you're probably going off to spend the night with that Baarova slut again! Bastard!"

Acting hurt and insulted, Goebbels proclaimed that as a man of honour he would *never* think of doing such a thing. At the front door he brandished a pistol and yelled that since she had so mocked and besmirched his honour the only thing for a gentleman to do was to shoot himself.

"So goodbye forever!" he yelled, waving the gun around, jumping into his car and roaring away. Which sent Magda running after him crying and shrieking into the night:

"No Josef no! Think of the children!"

Think of the children! The line reverberated in *mundfunk* retellings across Berlin. It was probably a new speed record, reaching the western forest areas by mid afternoon. And four days later it still filled Danziger's with whispers and very guarded smirks.

It was probably the best gossip so far. At least that was the immediate verdict from the *Haus des Mundfunk* editors, namely Herr Langen, *Mutter* and me. With a sizzling mixture of cheap wine and *Mutter's* former fluids dying on the wood stove, she slapped her enormous thigh and chuckled, "What could be better?" She wheezed and then almost as afterthought added, "So does anyone know if he shot himself?"

It was the only time I had ever seen Herr Langen laugh out loud.

"Yeah. Okay." said *Mutter* rolling her eyes at her own remark. "But where did he spend the night then? Baarova's?"

"No," said a voice behind us. We had not noticed Karin. She had glided, unheard down the hall while we were talking.

"Ahh," asked *Mutter*, "So he did not sleep with his actress?"

"No," said Karin as if she enjoyed saying the word. The Czech slut slept alone last night. They say Goebbels went to the home of one of his secretaries and spent the night with her."

"So he *was* a man of honour!" said *Mutter*, raising her glass in a mocking toast. "Our Josef. To whom we owe so much."

Usually *Mutter* never celebrated anything.

But here she was, arranging yet another little celebration. And she wanted it known that this one was special.

Neither Herr Langen nor I had any idea what we were supposed to be celebrating. All we knew was that she had been bartering for the best ersatz coffee available since rationing had started. She had bought two hundred grams of this imitation coffee made from chicory and barley. It was a luxury compared to the awful mixtures of beets or acorns flavoured with coal tar that was being sold as coffee now.

It was the closest approximation to coffee that we'd had since the old days of Auntie Voss and the Viennese coffee they served in the newspaper's cafeteria. At this celebration of *Mutter's*, we drank, slowly and gratefully, our taste buds acting like phantom limbs, filling in what was missing with memory that took over and made it all a treat.

Then she put in front of us a plate of tiny and very rare cinnamon pastries. That was when we knew for sure she had something else on her mind.

She put the refilled pot of ersatz coffee on the table. "Psalms," she said, proudly adding, "Verse 107: '*For he satisfies the thirsty and fills the hungry with good things.*' She said it in the thick Berlin dialect that she sometimes lapsed into when she was anxious or excited, mixing up letters like G and J.

" Mutter? What is going on?" asked Herr Langen.

Like a schoolgirl with a secret she couldn't wait to tell, she reached for the pad of paper and pencil she had positioned nearby. Slowly, secretively, she wrote something on the paper. We could not see it until she turned it around and we were looking at three big black letters in the center of the page:

BBC

"*No!*" I said. "You didn't!"

Mutter nodded. "I listened to the radio last night," she whispered.

Herr Langen pulled his chair in closer to both of us "Are you crazy? With walls as thin as these and you're listening to the *that*?" Like the rest of us, he did not even want to say the letters. It was a testament to the fear the Nazis had put into all of us, that merely mentioning the BBC or its broadcasts from London had become too risky to even mention.

"I put a blanket over the radio. And then listened to it under the blanket."

"You know that people have been executed because their neighbours overheard them listening to it and informed on them to the Gestapo."

"Do you want to lecture me? Or do you want to know what I heard or not?" *Mutter* said impatiently.

Both Herr Langen and I leaned in even closer. "Our *mundfunk* has made it all the way to London. The BBC—

Shh!

—*it* has heard our gossip and is broadcasting it on the radio!"

We looked from one to the other and then simultaneously all three of us burst out laughing. Her whispered account of the BBC newsreader announcing.

…the unconfirmed report that the high ranking Nazi official Goebbels had been punched by the husband of an actress…

set another joyous round of chicory and barley coffee. And for a moment we allowed ourselves a flicker of hope.

Days later, Herr Langen figured out what had happened

It was the British tabloid newspapers who had somehow heard our gossip and then, only after it was printed in those tabloids, did the BBC use it in its broadcasts beamed back into Europe.

"The British love the gossip as much as we do," *Mutter* whispered happily a week later after she had spent parts of the previous three nights huddled under blankets in her room listening to the BBC. "Our latest story to make their broadcast is Goebbels' secretary climbing into the guesthouse window to get to him."

"The British also love anything to make the Nazis look ridiculous," whispered Herr Langen. "It's almost a strategic matter now. And the Nazis will be going crazy trying to figure out how the BBC knows this. Goebbels career will be at stake. The SS and Gestapo and the Kripo and everyone else will be like hornets trying to find out who is holding the stick that has poked their nest. ”

"And Karin is holding the stick," said *Mutter*. "That is a problem. She doesn't understand this game she is playing. Her gleefulness is becoming a problem. In taking down that Czech actress, she's getting careless. If a few more Magda rumours come out, the image of the Reich will be at stake."

"Which means Hitler will get involved."

35

WE HAD TO FIND KARIN.

We hadn't seen her in a week, which was not unusual. When she was acting in a film she often stayed near Babelsberg for days, sometimes weeks at a time. But now she needed to know the way the tension and dangers were tightening around each piece of *mundfunk*. It was decided that I should go out to the studios at Babelsberg, find Karin and make sure she understood what was involved in replenishing our *mundfunk* supply. Caution was more important than ever.

It all seemed so simple. But I was anxious. And angry at myself for being nervous about such a little journey. After being housebound for all those weeks I had lost the confidence to do the simplest things such as walking down a street.

I went to sleep that night somehow dreading going to Babelsberg to see Karin. In my dreams Gestapo were knocking on my door and I woke up wondering how I could ever walk out onto the street without being spotted by Dick or Doof.

That morning I left *Mutter's* so determined to seem normal that I felt everything about me must have been blaringly abnormal.

I kept telling myself: Hadn't I walked down a thousand streets in Berlin with nobody looking at me? It wasn't as if I my face would be known to those outside the world I had worked in. Of course the higher up Nazis might know me: Goebbels and Helldorff and even possibly Hitler who had once shook my hand at the Italian embassy. But then again, without makeup I had more anonymity than I allowed myself to rely on. Besides, would *they* be on the streets looking for a former newspaper columnist whose name was on a list of those to be arrested? Would Dick and Doof have even read *Vosstiche Zeitung*? Neither was likely.

All I had to do was walk along the streets of Neukölln looking as drab as everyone else. And who would notice?

So I did.

But after walking for a block I realized no one was paying any attention to me. Even as I walked toward the dreaded Dick's domain I could see him smiling, partly visible behind an opened newspaper. Everyone else around him was sort of manic and holding up newspapers and cheering. Dick who never laughed was laughing with other men around him. I walked right past them and they never stopped laughing and yelling and cheering. Dick shouted, "First Austria, then all of it!"

All of it?

I looked at one of the newspapers. And realized from the headline that Nazi Germany had invaded Austria that morning. The crowds on the street were going wild, celebrating the Führer's glorious victory.

I could have walked down the street waving a British flag and singing *God Save The King* and no one would have noticed.

I took the S-Bahn to Potsdam and then a bus to Babelsberg where Karin was waiting for me at the studio gate. The scenes she was to be part of were not scheduled to be filmed until the afternoon. But already she was in the costume of a Prussian princess that made her look more than ever like a porcelain doll.

"I want you to know something," I said as we walked toward the entrance of the big sound stage where crowds of hurrying technicians were woven into a moving pattern with actors wearing flamboyant costumes of a 19th century Prussian court. I whispered, "The Nazis guillotined three young people yesterday. Two teenage boys and one girl. They dragged them to the death chamber in Plötzensee prison and cut off their heads."

"How awful," she said with that confused little smile that was always somehow a reaction you never expected.

"Their crime was passing out pamphlets—information, the Nazis didn't like."

"Oh," she said.

I looked around to make sure no one was listening to us. "And the BBC is broadcasting our gossip."

"Well that's wonderful then, isn't it?"

"Herr Langen and I think you have to be very careful. If this Goebbels' thing continues."

"The *thing*?" she almost spat out the words. "Well you can see for yourself. He's here."

"Did you hear me? We all need to be careful."

"The slut Baarova is stealing my roles," she said as if the logic was overwhelmingly obvious.

Before I could respond she was motioning toward something behind me. Parked beside the sound stage was one of those big cars, probably a Horch, that could only have been owned by one of the top Nazis or some rich industrialist. A driver twice my size stood beside it.

"Goebbels. That's his car," she whispered when I caught up to her.

The thought of being seen by Goebbels momentarily immobilized me. There were two choices: I could either take the safest route and leave, which would mean there would be no chance of being recognized by Josef Goebbels. Or I could take the risk and stay to watch a minor moment of history: The Nazi Minister and his mistress.

I decided to stay—but only after Karin had gotten me enrolled as an extra, one of about a hundred women, unrecognizable, in heavy makeup, wigs and ball gowns. We were filling out the background while the camera concentrated on Lida Baarova and Willy Fritsch, the stars as they walked through the film set of a Prussian castle.

For some reason I had thought Lida Baarova would be more beautiful than she was. I had expected a woman so magnetically striking in person that she left an imprint on the air around her. Instead, I found myself watching an attractive, dark-haired woman with a flawless complexion surrounded by a bustling entourage of fawning people who became the main reason you knew she was a star. With all the notoriety swarming around her, I had thought she would be grandly luminescent in a world of greyness.

Instead she was... thinking of a word here: merely *pleasant*.

Even though I had never seen a film being made, I knew this one was different from anything that came before. It had to be. With two stars, as famous as any we knew of, two mortals who, once the cameras were rolling actually did acquire that luminescence that no earthly being should possess. Only when the cameras were rolling did it become a kind of light that routinely outshone all those around them.

But this was different. What other film had ever had a Nazi in full uniform sitting beside the camera? The light of the stars was overshadowed by what came from beside the cameras, not in front of them. As Josef Goebbels sat in a folding chair as still as a sphinx none of the hundreds of people in that studio could take their eyes off him.

His presence changed everything. On a film set, which is as hierarchical as a royal court, here was the Director, usually lord and master of everything, looking nervously for approval from a man who—in theory of course, could have him shot.

But it was more than that. Goebbels was a physical paradox, a physically twisted man, swaddled and camouflaged these days by expensive tailoring yet still possessing what those movie stars craved: a visually magnetic presence. It was partly the strangeness of his face which when seen in person was even more tightly stretched over whatever lay below. And with his sunken features receding swiftly in opposite directions from his nose, interrupted in their flight only by the two bulges of his eyes that were like those of a frog, flickering at whatever they made their target.

Whenever Lida Baarova uttered her lines while playing the role of Princess Eliza, Goebbels' thin face would be stretched even more by his rictus smile and a nod of hopelessly smitten approval.

Beside him the director would nervously smile and nod in unison.

But what amazed me most was that no one could see what I saw: An even brighter star burning in the darkness, out beyond the lights. Burning brighter than either of the film's two stars, Fritsch and Baarova, as they acted in the lights. Or even Goebbels sitting in imperial supremacy.

It was Karin. She had a silent and combustible fury that gave her the magnetic qualities there. In that mass of hundreds of people, she was the one you'd notice most. But all her luminescence went unseen, shrouded. And like the real and distant stars I had read about, she was consuming her own existence leaving only ashes.

An hour later, she and I stood among the milling throng of actors, extras and technicians outside the sound stage. I could not change or even lessen what we had feared at *Mutters*. Karin was immovable in her rage. "That slut needs to be brought down into the slime which she came from," she said too loudly.

She was watching Lida Baarova step elegantly into the back of the Horch followed by Goebbels. I couldn't hear the rest of Karin's words as the big car drove away, scattering the throngs who jumped out its way.

Later in her dressing room she stared into the mirror. "That role was mine," she seethed. "You saw her. Baarova's a cow." I was sitting beside her, removing the stage makeup that had granted me an hour of anonymity. I had to whisper because others passed by the opened door.

"This is not the time to be reckless." I said.

"Reckless? Didn't you see how public he has become now?

"Fine. We need more gossip. But we worry. I'm concerned that stories could be traced back to you."

"Oh come on. Every doorman and chauffeur has a story to tell about Goebbels." She stared into the mirror with a look that could crack it and then got up. "You don't understand do you? You can't."

"What don't I understand?"

"That woman is stealing my salvation."

"I didn't know that you've needed salvation."

"Well then you weren't paying attention," she said, her tone hardening. She was standing behind me and we were looking at one another in the mirror I was using to take off the stage makeup. "You never were. You were always too busy being the smart one."

"That's unfair."

"Not really. You have no idea why I desperately needed to be an actress?"

"You're right. I don't"

"To save myself. I am an actress because of father's thing."

"Father's….?"

"*Thing*! I've told you! That day at the nude beach where father took off his clothes? Afterwards? What happened. Did you ever think to ask what he did? To *me!* A little girl. In his library. And he undressed me first. Then took off his own clothes. And then first he made me hold *it*. His *thing*!

"And do you know what saved me? At that instant, I became an actress. Suddenly I was Joan of Arc; I was Florence Nightingale; I was the Queen of Sheba; I was Cleopatra. I was all of them but most importantly *I wasn't me*. If I was an actress then none of what was happening was real. And *that* is what protected me. Saved me. And that whore Baarova, she should never have stolen my protection. I'll bring her down. Just watch."

"Oh Karin…."

"Spare me" She was staring at me as if I didn't exist. "Now do you want to know the latest gossip about Magda or not? It's the best yet."

Back at *Mutter's* I told them. It was agreed that with this new information, it was now like playing a children's game with a hand grenade.

What Karin had told me about Magda deciding to have a secret affair with her husband's assistant made Herr Langen and I wonder how to handle such a dangerous piece of information.

But Mutter was focused on other parts of the news. "*Him*? She chose a dickless wonder like him as her lover? Hanke? The most boring Nazi of them all?"

"And Goebbels' trusted assistant," said Herr Langen. "*Et tu Brute*?"

"If you're trying to impress me with that Italian it's not working," said *Mutter.*

"There's more," I said. "Hanke has the records of the women Goebbels has had them buy gifts for. He gave these records to Magda who is taking them to Hitler and is going ask his permission for a divorce from Goebbels."

"Wow," said *Mutter.*

"*Wow* is not a word I usually use," said Herr Langen. "So forgive me if I also say '*Wow*'".

"We have enough *mundfunk* to fill every empty mind from here to Munich," *Mutter* said dribbling wine all over her housecoat.

"Which is precisely why this is so dangerous." Herr Langen said. "Because those are the same empty minds the Nazis are trying to fill. They cannot stand competition. They will come after us. In one way or another."

What is now known:

Adolf Hitler is in the early stages of carving up Europe—first sending Nazi troops into Austria, then taking over a part of Czechoslovakia; then preparing to attack Poland, and soon after, France. All being done while he sets up a killing machine for Jews across an entire continent. Then he plunges the world into the bloodiest war it will have ever seen.

And what takes him away from all this? What disrupts his schedule of crisis meetings with his own generals and cringing foreign diplomats?

Magda.

Which is why gossip in Nazi Germany suddenly becomes even more dangerous than it has ever been before.

Magda, the scorned, the angry, the discarded woman. Careening into an affair with her husband's assistant that any Berlin psychoanalyst left prac-

ticing (being mostly Jews there are so few of them now)—would have recognized as needing several years of therapy.

It is Hitler who is pulled away from plans to conquer Europe and thrown into the middle of this lacerating marriage of Magda and Josef Goebbels, the marriage that is now becoming the scandal of the Third Reich. It is Hitler who finds himself counseling and consoling Magda.

The irony of it all: Magda—whom Hitler had loved.

Hitler? In love?

Is this not the title for a Broadway farce? A Hollywood comedy? A vaudeville skit by the enemy British?

Hitler in love? But yes, it is correct. Sort of:.

Historians in the decades ahead will come to understand what only a few know now: that Hitler has some deep and bizarre attraction to Magda Goebbels. Or at least as much of an attraction as he is capable of.

And not only historians. No less an authority than Josef Goebbels himself has fretted in his meticulous diaries about Hitler's attraction to his wife. In some cases it becomes a kind of flirting that no one has ever before seen or imagined coming from Hitler.

Seven years earlier, before he marries Magda, Josef Goebbels reveals to the sanctity of his diary: "…Magda is not acting properly with the boss. It's making me suffer a lot. She's not being a lady. Last night I couldn't sleep at all. I have to do something about this. I am no longer sure of how faithful she is."

The boss?

To the rest of the world he is the Führer, the demigod of the German Reich; the devil incarnate. But to Josef Goebbels, Hitler is "the boss." And in the years before Goebbels and Magda are even engaged, the boss has a habit of wanting to spend time alone with Magda, so much so that Goebbels insists to his diary that "…Magda will have to invite the boss around and explain to him that we are getting married. Otherwise such things as love and stupid jealousy will divide us."

Just over a year before the Nazis take over Germany, Goebbels steels himself and breaks the news to the boss: He and Magda will be married soon. It is a huge risk. After all, Hitler will lose the endless access he has to Magda. For lesser slights and irritations the boss has had people executed. But something rather touching happens (things here are relative of course): The boss is pleased. Almost relieved. How can this be?

Legions of German and Austrian psychoanalysts—most of course, then struggling for survival in Hitler's concentration camps, would know. Under normal circumstances they would be invoking Freud and subjecting Hitler and his strange sense of relief that Magda was marrying, to psychoanalysis, Which would have stripped Hitler down to the husk of his barren nonexistent sexuality caused by...

But that is not important. Not as the wedding approaches.

All that matters is that the boss *is pleased, so pleased that he acts as Best Man at the wedding of Magda and Josef Goebbels.*

It is a joyous affair. Mainly because Hitler sees the marriage as the way that he will always have Magda close to him. With her new husband slavishly loyal and subservient to him, Hitler will be with Magda whenever he wants to see her.

They all get something out of it, this threesome of a kind. Goebbels gets unparalleled access to Hitler, the kind that Himmler, Heydrich, Göring and the rest of the coldest-eyed Nazis can only dream of. Magda gets the kind of prestige she could never have imagined; being at Hitler's side on major social occasions when he needed the illusion that Germany had a First Lady. And Hitler gets a home and hearth whenever he wants it, dropping in on the Goebbels—often unannounced, and having dinner and playing with the children.

And talking to Magda. Endlessly.

But now, years later, during this terrible time of rumours and gossip, when Goebbels shows up for an event in Bavaria without Magda, Hitler is so infuriated by her absence that he sends a plane back to Berlin to bring her into his presence that same day.

And so things go on as usual until Hitler is confronted by this...

...this gossip!

Gossip is actually fouling up the smooth workings of the mighty Reich, creating the stench of scandal, all of it around Goebbels this serial fornicator, this Goat of Babelsberg and some film actress, not even a German actress either.

As Magda's hysterical reactions threatened to blow the carefully created and brutal majesty of the Nazi regime Hitler has meticulously created.

Even now Hitler hears that foreign radio and newspapers are making jokes about it all. And with his regime held up to mockery? On the BBC of all places!

When he is crushing nations? And now this, all this! *that he has to put up with?*

It will not stand!—especially after Hitler is told of the full scale of Goebbels' debauchery: the endless stream of women; the young actresses being cast in movies in exchange for sex; the love letters to Baarova; the cheating on Magda even on the same day their last child was born.

Hitler listens, seething, and yells, "The whole world will be laughing at us."

Hitler slams his fist onto a table and screams that Goebbels is a liar and a degenerate who shames the fatherland. Bringing scandal and gossip down on us, this endless, vile gossip.

It must stop.

It will *stop.*

36

THE NEWS COULD NOT HAVE shot through Berlin faster if we had taken a truck with a loudspeaker and driven the length of the city blaring out the news.

It should have been our greatest *mundfunk*. And in so many ways it was.

But *Mutter* had a different way of looking at it, an uneasiness that we hadn't seen before. "After the life I've lived, good news is just the icing on shit." To her way of thinking, a sudden big success was far scarier than a series of minor defeats. Big success attracted attention. And the one thing *Mutter* never wanted was attention.

People who attracted attention also attracted the Gestapo.

She began to be more cautious than usual. She decided that too many men entering her building would be a problem. She now insisted that her whores' customers enter and leave through back doors that opened up onto an alley. And when one of the men, a lawyer from Zehlendorf arrived at the front door dressed in a suit and tie, she told him that either he show up at the back door looking more like the local people or he could find another brothel.

The lawyer from Zehlendorf. who had become infatuated, maybe obsessed, with the whore from Cologne, began parking his car several blocks away and changing into a workers' coat. Still, *Mutter* yelled at him: "And you show up in those shoes? Patent leather? Shoes that only a Nollendorf dandy would wear? *Out!*"

The next day he showed up looking as if he'd crawled out of a sewer. "Finally," said *Mutter* approvingly, allowing him to hurry through the back door. And then adding, "Truly a tribute to the power and the glory of what is between the legs."

Mutter was not the only one who had changed. Herr Langen came into the kitchen while *Mutter* was cutting up mysterious ingredients that would soon become part of the soup she was making. Several times he almost said something but then retreated into his room, came out, and began the tentative process all over again.

"Verbal constipation," *Mutter* whispered when he disappeared again. "You see it all the time among the educated classes. They think too much." She was making another huge pot of soup, flavouring it occasionally with ash from the cigarette hanging precariously from the downturned corner of her mouth. She wiped up the overflow with a dirty cloth and after looking for a place to deposit it she went through what was now almost a ritual, flinging it against the grease-laden wall where it joined similar fabric carcasses, embedded in its death throes.

"I'm an artist," she said admiring the vertical mess. "I'm thinking about sawing the wall down and then taking it to one of those fancy art galleries. I'll be famous. And rich."

I wasn't sure if she was kidding. With *Mutter* you never knew for sure. But before I could say anything the phone rang and she answered it, her face, becoming a kaleidoscope of frowns and astonishment until she hung up. "Karin," she said. "You won't believe this,"

The next day Karin came back to *Mutter's*. Underneath a long, drab overcoat she was dressed stylishly in late autumn clothes with new boots that went almost halfway up to her knees. "Someone has been shopping at Ka De W*e*," said *Mutter* standing over the stove, inspecting the soup which was almost gone from the big pot.

"A celebration," said Karin twirling in a girlish exuberance I had never seen from her before. Everything about her was quicker, louder and more intense. "You understood the code, right?" she asked as if an answer was unnecessary.

The code as she called it was her phone call to *Mutter* last night from Babelsberg telling her that "That bird with all the feathers is in a cage and being taken to the east." It meant that Lida Baarova was being deported back to Czechoslovakia. Then she went on to say, "The bird was chased away by the big wolf," which meant that Hitler himself had taken charge and was deporting Goebbels' mistress because he was fed up with all the scandal and gossip at a time when he had nations to conquer.

But now, listening to Karin chattering excitedly, I just prayed that no Gestapo had wiretapped the Babelsberg studio phones. Because if they couldn't figure out that code of Karin's, then they had to be dumber than

Doof. Karin's vengeful glee would have splattered incriminating indiscretions all over the phone call.

"Finally people will know the truth about that woman," she said with the same seething glee that crackled through everything she said. "Just let her try to steal another role from people now!"

"*That's* what this is all about?" Mutter asked. "One actress wiping out another?"

For a moment Karin looked defensive, as if she couldn't quite decide how to respond. "Well?" she said sounding both aggressive and defensive at the same time. "You have to stand for something you know."

The next day as *Mutter* was on the phone fishing for reports of the previous piece of gossip, Herr Langen again emerged out of the shadows, looking distracted and somehow not himself. He was holding a small pile of newspapers and looking as if he was walking through someone else's experience. I made an '*Are you okay*?' gesture that he did not acknowledge.

Mutter hung up the phone. "All of Charlottenburg is talking about how Magda went to see Hitler. They're surprised she needs his permission to get a divorce. Imagine that." She was still chuckling until she saw the look on Herr Langen's face.

"What?" she said, switching to a frown.

"We have been fools. Total fools." His vehemence smothered the mood instantly.

"Is this just a bad day you're having?" *Mutter* asked.

"We have gotten people killed."

Mutter rose up, propelled between curiosity and indignation. "I am really hoping, you are not just making some stupid thinking-person joke."

"A joke?" He threw down onto the table the other newspapers he had been holding. There were two copies of *Der Angriff* and the *Völkische Beobachter.*

"Nazi filth," said *Mutter*

"Read them," he said.

"Why? They're toilet paper after it's been used."

"Read them. To find out how reckless we have been."

Our confused silence congealed for a moment until I could say, "Why are you saying this?"

"Because every time we make gossip, Jews die a few days later."

Mutter looked at me, as confused as I was.

"What on earth are you talking about?"

"Look at these Nazi rags." he said "Goebbels' newspapers. Every time he was humiliated by our gossip, he took his anger out on someone else. So Jews died." He pointed to one of the newspapers. "This is from two days after we sent out that story about Baarova's husband punching Goebbels."

The copy of *Der Angriff* he held out had huge headlines screaming:

The Need For A Jew-Free Berlin!

"And the next day's edition was filled with stories about rounding up Jews across the city." He threw down another paper. *Völkische Beobachter*, also Goebbels'. "This is from three days after we sent out the gossip about Goebbels' female assistants being caught by Magda crawling out of his guest house at midnight."

On the front page of *Völkische Beobachter* was a column with the byline:

By Reich Minister Dr. Goebbels.
The Jews Are To Blame.

"And on that same day, Goebbels sent the SA out to arrest Jewish store owners on the Ku'damm. None of them have been heard from since. "

Herr Langen was about to reach for another newspaper from the pile he had brought. *Mutter* stopped him. "Enough!" She threw the *Völkische Beobachter* into the fire. "We have been doing good."

"Good in the wrong place is evil's handmaiden" he said

"What makes you so sure all this couldn't be a coincidence? And happen anyway? Without us." *Mutter* threw another *Völkische Beobachter* into the fire.

"I have other *'coincidences'* if you want them. Like when we put our gossip about Goebbels wanting a threesome with Baarova and Magda? And what happens the next Monday? A hundred Jews are dragged off the streets and sent to the camps."

Mutter fell silent.

"We concoct gossip that sends Goebbels into a murderous frenzy against the innocent. There is a terrible link here." It was his turn to feed the fire. He rolled up *Der Angriff* and threw it into the woodstove flames. We looked at the words on those front pages again as they burned.

"So what do we do?" said *Mutter* in a very quiet voice.

"Do you need to ask?"

"Unfortunately yes," said *Mutter.* "Because I haven't heard you tell me that if we stop *mundfunk* totally, the attacks on Jews will stop."

"We at least have to try."

Mutter thought about it and then nodded. "*Jah*. Okay."

We sat around watching the flames devour the last of the Nazi newspapers.

"There's one problem," I said. "We've already sent out the latest gossip—what Karin told us yesterday about Hitler throwing Goebbels' actress, that Barrova woman, out of the country"

"Oh my goodness," said *Mutter* as if she remembered something. "Yes. The whore from Cologne. I just told her that gossip."

As Herr Langen threw another copy of *Der Angriff* into the fire, he said "Stop her,"

I was designated to go downstairs to the other wing of *Mutter's* building and talk to the whore from Cologne. In our little community she was renowned for being bad tempered in the mornings. Even from one floor above, we could hear her yelling at anyone who disturbed her before ten o'clock or sometimes even after that.

Ever since she had accused me of trying to steal her clothing, I had not said more than a few words at a time to her. And sometimes when we passed in the long dingy corridor, she would not even look at me or even say hello. So when I knocked softly on her door and it opened a little, I was prepared for the angry round face that peered out. Not having painted on her eyebrows yet, her face looked even rounder than usual.

"Hah!" she almost snarled. "Checking to see if I was away? To steal my clothes again?"

I held up a scarf I had once been given by the Italian embassy when they were hoping for favourable coverage in my *Vossiche Zeitung* column. It was a beautiful silk scarf with pale blue and green shades entwined and flowing the length of it. "Here."

She looked confused. "What is this? Some kind of trick? Is that it?"

"It's for you."

"*What*?"

I held it out closer to her. For a moment I remembered a dog our neighbors once had. It was beaten so regularly that when you reached out to pet it, it almost shook itself into a nervous collapse not knowing whether to cringe, bite or roll over to have its stomach scratched. "It's for you," I said again.

Her startled expression was frozen for a moment. "Why?" She feathered the word out as if it was airless.

"Why not?"

"What do you want me to give you in return?"

"Nothing."

"Nothing?" she said suspiciously.

I nodded.

"Look—I don't have anything to give you. Okay?"

"I know." I held the scarf even closer to her. "I'm not here to take anything from you."

"I don't understand" she said in a little girl's voice.

"I don't want to be your enemy. So I want this to be yours."

Looking confused, she took the scarf from me, caressing it lovingly as she stood teetering back and forth ever so slightly as if she was bracing herself in a strong wind. Then she burst into tears and opened the door as wide as it could go.

For several minutes I sat in the only chair in her room and watched her seduce the mirror. She tried what seemed like a dozen different ways of wearing the scarf. And with each one I could sense the compliments that only she could hear.

"Can I ask you one favour?" she said throwing the scarf over her shoulder. "Don't call me *The Whore from Cologne*. I'm not just some asphalt flower you know," she said using a term for prostitute I hadn't heard in a long time. "It's as if I have no name."

"I was going to ask your name."

"I never tell anyone."

"Then how do I know what to call you?"

"Make up a name for me." When she saw I didn't understand she said, "If you came from a good family like I do, you wouldn't want anyone to know your name. My family back in Cologne would be appalled to find out what I do. So make up a name for me."

I thought for a while and said, "How about Ursula?"

"Ursula!" She clapped her hands together. "I like being Ursula!"

"But I don't understand something. If you come from a good home, why are you doing this?"

"Because I like being desired." She found yet another way to tie the scarf. "I wasn't desired very much," she said looking at me as if it was the most obvious response imaginable. "Don't you want to be desired?"

Why was I feel so uncomfortable by such a simple question? I could feel myself getting red in the face. "Yes, of course I do," I said quickly. Too quickly.

And thought about the question and my answer to it for days afterward.

An alarm clock rang. "Oh I'm sorry," she said shutting it off. "I always set the alarm for an hour before my first client arrives. I need to prepare. I'm not some common streetwalker you know. "

I got up to leave and when I was at the door, I said, "Oh one other thing—we're starting to think you shouldn't say anything to your clients about what *Mutter* told you last night."

She looked confused. "But this is the best gossip of all. Baarova being thrown out of Germany. And by Hitler himself!"

"It's possible that bad things might happen if anyone knew about it."

"What bad things?"

For an instant I realized how unprepared I was for such a question. Suddenly reason and logic seemed completely wrong. Without a conscious thought I just blurted out, "I went to a fortune teller last night. And was told that bad things would happen to anyone who talked about all that."

"Oh," she said, puzzled. "A fortune teller? Really?"

"Really."

She thought for a moment as she was painting on her large, sharply curving eyebrows. "Then I guess it's our secret isn't it?"

Karin's returned later that night, needing no words to signal what was coming. Merely her sense of indignation and the way she glared at us, holding her palms out in a *What?* motion made words almost unnecessary.

"Girl, sit down," said *Mutter*. Each of her own words made the cigarette wedged into the corner of her mouth jump up and down like a tiny baton. When she wanted to be, *Mutter* could be one of the few people Karin would not argue with. Her tone of voice could come at you like a truncheon doing its work.

"I've haven't heard any talk on the street about Baarova—"

"Sit!" snapped *Mutter*. Karin turned suddenly obedient and sat down. "Now then. Your sister has something to tell you."

I had neither expected nor wanted to be the one to tell Karin what we had decided. I looked from *Mutter* to Karin and back again. One glared at me; the other just kept staring into the soup she was stirring.

"Tell me what?"

The only sound came from the wooden spoon hitting the sides of the big metal pot as it stirred the remains of the soup.

"*What?*"

"We need you to understand," I said, not wanting to say anything at all.

"What is there to understand?"

"We are not going ahead with sending out this latest gossip."

"This is a joke, right?"

The wooden spoon kept breaking the silence, clanking against the pot.

"You're teasing me, right?"

"No. We're not. We had to tell the whore from Cologne—Ursula, that—"

"Tell her *what*?" Karin's face was turning red.

"—that she should not tell the gossip to any of her clients."

"I risk my neck for this? The juiciest gossip anyone has ever heard. It's history even. With that role-stealing Czechoslovakian slut finally getting what she deserves?"

"We have had to evaluate everything."

"Evaluate what? Hitler himself is in the middle of this." she interrupted furiously. "*Hitler*? Playing marriage counselor to the Goebbels after Magda went crying to him? And he ends up kicking Goebbels in his skinny Nazi behind and orders the SS thugs to grab his slut Baarova and throw her out of Germany? Name me one other *mundfunk* we've ever done that is anything close to that!"

"We believe people are being hurt by what we're doing. We need you to think it through," said Herr Langen finally speaking up.

"No *we* do not need to think anything though." Karin stood up spinning in her fury from *Mutter* to me. "I finally get to watch that bitch Baarova find out what happens when the whole world sees her for what she is." And then she stormed along the corridor and down the stairs.

After a while *Mutter* said, "The soup is best when it's been left on the heat for a while. Like most things."

Not long after the soup was finished, *Mutter* made a puzzled motion, nodding toward the corridor behind me and whispered, "The whore from Cologne." I turned to see Ursula standing in front of the one tiny mirror *Mutter* had hung in the hallway. She was adjusting the scarf I had given her and when she saw us watching she called out, "I think it looks best with a big fluffy knot off to the side, don't you?"

"I never see you on this floor," *Mutter* said.

"I am doing things differently this morning."

"Obviously. Isn't Wednesday the day for your priest?" Mutter said turning to me. "Her best client."

"The chatterbox," Ursula laughed. "The one who loves to talk and talk. I call him the holy telegraph. Everything I tell him goes all over the city."

"Father *Mundfuck*," whispered *Mutter* laughing at her own little joke.

"He lives for gossip. And sex. He hates it when he gets a funeral on Wednesdays—that's our day here. To make up for it he sits alone in the confession box at night and does things to himself. He suffers when he misses his Wednesdays"

"So, then...?" I didn't quite understand. "...Does he have a funeral today?"

"Oh no," Ursula said cheerfully.

"Then why aren't you down there with him?"

"Oh he's with..." She thought for a moment and giggled. "...my assistant."

"Whores have an assistant now?" said *Mutter*.

"Just for today." She giggled again and then looked at me as if I should know what she was talking about. "You know."

"What do I know?"

"Your sister."

I stood there, those two words disintegrating in my jumbled thoughts Then I ran.

I ran all the way to the stairs. Then I clattered down them, swinging around the banister knob where the steps reversed direction and then blasted out into the darkened corridor where the other women had their rooms. Way down at the far end, a shaft of light spilled into the corridor.

Caught in the brightness of that light, something moved. It was a tiny child, a boy, his back to me peering around the edge of the open door. He turned when he heard me, a flurry of blonde hair catching the light.

"Max? Sweetie? What are you doing here?"

He looked around confused as if he was going to cry. "Mama?" he said.

I looked into the whore from Cologne's—Ursula's, room and what I saw wrenched all understanding from the image before me. Except for the nun's headdress, Karin was totally nude, tied to the bed and gagged so she couldn't talk. The headdress was a great white contraption that billowed out at each side as if her head had sprouted huge wings.

I swooped Max up into my arms and ran with him as fast as I could, back up to *Mutter's* floor. As I ran, I yelled and yelled. For Inga, for *Mutter*, for anybody to help me with Max, but no one could hear me over his wailing.

Leaving Max with Mutter, I ran back downstairs. "I was Sister Agnes," she gasped laughingly when I took the gag out of her mouth. "He kept calling me Sister Agnes. While he was on top of me. And then he got upset afterward when I wouldn't pray with him asking for forgiveness. I told him we didn't need forgiveness."

Sharp little footsteps sounded outside the room and Ursula hurried in as I was untying Karin's wrists from the bedposts. "Oh no! Not the Sister Agnes routine," Ursula said, "Dear me, I totally forgot it was the first week of November. Right after All Souls Day. Right after all the big holy days is when my priest always wants sex with Sister Agnes."

"I sort of liked being Sister Agnes," said Karin.

As she looked up at me while the final knot came untied, freeing her from the bedpost, I said. "Can I ask you something? Aren't you embarrassed? Even a little?"

"Why?" she said with the innocence of a kitten.

Ursula grabbed the white wings from Karin's head. "He's made me keep this nun's headdress in the cupboard for over a year. He gets upset if it's not properly cared for."

"He loved hearing all the gossip about Goebbels and that slut of his being kicked out of the country by Hitler," Karin said.

"Oh god no! Karin you didn't," I yelled.

"What exactly is the problem?" she said with that mixture of defiance and triumph she sometimes showed.

"How could you?"

"*What*?" She looked at me perplexed. "Do you think a priest should have sex with me for nothing? I'm not that kind of woman."

"*Not that!*"

"What then?" She was walking around nakedly as if everything was normal."

"The gossip! You told him the gossip!"

"And all of Berlin will know about it by tonight," she said, pleased.

"I told you, we don't want that! Not now."

"Why are you being so nasty? Baarova deserved this."

"Lives are at risk."

"Oh don't be silly. Has anyone seen my clothes?"

37

WE WILL NEVER KNOW.

We had no way of knowing for sure how much our gossip added to what happened that week. And to Goebbels murderous furies. The first sign was two days later when we heard noises out on the street. Something was being broken.

The Night Of Broken Glass had begun.

In the next two days, most of Berlin's synagogues were either set ablaze or vandalized; Nazi mobs destroyed and looted every Jewish store they could find; nearly a hundred Jews were murdered on the streets, and twelve thousand Jews were arrested and sent to concentration camps. And for all the resulting damage and broken glass strewn everywhere across the streets, the Jews of Berlin were given the bill and told to pay a billion Reich marks.

But first:

Josef Goebbels is lonely.

Not only that, he is sad—"increasingly melancholy," as he laments in his diary. More accurately, he is almost crazed. The great love of his life, Lida Baarova, has just been wrenched away from him by Adolf Hitler who sends his personal adjutant to her house with orders that she must never contact Goebbels again and is to leave Germany immediately. SS guards surround her just to make the point absolutely clear.

Baarova's reaction is hysterical, flailing in rage, longing and fear, not knowing where to turn. Or who to turn to. So extreme is her anguish that she disregards the warning and tries to reach Josef on the phone. But Herr Reich Minister is "out of town" and "on official business". Baarova has what looks like a heart attack. So severe is her reaction that when Hitler hears about it, he dispatches his personal doctor. Having Goebbels' lover die on them like this would be ridiculously inconvenient and needlessly messy.

Goebbels is just as devastated, He longs to contact Baarova but he cannot. To disobey Hitler—even once, would leave his life, his career and any chance of a family life, in ruins. And he understands the odds as they all do, the odds of physical survival after disobeying Hitler.

The odds are close to zero.

"Life is hard and cruel," Goebbels tells his diary. He quickly becomes vastly diminished from the searing and feared presence he has been for years. He rambles around in search of people he can talk to with his indiscreet stories of longing and woe. He begins pouring out personal details to other powerful Nazis, some who are not friendly to him. Others like Goring listen patiently and try to console him.

But he is inconsolable. He sits alone in his private screening room watching A Prussian Love Story and crumbles inside at the sight of his beloved up there on the big screen, aching, longing to talk to her, to be with her, to....

He goes to bed—alone and with a fever. He drinks too much just to be able to sleep and his mood swings become more noticeable. His stomach pains are so bad that he is convinced he has a tumor and is about to die. A famed surgeon is called in to operate.

But operate on what? Nothing can be found. Nothing except for "serious nervous disorders".

Even worse, he has to face Magda's cold, pitiless fury. For now it is Magda who holds what might be called the whip hand. And Hitler is on her side. Always. Because what Josef Goebbels has never figured out in all his fornicating rampages of infidelity was that Hitler would be the one who was faithful—to Magda.

Adolf Hitler is not willing to abandon the only female companionship he now has in his shriveled existence with women. Nothing in the past seven years has diminished Hitler's need for the kind of female companionship that Magda has so often provided.

So Hitler allows Magda to draw up a contract, an actual written document that treats the feared Minister of Public Enlightenment and Propaganda like an errant child. He is given strict rules about his conduct, when he may have contact with his own children, when he may show up at their home and how he must get Magda's explicit approval to be in her presence. The rules go on and on.

Magda's rules.

And it is pointed out to him where he must sign. Right above the signatures of Magda—and Hitler.

At the end of October it is his birthday, his forty-first. Usually it is an occasion when he is showered with presents and affection. Magda has always made it such a celebration. And in recent years even Hitler, normally remote and calculating, had shed the traces of his awkward rectitude and showers Goebbels with birthday wishes.

But not this birthday. It yields only the iciest of acknowledgements from Magda and a stiff, cold telegram from Hitler. Goebbels records the day in his diary as "no doubt the emptiest and saddest birthday of my life".

But more than sad, it is dangerous. Goebbels is aware that the telegram from Hitler is just one more sign that he has fallen out of the favour he so desperately craves. After all the years of playing to Hitler's every whim and being the one that the Führer most relied upon—and now this? This purgatory? This distance? This coldness?

As Himmler, Heydrich, Göring, Bormann and all the other Nazis were jostling for power and taking his place in Hitler's esteem.

Goebbels is sure he has a tumor growing somewhere. He just has to be dying no matter what the idiotic doctors say about nerves. He is desperate and alone. And then suddenly, the answer appears. Not merely the answer but the cure!

Why, of course:

The Jews.

The Night Of Broken Glass—or Kristallnacht as it became infamously known. On the day before it begins, Goebbels is still reeling, distraught and alone as he leaves for Munich to attend the kind of mandatory celebration that he now tries to avoid, a raucous tribute to the earliest Nazis who tried to seize power fifteen years ago in an uprising in a beer hall.

But then as Goebbels is preparing to go to the ceremony in Munich something amazing happens. Something so far out of what is expected or even possible that it leaves everyone momentarily stunned.

A German diplomat is assassinated in Paris. For others, it is a tragedy, an outrage, a foul murder.

But Goebbels recognizes it as a momentous gift—because the assassin is a seventeen-year-old Jew. Goebbels is not religious but Mirabile dictu!—this surely must have been divinely inspired. Because what is one dead diplomat when you are given what you can mold into a sanctifiable case of martyr-

dom!—our poor dead hero!—whoever that dead diplomat was who perished at the hands of a Jew.

And so Josef Goebbels is there to start it all—and even better: he knows Hitler will be there to watch him in action.

So on this night—November 9, Goebbels ascends the podium in the Munich town hall and with the sheer force of his mesmerizing oratory he seizes on the pent up furies of the thousands of personal failures in those ordinary men he is speaking to, whipping resentment into a malleable and lacerating force that he can direct out into the streets as the old fighters stumble out with blood in their eyes and flames at their heels.

Soon Goebbels is hearing reports from other areas of Munich where Jews are being beaten in the streets by these old fighters; and of Jewish homes looted, and businesses destroyed.

With the skillful instincts he has honed as the Nazi most responsible for imagery and narrative, he hastily confers with Hitler—just like the days before all this Magda-Baarova mess! And the Führer actually makes time to listen to him. As he used to do. And agrees with Goebbels' strategy that all this flame fanning by Goebbels' men must be completely invisible. In the mind of international public opinion there can be no perception of arson by the Nazis. It must be... how to put it—spontaneous?

Or something like that.

And so with Hitler's blessings raining down on him, a grateful and relieved Goebbels sets out to create the most spontaneous Kristallnacht he can.

And what Goebbels creates becomes the bloody divide where no more illusions about Nazi intentions were possible. Until November 9, 1938, there were still many among the Jews of Germany, who believed the deadliest myths of all: That This Too Shall Pass, and, It Will All Go Away and "normal life" will prevail.

The cities explode. Jewish families are driven out of their homes which are then looted. Teenage boys and men are rounded up. Synagogues burn as firemen valiantly fight to stop the fires from spreading to surrounding non-Jewish properties. Policemen stand and watch as Jews are beaten or thrown out of windows; the sidewalks fill with so much broken glass that they become dangerous, and shops and businesses owned by Jews are stripped bare.

But Josef Goebbels again senses a certain divinity in it all. Because of that most profound of all conferred blessings: Redemption. For Hitler is pleased with him. Once again.

What else matters? Or so he tells himself sitting in isolation at his huge and secret home in the woods at Bogensee, remembering when Lida was there with him.

Indeed: what else matters?

David Buffum sees that absolutely nothing else matters to the raging Nazi hordes.

He is the American consul in Leipzig, He watches what is happening and he writes that what he sees has "no counterpart in the course of the civilized world."

On the two nights of Kristallnacht, he goes out onto the streets of the small city in eastern Germany to report on the same brutal events happening across the nation He records significant moments that the world needs to know about.

And of course, ignores.

Buffum notes that with Goebbels' words driving them, the rampaging Nazis forget that this is the land of ultimate civilization, the land of Beethoven and Brahms and Bach and Schumann and Handel and...

None of them matter now for culture is what is being played out in this brutal street opera as Nazis take up the hunt for the Jews who are—of course! the cause of all their problems.

Which is where Buffum makes an observation that will be forwarded to Washington and where it will be filed away in obscurity:

It is about the role of the so-called Ordinary Citizen.

He observes the Average Person, the Ordinary Citizens, the Civilian Population as they watch what is happening all around them: the beatings; the vandalism; the killings; the arson.

They watch.

And watch.

And do nothing. For two days the Ordinary Citizen continues to do nothing except watch. And who, in later years, will ask in varying degrees of indignation:

"What exactly could we have been expected to do?"

Herr Langen gripped the rooftop railing.

Below us, the street had exploded. Again. It was the second night of *Kristallnacht*. The Jewish butcher store had been smashed and stripped bare. Then while the police stood and watched, a junk dealer had his cart overturned and was beaten until he stopped moving. When they couldn't get even an upraised arm from him they went looking for others.

Dick and Doof acted as traffic wardens for the riot, guiding the Nazi hordes toward where a trove of Jews might be. Dick especially was florid in his actions, swinging his arms around, pointing to various homes as men, women and children were driven out onto the streets and the wooden clubs that awaited them.

"I am a coward," Herr Langen said.

Mutter had just arrived, out of breath and agitated. "Don't be stupid."

"I should be there!" He was pointing down toward the street below.

"And do what exactly?" she wheezed. "Get your head bashed in? Do you have any idea what I just saw? I watched them smash Brünn's store to pieces, steal all the furniture—carrying it all right through the big, smashed windows and then beat up his whole family. His son is probably on a cattle car right now."

"I am doing nothing. I am just watching."

"We all are," said *Mutter*, gradually stepping backwards until I realized that what she was really doing was barring the entrance to the stairway door. With her feet apart she looked bigger than I ever remembered her. Herr Langen would never have made it past her.

But something on the street has drawn his attention. "Your sister," he said.

Even from the end of the block it was unmistakably Karin, almost stylish and solitary as she picked her way through the shattered glass and debris. She passed store after store, all of them disemboweled, their most private anatomy ravaged and made public. All around her, men with rifles and clubs were running in packs seeking prey. She stopped when she came to the ragged form of the junk dealer lying on the street. With one hand he made the slightest motion to her.

"What's that girl doing?" said *Mutter* who had returned to the railing.

"The old man isn't dead," said Herr Langen. "She's helping him."

Karin had knelt beside the junk dealer. She took off her white jacket to put under his head.

"This cannot end well," said Herr Langen.

From where we were, we watched Karin kneeling over the junk dealer as the swarm reformed, broke and then circled around her. A man stood over her. She looked up and seemed to be talking, pleading or arguing with him. The man leaned toward her, his hand pushing on her shoulder.

She swatted his hand away. He shoved her. She slapped his face and then knelt down on the street.

"Oh no," said *Mutter*.

The man stood over the junk dealer and fired several shots into him. Even from here we could see the blood that had splattered across Karin.

She would not let us wipe off the blood.

Staring out into the darkness and slowly rocking back and forth, she sat with the rest of us on the coarse surface of the rooftop. Finally Karin said, "The gossip had nothing to do with this. You know that."

We were silent.

"There was no reason for this to happen," she said.

Our silence went on until *Mutter* grunted. She was the only one of us sitting on a chair, an old wooden construct whose groans under her weight mingled with the distant cries in the night. "I keep telling you—reason has nothing to do with it," she said. "That old man—did he hurt anyone?"

As Karin spoke, I caught *Mutter's* look that silently shredded whatever she said.

"And they shot him."

Mutter drank slowly from a bottle. "Why are you surprised? When wolves hunt, they kill. What else do you need to know?"

"People are not wolves," Karin said. "People are meant to be good."

"Child, child, child," said *Mutter* rolling her eyes. She got up, groaning slightly when she rose and glared at Karin, weighing whether or not to explode in one of the tirades she was capable of.

Then she put on her coat and muttered, "We are missing some ingredients for the soup."

SIX

38

WE HAD ENDURED TWO YEARS of listening to Goebbels' triumphant broadcasts of conquest and quick military victories. And even those of us who hated the Nazis began to wonder if we had underestimated the ruthless genius of Hitler.

But then the triumphant broadcasts stopped. First there was the shocking defeat in Russia where a large part of Hitler's army froze, starved, died or surrendered at Stalingrad. And then came the bombing that now terrorizes us almost daily, with the shiny American planes, silver and beautiful and so high above as they rain death down on us with their bombs. At least at night when the British planes come, we can see nothing until the darkness explodes with phosphorus and death.

Now instead of the triumphant bombast coming at us through the radio like a battering ram, we often get the vague and angry calls to focus on the glory that surely lies in the better days ahead. Gradually we have sensed what is coming. Because after the debacle at Stalingrad, no one needed *mundfunk* to figure out that something was seriously wrong with what we were being told.

Especially when Goebbels took to his radio broadcast to announce that this crushing defeat in Russia showed that *"we are a trifle susceptible here and there on the periphery of some of our military campaigns."*

a trifle?... A large part of the German army wiped out? A million men killed? And so we are now '*a trifle susceptible*'? Even *mundfunk* could not compete with that.

But we had other concerns now, mostly involving mere survival.

Mutter had returned one day from her foray into butcher shops and bakeries with tales of Gestapo bursting into nearby apartments. Any remaining Jews, communists or others whose names were on lists had been dragged out of their homes.

Mutter told Herr Langen and me that survival would require us to do something we had never even imagined—become construction workers.

She had decided that several places needed to be covered by false walls that looked as they were real. Hiding places would be constructed within our rooms, corridors and even next to the kitchen—anything that could hide us in case the Gestapo barged in.

"I've never even held a hammer," I said.

"You won't be saying that a week from now," *Mutter* replied.

At first our efforts were pathetic. Herr Langen had as little experience in this as me. In the first week we accidentally destroyed precious wood and some of the tools we found in the deepest basement of her building. But over the terrible months of 1942 when the Nazis announced quotas for rounding up people they needed as kindling—really; they were hunting for people like us who would keep the ovens burning at Auschwitz, Sachsenhausen and Dachau. So we struggled and learned to build hidden compartments that the Gestapo would never find. Or so we hoped.

After those first weeks, occasionally covered in plaster dust and sometimes festooned in bandages, Herr Langen and I actually began to enjoy what we were doing. Not only the trial-and-error part of it but also a strange bond that was developing. Herr Langen's cloak of invincibility had long ago fallen away revealing a vulnerable man shielding his basic shyness. And what had been buried under an irascible exterior was a sense of humour that now so easily burst through when confronted by absurdity. Such as what often happened when he first tried to build something.

I had never seen him laugh before. Not like this. The kind of laughter that made him shake all over when he aimed for a nail and accidently hit the light switch, plunging the building into darkness. Or, discovering that he had inadvertently fastened a frame to the floor with the dozens of nails he had driven right through it. Gradually the mistakes decreased. The humour did not.

For two months we built false walls and hidden entrances that were at first anything but hidden or false. In a good way, building our walls and secret doors exhausted us. and slowly we became good at what we were doing. Herr Langen took pride in the smooth plaster surfaces he created, and I became a minor-key artist in delicately smearing those surfaces with traces of dirt and old paint to make them look as if they had stood there for a century.

There were many things about Herr Langen that were different now. But also there was an odd recklessness, even defiance as he walked the streets with purpose and counterfeit identity papers. And not once was he stopped by the Gestapo. In so many ways this recklessness freed him as he went on his journeys to Danziger's to get the letters from his wife. Merely the trek across Berlin gave him the sense that he would soon be with Emma again.

But when even Danziger's became too dangerous for him, he began receiving her letters at a coffeehouse in Moritzplatz and would return smiling, even before he opened the envelope. "My light, my beacon in the darkness," he said. I had never heard him talk like that before.

Several times while we were constructing these hiding places, Herr Langen would vanish for hours at time and then return with a letter. For the last few months every time he returned with one of Emma's letters, it had sent him into hours, sometimes days of silence. And not once would he ever say why.

One day he emerged from his room in an even more somber mood than usual. I decided it was time to ask what was wrong. He acted as if he had not heard me. Hours later, after we had finished hoisting several heavy pieces of wood to support the back of one of our walls, we sat on the floor, breathless and covered in sawdust.

"I never talk about personal matters," he said. "Forgive me but maybe it was how I was raised. And why I was never a natural for all that gossip business. Or things that are best left secret."

I waited.

"You know there has been trouble in France."

I knew the French had been rounding up Jews as fiercely as their Nazi masters. "Is Emma safe?"

It took him a long time to answer. "Yes." He said the word twice. And then after a pause, he said it again.

"And?"

"She had to flee. The French were rounding up all the Jews in Paris and putting them into a bicycle-racing stadium before they had enough trains to transport them to Auschwitz. But she escaped."

"That's a good thing."

"A very good thing." But he didn't say it like it was a good thing. "You see she had a friend in this French underground organization, *Amelot* it is called. He saved her. Got her away from the platform where the trains were coming to take them." Herr Langen got up and brushed off the saw-dust. "May I ask you for a very personal favour?"

"Of course."

He got up and went to his room, returning with several letters that he handed to me.

"Read them. Please. And tell me if what I believe is correct."

"What do you believe?"

"That she still loves me."

My expression must have shown more than I wanted it to. Instantly the last shreds of his usual certainty left him. I had never seen him so uneasy, so vulnerable.

"I need a woman's opinion."

I held the letters with a kind of dread, as if I was about to become a voyeur, peeping through a window into the life of someone who had always been so intensely private. As if there was some mistake and he would come rushing back to grab them away from me.

I waited. And I finally I reached inside one of the envelopes.

I read the letters in fragments. At first rapidly, and then slowly. I was trying to absorb not merely the words but the feelings that flew from them in pain and love. No matter how I read them, they remained fragments in my mind:

> *Dear Paul ...things have changed quickly here...scarier...the French are doing here the same as what the people in power are doing where you are. ...they called it La Grande Rafle— the Big Roundup of all the Jews—I was one of thousands.... but I escaped...with help...great courage by a marvelous man... Explain in later letter...with eternal caring.*

The earliest of the letters he gave me were the easiest to read. Then came more difficult, more recent letters. About Eugene.

> *....I am in hiding now, maybe like you....Paris is no longer safe...but for now I am....An amazing organization...it is called Amelot....saving so many of us....Eugene, did I mention him before? ....he is one of Amelot's founders...all so brave...I am*

helping them from my hiding place....He has saved so many children...smuggled them to Switzerland...I think of you often...and wish you love.

And:

...Very short letter...Eugene needs my help organizing forged documents...I can only do much from my hiding place....but I feel a purpose I have never felt before....I am wishing you love and kisses...

And:

...Paul I am in terrible confusion...Of course I have loved you.... please, it is difficult all around...I am trying to help Eugene...I think you might even like him...

Then what had been flowing, churning unspoken from within the lines, overflowed some unseen bank of pain and remorse.

....Paul, of course I love you. I always will. But I am tormented by the terrible gap between "love" and "being in love" Can you understand? ...I am sorry. I am not being fair I know....... I am confused, terribly...You are a wonderful man... But I must be with Eugene. I love him as I had loved you...I pray for you...for both of us

And:

...Please. I beg you for your understanding even though I do not deserve it...Eugene was taken in last night...there is still a chance he will not be sent to one of the camps...I am consumed...

And:

> *…You deserve better…you are a wonderful man…Pray for me*
> *as I do for you…I will not be able to write again…*

I stared at the letters until late in the night, dreading having to give my thoughts, my verdict, to Herr Langen who I now saw as a man condemned. And then I hurried as silently and as quickly as I could to the kitchen.

Mutter stirred the soup with one hand and held whichever of Herr Langen's letters she was reading with the other.

"I shouldn't be showing you his letters," I said.

"You're right."

"But I wanted you to read them."

"Life is full of paradoxes."

"He wants me to tell him that what he already knows is not true," I said.

"*Aach*, he never really wanted your opinion, He knows. He doesn't need you telling him his beloved wife is in love with another man. He gave you these letters because the pain is unendurable. He just needs someone else to know. Someone he can talk to."

"He is a very private person."

"Private people have their own kind of hell," *Mutter* said. "I was married to one once. When they become un-private, they are in trouble."

She stirred in aimless circles as she read the letters, occasionally grunting and mumbling things I couldn't understand. Only when she gave me back all the letters could I understand:

"Who knew our Herr Langen was 'Paul'? I had him figured out as a Joachim or a Roland."

She reached up to a shelf behind her where a long row of glass jars was waiting to be filled with the beans being cooked in another pot. Preserving whatever was edible in wax-sealed jars was one of *Mutter's* ways of creating something to trade in the months when the coupon rations ran out. She was constantly quoting the Bible as she sealed beans inside the jars: "Matthew 14," she would remind anyone who would listen. "He fed thousands with just five loaves of bread and two fish. But then He didn't have those whores downstairs eating us out of existence." Then she would laugh, bouncing the cigarette at the side of her mouth in little detonations of ash.

"Tell me why you came here to have me read the letters. What is it you want girl?"

"I didn't come here wanting something."

"Yes you did. You may not know it but you did."

"I think we need to do something. To keep him from going mad in that little room every night."

She nodded. And stirred until she looked over. "And?"

"*Mundfunk*," I said.

"What about it?" said *Mutter*. "You think that if we start it up again, that keeping him busy will cure him?"

"Nothing will cure what he has."

"Yes." She peered from the soup to the other pot on the stove. "Hold the sieve over the sink while I pour the beans into it." For several minutes *Mutter* expounded on the values of canning in the pressure cooker. Then she said, "If you don't do it right, bad things can happen. People can die."

"Are you talking about canning beans or *mundfunk*?"

"Both."

Late that night, I heard *Mutter* humming to herself in the kitchen. As quietly as I could I went to the chairs around the table and said, "I've thought more about it. I want to begin again."

She just looked at me. Or maybe through me. She never even blinked.

"For his sake I want to find a different kind of gossip."

"For *his* sake...?"

"For other reasons too," I said quickly.

"Like what?"

"Do you remember what we said? About *mundfunk*, our gossip, being a sharp little stone in the jackboots?"

Her eyebrows rose. "Well child, tell me exactly where do you find this gossip now?"

I had no answer. What had once provided us with reams of gossip was gone. Since Lida Baarova had been deported there had been none of Goebbels bizarre libidinous outbursts, no more female assistants crawling out windows at midnight, no more deluges of flowers being sent to young actresses or crockery barrages from Magda. The fear of Hitler's wrath alone would have been enough to pry Goebbels loose from his actresses.

So *mundfunk* was impossible—until one day, suddenly it wasn't.

It came to me. Just like that. Listening to Karin, I realized the answer had been there all along. Just waiting for us. Right back where we started.

"The movie business?" Herr Langen said when I told him.

"The movie business," I said back to him.

"Don't be silly. Why would we risk our necks for a bunch of stories about silly people in an irrelevant profession?"

"It's the opposite of irrelevant. The movie business in Berlin has been turned into a military weapon."

Herr Langen rolled his eyes.

"Karin has said that they talk about it at Babelsberg—how Goebbels has convinced Hitler that movies are a vital component of the war effort. And that if civilian morale collapses, then everything collapses."

He stared into the floor, said nothing, and then went back to his room.

"Let it sink in," said *Mutter*. "With those thinking types you have to do that sometimes."

The mere existence of a movie business in the middle of the war astonished us all. And once again it existed because of the obsessions of the same man: Josef Goebbels who had willed his movie industry to be far more than just a diversion. In these, the worst days of the war, when Berlin and so many other German cities were being reduced to rubble, Goebbels had managed to divert the enormous resources needed to keep movies being made at the studios he controlled.

Movie plots had become militarily strategic, necessary to keep up the resolve and morale and obedience of the people being asked to fight and die for the Reich. Goebbels solution was simple: get them laughing! Engross them in heroism! Hurl them into fantasies—anything to wrench their minds out of the bombing, the hunger, the misery. In other words, make weapons out of the movies. And so even while entire movie sets and studios were sometimes obliterated by British and American bombing raids, filming continued with big movie stars like Emil Jannings, Hans Albert, Marika Rökk and Zarah Leander.

A day later Herr Langen emerged from the silence of his room, he looked at the scraps of movie gossip I had collected and read them over several times. "We stopped *mundfunk* for a reason," he said.

"And that reason no longer applies," said *Mutter*. "There are no Jews left for Goebbels to attack."

Later that day later he said, "Okay. As long we are not just dealing with mere movies here. Where do we start?"

We started with Zarah.

What is now known:

Zarah Leander is so famous, so imperious that she could supply a week's worth of gossip.

Dark haired and beautiful with large brown eyes and full lips, she could stare down the most temperamental Hollywood actresses. In her stardom, she sees herself as a regal presence whose whims are to be catered to. If she wants to go shopping at one of the Kurfürstendamm's most elegant stores, she demands that all other customers are told to leave.

When she surrounds herself with adoring homosexuals, Goebbels orders her to get rid of them. She refuses.

And Goebbels dares not overrule her.

Beautiful, scheming and demanding, she is easily the biggest movie star in the nation as well as becoming the highest paid actress, negotiating her own contracts and having no hesitation arguing with Goebbels if the terms of those contracts are not lived up to.

Audacity is a dangerous game to play with Goebbels. But Zarah Leander has carefully calibrated her behaviour, understanding that he needs her for his next big film, Die Grosse Liebe—The Great Love. She knows that in his mind no one else but her can play Hanna the beautiful singer in love with the courageous fighter pilot flying missions against the British in North Africa.

And she also understands that Die Grosse Liebe will be Goebbels' way of rousing the people, the Volk, with a love story so patriotic, so moving, that movie audiences everywhere will leave the theater in tears of joy—and most important of all, with gratitude to the Fatherland and the Führer.

So while the German army battles Russia on the eastern front and the British and Americans on the western front, filming on Die Grosse Liebe begins in the vast sound stages of the UFA studios at Babelsberg. There are huge sets and complicated musical scenes with choreography and costumes that rival anything Hollywood has done.

But it is soon obvious there was one problem that urgently needs to be corrected. It is a problem so explosive that even Goebbels backs away from confronting it.

Zarah Leander's weight.

None of the studio executives wants to face the fury they know would result if they even hint at the problem of a movie super-star who has become...how to put it delicately? ...A tad pudgy?

No one is going to tell the most willful and fiery actress in German film that she the seams of her costumes are straining. Or that the camera is picking up ripples and bulges where once there were none.

Or that there is now a problem of—again, how to put it?—perception? She is no longer that lithe creature from La Habanera *or* Heimat—*which were only filmed a few years ago.*

The studio executives try different descriptions of the problem, each fearfully imagining that he might be the one sent to explain it to her.

Among the possible ways the nervous studio executive come up with to explain the problem to Zarah:

—The wartime wide-angle lenses are unfairly making you look heavy.

—Script changes now require the character to be almost starving.

—When movie audience are on rations Hitler does not want to upset them with anyone looking 'normal'

After each days' filming and more of the raw film comes back from the labs and is shown in the UFA screening rooms the problem becomes a crisis. Various executives, experts and committees tiptoe around the topic. Perhaps it is lack of exercise? Or eating a bit too much? Or what if, what if.... after all, she is getting close to forty.

With each executive suggesting others break the news to her and none of them willing to do it, the responsibility is foisted onto UFA's lower echelons with the order: Make Frau Zarah look thin. Or at least thinner. So the orders go out to the various departments.

But Costumes say they could only do so much.

And Lighting say the same.

And Lenses? The wizards of Carl Zeiss AG reply that their lenses can only do so much. Which means practically nothing at all.

With the scenes about to be filmed where Zarah will be shown from head to toe, performing on a huge set in front in of pretty, and petite chorus girls, panic sets in.

As Goebbels is demanding a solution, some unknown UFA executive comes up with an idea "If we can't lower the water let's raise the bridge."

Which is met with a collective, "I beg your pardon?"

He explains that if Zarah is going to be filmed in front of pretty and petite chorus girls, it would only accentuate the problem. So why not bring in enormous chorus girls—so huge that Zarah herself would look almost tiny standing in front of them?

And where exactly are we going to find these enormous chorus girls? Someone, in a UFA meeting said the unthinkable:

The German Army—dressed as women. As chorus girls to be precise.

Preposterous! Ridiculous! With the war all around? Our Army dress up as chorus girls? The howls of scorn rain down until the studio bosses realize no one else can come up with anything better.

So, using Goebbels power, an order goes out. And as if by magic: an SS unit just happens to be stationed nearby during the very days when Zarah Leander's big chorus line will be filmed.

And not just any SS unit. No, the men in this unit are monsters, both physically and in every other way. This is one of the army's most effective killing units: the feared and goose-stepping killers from the Leibstandarte SS Adolf Hitler *Division.*

And not a single citizen can ever imagine these murderous goliaths in dresses.

Which is where our gossip came in.

Even *Mutter* was grudgingly impressed when I told her what Karin had learned about soldiers from one of the most fanatic SS Divisions being ordered to dress from head toe in women's clothes that made them look voluptuous.

Originally formed to be Hitler's personal bodyguards, the *Leibstandarte SS Adolf Hitler* had been used to ravage Poland, France and Greece leaving behind stories of atrocities and mass executions.

The troops of the *Leibstandarte SS Adolf Hitler Division* were briefly back in Germany, sullen, gaunt, battle-scarred and vaguely murderous. And also tall and physically formidable.

In other words, perfect chorus girls in the eyes of the desperate studio executives. They had decided it would be less dangerous to tell these SS killers they would soon be dressed as women, than to talk to Zarah Leander about her weight.

But we needed something to dispel the natural skepticism anyone hearing such gossip would have: *The SS in dresses? Oh right. And of course*

Göring was there wearing a ballet tutu. In other words we needed Karin to come up something to make people believe this gossip. But she was in another of her crises For the last year or so she seemed stranded in that actresses' neverland, floating between the hope of landing the big role and the reality of watching true stardom slowly slip away. "I'm sorry." She sank into a chair as if air had escaped her. "I'm just tired. Of trying to be a star. And I don't know why."

"Don't know why you're tired? Or you don't know why you're trying to be a star?"

She stared at me as if she was thinking. It took me a moment to realize that she was about to burst into tears. It came first in peristaltic waves, as if some invisible force was slowly shaking her. I thought maybe she was upset over something at the studio, or the problems of not being a star. I was not expecting what she blurted out in an explosion of tears:

"Don't you ever miss father?"

I wasn't sure I heard her right. "*Father*?

She nodded and turned away angrily. "I don't need a lecture, okay?"

"He wasn't all bad you know."

I said nothing.

"At least I found a way to get someone to approve of me," she said. After a long silence she said quietly, "I am ridiculous." She waited for a response which I never gave. The silence made her more anxious. "Maybe I'm trying to make him seem better so I can look at myself as a horrible mother and not feel guilty."

"Maybe being a mother is not one of your strongest skills."

"No kidding."

"Inga's practically raising Max as her own you know. She wanted to get him almost like she was the real mother."

"Maybe that's for the best."

"Yeah. They're both really needy." Then she got up and left without another word.

The next day she returned as if nothing had happened. She was back to being her self-contained presence with an emotional moat around her. "Here," she said handing me an envelope. Before I could ask what was in it she said, "I flirt outrageously with the *Die Grosse Liebe* assistant film editor. He will do anything for me." Then she turned and left, calling out behind her, "It's been snipped off one of the unused takes from the filming."

In the envelope was a little piece of 35-millimeter film. When I took the envelope to *Mutter,* she held the piece of film up to the light. "Three frames," she said. Downstairs in one of the rooms that her pornographic photo studio once occupied she put the three frames of film on what she called a lightbox, a flat, white surface with light coming from below. Attached to the top of the lightbox was an enormous magnifying glass.

"Look," she said chuckling.

And when I looked through the magnifying glass what I saw would become the resurrection of *mundfunk.*

"Your chorus line." She was close to laughing. Which for her was amazing.

I was looking at a row of enormous, angry looking SS killers in beautiful taffeta gowns that accentuated their perfect breasts.

By the time the night was over, Mutter's dirty picture photo developing equipment had churned out a dozen prints of the SS as a chorus line.

And looking at those frames of film, unless you used a truly strong magnifying glass, they appeared rather glamourous.

39

HERR LANGEN WAS NOT INTERESTED.

He showed up at the stove that morning completely different from the man he had been the night before. Cranky, distracted and completely indifferent to the bizarre photos of the SS chorus line, he retreated to his room soon after silently drinking his ersatz coffee.

"It's obvious what his problem is, isn't it." said *Mutter.*

It was.

For several days in a row, he became increasingly insistent about the letters from Emma, his wife. He wanted to talk to me about them but I had been avoiding the topic. I dreaded the conversation I knew I would have to have with him. I had some futile hope that our renewed efforts in gossip would deflect the need for such a talk.

They had not.

I got up, went down the hall to his room and knocked on the door.

Ten minutes later I sat across from him, the letters from his wife lying in a pile between us, saying nothing as he talked about how Emma was still in love with him—it was *obvious*, was it not? To *anyone* with *any* intelligence who read the letters.

Well? Was it not?

He talked because he needed to. I was there because he needed someone, anyone, to listen. Someone who would not contradict or mock. So I had merely listened in silence as he talked. I wondered at what point the tough-minded editor within him would intervene. I wondered at the amazing ability of self-delusion as a defense against a pain too great for the emotions to endure. And I wondered about how this fierce man could have hidden this vulnerability from so many. And for so long,

He had talked, convincing himself that he was convincing me. Until he suddenly stopped. "You're not saying anything."

"No." That was all I said.

He waited for more, summoning up whatever shreds of indignation he could find within himself. And then he seemed to slump backwards into the chair. He sat there for a moment.

"I believe she loves you," I said, and then made the mistake of hesitating.

"But..." he said looking at me accusingly.

"Please."

"What comes after the, 'But' you were going to say?"

"But...." I did not want to say it.

"But she is no longer *in love* with me. Is that it?"

I didn't know what to say. After a while he picked up the letters and quietly walked back to his room. Swirling pain in his wake.

He was gone all that day. When he returned it was late at night and the next morning his door was locked until *Mutter* and I knocked on it. *Mutter* told him he was needed in the kitchen.

A few minutes later he could barely look at us and refused even to examine the little piece of 35 mm film. "Why are you even talking to me about such filthy little speculations. Leave that to the *lügenpresse*."

"Herr Langen," said *Mutter* in a voice she reserved for those who irritated her, "May I remind you that with these filthy little speculations—as you call them, the three of us postponed the war."

"Postponed? By what? An hour? A day?" The words were flung out.

Mutter matched him. "So let's suppose it was only one day. And also let's suppose ten young men weren't killed on that one day because the war hadn't started yet. Is that what you scoff at? Is it?"

"You are absolutely right. You are doing fine. You don't need me. I am just in the way right now. I apologize."

He left and we heard the outer door to the street close below us. *Mutter* waited a few seconds and then went to a cupboard and took out a metal ring with several keys on it. "I saw something when he opened his door yesterday." She walked down the corridor and tried several keys in the lock until she found the one that unlocked Herr Langen's door.

"No," I said. "You shouldn't do this."

She turned to me with that look she sometimes got. "I have to."

Then she went into his room. When I got to the open door, she was standing beside the small desk holding something in her hands. "These things would get me shot."

On the desk were about a dozen small frames, each one holding a photograph of Herr Langen and his wife Emma, dark haired and pretty in the photos where they were youngest, maybe in their teens. The later photos showed an imposing woman with a relentless gaze and a knowing smile.

The photograph that *Mutter* was holding showed Emma at what looked like a celebration of some kind. "They're Jewish. Look at the Hebrew signs. I told him. Never leave anything like this lying around. Nothing the Gestapo would find if they barged in here. And this he leaves out in the open. Hiding a Jew is the death penalty. He knows that."

But I was looking at something else. On the top of a bureau were his forged identification papers with his photo and the name Horst Schmidt. *Mutter* looked over. "He went out without any papers?"

"If they stop him on the street he's as good as dead," I said.

"Maybe he wants to be."

"Okay. I'm taking over. I'm going to handle this," I said putting the little photographs back where they had been.

"You?"

"Me," I said sharply. She shrugged and returned to the kitchen.

I set a bucket of water by the open door in front of his room and soaked one of inner the walls and part of the floor. It was late afternoon when I heard the outer door to the back alley open and close. I was ready for him, waiting just inside his room when he came up the stairs.

He stopped, caught somewhere between fury and disbelief at seeing me in his room.

"There was a leak in the pipes," I said pointing to the soaked wall. "We had to make sure it wasn't going to be a flood,"

He hurried toward and then past me. When he saw the photos where he had left them, he wheeled around. "My room is private." It was more an accusation than a statement.

"I understand. But this was an emergency."

"Private means private."

"And emergency means emergency." I said, matching his glare.

"Get away from those. They are *my* photographs which—"

I interrupted. "Which could get us killed."

"Mind your own business."

"Which is precisely what I am doing." I walked past him toward the bureau and held up the forged identification papers. "You went walking around Berlin and didn't even take *forged* papers? Are you trying to get caught? Is that it?"

"I do what I want." I had never seen him so angry.

"Really? Well then let me ask you one question. Just one." I took a sharp, angry half step toward him. "Are you *that* convinced that under Gestapo torture you would not betray us? Telling them about all of us here?"

The question stopped him.

"If you are certain beyond any doubt, then fine, walk all over Berlin with or without your forged papers and get yourself tortured and killed. I don't care. But if you cannot, one hundred percent guarantee that you would never break under torture, then you are nothing more than a stupid, selfish fool."

We stood a few coiled meters away from one another. He started to answer but somehow could not find words.

"And once the Gestapo have you spilling out everything they want to know, then Mutter, me and the other women are faced with them breaking into this place. And finding all your Jewish trinkets, enough evidence for the Gestapo to decide that Mutter knew exactly who she was protecting. It would be enough to send *Mutter* to the gallows for hiding Jews."

He sat, maybe slumped, onto the edge of the bed, looking at several of the little painted glass scenes.

"I'll get rid of them." he said quietly.

I did not have the time even to reflect on what he had said.

Clack-clack-clack-clack-clack.

A bizarre noise reverberated from somewhere below us. It was a strange sound that made no sense—a loud *clack-clack-clack.*

It started and stopped. *Clack-clack-clack-clack-clack-clack.* And then a few seconds of silence. And then *Clack-clack-clack-clack-clack-clack.* It was coming from the front stairs. Almost no one used the front stairs now,

We went into the darkened corridor. *Mutter* had heard it too. She was drawn in from the kitchen, standing in silhouette, blocking the light behind her.

Clack-clack-clack-clack-clack-clack.

The door from the stairs swung open and a small figure barged into the corridor. A boy. Eleven, maybe twelve years old. Dressed in some kind of Nazi uniform complete with swastika armband and hard soled shoes that made the *Clack-clack-clack-clack-clack* noise. When he saw us he beamed like a missionary finding some Lost Tribe. He almost marched down the corridor and raised his arm stiffly into the air.

"*Heil Hitler!*" he shouted.

After a long pause it was *Mutter* who came like cat inspecting something dangerous. "Who are you?

But I knew instantly. "Hello Max," I said.

Soon after Karin had gladly turned Max over to Inga, he had been taken from *Mutter's* when she moved. After all those years of feeling like an ornament and wondering if she would find a man before her breasts betrayed her, Inga had finally found someone to marry. All we knew about him was that he was a *Hauptscharführer* in the SS and that he made her cry a lot.

Max had left us as a sweet little boy. Now what stood before us was a child who could have stepped out of a Nazi propaganda poster. Blond haired, blue eyed and with all the certainties that come with never having been tested, he looked around. "Where is the Führer's picture?" he demanded.

None of knew what to say. But *Mutter* had not survived for so long by being timid or unprepared. "Where we keep the Führer's picture is none of your business."

"The Führer's picture is not here. I can report you."

"Report me?" said *Mutter*, her face cinching up behind a scowl. "You little half-wit."

Max instantly became shrill, talking as if he was trying to remember lines he had heard someone else say. "It is the duty of every Hitler Youth to report all conduct that does not live up to the standards of the Reich."

Mutter swelled in front of him. I really believed I was watching her get bigger, angrier. She peered down at Max and held out her hand crooking her finger, beckoning him to come closer. For the first time he looked uncertain; he approached her and when he was close enough her hand shot out like a serpentine flicker, grabbing his left ear and twisting it.

"*Ow, ow, ow, ow, ow, ow,*" he yelled as she led him toward a cupboard, bending down and pulling out a magazine-sized poster showing Adolf Hitler.

She swung him around by the ear. "Do you want the Führer to be covered in cooking grease?" she said pointing to the wall behind the stove. "Do you want me to hang the Führer in a slime-filled wall of grease? Is that it?"

"No, no, no, no." Max cried.

"So you think the Führer should be covered in grease? *I* will report *you!*"

"No, no, no, please no!"

Mutter released Max's ear and kicked him in the seat of pants, sending him sprawling onto the floor. "Enough is enough. I'm going to report you to the Hitler Youth," she said standing over him.

"No, no, no, no." Max blubbered before exploding in the tears of a twelve-year-old.

From behind us on the stairs came another staccato burst of footsteps. "Oh I am so sorry," said a voice I recognized. It was Inga—at least until I turned around. I barely recognized her. If we had passed one another on the street I would not have known her. She had changed so much, gaining weight in some places and hollowed out in others. Her face somehow seemed to have collapsed into the map of a forgotten battlefield, discolored and cratered in places where a fragile beauty had once resided.

"His father has taught him to be like that," she said nervously.

His father? For a moment Helldorff appeared in my mind. But this was a different father, the *Hauptscharführer.*

"His father always demands that Max do what is proper for future Nazis," she continued as Max sniveled on the floor and yelled "Heil Hitler." Inga hurried toward him, tugging at his hand until he stood up. "Say hello to Aunt Bella and to *Mutter.* And to—" she said turning back toward the corridor. "Where did he go?"

Herr Langen had vanished.

Inga talked in confused half-finished sentences until she came to why she was there: she wanted to move back to *Mutter's.* "Even for just a few days," she added quickly, sensing a change in *Mutter* the moment she made her request. Her reasons for wanting to return tumbled over one another, twisting into impenetrable explanations. All we could understand was that her husband, the SS *Hauptscharführer* whose name it emerged was Lothar, had been sent back to Berlin to be part of some new unit being formed here.

And it had been difficult. With the outbursts of temper.

Lothar needed time alone. He was under such stress poor man.

The war does that to them.

Oh, and did she mention his accusations about her drinking too much?

"Father says we are smashing the enemy," Max announced sternly before Inga sent him outside.

There was a feral quality to her now. Beaten down yet sharp and in an unseen and muted way, cunning. It took a while to understand that she had already put a suitcase in her old room downstairs. And a small bag in the next-door room with clothes for Max.

I looked to see if Herr Langen was listening to the possibility of one of the Hitler Youth moving in with us. The door to his room was a few centimeters open.

Mutter looked as if she was thinking. Then she said, "Tell me about you and this..."

"Lothar."

"Yes, Lothar. Tell me, are you happy, the two of you?"

"Oh yes, yes," said Inga quickly. Too quickly. Then she looked confused about what to say next. "He is good to me. When he can be. But you know the stress that men are under now."

"Of course," said *Mutter* in a flat, dry voice.

"And I try to please him. Even though he doesn't think I do. I show him that I can help the Fatherland too."

Mutter looked as if she was thinking for a moment. "You know my last two whores are working on that floor below, the one where you would be staying," she said to Inga's hurried assurances that it would only be for a few days.

But then *Mutter* confused me. She began talking about how she had so many cupboards here all of them full of preserved meat and vegetables. Which I knew was not true. What was she doing?

And she embellished what she told Inga to make it seem as if she had food and provisions hidden all over the kitchen. It made no sense. I knew there was nothing hidden in the kitchen.

"All very illegal, so don't tell anyone." *Mutter* said. When I cast a questioning look her way *Mutter* ignored me as Inga nodded theatrically.

And when Inga was heading back toward the stairway *Mutter* put two fingers to her lips. I nodded. When all was silent, she said, "Did you smell the liquor on her? She smelled like a schnapps factory."

"I was concentrating more on the bruises."

Late that night, when all was still and silent, *Mutter* stoked the fire so it roared and crackled and then gently tapped on Herr Langen's door. Minutes later the three of us sat around the fire as she whispered to us that we were to clear out all personal belongings from our room—"especially the photographs and letters," she said looking straight into Herr Langen's eyes.

"That little Nazi Max is one thing," said *Mutter* "but our girl Inga, she gives me the shivers. My daughter Erma, before she left for Mecklenburg, said Inga was not the same. Not since she met this Lothar."

Herr Langen was very different from a few hours earlier. Subdued and serious, he asked *Mutter*: "I don't understand something I overheard you telling her. About having a huge amount of provisions and food stored in here. There's no illegal stashes of food in—"

"No need to go into that now," interrupted *Mutter*.

"Wouldn't it be easier just to send Inga and her little Nazi away?" he asked.

"Then it would look like we have something to hide."

"We do. Just be ready."

"For what?"

"We are going to be raided by the Gestapo."

"*What*? "Both Herr Langen and I sat back. "How do you know?""

"Inga will bring them down on us. There is now nothing we can do to stop it. She came here to escape this Lothar—but also she's desperate to win him back. And now that she thinks I have this vast horde of illegal food hidden away, she has all the evidence she needs to make herself a Nazi hero."

"You shouldn't have told her about illegal food," I said. "We don't have any."

"Of course I should have told her. Better that she seizes on the one thing that is not true here than all the things that are true."

"Be ready?" I said asking myself more than her. "How?"

"Sleeping in your clothes would be a good idea." *Mutter* looked from me to Herr Langen.

"You really think Inga is an informer?"

"Here is all I know," *Mutter* said. "She is a weak person trying desperately to please a brutal man. *Acchh*! I've seen this a hundred times with my whores—the abused ones. It's just what they do. Nothing is more dangerous. So sleep in your clothes. The Gestapo usually arrive very early in the morning."

Over the weekend a strange rhythm played out at *Mutters*. Herr Langen and I had cleaned out our rooms of everything, right down to the toothbrushes which we now kept in our pockets. He had put everything, including his photographs in one of the hiding places we had built. The door in our corridor, leading to the stairway had a bolt that was slid into place whenever Max's *Clack-clack-clack* was heard downstairs. Several times in the late afternoon we heard *Clack-clack-clack* on the stairs but for an hour, maybe more, the door handle to our corridor never moved.

On the second night, Inga came upstairs to apologize for Max being so noisy. He was excited she said. He had been allowed to accompany some older Hitler Youth boys as they were being trained to operate the 88-millimeter guns at the flak tower, the massive concrete structure that loomed over the Tiergarten and the zoo like some medieval fortress. With walls as thick as a house, it was thought to be indestructible, even from a direct hit by one of the bombs coming from the American or British planes that the gunners in the flak tower were trying to shoot down.

Before she left, she asked again about the food that *Mutter* told her she'd hoarded. "You've really stored that much? Why isn't that marvelous," she said.

"It is," *Mutter* replied.

"And it's all here. Amazing. Can I see?"

"No."

Inga retreated to the stairs with a jagged smile that flickered and could not stay in place. As her footsteps faded, the bolt on the door was quietly slid into place. Herr Langen climbed out onto the rooftop garden and watched Inga hurry up the street and vanish into the mist. "She's going to tell them," *Mutter* said from the shadows.

That night I had a case of the nerves. I sat by the stove and said, "I understand what is happening, why we have to do this."

"I doubt that," said *Mutter*.

"Maybe you're wrong," said Herr Langen. "Maybe we both understand. From the moment Inga walked through that door I knew something was wrong and maybe could not be fixed. And if we're right, the only way to get through it is to take control."

Mutter made that whooshing sound with her mouth as something indescribable flew from it making an arc and sizzled on the stove. "We won't know if we are in control unless we take the risk."

"What risk."

"Of finding out if she's what I think she is."

That night Herr Langen stood on the roof until Inga came back. "She got out of a car a block away and walked the rest of the way here," he told us. Then he checked to make sure that the false wall in front of his hiding place slid and locked in place noiselessly, and then he went into his room, closing the door.

I lay on the bed in my room, fully dressed in that half-sleep state that comes from expecting to be flung into a heart pounding consciousness at any moment.

Dawn came and the only sound was the quiet clatter of the rain and the sound of the water running in the bathroom down the hall. I felt suspended in time, waiting for the hands of the clock to begin turning again. I almost wanted something to happen—*anything*, just to set fire to the debris of worthless minutes dying in my thoughts.

It came in a way none of us expected.

Herr Langen was watching from under the leaking tarpaulin strung above the rooftop garden area. He came hurrying into the corridor "A black car! It stopped outside," he whispered sharply pointing toward the street.

But in his haste, he did not notice that he was tracking wet footprints all down the corridor. "*Idiot!*" hissed *Mutter* pointing to the floor and the trail of watery footprints he had left. As a rasping voice sounded below, we grabbed towels and frantically wiped the floor.

Heavy steps sounded on the stairway. Wheezing, gasping and then a fit of coughing, "Shit, shit, shit," said a voice from the other side of the door at the top of the stairway. *Mutter* retreated quickly to the kitchen, grabbed the poster of Hitler and slapped it against a nail on the wall. Then she opened a drawer and pulled out a red tag that she tied to the radio as a banging noise sounded on the door.

"*Gestapo!*" yelled the voice on the other side of the door with more banging on the door. "*Gestapo! Aufmachen!*" said the voice sounding almost bored.

Mutter was furiously flicking her hands at us as she called out. "Coming, coming." Neither Herr Langen nor I had time to get to the hiding places in our rooms. For a moment I froze; he grabbed my hand and pulled me into the closest hiding place. It was also the most dangerous and the smallest, located in a former storage closet right off the kitchen. When it was latched from the inside it presented a smooth wall to anyone sitting in the kitchen.

As Herr Langen dragged me inside, *Mutter* opened the door further down the corridor. I saw a heavy, older man lumber through the door, wheezing and holding out some kind of small metal shield that he thrust toward *Mutter*.

"Gestapo," he wheezed.

"Oh for godsakes Bruno. Is all this really necessary?"

40

THE HIDING PLACE WE HAD rushed into was not meant for two people. Through a tiny crack we could see *Mutter* look from the man's hand to his face and back.

"Sorry *Mutter*," said the Gestapo man. "I have orders you know."

"Bruno, honestly. You and your stupid orders."

"Can I come in?"

"You're already in."

"Yes."

"You've gained weight."

"Thank you so much for pointing that out *Mutter*. I need to sit down."

"You're the Gestapo. Do you even need to ask?"

"Arthritis."

Listening to them talk was already fraying my nerves. Our tiny hiding space was at an angle to the corridor but looked out onto the kitchen through the thinnest of cracks where this wall we had built did not close properly. That crack was next to the latch that I was clinging to. I could see *Mutter* and the Gestapo man—Bruno apparently, standing around the table. And then—*what is she doing? Inviting him to have a tea or an ersatz coffee? A Gestapo! No, no no ! Impossible.*

But she was.

While I was trying desperately not to cough? Or sneeze? Or even tumble out of our hiding place? And here was *Mutter* playing hostess? To some wheezing. arthritic Gestapo officer?

I didn't know how long I could hold out. Jammed in together, Herr Langen and I were pressed at right angles to one another. I could feel his breath on the side of my face, feel the single drop of perspiration as it fell from his forehead down onto my wrist, and wonder if the pounding heartbeat I felt was mine or his.

I could not make even the slightest move because the inside latch was in my hand. I had quietly tugged on it and nearly panicked when I found that the partition would not completely close from the inside. I had to hold the latch and pray I would not let it slip out of my hand, sending our so-called wall flying open. Soon it was my perspiration that was trickling down onto his arm that had nowhere to go but around my waist.

I realized that on top of all the other physical challenges, I was sucking my stomach in. *At a time like this*? *That's* what I'm concerned with? *How I look*? Why? Survival? No! Vanity: so he wouldn't feel the softness around my middle.

I was ridiculous.

But it still didn't stop me from sucking my stomach in.

In the kitchen, mere meters away, Bruno sat, his bulk engulfing the chair and the mass of his back and arms straining against his suit jacket in horizontally creased rolls. What was happening now? *Mutter* was actually joking with him!

In that little hiding place, struggling to keep my balance with Herr Langen and I pressed together, and desperately holding onto that latch I couldn't believe what I was hearing:

"Why is there no long leather coat Bruno? I thought all you Gestapo types wore those long leather coats."

"I'm too old for that *Mutter*." In that raspy voice he rambled: "My partner Klaus the drunkard, crashed his car in the rain last night so I told them I would handle it on my own. A joke—I can barely climb those stairs now *Mutter*. Usually I can fake it. But with you I figure I don't have to. I'm hanging on for two more months. Then I can retire. Mmm, good ersatz coffee. And why am I not surprised? You always could work the black market like no one else."

"But you always knew that Bruno," she said.

This small talk seemed to go forever—*Mutter* and Bruno: friends? Or maybe just adversaries from back when he was a young *Kripo*—a criminal cop, and she was the beautiful mistress of his boss, a corrupt inspector in the *Kriminalpolizei*.

"We can both agree now *Mutter*, that Inspector boyfriend of yours was a complete bastard."

"Yes, yes. But he was good for some things."

Laughter.

And then Bruno said, "I came here on my own today. Just because it was you *Mutter*. Because of old time's sake. You saved me, you know that?"

"Not really," *Mutter* said. "I just told you what I found out. That you had enemies. Who wanted to hurt you. Besides remember the first whorehouse I had?"

Bruno was laughing. "Oh that Italian girl you had. How could I forget? So each of us owes the other."

"Yes Bruno, we saved each other".

"God I miss those days. When I was in the Alex and you were just starting your... can I call it your profession, *Mutter?*"

"Your boss back then was a Jew, remember?"

"Ah Weiss. I liked him. Imagine, a Jew as *Regierungsdirektor*! In charge of all us fools. Too bad about him."

"Do you ever think of that now?"

"About what?"

"When you take Jews away?"

"*Mutter, Mutter*, don't make me talk about that. Not when I'm about to retire. It was different before."

"Before?"

"Before it changed. Before *Gleishschaltung*. I was one of the lucky ones. Most of the Kripo men I worked with never got to make the change. Most of them were fired. Only a few of us got to transfer to the Gestapo."

"Are you glad you did?"

"Ah *Mutter* you keep asking me question like that. Even the walls have ears."

"Bruno, why are you here?"

"Do you know how many people are informing on their neighbours now?"

"You're not answering my question."

"We were told things."

"You were told things?"

Mutter, Mutter, Mutter hurry up! I can't keep holding this latch forever so please—

"Someone made a report on you. They said you are hoarding. Huge stockpiles."

"Stockpiles?"

"Of food. The report said you had food hidden away in every cupboard in your kitchen. Huge quantities. Hoarding is a serious crime. You know what Goebbels said."

"Bruno, look around you. See that red label there on my radio?—how many homes do you go into where the red label warning about listening to the BBC is still attached? Put *that* in your report I know you have to write. And while you're at it, look up there on the wall. Who's in that big poster I have hanging up there? Rumpelstiltskin? Little Red Riding Hood? Put that it your report—'Subject has big poster of the Führer and—"

"*Mutter* please-"

"And hoarding? You know what Proverbs says."

"*Mutter* for christsake—."

"Him too. 'He who withholds grain, the people will curse him' Proverbs eleven or twelve."

"Since when does the Bible get quoted in a whorehouse?"

Exactly! Mutter enough, enough! I can't hold on much longer. Herr Langen and I are...

What is happening? Something I feel against my hip.

Something suddenly becoming hard! Herr Langen? No, no it can't be. But it is!

I can turn barely few degrees, enough to see the panic in Herr Langen's eyes as he mouths 'Sorry. I am so sorry.'

"Since when do you ask Gunter? Since some poor innocent woman in a respectable whorehouse is accused of crimes like hoarding. That's when!"

"C'mon *Mutter*, be fair. I told you, I'm just doing my job and-"

"Bruno, open any cupboard you like. Go on open them all. Get off your fat behind, do your Gestapo job and look in my cupboards. Go on!"

"All right, all right." His grunting and wheezing rendered him mute for a moment. Then, the sound of cupboard doors opening and closing. "Nothing. Nothing. One jar of beans. That's it? That's all?"

"Of course that's all. Make sure you put that in your report Bruno."

Yes! And just go! Leave! Write your report!

While I have Herr Langen pressed against me in ways I could never imagine as he silently shakes his head in apology for his hardness. But wait— that word. I just heard that word:

"Gossip? What does the Gestapo care about gossip Bruno?"

"You have no idea how we have to care. The SS keep doing their damned *Lage und Stimmungsberichte* and they go all the way to the top."

"What do you care about Situation and Morale Reports?"

"Because the SS now has a whole department just to find out public opinion. Mostly because of all that gossip that makes Goebbels crazy. And Hitler too. It started when Goebbels was chasing after that Baarova woman."

"I'm shocked Bruno."

Mutter, Mutter! Wind it up! Enough with being shocked! While we're clinging to the latch with what strength I have left and firing looks at Herr Langen to see if he's listening.

"You have no idea *Mutter*. Those damn official reports have to include page after page of gossip that the average people are talking about. It makes our life hell. Goebbels, Himmler, Göring, they all have fits over the gossip. It makes them look ridiculous. You heard Goebbels on the radio."

"No."

"Yelling about 'fishwives' gossip'"

"Fishwives?"

"And 'rumour-mongering low-lifes'"

That's us, that's us! Fishwives! And low-lifes!

"And they want us to find out who started this nonsense."

"Of course they do Bruno."

"It makes our life hell."

He was leaving! Passing mere millimeters away from our hiding place.

"Now remember Bruno, put in your Gestapo report that a poor innocent woman was slandered by some malevolent informer. Hoarding! Where do these evil minds come up with such rubbish?"

"You have no idea *Mutter*—we are flooded with such lies from informers who are just trying to destroy their neighbours so they can benefit in some way."

"I'm shocked Bruno. Now take care of yourself. Good-bye."

Yes goodbye!—as the door closed and a moment later we tumbled out of the hiding place, gasping for breath.

Herr Langen could not look at me.

Inga was dead before the bombs fell.

We didn't know she was being murdered until just after it happened, when we were fleeing for the bomb shelter. I raced down the stairs as the air raid sirens were sounding, stopping on the floor below us. The door to Inga's room was open. I hurried toward and stopped, frozen by what I saw.

On the small bed, *Mutter* was sitting quietly on a pillow that was completely covering Inga's face, smothering her as she lay on her back, utterly still.

With a cigarette hanging out of the side of her mouth as she was suffocating Inga, *Mutter* was turning the pages of her Bible.

She looked up for a moment and then went back to turning the pages of the Bible. "She's dead," she said as if she was talking about the weather. "She's been dead for at least ten minutes. Never felt a thing. She was too drunk."

"You murdered her?" was all I could think of to say.

"Just be thankful that it was Bruno the Gestapo sent to investigate us. He couldn't catch his own shadow. But the next time Inga wanted to grovel and please her husband by showing him what a good Nazi she was, we could have gotten the SS. Or a competent Gestapo agent."

Bombs could be heard far to the west.

"But this is giving me trouble," *Mutter* said, "The Bible is tough. The best I can find is Deuteronomy: '*Vengeance is mine, and retribution*'. But is this Him talking about His vengeance? Or can it be anybody's?"

Bombs again sounded in staccato explosions somewhere not far away, maybe Wilmersdorf. *Mutter* raised herself with a grunt. "Sometimes the Bible doesn't work the way it's supposed to. It doesn't always apply in times of war you know." She got up off the pillow, picked it up and looked down.

"We'll have to get rid of the body after the bombing."

41

ALL OVER THE CITY THERE were air raid shelters. Some were huge that could handle thousands in the subways and the flak towers; other were like ours that were really just basements.

Ours was beneath a storage hut in an empty lot behind *Mutter's* building. Even though there was far more space in her basement, *Mutter* refused to turn it into an air raid shelter after what happened to thousands of people in Hamburg last July. Big buildings there were hit by bombs and collapsed, entombing or roasting alive those in the basements, trapped under tons of stone and steel rubble. "If a bomb falls on my head there's nothing I can do about it," *Mutter* said after hearing about the Hamburg bombing raid. "But I refuse to be trapped in a coffin of my own making." Instead she hired workmen to install heavy metal doors and to reinforce the basement ceiling in the hut. When they were finished, *Mutter* asked their opinion about the chances of surviving a bomb falling right on top of the hut now that all these big beams had been installed. The workmen talked among themselves and then gave a one word answer:

Zero.

As we hurried across the empty lot toward the hut *Mutter* stopped and looked up into the rain. The noise of a single approaching plane got closer. In a roar it wove through the thick clouds and dropped a bright flare somewhere over toward Tempelhof airport. "Not good. A pathfinder plane. He is marking territory. Not good at all." We got to the hut where a man was waving at us to hurry. "Oh god not that fool Doof," *Mutter* wheezed as the noise from the planes drew closer and bombs could be heard leapfrogging toward us.

"Doof was yelling, "This is a *Luftgefahr* 15 category raid." "Papers," Doof demanded as he checked everyone going inside the shelter.

I looked over at Herr Langen as we were running. He stopped. And I knew he was thinking of the same thing I was: those counterfeit papers of his on the bureau in his room.

"Papers?" I blurted at Doof, "Are you crazy?" In the chaos and panic of the moment it just came out of me. "We're running for our lives. Our papers are back inside." No one ever talked this way to Doof who was always looking for new ways to rule his little parcel of streets and houses like a despot. He seemed to have some inner inflating mechanism that swelled him up as he bellowed at me "Fraulein if you are not careful I will have you—"

He never got to finish what he was saying.

A massive explosion rocked everything around us. It came somewhere up the street on the other side of *Mutter's* building; in an instant the air around us seemed to turn solid. Like the force of a massive hammer. I saw Doof knocked backwards and covered in dust as he gagged and spit, stumbling back into the entrance to the shelter. Herr Langen pushed him aside as we entered, and then pulled the heavy metal door behind him. It slammed shut with a clanking noise.

The shuddering darkness was jarred with every distant blast, about twenty, maybe thirty. People huddled in shadows that were pushed away by a naked light bulb swinging on a cord fastened to one of the big reinforcing beams. They were huddled on benches or on folding chairs that some had brought. A few were rocking back and forth muttering prayers while others sat staring into their own thoughts as the tiny world around us shook with each explosion. Then came a blast outside that slammed us all onto the ground with shrieks and cries to whatever gods were implored. The ceiling of the shelter heaved and groaned as the great beams lifted and slammed down again in an explosion of dust and debris. I found *Mutter* beside me on the floor and started to help her up. "No! Stay down here. It will be safer."

The air had somehow hit us like a fist. My ears filled with screams from somewhere far away yet someone was yelling from right in front of me but I could barely hear. It was Doof, pointing hysterically toward a light that was suddenly intruding. The big steel door had slammed open, blasting the locks off it and twisting on its hinges with the very top of the door bent backwards as if it had been pried open by a giant.

"The blast!" Doof was screaming. "The blast did that!"

What is now known:

The deadliest part of the bomb comes not merely from whatever fires of hell it creates but also from what happens to the air around it. Air, or in this case, a form of it known as blast overpressure, is better understood now than it was on that night toward the end of World War Two.

But what was best understood back then was that this terrible kind of air produces rather immaculate corpses.

As Berlin shudders under the latest in the Allies' High Explosives dropped on it from above, the aftermath will leave a platz full of dead people, many of whom look as if they are sleeping on the roads and sidewalks. But again, that is how they appear until you look more closely. And sometimes only if you know what to look for.

Destruction of the eyes would be the most obvious. Or perhaps trickles of blood beside the mouth. But so much of what has killed this platzful of people cannot be seen. Like the air bubbles blasted into veins and arteries creating embolisms that are more lethal than a bullet. Or the bleeding and ruptured organs, the kidneys, the liver, the heart. Or the inner ears that are turned into sludge. Or concussions, worse than being hurled headfirst into a brick wall. They are all the work of this air that has suddenly turned more violent than a hammer attack. All the worst words come into play: ischemia; infarction; hemorrhage; sepsis; rhabdomyolysis—and on and on through the diagnostic horror chambers of the human anatomy.

But this air that does such terrible violence has first had violence done to it. In a sense, the air is taking revenge. In that instant when the explosion expands at supersonic speed, a shock wave is created in a millisecond—which is another way of saying the air is unbelievably compressed and travelling outward like a vast and circular battering ram, destroying all it encounters.

This nearly invisible vengeance is the blast overpressure and people have spent careers studying it and quantifying its lethality with measurements like psi's and kilopascals.

But in Berlin almost no one knows about such measurements. Or cares that at 20 psi, air alone can turn concrete buildings into powder.

All they know is that their cities are exploding around them. And so many of their citizens are dying immaculately.

The screaming went unheard in the next blast. We could barely see what was happening. The electricity for the single light had ceased shortly after several of the men heaved against the big door and managed to wedge it shut again. Now the candles were being snuffed out with every blast and the only light in the shelter came from a battery-operated torch in the hands of one of the men we did not know. Most of the time there was no light at all until another bomb landed nearby and an angry flash of light drove its way through cracks in the ceiling.

Like most raids now, there were people in the shelter we barely knew from nearby apartments, and several men and one woman who just happened to be in the area when the sirens went off. The raids had a way of stripping character right down to the marrow. You could never predict who would be strong and stoic and who would shriek and flail in panic.

Like Doof.

It took one bomb to strip away his overbearing *blockwart* act and leave only a terrified, chattering nuisance in a time of peril. With every heaving shudder of the shelter he yelped and clutched at whoever was sitting closest to him. For a while that was the whore from Cologne who had now decided she didn't want to be called Ursula. As the bombs rained down, she revealed an almost heroic side. With the Swabian adding details, she provided a desperately needed diversion with their anecdotes about clients. It became a kind of parlour game that for a moment at least, took peoples' mind off the terror: *Guess which boss of yours I've had at least a dozen times?* she said to Doof who screeched as part of the ceiling burst.

I had found a place on a bench and balanced myself on it as it shook in the darkness. A woman's voice could be heard from somewhere nearby quietly saying the Lord's Prayer. Other voices, with other beseechings drifted in and out of the shattering crashes.

And then there was Herr Langen. It was as if he was preoccupied with something into which no amount of aerial violence could get through. He was strangely unmoved by the sound of the world outside being shattered.

He leaned closer in order to be heard as he talked to me in a low voice. "I would be grateful if you would listen to me. In case the worst happens here. I would not want to die and not have said this. I am ashamed of what happened back in that hiding space."

"Don't be," I whispered as another blast shook everything.

"Well I am. I am sorry. I do not know what happened to me."

""It's okay," I said. And took his hand in mine. Just the warmth of another human's touch lessened the torrent of fear about to overflow the banks of my crumbling fortitude. Then I said a single word. "Paul." I whispered. He looked over at me for a moment surprised and then with a faint smile.

He was no longer Herr Langen,

It was as if I had stepped into some hidden place and Paul was with me in that warm and secure refuge the instant before we all screamed as the most terrifying blast of them all went off somewhere so close that it felt as if the earth under the shelter became a roller coaster, flying upwards and then sinking.

"Oh dear god!" a woman shrieked. "When will this end?"

What is now known:

End? The end is not even close. On this summer night, the Royal Air Force is only beginning its nineteen separate and massive attacks on Berlin in a seven month period. In those months almost 11,000 bombers will drop 17,000 tons of high explosive bombs and almost as many incendiary bombs. For each raid, five or six hundred bombers will drop fire, explosion and terror from the air.

All this death originates six hundred miles to the west in the quaint and leafy British town of High Wycombe, just outside London. It is where the Englishmen at RAF Bomber Command send out planes night after night to carry out a simple strategy: Bomb the German civilian population into the ground,

Then bomb them again until they cannot go on.

And then bomb them some more.

It is a tried-and-true strategy; Bomber Harris is sure of it. After all, it is the strategy that he created back in the 1920s in Iraq—or, as it was known then, Mesopotamia.

Iraq was where Bomber Harris—later to be known more properly as Air Chief Marshall Sir Arthur Harris, first attracted notice as a fierce and innovative wing commander. Harris is quick-tempered, loyal, and looks every inch the proper Englishman with a round, ruddy face and a piercing gaze framed between sandy coloured hair and a formidable mustache.

Sent to Iraq in the 1920s he becomes convinced that the way to win the war against Arab tribesmen who have united against British rule is to bomb them back into the sand.

It works.

The tribes surrender in droves.

And if those Iraqi tribesmen could be brought to their knees by bombing then so too can these Germans. Bomber Harris is sure of it.

But for some reason, the Germans just aren't cooperating. They are not acting at all like those tribesmen in Iraq. There is no wave of surrender that the British can see on the horizon.

So Air Chief Marshall Sir Arthur Harris loses patience with these Germans who will simply not surrender as they should. He draws up a list of sixty more German cities to bomb into rubble.

So yes, on this summer night there is no end in sight. Berlin will be bombed. And bombed again. And again.

Until they see the light and act like Iraqi tribesmen.

Darkness.

In the air raid shelter, fear burns away the images within my mind.

I sit there as the bombs fall outside, and in those moments of life and death I wonder if what *Mutter* says is true—that all over Berlin there are other women just like me, women in hiding. Women whose men have been killed. Women who wonder when their ovaries will fail them forever. Do they experience desire as I do? Do they long to feel another body next to theirs?

To be touched?

And just to feel the warmth of a hand?

Paul's hand.

We stand up, shuffling uncertainly in the darkness and I feel him reaching out, steadying me. As I knew I somehow was also doing to him.

When the droning roar of the planes had faded and all we could hear was a kind of howling windstorm, two of the men struggled with the big metal door that would not fully open. It was warm to the touch and one of them used a piece of wood to pry at its edges. There was a loud clanking noise and as the door fell inward, an orange light flared into the air raid shelter. It came from the earthly hell that Berlin had become out beyond that doorway.

Herr Langen—Paul, went out first, calling to us from somewhere past the shadows. We stumbled chaotically up the stairs; in that moment where nothing was unusual but stillness, I was vaguely aware of a figure in the darkness, completely still while everyone was lurching toward the light. It was Paul. "Why are you just standing there?" I yelled over the roar from outside.

He did not move, merely looking calmly from the raging light over to me. "When you worked for me did you ever wonder why I was always so fanatical about the truth?" he asked.

"This is not the time for such talk." I yelled. "Let's go!" In that chaos he looked almost indignant. I yelled again, "I am not going to wonder about it right now."

"It was not the noble motives I told myself."

"Fine. Come!" Nothing. I yelled, "Paul!"

We stumbled past all the small structures that had totally ceased to exist. And the people who had been inside them lay dead, flung across a plain of devastation like so much scattered debris.

"My life—the important part of it, has been a lie."

"Can we talk about this later?"

"I didn't get Emma out of Berlin to save her. She left me. Because she could not have another child. At least that is what she told me. I could never acknowledge that she was gone for good. It's quite terrifying how the mind has its defenses. Its delusions."

It was the strangest moment for him to be talking about something so personal. I had never seen him looking so untouched by what was happening around him. Even as he was helping others evade Doof who had found some inner inflation mechanism and was marching around again near the entrance to our shelter, demanding to see identity papers. Paul paid no attention to Doof, guiding the confused and the terrified past Doof, leaving him waving into the fires and making threats that no one heard.

The most astonishing sight was *Mutter's* tenement building. Surrounded by devastation, it had barely been touched. It loomed in front of us, a darkened hulk silhouetted against a fiery sky. Inside, we groped our way using candles that flickered and failed in the hot, swirling air that was so thick you could taste it. We stumbled up the stairs past a room with only part of its exterior wall. Through the gaping wound in that walls we could see that every structure to the east of us had been completely flattened or left as jagged remnants.

Fires were burning everywhere and in the distance I could see people struggling to escape from the pull of the terrible winds that were sucking them into the fires. Some struggled, fought and clawed to free themselves from the inferno's clutches.

And did not make it.

42

AFTER THE BOMBING IT WAS obvious that Berlin as we had known it was becoming a time capsule existing mostly in our memory. What were once buildings are now just stalagmites growing out of the wreckage.

It seemed that every night, more of its grand architecture was being pulverized, reconfigured in the streets as rubble. Almost every day we could look out on what memory told us should be a different scene. Gone were so many of the buildings that we looked out on only days earlier. And in our sanctuary at *Mutter's,* stories came back to us about the grand boulevards like Unter den Linden where palatial buildings were now mere shells, their innards blown out like corpses torn apart. The bombs are hollowing out entire streets, leaving only teetering facades. They respect neither beauty nor need. Ornate palaces like the one in Charlottenburg are obliterated as routinely as workers' housing. It is as if all that has made Berlin recognizable has been ripped away.

Yet on some of the wider streets, the ones that are relentlessly and quickly cleared of debris, we still sometimes confront an image that glides right out of our past. Like a part of a barely remembered way of life, big Mercedes staff cars flying small Nazi flags from the fenders occasionally roar though the streets scattering whoever gets in their way.

In the relentless July heat after the bombing, Karin was crossing a street when she saw one of the big Mercedes coming toward her. Unlike previous encounters, this one was moving slowly, edging around the uncleared stone remnants of buildings that no longer existed. Through the rubble-piled gaps where those buildings once stood she could see the massive, red-tinted police headquarters building at Alexanderplatz. Any big Nazi vehicle near *The Alex*, as it was called, could possibly be carrying the one man she had never stopped obsessing over.

Karin stepped into the middle of the road, blocking the slow path of the Mercedes she was sure would be carrying Helldorff. Even the thought of him had sent Karin into little fits of indignation whenever she saw one of these massive, rolling symbols of what was crumbling around us. And now she was sure it would be him, sitting there encrusted in weakness and cruelty, extracting pleasure from the view from behind the driver, framed through the windshield, showing mere mortals looking on in awe.

Or better yet, fear.

As the beast approaches, shiny and massive, it does not slow down as Karin expects. The horn sounds, a battering ram at the ears, as people nearby call out to her. At the last moment someone grabs her arms and pulls her back, just in time…

…just in time for her to see Helldorff just as she knew he would be, a unformed pasha scowling and indignant at this momentary hindrance. But he sees her. And then looks away. She is sure he has seen her.

"After all these years? What do you care if he sees you? As you almost get run over." You can always tell when *Mutter* is disgusted, by the way she chops whatever now passes for meat going into the stew. She was wielding the cleaver like an assassin, "You had a child with him; isn't that enough?"

"I never finished what I started with him so—"

"You mean what he started with you" interrupted *Mutter*. "You threw yourself out of his car and ran half-dressed through the zoo."

"I could have brought him down. He was afraid of me."

"Girl, girl."

"I'm serious."

"I know you are. That's what worries me."

"Oh *Mutter*," said Karin not sensing the mood around her, "you're probably just wishing you were back in the days when you did just what I'm doing."

"Oh you are only partly right sweetie."

"Really? What part is right?"

"I do wish I still had what you have now." *Mutter's* eyes narrowed into that face still sculpted by its lost beauty. "But not what you are doing with it."

"What am I doing with it?"

Mutter's eyes narrowed more. " You obviously want to see him again."

"I could make him pay for what he did. He just assumed he could do whatever he wanted to me."

"You don't play dangerous games with Nazis."

"They're just men."

"And *that's* an answer?" said *Mutter* as she turned toward the wood stove and spat whatever it was that landed on the hot iron surface and sizzled until it vanished. She turned to me after a drink from the bottle. "What is this new language your sister's generation is speaking? *'They're just men.'* Nazis? Do you understand any of this nonsense?"

Karin became defensive. ""Everyone can see how badly the war is going. So Helldorff and all the other big Nazis will be scared now."

"Cornered dogs are always the most vicious." Meat was chopped like it was something that needed to be subdued. "This one," she said to me, motioning at Karin, "she won't know she is playing with fire until her dress is in flames. Or more likely what's under the dress."

If a man thinks he can do to me whatever I don't want done, he's going to be sorry he even tried. Is that better? Clearer?"

"Sweetie that zoo in the Tiergarten that you go to—there are lions there that you adore. But you don't get in the cage with them," said *Mutter.*

"I don't adore a Nazi."

"But you're talking about getting in the cage with him." I said.

Karin erupted as she always did when something irritated her. She got up and stormed away. "I don't need another lecture to the stupid little sister?"

I got up to follow her.

"No. Let her go," said *Mutter.* "Some things, you can't heal."

Darkness. Again.

Now it is memories only I can see in my own little cinema projected on the ceiling of my room at *Mutter's.* As I lie awake while searing fragments of my life pass through the darkness.

Why am I seeing Karin as a little girl? Angelic almost, she is leaning forward, listening fervently to the latest of my fairy tale stories that I wrote especially for her.

It was from years ago, when she was maybe seven or eight years old, and I would have been about fifteen. She loved my stories as much as I loved writing them for her. They were about colourful characters I invented: the milkman, the dowager, the butcher, the aristocrat, the policeman.

Reading those stories to her was a magical time.

But then it changed. Terribly.

Terribly because I later realized it was after a night when we discovered father had taken her to the room he slept in and closed the door behind him.

Soon afterward she demanded to meet the characters I had created. No matter how many times I explained to her that the Duchess was just someone I had created, she refused to listen. She kept demanding that I let her meet the Duchess and then the Aristocrat. She simply refused to understand that they weren't real.

Finally I decided to tell her that I had sent them away. It was the only way to stop the incessant demands to meet these imaginary people. But when I told her, Karin went into a howling, thrashing tantrum that lasted for days.

Somewhere in there was the moment I realized the real difference between Karin and me:

She sees it when she believes it. Reality is whatever she believes it should be.

If Karin believes my fairy tale characters are real then they are. And she has known those characters all her life. In fact they were probably here for breakfast yesterday. She is sure of it

And on and on.

But I had missed the reason for it all. I had never understood that this was her protection. On that night when *things* were being done to her it was the only way she could erase what had harmed her. The Duchess and the Aristocrat and the milkman were her best friends.

They would protect her. When I hadn't.

Maybe Karin was right.

As different as they were, both Helldorff and father were oddly similar in one fundamental way. Both were irritable functionaries hiding behind whatever protection their uniforms provided. Yet Helldorff in his own way was unique, with that watery stare of his that could simultaneously flash cruelty and vulnerability.

I later wondered if that was what had attracted Karin, what had kept them circling one another in tightening emotional spirals while she casually laughed at whatever it was about him that made others fearful.

It all changed years ago when Karin got pregnant.

They had already used each other up, exhausting any response from one another even when she scorned him dangerously. She was both amused and relieved when she discovered he was casting her aside, interpreting it as a surrender. She was not even upset to find he had so quickly turned to a young blonde who she could not match as her stomach began to bulge four months into her pregnancy.

In the end, all that Karin got from Helldorff was a son and, for a while, protection.

Three months before she gave birth, Helldorff cut off all contact with her. She decided his absence was a sign of fear and in a way she may have been right. He paid all her hospital expenses while ordering his secretaries at Police Headquarters not to put her calls through to him.

Ever, he said.

Months later one of his secretaries told him the same woman was calling again, wanting to know what she should call the baby. Helldorff shrugged, looked out the window of his corner office in the Alexanderplatz and said the baby's name would be Alexander.

A day later the same secretary nervously entered his office saying the woman had called again asking that Herr Helldorff be told the baby's name would be Max.

Or Maximilian if he wished to be formal.

But Helldorff, at the height of his power within the human machinery of fear and power, does not have time for such trivial banalities.

What is now known:

It is, for Helldorff, with his fascination for clairvoyance, a blessing that he cannot see what awaits him. For now, at this height of power and arrogance he, cannot imagine his terrible fate that looms ahead. For now he is content to go on using his vast power in Berlin to extort Jews who are desperate to save themselves. Their panic enriches him. And fascinates him. Like pulling the wings off flies.

Not knowing that in a few years he will become the fly.

His is a fate that leads us to something that so many have wondered about—and then put quickly out of their minds. It is simply too terrifying.

What Count Wolf-Heinrich Graf von Helldorff has bequeathed to the ages is the terror of that last moment of life, the instant when the scales of life and death that have been balanced so exquisitely for each of us suddenly plummets down on the wrong side. That instant? What is that last awful flicker of consciousness like?

What is that awful moment when you are about to be sucked into the abyss and there is nothing you can do about it?

It could come in any number of guises—like knowing with a terrible certainty that you've been fatally stabbed and in the onrush of your blood, there is nothing you can do but cling to the few precious seconds you have left when you know for sure that you are dying and there is nothing that can save you from that blackness that awaits.

Or maybe that moment, having jumped off the bridge with the hard, killing ground rushing toward you, and suddenly you think maybe you've made a mistake. Or in that flash of an instant when the Arabian executioner swings the sword and your head goes flying—are you still thinking thoughts for a second or so? Clear, lucid thoughts about just trying to keep the lights on as blackness descends?

Helldorff would never have intended to teach a master class in all that.

In life he could be seen as weak and evil and vicious all at once. But there was one constant that ran through Helldorff's life: he was always looking for the angle, some loophole, some way to gain an advantage over the situation he is in.

Whether it is with Hanussen or with the rich Jews, there is always that angle that he plays so brilliantly. So coldly. With Hanussen, it is simply abandoning him as he is about to be murdered. And with the rich Jews it is figuring out the precise value of their desperation, and then charging them to buy back their passports and travel documents they need to flee Germany while they still can.

But it is that same mentality, that same playing the angles and finessing the odds which will destroy Helldorff.

Because now in the heat of July, as the war drags on and the German military defeats mount, Helldorff realizes his side will lose. So of course he looks for an angle. He has heard of a plot to overthrow Hitler and he becomes involved just enough that either side would think he was with them—the ultimate playing of the angles! But it backfires and Helldorff is left exposed with all the other plotters.

The others will die hideously but Helldorff has a special death reserved just for him by Hitler whose rage is volcanic. Helldorff? Whom he had trusted! Whom he brought into the circles of power?

And so vicious is Hitler's fury that he minutely choreographs Helldorff's death in a way that will extract maximum horror. He wants to extend that mind-scalding moment of plummeting into the abyss. Hitler is a master of such things. He knows that horror depends both on conscious thought and on recognizing the agony that lies just ahead. A quick bullet is not horror. It is just instant blackness. No, there must be that drawn out moment of sheer terror—giving consciousness the time to explode into the full horror of what lies just moments ahead.

And who better to assist Hitler's horror show than dear old Frau Bechstein? She of the renowned Bechstein piano company. And it will be, in its own terrible way, a hideous kind of music that dear old Frau Bechstein provides.

Because those who Hitler wants to suffer unimaginably and die in agony, are to be hung by piano wire.

And dear old Helene Bechstein, who has cooed and fawned over Adolf long before he was the Führer, who called him Wölfchen!—my little wolf, is here to help. With only the finest piano wires of course. The best that can be provided by the Bechstein Piano company.

Which is where octaves become important.

Ask yourself this question: What octave am I? Middle C probably. Schloss-C in German. Most people are schloss-C.

Wölfchen's people are getting good at knowing what kind of piano wire to use on those they have to hang. The fat ones get the heavier, lower octave wires, a sturdy C2 that Frau Bechstein's technicians would have made sure was pitched at precisely 65,4064 Hertz.

But the skinny ones get to dangle in agony from the thinner wires, usually 5th or 6th octave wires. And those in between—like Helldorff, get schloss-C, middle C.

Wolfie's people learn by practicing, and those Nazis in the Plotzensee prison execution chamber in the north of Berlin, are becoming experts at judging octaves. After so many hideous executions they have become proficient. As the condemned are led to the execution chamber, they can instantly size up the kind of piano wire that will be used on these, the wretches who Hitler wants to suffer most as they are dangled from a steel beam near the high ceiling across the width of the Plotzensee prison execution chamber. For added horror, there are meat hooks that dangle from that steel beam with Frau Bechstein's piano wire wound around the hooks and then hanging down in the form of a noose that will inflict pain and terror unimaginable to ordinary mortals.

But in Hitler's late-stage ravings even that is not enough for what Helldorff deserves. No, there must be more. Worse. Unimaginably worse.

As Helldorff is dragged toward his awful fate, there are no more angles to play. Already stumbling in terror he is confused because the execution chamber turns out to be nothing more than a banal little workmen's' shed behind the looming prison, a shabby brick bungalow of death and pain. He is pushed inside and forced to....

…watch.

Because Hitler, that genius of terror, has ordered that Helldorff be the last man to be hanged, forced to watch others shrieking in their agony, twisting in their unimaginable pain as the Bechstein piano wire strangles them, cuts them slowly, with bowel and bladder explosions that accompany their gagging gasps as their beltless trousers fall down to their pathetically kicking ankles, just to add to the grotesqueries already shredding whatever consciousness they cling to.

And Helldorff is forced to watch it all. To cry out in fear at what awaits him just minutes away.

There can be no turning back. No angle can save him.

And then he is shoved and dragged to the gallows and the piano wire is looped around his neck. But in his terror he is incapable of registering the final sadism—a camera crew that has been sent to record his agony on film so Hitler and others can, in a day or two, sit back in their screening room and watch at their leisure as this Hell on earth plays out with the shrieks, the kicking feet, the gagging and puking and shitting and slow dangling partial decapitation.

It will make for such an enjoyable evening's entertainment.

The camera crew is part of UFA the big movie studio out in Babelsberg. Josef Goebbels, who is now in charge of UFA, has made sure the best cameraman and soundman are there to capture every tiny moment of terror and agony.

And when it is all over, when Helldorff is dangling, still, bloody and quiet, the camera crew silently packs up their equipment.

Then they go outside to vomit.

And weep uncontrollably.

43

ON THE NIGHT AFTER THE bombing I helped *Mutter* move Inga's body.

I took her by the arms, and with *Mutter* holding her feet, we carried her out onto the street. In the cold damp night people were groping their way through the fire-driven winds that still occasionally flared around us. No one paid any attention to us. Not when there were still bodies all over. We took Inga to a place where she would be found when the men came around to collect the dead. *Mutter* stood looking at her immaculate corpse, propped up on the giant shards of concrete.

"And the dust returns to the earth as it was, and the spirit returns to God who gave it," *Mutter* said. "Ecclesiastes," Then she added, "Do you think Ecclesiastes will include people who were sat on?"

Then there was an even stranger moment. Strips of silvery metal foil began falling out of the air. They were the radar-jamming paper streamers dropped from the bombers; some would swirl in the atmosphere for an hour before coming down. These were now raining down on the ruins and on the dead. Inga was soon covered in strips of silver streamers, sparkling in the reflected light of the flames.

"She'd like that look," *Mutter* said.

The familiar and menacing sound of planes came at us quicker than usual and the huge flak towers erupted in the distance, blasting metal into the air in which the planes would be flying. With explosions and fireballs erupting somewhere north of us, *Mutter* and I hurried back toward her tenement building. I was turning toward the shed behind the building when Mutter grabbed my arm. "If I'm going to be flattened, it's not going to be next to Doof. Who knows if you don't get all mingled together which means I could end up in eternity with that moron."

As a jangled tempo of massive explosions sounded from somewhere distant, we got upstairs to the long corridor and then to the kitchen. I almost jumped in startled confusion by what suddenly happened—the phone rang.

In all this. maelstrom? A phone?

Mutter answered it and said "What?" several times before handing the phone to me. "It's your sister. She's in trouble."

"What kind of trouble?"

Mutter said, "I'll let you figure this one out."

On the static-filled phone line, Karin talked in panic-stricken words that never became sentences. "Please!" she said several times. "The crocodiles! Hurry!"

Down on the street there was no way anyone could think of travelling across Berlin to the zoo. Entire sections of the city were smashed and blazing. *Mutter* came up with as close to a solution as could be found: she put two fingers into her mouth and whistled.

The only vehicle on the road, an older Opel lurched to a halt. It had blackout slits for headlights and two SS runes painted onto the driver's side fender. "Gerhard!" she yelled. The side window of the car rolled down and a heavy-featured young man looked out. "Don't leave," yelled *Mutter*. "She's going with you."

"No!" he yelled back. "I have to go to Zehlendorf."

"It's on the way to where she's going."

"I have orders! My commanding officer. He lives on the edge of the Grunewald."

"Even better," Mutter said grabbing my elbow and propelling me toward the Opel while whispering "The plumber's son. Started out as a good boy. But stupid. Be careful." Mutter opened the passenger door and almost shoved me inside."

"This is an SS car," the boy yelled.

"Gerhard I've known you since you were smaller than that clogged sink you never fixed properly for me. So please remember that and take a look around you! Berlin is on fire—and you're worrying about helping someone?"

Gerhard grunted and the put the car into gear. For a while we drove in silence. On either side of the street entire walls crumbled in this latest inferno of massive fires scattered across the city. It was as if the walls had been shot. One moment they were standing; the next they collapsed. The dust was so bad that I put my scarf over my face but Gerhard had nothing to cover his mouth. He began coughing so heavily that I told him to stop as I tore at my scarf with a hairpin and then ripped it lengthwise giving him half. He nodded in gratitude and then reached under the seat pulling out two pairs of large military goggles.

For the rest of the drive we were wiping layers of dust off the goggles and even then it was difficult to avoid hitting objects in the road. Some roads were totally impassible. "Unter den Linden and Wilhelmstrasse were hit hard," he said.

"Try Lützowstrasse," I said. He nodded and drove as far he could before the road became impassible. "Too many bodies," he yelled over the noise of the inferno. "You see how their stomachs are huge? Sticking up through their clothes? Smoke poisoning. It does that to anyone dies from smoke."

He stopped the car and got out, bending to touch the road. Quickly he got back in the car and turned around. Gerhard turned into a nervous talker. His round, knobby face sent the goggles bouncing and the scarf flapping as he talked "The road is too hot. The asphalt is melting. In another hundred meters a car on that road won't have any tires left."

We wove slowly through the streets, some darkened and untouched, some lit by the showers of sparks raining down and others impassable and illuminated by the fires. Gerhard didn't want me to get the wrong idea—he would have been happy being a plumber like his father. But being in the SS was helping the Fatherland. And besides he was convinced that God was on the side of the Fatherland.

Over and over he talked about God being on our side.

It was the sheep that had convinced him of that he said as he turned onto Budapester Strasse. The sheep? Yes, the sheep. He once watched a friend working in a butcher shop as he killed sheep. The friend would hit them as hard he could on the head with an iron mallet and then while they were unconscious slit their throats.

Was this not a sign from God? That God was not on the side of sheep? A sign that sheep who went quietly and stupidly to get their throats slit did not have God on their side. Even though SS men were not supposed to talk of God. But still, there were those sheep. Cast out by God—who chose not to stop that knife at their throats.

"But that is why I follow the Führer," he said as we drove toward the Tiergarten. "He has the answers to all the questions." The Tiergarten had been set ablaze with many of its trees burning in the night. "Are you with the Führer?" Gerhard demanded in full SS tones.

I had a moment of quiet panic that subsided just enough for me to think of what to say: "What a silly question," I said sharply.

Instantly the SS façade fell away and the boy returned. "Oh I am so sorry. I did not mean to insult you. Please forgive me," he stammered. Of course, of course, *everyone* is with the Führer. I meant no offense."

He turned a corner and then leaned toward the windshield crying out as he slammed his foot on the brakes. "*No. no, no!*"

The most beautiful church in Berlin was gone. Obliterated.

The Kaiser Wilhelm Memorial Church, gigantic and inspiring was now rubble. Firemen's hoses spat through the beams of light as walls groaned and crumbled into the flames. Gerhard the SS boy was out of the car yelling, "How can this be? *They* did this?" he gasped "To God's house?"

Only the part of the spire remained. Silhouetted against the swirling smoke it protruded high into the night like a vast and lacerated finger pointing to the skies.

He raged at the skies and yelled into the inferno. "We are not your sheep! Do you hear me?" He spun around motioning to me to join him in his tirade.

I left the car and hurried away.

Turning back into the direction we had come, I stumbled into a small silent street where people lay dead in the darkness. Out past the end of the street were fires that pushed back shadows. I walked up to a woman who was balancing awkwardly on what was left of the low window ledge of what had been a bakery. Her back was turned to me when I asked if she need help. She shook her head without turning around. She was sobbing and writing with chalk on the outer wall:

> *Liebste Frau Lorenz wo sind Sie. Ich bin in*
> *grosser sorge. Ich habe platz fur Sie.*

"Frau Lorenz?" I said.

"Above the store. She slept there sometimes. When she had very early mornings. And it's gone. All gone." She wiped away tears. "I used to buy my bread from her. I want her to stay with me. If we can find her I will—"

Something interrupted her. A terrifying unearthly noise reverberated through the narrow street. It was not the kind of sound that comes normally from anything living, Whatever it was came wrenched, not expelled from a throat, ripped out in pain or fury as a shriek a bellow or something unknown.

"Be careful," the woman said. "Terrible things have happened over there in the zoo." And then went back to writing in chalk.

I walked toward the unearthly sound and to a place where the night opened up again.

When the latest air raid began, Karin had been waiting to spend one of the rare hours with her son Max. It was to have been a chance for both of them to wander through the zoo, the place Karin loved the most. Even in these terrible times she found every excuse she could to visit the animals, convinced she had ways of communicating with them that others did not have.

But waiting for Max, she couldn't remember why she had wanted to meet him. It was such a difficult time. Maybe there was another time that would work better. Especially since she was waiting for the boy to finish this training course or whatever it was in that huge ugly place next to the zoo, this flak tower it was called, where mere boys were now being trained to operate the big guns to shoot down the enemy planes.

When the sirens sounded, she was hurrying past the little Russian Orthodox church next to the zoo. Inside, the choir had just begun singing and they continued even when the roar of planes drove out any other sound. The church shook with vibrations so overpowering that dust fell from cracks in the ceiling. And when the bombs fell nearby, the candles swayed and then those that didn't topple were snuffed out in a rush of smothering air. The choir continued in ragged melody until the last few quavering and high-pitched voices spiraled into a silence that was quickly filled with loud and sobbing prayers. There was nothing to do but wait.

A middle-aged woman beside Karin collapsed in fear and had to be helped up by others. There was something about the woman's hysteria that irritated Karin. Such displays were fine for a film. But here? Mere weakness. Karin got up and groped her way toward the closed doors that were buffeted by the winds outside. Was this not God's house they were in? So would not God look down and see all these creatures—human and animals in one little area where the bombs were coming down. And would not God make it a kind of zero-sum game of death? If one side lost a human—say that hysterical woman over there to a bomb, would that not mean that an animal in the zoo would be spared on the other side of the ledger?

Karin looked around and immediately selected a dozen or more churchgoers who should die so God could spare some of the animals in the zoo next door.

Surely the doddering old fool conducting the choir could go. He was worth a bear at least. And that wispy, fluttering woman, definitely could go instead of a stork. And the bulbous old Prussian with the enormous mustache that was always a refuge for bits of the last meal he'd eaten—he should easily be worth a giraffe. And that fussy old—

The windows at the back of the church blew out.

An hour later when the planes had gone and the night filled with bellowing cries, someone was opening the charred and battered doors of the church. When the doors swung open, a massive crocodile was standing outside on the path. It was looking straight ahead as if it was asleep with its eyes open. And then its front foot moved, its claws clattering on the hard surface. As if prehistoric gears had found one another, the second foot slowly moved and the whole beast turned stiffly.

The crocodile stared at the open door. And plodded forward, one foot raised and falling in front of the other. Again. And again. And again.

It got to the two little steps leading to the church door where dozens of terrified people moved backward. It took another step. And another.

And then the crocodile's head exploded. From only a few feet away the older man put down the big rifle he had just fired.

That was when Karin had screamed at the older man. Killing this magnificent creature? How could he? With his military bearing, the older man looked in amazed fury over the slowly lowering barrel of the rifle. He was tall with close cropped grey hair and eyes that burned holes in the night. Standing over the dead crocodile at the entrance to the church, with Karin screaming at him for killing it, he looked from the churchgoers thanking him over to Karin. Incomprehension turned to silent disgust.

The man with the gun turned and walked toward something he saw in the darkness. Something that moved close to the ground. He raised the gun and fired again.

It was the zoo; the enormous Berlin Zoo that had enchanted the city through endless childhoods was now a twisted inferno, shrieking in the night.

Cages and enclosures were ripped open. Bomb craters were where the Aquarium and Primate House should be, and fires burned in geysers as far as you could see. It seemed as if the whole place was crying out. I walked closer into the hideous symphony of a thousand creatures loudly dying. Flamingos on fire flew past me, crashing into the pavement when their wings burned away. Monkeys howled from the highest branches as flames raced closer up the trees they were on. A lion pirouetted wildly and in pain, trying to extinguish the fire that was burning off its mane. A camel quietly, almost regally, walked past and except for the steam it was giving off, seemed normal until it collapsed as if hit by an invisible wrecking ball.

I went further through what had been the main entrance, past the Primates House that had been blasted into tiny canyons of wreckage. When she phoned, Karin had kept yelling that she was near the crocodiles. There had to be some place where she—

I tripped over something and tumbled onto the ground. As I rolled over and sat up I found myself looking at a long pipe about the diameter of a breakfast bowl, lying across the road and glistening in the light of the fires.

The pipe moved.

It not only moved, it revealed markings, strange, stretched circles as it ebbed in a swift tidal motion, slithering backward until two eyes came into view. It was a snake. The biggest snake I could imagine. Staring at me with pitiless eyes above a tongue that flickered out and vanished. Slowly it moved toward me, its head staying almost still, its eyes never leaving me as the rest of its massive body slithered in menacing, horizontal sweeps back and forth. Closer and closer. The eyes never leaving me, paralyzing me. Why could I not get up? Run?

Slithering. Closer.

And then it stopped.

Its eyes remained fixed on me. The tongue flickered toward me. And then something let go. As if some force had gone away.

"It's dead," a voice said from the shadows. A woman came toward me holding a big stick. She dropped the stick. "I would have done what I could. But African pythons…" She was already hurrying away, not finishing her sentence.

"Wait," I called out, stumbling to my feet. "I know you."

Katherina, the zookeeper in charge of the apes was in tears as she hurried forward into the howls and screams of what once was the zoo. "The damnable flak tower " she cried pointing at the monstrous structure looming in its own darkness beyond the zoo in the Tiergarten. "From the moment they announced a flak tower was to be built next to us I knew my babies were doomed." In the flickers of light I could see her once serene face was now a reflection of what she was living through. "The animals. Look!" she waved into the darkness.

We were stumbling through a darkness momentarily erased by fireballs that blossomed whenever something exploded. Ahead of us was a smoldering jumble of rocks and shattered trees that we threaded through, coming closer to the source of the bellowing, unearthly sound that had drawn me in. Standing on what was left of a little bridge over a pond was a huge elephant thrashing and turning madly in rage and futility.

"Siam! Siam!" she called out and hearing its name, the elephant grew even more agitated. "Oh no! Oh no!" she said over and over as it fixed its fury on us. It took me a moment to understand what Katherina was pointing at. In the pool of shallow water under the little bridge was what I first thought were small, vertical logs. In the roaring light they became the legs of a baby elephant lying dead on its back. "Siam is the father and he—," was all I heard before the trumpet of Siam's rage sounded again. "All he knows is that humans are to blame."

Siam began a thrashing rush toward us. The beast charged and stumbled when the little bridge collapsed under him. "Leave! Quickly!" Katherina tugged at my arm, running and stumbling deeper into the wreckage as the elephant flayed the night with its trunk, crashing and falling in a crazed hunt to find someone to pay for all this anguish.

The animal hospital was the only structure in the zoo left unscathed. The kerosene lights coming from inside gave it an eerie feeling that intensified as we got closer to its shattered windows and moans coming through them.

A voice was yelling the same words over and over again. I couldn't make out what it was saying.

We went inside, through the demolished doorways, into a shadow-cast charnel house. It was a Noah's Ark of the apocalypse. Dead and dying animals lay all over the floors. Dr. Heck and several assistants were doing a kind of triage, separating creatures with a chance to survive from those with no hope. Hyenas, gorillas and chimpanzees lay entangled and barely moving. Katherina rushed to help, shedding her coat and going to one of the big apes in the corner, lying against the wall and breathing heavily. No fish could survive. Nor crocodiles and snakes. Birds fluttered helplessly on smoldering wings.

Other assistants arrived, one carrying two indignant looking penguins, and another older man who carried a big rifle. I didn't understand what he was doing until a panther came crashing in, confused and slashing, seizing a baby African piglet by the throat before the man with the gun could fire. The panther crashed to the floor covered in its own and the dying piglet's blood. A few people looked over and then went back to whatever creatures they were trying to save.

There was that voice again. I could hear it more clearly now, "*Heil Hitler!... Heil Hitler!... Heil Hitler!*" Over and over. It came from further down the corridor, calling out for a minute, falling silent and then starting again.

I walked through several empty rooms, and then one filled with carcasses. A man and a woman stood over a dead zebra wielding huge knives they were using to slice up the animal. Dripping chunks of meat lay on a metal counter. The woman looked up, an oozing sabre-like knife in her hands and guilt written all over her face. "We have families, you know."

The man looked up from where he was kneeling over a flank, also in need of justification. "We'll give you some."

"Thank you," I said and kept walking. Ahead, through open doors I saw Herr Riedel, a serious, balding man swaddled in a flapping apron. He was the lion keeper and was forcing a surly, silent tiger back into a big metal traveling cage. He saw me and yelled "Next room," as he prodded the tiger back into its cage. I continued toward the faint shaft of candlelight coming from another room.

It was where Karin sat on the floor, staring off into that world of hers that only she could see. With her back to a wall, she had a baby lion cub in her arms, holding it close and nursing it with a bottle. Just over an arm's length away a female lion lay on its side, groaning and clawing at the air as Karin held her cub. "She's dying but still she is trying to protect her baby," she said. "Isn't that beautiful?"

I had never seen Karin so peaceful.

"In normal time she would kill me for touching her cub. But I feel her love for her cub. So I'm trying to let that love flow through me. You can feel it too, can't you?"

"Maybe I'm too far away."

"Come closer."

The mother lion raised its head and tried to snarl, making only a rattling sound from its throat. Its back legs scratched weakly at the tiled floor trying to get the traction to raise itself. "There, there," Karin said soothingly. She held the lion cub out in front of her and then pressed it closer to the mother's face. She was lying almost next to the mother as she nuzzled her cub, licking it once and then groaning.

And then after a wheezing sound, dying.

The lion cub made scratchy mewling pleas to its mother. Karin gently pulled it back to her, soothing it and singing lullabies that were lost to the din of dying creatures all around.

I sank to the floor wondering. A baby lion cub? And all that love flowing onto it, sustaining it?

"Have you seen your son?" I asked.

"My son?"

"Max."

"Oh. Yes." It was as if she'd forgotten about him. "I just got used to thinking of him as being Inga's now."

"Inga's dead."

"In the raid?"

"Yes."

"How awful." She pulled the tiny cub closer to her.

Max stood in the doorway suspended somewhere between a twelve-year-old boy and old age.

Behind him the damp dawn was draining away the darkness. For a moment he couldn't say anything even when it looked as if he was trying to talk. He leaned against the wall, his eyes red with exhaustion and his face grey.

"They wouldn't let us leave the flak tower last night. All of us. They made us stay and shoot the guns into the air. The smaller guns. Out on the roof."

"But that's awful. Were there no men there?" Karin sat on the floor holding the lion cub in her arms, nursing it again with a baby's bottle.

"There were a few men."

"But since when are boys like you doing this kind of thing?"

"It's because a lot of the men have died."

She stroked the lion cub under its chin, barely looking at Max. "Bella has something to tell you." Karin's remark caught me by surprise. I tried to signal her with my eyes. She was not looking in my direction. "About your mother."

"Karin!" I said, "Don't do this—"

"What about my mother?" The boy looked from me to Karin. Then he blurted, "Which mother?"

"Inga." Karin said. "Of course."

"She always told me she is not my real mother."

"She said that?"

Max's face gave way to a slow rising anger that was overwhelming his exhaustion. "When she drinks too much she says things like that. Once she said you never wanted to be my mother."

Karin continued soothing the lion cub.

Max looked as if he was either going to yell or burst into tears. "She said that. So she has to pretend harder to be my mother." His words came out in jabs now. "*Pretend* to be my mother. She's said those kind of things when she's really drunk, so drunk she could barely stand."

"A shame."

"No it's not a shame!" Max was yelling. "You know why? When she's sober she wants me. You can tell. She does. She's the best person I have."

I instantly moved in front of Karin, knowing what would come next. "Karin! No. Not—"

"The boy needs to know."

"What does *the boy* need to know?" Max almost yelled before I could respond.

"I'm sorry."

"Sorry for what?"

"Inga's dead." Karin said.

"No!" He yelled again and pointed his finger at her. "You stop that!"

"I'm sorry. Really, I am."

"You're not! " He swiveled toward me in fury and pleading, "Make her stop saying terrible things like that."

"She died in the air raid last night." Karin said.

When I started to say something but faltered, Max lost whatever had been holding him together and became a boy even younger than his years, exploding in tears and pounding his fists on the wall.

"I will do what I can. To help," said Karin holding the cub closer.

"No you won't." Max spit out the words. "You never do."

"I'm sorry," said Karin. "I understand how you feel."

"No you don't. You never have!" he yelled, pulling himself up by his own vehemence as he stormed into the corridor. "I don't need you. I have the Reich."

His departing footsteps made staccato volleys all the way down the corridor. "He's just a boy," Karin said. She held the lion cub out in front of her and then put it down beside the muzzle of its dead mother lying on the floor. "She wants its mother. Its real mother." I watched her for a while. She wouldn't look at me.

"Please," she said, "don't lecture me."

As I was leaving she said quietly, "I understand more than you think I do."

On my way out I walked along the outer corridor toward that same voice that had started yelling again. I pushed open a door and the voice came at me in a shriek. A parrot jumped back and forth in an enormous cage, yelling loudly, "*Heil Hitler!… Heil Hitler!… Heil Hitler!*" With a bright red front and head and blue wings and streaks of yellow, the bird could be heard all the way out of the building and onto the smoldering ruins of the zoo.

The way back to *Mutter's* was a journey through images that the mind sometimes refused to accept. The Memorial Church was still there in my mind, towering and awe inspiring, not the smoldering wreckage that it was now. And the shattered Ku-damm—my mind rebuilt all those fine shops as I looked away. But *Mutter's* street, the one where Dick and Doof still patrolled, was beyond the power of memory; it looked like a giant mouth that had been punched, leaving some of its teeth missing, with some buildings standing intact next to wreckage filled spaces on either side.

Even after the latest bombing, the damage to *Mutter's* building was mostly superficial, losing only part of the façade at the far end of the ground floor. When I went inside all was quiet. After the exhaustion of the previous night, everyone was still sleeping.

I went quietly along our dimly lit corridor, stopping and then backing up until I was in front of Herr Langen's—Paul's, door. Gently I opened the door, went inside and closed it silently behind me.

I stood waiting for my eyes to transform the darkness into vague outlines in shades of black. He was asleep, lying in his side facing toward me. I remained frozen in the silence of a voice in my memory. It was my own voice rushing through all the encounters with him that I could remember—from the timid first meeting in his office, to a gradual easiness and then to the first names of where we were now.

And for the first time, I allowed myself to understand that somewhere on that journey, possibly long ago, I had fallen in love.

As I gently lay beside him, I had never been naked as I was then. He stirred and there was a moment of touching, a spark of something that shot through me, something I did not at recognize until for the first time I understood ecstasy.

I did not know I wanted, *needed* to be touched, craved it even, and with the warmth of his hands turning me toward him, *oh Paul*, and thankful for the darkness because I am not young; my body is not old but it is no longer the way I want it to be. And could he be thinking the same thing? but I am glad not to be seen in my nakedness in case I do not...am not desirable... in case he is disappointed... And why am I thinking like this? I give thanks for the darkness so my flaws... did Karin ever wonder about this? Flaws? With all that beauty of hers, could not some of it have been divided between us? Surely she cannot ever have craved darkness, she must glory in the light with that perfect body like a trophy that her soul won in a lottery, but I cannot think of that now as his lips are searching for me in the darkness.

Mutter amazed me.

She missed nothing. And at the same time she yielded nothing. Unless she wanted to. Which is a way of saying that you never really knew what she was thinking unless she wanted you to know it. She would just sit by the stove brewing her stews of increasingly suspect ingredients. For instance when a horse died on any street within three or four blocks of us, you knew that her fierce bartering skills would fuse with her survival instinct and the result would be a half-kilo or more of horsemeat. But it was when no horse had died recently and she was adding something that looked like meat to the stew that her meals were a perilous crossing. And relief only came when we got to the other side.

On the morning after that terrible bombing raid and the zoo, I left Paul's room, coming out into the corridor so silently that no one could possibly have known my starting point. To make it look as if I had spent the night in my own room, I made noises and took a bath—this was when the water was still running. And then when I finally made it to the kitchen, drying my hair in a towel, I was convinced that *Mutter* knew nothing about where I slept the night before.

She was reading while stirring the big iron pot on the stove. For a while she would turn the pages of one of the pornographic novels from the Weimar days that she had stashed away. Occasionally she made grunting noises as she read from the dirty parts. And sometimes she would whistle quietly or come out with a *yes*! before putting the novel down and picking up the Bible, usually heading straight for *Matthew* or *Corinthians*.

When she saw me, she looked over her glasses and grumbled something about redemption being the best part of sinning. And then belted out biblical verses about fornication.

But on this morning she soon abandoned her usual practice of going back to the pornographic novel after a brief foray into redemption. She put the Bible down and peered at me over her glasses.

"So it's 'Paul' now, is it? No more 'Herr Langen'?"

I gave the slightest nod I could and shrugged.

"Neither of you are teenagers," she said. She waited for me to reply. I merely nodded. "Time is not on your side. You must mate like minks. Do you hear me?"

Again the stew was stirred. At first slowly but then faster and faster until she threw the big spoon down and went back to the pornographic novel. She read for a moment, grunted, and then said, "I know you. Both of you. You are a type. The type that still hears some dried-up minister's voice from when you were a child. spewing all that fire and brimstone stuff about sex that they scared you with. Or maybe it was some old maid aunt lying to you about how thankful she was to escape all that sweaty, sticky fornicating business.

"Just go back in there and fuck like you'll die tomorrow. Because you might.

"Do you understand?"

I nodded. And did as I was told.

44

THE GREY LIGHT OF MORNING reveals the wreckage of the Ufa-Palast am Zoo, the grandest movie theater of them all. It is across the road from the Berlin Zoo, and like the Zoo the once glittering movie palace it is now rubble.

After the worst of the bombing on the night before, the animals fled from shattered cages, some of them racing or lumbering toward the steaming wreckage of the cinema, lured by the scent of incinerated food that has been blown through the rubble like shotgun pellets. In the splintered remnants of the balcony, now open to the skies, a band of monkeys found a few morsels before they were chased away by a hobbling lion. The lion snarled his way toward chunks of uncooked meat that once were to have been sausages. It limped up to the top of the rubble, looked around, and was shot dead by the older man with the gun.

On both sides of the boulevard all that grandeur lay in ruins.

Which we learned, was the state of so many cinemas across Germany as the British and American bombers were blowing the great cities and towns, to pieces. And with them the cinemas.

For days after the raid, bombed-out refugees struggled around the remnants of the Ufa-Palast am Zoo, pulling their few belongings behind them searching for somewhere to live, lining up for assistance from the regime and begging for food.

Movies were the last thing they wanted.

Which is where we came in. Because if theatre, cabaret, concerts, rallies, sex and movies were all finished as public entertainment, then at least there would still be what people now craved more than ever:

Gossip.

"Forget my whores," said *Mutter*. "They can't help our gossip now."

"Why?" asked Herr Langen. Paul.

"Not enough clients now. Their clients are like the bees spreading the pollen around. Only in their case they spread gossip. You need a lot of bees. And we no longer have a hive."

"So what do we do?"

The three of us sat in the kitchen warming ourselves by the stove and agreeing with *Mutter* that even though it would be difficult, gossip was like the weeds that grew in the cracks in concrete: there was just no way to stifle it. But it was even more perilous now because the Gestapo saw treason everywhere and all around us people were vanishing at an even faster rate as the war became grimmer.

The SS had refined the terror they created and with it the language they used to polish the hard surface of fear that encased us all:

Protective custody.

Politically unreliable.

People's Court

Such simple words. Melodic almost. But they were like silk flowing over the blade hidden within. They were routinely used as a rationale to execute so many people.

Such truly simple words.

And gossip about the Reich was one of the quickest ways to be *sent east*.

Which left us pondering how to move out our gossip without being ensnared in the traps that lay all around. Suddenly *Mutter* acted as if she'd had revelation, "The water pump!" she said.

"In the mornings there is a long line at the pump, most of them women, waiting for their turn to fill their pails with water. That is the level of civilization we have been pushed down to. Sometimes it takes an hour to get to the pump so there's this long winding line, and all they have to do is talk. If we're smart we can use it to spread the gossip. Three times a week I'll be in the middle of that line. Asking if anyone has heard about whatever piece of *mundfunk* we come up with."

There was a silence. Neither of us knew what to think of the idea which made her impatient, especially because Paul was staring into the floor "Well Herr Langen? Searching for big words are we?"

Paul took his time looking up at her. "Think of each piece of gossip as a Lilliputian," he said.

"Here we go," said *Mutter*.

Paul ignored her eye-rolling. "Each one is infinitely smaller than Gulliver, their massive opponent. But because there are so many of them, together they bring Gulliver down."

"*Wunderbar!*" chortled *Mutter*. "Now tell me what the hell you are talking about"

"I am saying more or less what you said. We release only the smallest fragments, one at a time. The chattering people out there will put them all together."

That night Mutter began dividing the gossip we had heard into items, writing them on a scrap of paper. The first ones were more stories about Zarah Leander and the SS. But there was grim gossip too, like the actor named Robert Dorsay who had just been executed for making jokes about Hitler.

And there were Goebbels' rages. He had ordered a complete reshoot of Marika Rökk's vivacious dance scene in *Die Frau meiner Träume*—The Woman of my Dreams. *Dreams*? Goebbels was livid, "A German woman should not dance so provocatively and shamelessly," Goebbels was supposed to have screamed at the producers—who scrambled to reshoot the scene with Marika Rökk who had now been ordered to dance as if she was arthritic.

Paul put a checkmark beside the stories on *Mutter's* piece of paper. She beamed the way she always did whenever he approved of her suggestions.

"*The words of a talebearer are like tasty trifles, and they go down into the inmost body,*" said *Mutter* in triumph.

"Proverbs " she added.

"No," Paul said. "Lilliputians."

SEVEN

45

The End. April 1945

33.09%

I think of it all the time: Thirty-three and point zero nine percent.

In other words almost exactly one third.

One out of three. Which is the percentage who voted for Hitler and the Nazis in the election that allowed them to take power. To cause all this horror and cruelty and murder.

But the bombs from the planes high above us do not discriminate. They fall on the other two thirds of us just as they do on the 33.09.

We are being incinerated. Entombed. Torn apart.

Many will say we deserve it. All of us. Maybe. Yes. We, the two thirds, stood by until it was too late. But it became too late so quickly. That was part of the terrible national folly—it became *too late* before people thought it would.

In their own terrible way, the bombs are the ultimate moral judgement. Their way of killing whoever just happens to be there is as uncaring as so many of our people were when there was still time to stop all the madness. No one cared enough to really do anything. Just as the bombs do not care now.

So we are being incinerated for not speaking out. For not standing up in that moment when we could have. For not mocking all the *Seig Heil* types in the early days. The buffoons who were enthralled by how they looked in the mirror.

But now it is truly too late, For everything. We are burning and yes, there is the matter of our guilt.

Is it guilt for not having the courage to die the painful deaths of martyrs, hanged by piano wire a decade ago?

Would you?

I also think about that all the time.

Waiting to be conquered is a strange way to live.

And even more bizarre, is cheering on one set of conquerors over another. Now that the war is almost over, the awful irony is that we are praying for the Americans. And for the British. We want them to conquer us.

All of us, everyone but the Nazi hierarchy who will have to shoot themselves anyway, are praying that either the Americans or the British get to the wreckage that is Berlin before the Russians.

We are surrounded.

Fear registers on the face of anyone hearing a noise in the distant east. It is the Russians who are coming from the east. Is it their guns we hear? Artillery? We know they are there and getting closer. And we have heard what the German troops did to the Russian civilians when they still thought they would conquer Moscow. And now we are hearing what the Russians are doing to us in return.

The stories make us tremble.

The view from our little rooftop area had changed. After each bombing the street would be cleared of all the rubble from the buildings that had died theatrically More than half of the buildings were still standing but they were just walls with no roofs, floors or windows. It was like looking out on the ruins of an ancient civilization whose inhabitants had not yet vanished into history. Occasionally an architectural death rattle would give warning in the form of a low groaning noise just seconds before another wall collapsed in a cloud of dust and flying debris.

The American and British bombers had not hit our little area of Neukölln as hard as many other areas of Berlin. Even with some of its windows blown out, *Mutter's* building was one of the few on the street that were still standing.

But in all its grim greyness, almost everything about the area was different now. Dick and Doof had reappeared with orders from the Berlin *Gauleiter's* office that any unused rooms were to be given over to people who had been certified as "Bombed out" Within days the new arrivals on our downstairs floors were locked into shouting matches with the Swabian whore, yelling at her to stop singing her filthy Bavarian songs at night. And to hell with this Jürgen, whoever he was. And their cooking smells seeped up into our corridor, some so strong that not even *Mutter's* most fortified soup could fight them off.

These new people, urban refugees, living downstairs made it treacherous for us. In their pain and confusion you never knew who could become an informer. Especially those who were most vulnerable, those with a desperate need to please Doof who was gorging himself on self-importance.

In order to avoid them, whenever Paul or I left or entered *Mutters*, we would always use the farthest of the rear entrances at the eastern side of the building.

Which is what I did after I heard the words *Philharmonic* concert over the phone on one of the few days when the phones worked. It was Karin's code. I could barely hear her over the static. It was obvious that she did not want to say much in case someone was listening. She hurriedly said that she would phone me again. And that it was important I do what she said.

The war was lurching to what most of us knew would be its strangled end. And as it did, Berlin, once the great mecca of entertainment, hedonism and culture had become a grim, grey and fearful place. Any act of pure enjoyment seemed almost frivolous with all that death around us. The nightclubs were long closed; a few theaters like the Deutsche near the Friedrichstrasse station struggled to stay open; and so many of the grand café areas like Haus Vaterland were now just incinerated shells held up by twisted girders.

All of it has gone; all the life and sensuality. Gone.

Ah yes but this is Germany and where else in the midst of the death throes of a nation and the annihilation of a regime could music be considered a priority?

Even though it is now just eighteen days before Hitler will put a gun to his head and pull the trigger. No one can know that of course. Yet everyone understands that the end is near.

But Albert Speer, Hitler's architect, designer of the Third Reich—creator of the awe-inspiring Cathedral of Light at the Nuremberg Rallies, orders the Berlin Philharmonic to perform.

Merely finding a place for the orchestra to play is a problem because the Philharmonic Hall has been bombed into rubble. Another hall is found but this one has no heat, so both the orchestra and the audience are wrapped in extra clothing to fight off the cold.

Speer has decreed that the usual Beethoven violin concertos and Romantic symphonies be played. But most of all he wants the concert to end—as maybe the Third Reich is ending, on the finale from the Wagner opera Götterdämmerung. And what better way to go out than with this brooding music that drags all who hear it into the terrible prophesies of wars among men and gods?

But someone has decided there is another way to go out. Perhaps a better way.

As the concertgoers leave, smiling boys from the Hitler Youth are standing at the exits holding what looks like baskets filled with candy for all to take. But it is not candy in those baskets. They are filled with cyanide pills. Crunch down on one and you're dead in seconds. Just to be helpful you understand.

Because after all, the rapacious Russian army is just beyond the city limits.

The real Götterdämmerung.

I left on a cool Thursday afternoon in mid-April, telling Paul and *Mutter* that Karin had two tickets to the Berlin Philharmonic, which amazingly was still having performances.

I got part way to Beethoven Hall on the U-Bahn and then walked the last few kilometers. I arrived there as people were hurrying into the Hall. I walked up the steps and looked around; Karin was nowhere to be seen. I walked around the side of the building and saw an old car idling on the street. Memory kicked in. I walked closer thinking surely it could not be.

It was.

Uncle Rudi was sitting behind the wheel of a car that did not fit what I remembered about him. It was such a shabby and ordinary vehicle, not like the big, expensive cars he once drove. And there were no stanchions flying Nazi flags from enormous fenders. For a moment I wasn't sure it was him; to make sure I walked around to the front of the car. He sat as still as a sphinx, looking straight ahead. Only his eyes followed me.

There was a moment where we just stared at one another, him looking through a cracked windshield. Then I said, "Uncle Rudi?"

"Well at least *you* still recognize me. And will still talk to me. I was concerned on both counts."

"Tell me—explain to me, what has brought you to meet me in a car you would once never have been seen in?"

Instantly he answered, "Humiliation."

We sat in the remnants of a café, not far from the Ku'damm. His hands no longer shook the way they used to whenever he lit a cigarette. And while he wasn't actually smaller, he just seemed that way. He had regained some of his aura of mystery but the scars on the side on his face no longer enhanced it. Instead they just looked like some tribal disfigurement that you had trouble keeping your eyes away from.

I told him how I marveled at how relaxed he seemed.

"It happens when you stop caring," he said. "I have almost been dead three times. Last summer I thought they would come for me and kill me. After July 20 when people tried to assassinate Hitler. But somehow they forgot about me. I'm not important enough anymore. Out there in the hinterlands of Cologne, the place they banished me to. Or what's left of it."

"Why did you need Karin to reach me?"

"Her, I know how to contact. You, I don't"

"Why are you here?"

"Before I go into that, I want you to understand something: Surrender to the Americans, not the Russians."

"Everyone is saying that."

"Then they've heard the stories. The Russians are raping every woman they can find alive."

"Why haven't we just surrendered? The whole country?"

"Because so many people still in power here know they are war criminals. And they know they will pay a hideous price for it. So there is no choice."

He reached into a leather briefcase. "Stettin," was all he said at first. It was a photograph of an official document: Father's birth certificate. "I told you there were still documents I could not get to."

"And now...?"

He pulled out a piece of paper. "I went back there a month ago. The documents have all been moved to the new archives." He handed me a photograph of an official document. "This is the best I could do. A photograph. I couldn't get the original document out of there." It was father's birth certificate He pointed to a line on the photograph. "Look here."

On that line was the heading, *MOTHER.*

Under it was Birgit's name.

And next to her name was the word *Jude.*

"We talked about this. I know this."

"But they don't. At least not yet. But because of this document is now available to be viewed they will. Soon. They are beginning to look through these documents, looking for anyone they may have missed."

"What will happen when they find out father is half-Jewish?"

"It depends on how long the war goes on. Some Gestapo offices are in chaos now. But I still have contacts," he said. "I can help. A little. But not much."

"Why are you showing me this?"

"Your father would never listen to anything I said. He needs to know that he's half Jewish. Before the Gestapo comes for him. If it's not too late already."

Images of wedding rings, piled on a desk stopped me from saying anything. I was about to tell Uncle Rudi that it was not fair to ask me to do anything to save father. But another image took over. "What do you think he would say if he knew his real mother was a Jew?"

"Are you smiling?" he asked. As he too allowed himself a tiny smile.

"Am I?" I didn't mean to. "All right, I will go and see him. I think he needs to know this."

"You haven't asked me about yourself. Or Karin. After all, this makes you one quarter Jewish."

"Will they come looking for us now?"

"No."

"Why just him?"

"His files had already been sent to the Gestapo before Stettin was bombed again last month. Yours would have still been buried deep in a mountain of paper that went up in flames. It will take them too long to make the connection."

From somewhere far away came a low rumble that we would once have thought was thunder. He looked sharply in its direction. "The Russian artillery," he said trying to sound relaxed.

"Are you going to be all right?"

"I'll be fine," he said with as much of a smile that flickered. But we both knew he didn't mean it.

I left thinking that Uncle Rudi was a chrysalis in reverse, going from beauty to a shell of what he had been. I hugged him, almost clung to him because of what I needed to believe, not just about him but maybe about all of us.

On the way to father's, the streets seemed to empty out and there was an eerie, deserted quality because for several days in a row the American air force had carried out daylight bombing raids. Even though it was in the middle of the week, on one of a warm and sunny day, there were parts of Charlottenburg where it seemed as empty as a Sunday.

I got close to Wilmersdorf and the streets that seemed so familiar suddenly became menacing for no reason that I could understand. I remembered us running and laughing and now there was only an odd stillness. Or maybe it was because the little enclave of houses was mostly untouched by the bombing. The concept of normal—whatever that was, was eerie.

I turned a corner and found myself staring at the house that had once been my home but now stood emptied of any attachment that mattered to me. Outside the entrance was a black car that didn't belong there. I had seen cars like that in other places and these days they all meant Gestapo. For a minute or so, all was still and quiet. That ended in an instant with the loud wail of air raid sirens. It was like a starting bell that sent the front door swinging open with two Gestapo men hurrying out to the car and then speeding away. A plump older lady came to the open door and stood looking up into the sunlight like a flower waiting to bloom.

When the Gestapo car had vanished she lowered her head, opened her eyes and when she noticed me said, "Hello Bella."

"I don't know you," I said approaching. She didn't answer. "How do you know my name?"

"The photographs of course. They're all over the house. Every day since I first came here four years ago I've watched you and your sister grow up in the photographs. I'm Greta. His housekeeper."

"Those men..."

"Gestapo."

"Yes. Why did they leave like that?"

"Your father told them this house has no air raid shelter. They said they will be back after the raid. Then they ran away."

From high above a faint noise intruded, as if the sky was being scraped.

"What do you do in air raids?"

"I just sit here. And we wait for them to end. They always do." She pointed toward the library. "He's in there."

The noise from the sky had changed into a distant droning sound.

I wanted to arrive unannounced at the door to his library but the hallway floor creaked treacherously under me as I approached. Alerted to an intruder, father sat behind his desk, as straight and stiff as a mannequin. He had aged. His face that once had a kind of weak elegance was now cinched up around his mouth as if some inner drawstrings had been pulled tight. His head seemed to have shrunk and the hair on top of it had thinned to a collection of strands. The only part of him that had not changed was his Nazi bureaucrat's uniform.

His glare came at me like darts. "Well, well," was all he said.

"Hello father."

"Did I ask you to come?"

"No. You didn't." I waited for a response. "What were the Gestapo doing here?"

"That is none of your business."

"I think I already know."

"Lies, all lies."

"But those men are coming back?"

"So you are here to cheer them on. My, my. You and your mother—sainted as she was, have a lot in common."

I looked at the small pile of gold wedding rings on the corner of his desk. "The last time I was here there were hundreds of rings. Thousands probably."

"And?"

"There's only a few on your desk."

"Is it my fault we're running out of raw material."

"You mean running out of Jews."

"I received a letter of congratulations you know. Eichmann signed it himself. Do you know that?"

"No."

"Well you should. I brought millions into the Reich."

"You know don't you?"

"Know what?

"Mother told me. I know. I've always known. So you must have too."

"What drivel is this?" His eyebrows shot up.

"You're half Jewish."

He screamed: "You will not come into my house and spout your filth!"

"Birgit was your real mother."

"*Get out!*"

"Mother told me as she was dying. About Birgit being your mother. My grandmother." I pointed. "Those rings. They're from people like you. Or me."

"*Out!*" he reached into his desk drawer and took out a pistol.

The droning sound in the sky was becoming a roar. I sat there, for some reason utterly unafraid. "And you knew too. You saw grandpa, your father, break down at Birgit's funeral. She was the great love of his life."

His face blossomed into quivering redness. I heard part of what he yelled at me, something about never having been respected. Everything else was drowned out by the terrifying roar that sent the windowpanes shaking and snapping in their frames. It was if he heard nothing but his own voice. He leaned from behind his desk, yelling and lecturing me but not one word could be heard.

Not even the first explosion interrupted his fury. He clutched and pounded the desk as if that would make his words intelligible. The explosion sounded as if it came from somewhere up around Spandau. But then other ones followed quickly like some monstrous castanet.

Father just kept standing there, yelling and waving his arms. More explosions. Closer.

I got up and left the room with him still yelling. Somewhere upstairs, a window blew in. Still he raged.

Greta, the housekeeper sat near the front entrance, her eyes closed, a rosary in her hands with her fingers, like fat little sausages, drumming on its beads. Everything was shaking now. I climbed the stairs to my old room, clinging to a banister that throbbed under my grip. If I was going to die, let it be in the room in which I was born. Nothing had changed since I last saw it. The heavy curtains were closed and a musty smell clung in the still air that instantly turned violent as I was thrown off the chair I had just sat on.

The explosion was so brutal that it twisted the house and felt like a hammer that smashed my bones. Everything was blown away for an instant, then sucked back with a noise so loud that blood came to my ears. From the floor, behind an overturned armoire that might have saved me, I looked up at where there should have been ceiling and saw the sky. In all that blueness, bright silvery things streamed past high above.

Pretty, bright, silvery thing that dropped death on us.

I was no longer in a room; I was on what now was a ledge, dazed and surrounded by sunlight. And soon, by silence. And dust. And things floating in the air until that air became clean again.

I clutched at what had once seemed eternal and now were wisps. Bannisters: walls, stairs, all quivering to the touch, some crumbling completely as I edged and crawled my way down the stairs that had once been at the center of our house but were now open to the skies. It was as if the house had been sawed in half.

I wobbled and groped my way to the ground floor that had become a kind of gravel quarry, strewn with maimed fragments of what had once given support and strength. Everything was being covered in a fine dust. Which was why at first I didn't see Greta, the old housekeeper. She remained utterly still in the same chair I had last seen her in, sitting looking straight ahead. But now she was covered in a fine plaster dust, looking like a statue. I touched her shoulder. Gently. Out of concern.

She fell sideways and lay curled and still on the floor with dead eyes, wide open and seeing nothing.

I walked through debris and maneuvered myself across fallen beams until I reached father's library. He was standing in the middle of the wreckage looking out through chasms that once were windows. He turned in a shuffling semi-circle, in that arthritic way that people turn after a certain age. He stared at me as if I was something he had misplaced and found again.

"The housekeeper," he said, "Is she dead?"

"Yes."

"Oh," he said, brushing away debris from his chair. He sat down behind the desk and looked lost. "She was nice you know. Very nice."

"Yes. She seemed nice."

"She gave me sex."

"I'm your daughter. I don't need to know this."

"Don't be ridiculous. It wasn't sex like most people think. But still it was sex." He looked up at me almost desperately. "You people, all of you, never understood, did you? That was all I asked for. There's nothing wrong with that you know. It didn't have to be perfect. The sex I mean." For what seemed like the longest time we stared at each other through all that wreckage. He never blinked. I don't know how he did it.

Finally I turned and went toward the front door, crawling over the wreckage. I stumbled across fallen beams in what was left of the doorway and got to the driveway.

A gunshot sounded.

When I heard the sound I was almost at the street. It was a single shot and came from inside the wreckage of our house.

I waited to see if there was anything that followed. There was nothing. And then I remained, waiting longer for some wave of remorse or sorrow to surge through me. It never came.

Instead, I stood caught between the rushing torrents of my life. I walked forward.

When I got to the street there was only silence that was occasionally broken by an odd fluttering sound. It came from the few birds left barely alive after the blasts from the bombing raid.

Everywhere there were dead birds that had just fallen out of the skies. Those few that were still alive, made noises and some tried to walk or fly before toppling over.

After a few minutes the stillness was complete.

46

THERE IS SOMETHING SEXUAL THAT happens in the face of doom.

Berlin went from the exhaustion of war to the frenzy of incoming defeat that everyone knew was mere days away. And with it, came a desperate need for sex. We heard stories about it everywhere: in the lines at the water pump, picking nettles for tea, or scrounging for leftover lumps of coal on the tracks of the S-Bahn trains.

Stories were all over—even of the young women at the *Haus des Rundfunks,* many of them still in their teenage years, setting out in battalion strength to lose their virginity before Berlin was conquered. And we heard of young soldiers desperate not to fall on the battlefield, unloved in the most physical sense they could imagine. No one condemned it. All of us discovered some primordial urge to ward off the impending terror that awaits us. With every distant rumble of the Russian artillery, propriety crumbled.

Copulation was everywhere. And not just among the young who wanted to know lust before they died. The wrecked forests of the Tiergarten, the bunkers, the darkness, the shattered offices—all of them became setting for the desperate mosaic of sexual frenzy and unrequited life. It went on amid grim military men fighting and knowing that their lives would end soon in a broken city filled with the shattered and the homeless; and amid the corpses of young men hanging from lampposts with signs pinned to them accusing them of deserting their army units, and amid the fear of what lay ahead when the Russians came—amid all that there was an invisible and frantic demand that desire be fulfilled.

Mine was simple: Paul.

Shamelessly I cast aside all declarations of independence. I wanted to possess and be possessed, to fling aside the past and care nothing for the future. For three nights I did. We did, And on one of those nights we lay naked while bombs began to fall not that far away as he was over me moving rhythmically as neither of us thought to flee to safety. This *was* safety.

If this was to be the end of us then *God we give thanks for this bliss from which we are now to be taken* and when the bombing ended we lay there entwined in one another's arms and fell asleep.

It was after these nights that I learned a fundamental difference between us. For me life has no compartments; whatever happens in one area of my life floods into all the other areas of it. Paul had that ability to lead life from its compartments. They exist within him so that no matter what happened in one, it will not interfere with what he is doing in another.

It is just the difference in how we are. I saw it most clearly on the morning after that night when we ignored the falling bombs. I came into the kitchen and could barely think of anything but the night before. *Mutter* said something to me that I ignored and just smiled at her. She gave me a strange, puzzled look and then rolled her eyes. I sat in front of the stove, grateful for the watery ersatz coffee and adrift in the memories of last night.

Paul came into the kitchen, smiled to us both but before he sat down *Mutter* had said one word to him, the same one she had said to me:

Kolberg?

He repeated the word.

Mutter nodded.

In less than a minute, instantly he was in that compartment. While I chose to remain drifting on memories for a little while longer, Paul was at the table mapping out a strategy. It would be our grand finale. Never had gossip and the fate been so intertwined.

Josef Goebbels cannot let go.

Like a gambler having lost his fortune, he is sure that just one more roll of the dice will change everything: Just one more spin of the wheel. That's all—just one more and it will all change! But now? With Germany crumbling? With death and defeat all around, a movie?

The official German records will say that a mere 1,105,987 German soldiers have been killed in Russia. And they say another million or so are missing. Both are lies. Everyone knows the carnage is worse, far worse. Three, maybe four million Germans have died there. And an entire Nazi army group has surrendered and is being marched off into the prison camps of Siberia.

And now with German cities terrorized nightly by falling bombs and with devastating reports coming in from the fronts on a daily basis, it is beyond what anyone can comprehend. The ultimate catastrophe is looming.

So Goebbels decides that what the nation needs is another movie.

Why of course!

What better way to rouse the masses than the amazing true story of the brave little town of Kolberg. A stirring tale of German heroism and victory.

But now? A movie?

Is he trying to hold on to his one, last link to Lida Baarova? She is in exile in Italy where he hears she is acting in bad movies. It must be hard for her; Gobbels is sure of it. But surely from her lonely exile she would have to have heard of his accomplishments in such important motion pictures. She must have heard.

Surely.

And Kolberg will be a film for the ages It is the perfect heroic tale for these difficult times—even if it happened almost a century and a half ago, way back in the Napoleonic wars of 1807. When one courageous German citizen rallied his countrymen in the encircled town of Kolberg to fight against the overwhelming foreign army all around them.

Exactly like what we face now, Goebbels announces. Who could possibly miss the similarities?

Using his power as Reichminister, he makes history in the movie business. Kolberg will be the most expensive film he has ever put into production. Even as the war is taking its final devastating turns, with the German army now losing ground at an alarming rate, he makes a momentous decision:

The movie comes first. It will get whatever it needs.

When 187,000 film-soldiers, all in proper costume, are needed for the movie, Goebbels orders them to be found. But then the director demands they be real soldiers and sailors. For authenticity of course.

Real soldiers? At a time when the army is desperate for men needed on the front to fight the war?

Goebbels makes sure the movie gets its real German soldiers.

At times it gets even more bizarre. Nazi officers are pulled away from the battlefields to screen test for possible roles in the movie. And as bombs are destroying houses and apartments all over Berlin, workers using precious building materials, construct a version of the town of Kolberg at the UFA studio.

And when snow is needed for a winter scene being shot in the summer, over a hundred railway freight cars that should be carrying military equipment are instead loaded with salt that will look like snow when it is spread across the ground.

And while this is happening three German army divisions are completely wiped out on the Eastern Front in the Baltics.

But the movie battle scenes are spectacular. No film in the entire history of motion pictures has ever had so many cast members for its battle scenes.

After months of filming, Goebbels urgently wants to get his heroic movie into the theaters around the country. But by the time the film is finished there are almost no movie theaters left. They are all in ruins.

But Goebbels sees an opportunity to have a spectacularly different kind of premiere of the movie—one that will make it a glorious publicity event. He decides that the triumphant premiere should be held in a little town on the coast of France where the German army is completely encircled and fighting for its survival. The only way the German troops there can get food and ammunition is by the Luftwaffe, military planes that have to break through the anti-aircraft fire and drop supplies.

Which for Goebbels, make this movie premiere even more dramatic. Because if German planes can drop supplies, then they can also drop cans of film he announces. Surely the nation will thrill to hear about encircled Germans fighting for their lives watching a movie about encircled Germans fighting for their lives. Just like Kolberg!

How perfect can it be?

The dying young Luftwaffe pilot knew.

His anguished mother was one of the women standing in line at the water pump with *Mutter* and when she broke down, on the verge of hysteria, the other women in the water line surged around her, comforting her as she sobbed about the pain, the terrible pain, he was in. And for what? He had flown cans of film—*film!* and now he was dying because of it.

"They brought him back home—or what is left of him,'

He had insisted on coming home to die. For some reason his request was approved, and he had been carried in to his family's apartment in Neukölln on a stretcher.

That afternoon *Mutter* took her small supply of dried chamomile, made it into a paste and then went to the young pilot's home where she applied it to the lacerations on the young pilot's one remaining arm. While he was dying, he wanted to talk, *needed* to talk. He told *Mutter* of many things: of growing up in Kreuzberg; of the girl he loved, the one who married a U-boat officer; and of how flying the Junkers military transport plane for the first time was such a thrill. He told *Mutter* all that and was just glad to have someone who would listen while his mother was out trying to find food.

But his mood changed when he talked of the terrible flight in a late January blizzard. Flying almost blind, making pass after pass over the French coastal town where the German army was trapped, until he had the encircled fortress beneath him and his bombardier could shove the package of film attached to the parachute, out of the plane.

Telling it he changed, growing angrier *Film! Stupid cans of film!* until *Mutter* whispered to him and pressed the chamomile compress a little tighter. He told the story every time *Mutter* went to see him, as if he was trying to expel it. The dangerous passes at low altitudes; dodging the American anti-aircraft fire; the heroic climb after the drop, all that. But then what was left of his legs would kick as he relived that Russian fighter plane that came out of nowhere, blasting in from the Baltic just as he was a few thousand meters away from landing.

"Look at me," he shouted waving his one remaining hand across what was left of his body. "*This*—because of a movie!" he would rage as *Mutter* tried to calm him. "A *fucking* movie dropped on the heads of our troops fighting for their lives."

The dying young pilot knew more than he should have. Some of his friends, the young pilots he had flown and drank and laughed with would show up occasionally, sitting beside his bed for awkward hours overflowing with memory. Talking about the debacle of the movie premiere at that encircled French town where numb and battle-twisted troops were marched into the *Theatre de la Ville* and told to watch a something called *Kolberg*, a movie with a lot of boring speeches.

And other friends brought the bloody news from what happened only a few weeks ago where the movie was based, at the real town of Kolberg when the Russians attacked it. The town surrendered in two weeks. But nothing was ever written about it in the newspapers that Goebbels controlled.

It was as if the surrender of the real-life Kolberg never happened.

But the young pilot knew it did. And just before he died, he made sure that *Mutter* knew it too.

Kolberg was our last, grand piece of gossip.

The morning after they took the young pilot's body to the cemetery, we sent the *Kolberg* gossip on its way. In the lines for crisis rations and the water pump queues and in air raid shelters it was being talked about. Like some raging pathology it was communicable and soon everywhere you went in Berlin someone was whispering about the madness of *Kolberg*.

Later that night, with what we thought was the rumbling of guns in the distance, Paul whispered, "We've changed places. You're the editor now."

"I like that," I murmured.

"I know you do," he said kissing the back of my neck. As I said a tiny prayer, hoping it would be heard somewhere.

47

IT WAS NOT EVEN DAYLIGHT when the pounding on the door began. Our instinctive reaction—*Gestapo*! had us hurtling toward the hiding places as we heard *Mutter* mumbling curses all the way to the door down the corridor.

When she opened the door we heard Dick and Doof, their voices alternating between panic and the indignation that erupted when *Mutter* bellowed "Don't you know the man has a heart condition?"—which was not true; it was just a cover story we had created in case they came looking for men to become cannon fodder.

This intrusion ended abruptly with more screeching from Dick and Doof and a loud curse from *Mutter* yelling at them to go away, followed by the sound of the door being slammed loudly. And then their footsteps fading on the stairs.

Mutter came bustling down the hall calling out. "Herr Langen there is a problem. They know there is a man in this house. And they will get you for the *Volkssturm* in one way or the other."

The *Volkssturm* was Hitler's last mad, desperate scheme—the Nazis attempt to scour the civilian population for any available men who could be sent into battle. From boys to sixty-year-olds, they were swept into what was intended to be a fighting force. Instead, what emerged were pathetic collections of the lame, the fat and the ailing, mixed in with a few terrified or reckless teenagers. All who were called, were expected to report for service wearing their own grey or brown clothes—nothing colourful, and then be handed what was usually either an ancient rifle or a *panzerfaust* and be sent off to defeat the enemy.

At least that was the plan. In practice, it meant that a collection of diagnoses were sent off to battle: astigmatism, arthritis; stenosis, flat feet, cataracts, arrhythmia, gout, emphysema, osteoporosis and whatever else had been caused by time, decay and the German diet.

And it also meant that salesmen, retired factory workers, dentists, chemists and bartenders were now supposed to be soldiers, ordinary men sent off to war in civilian clothes with a black armband embroidered with the words *Deutscher Volkssturm Wehrmacht.*

And it really meant was that a lot of boys and old men were being slaughtered in tragically bumbling attacks.

After another loud encounter at the entrance to our floor *Mutter* barely knocked before flinging open the door to our room. "They told me they want 'the man' living here to go with them. I told them we are all asleep. They'll be back with the SS man who has been assigned to our block. Make sure your papers are the right ones."

My first instinct was to flee or hide but *Mutter* was adamant. "They know he is here. And they are shooting deserters or hanging them from lamp poles. Even boys and old men they hang."

Paul's forged papers had his photo over the name, *Werner Albrecht*, 44 years old, brown hair, 182 centimeters, 79 kilograms. Another paper was a notation from a doctor saying that Herr Albrecht had a heart condition and should be excused from any form of military service. The doctor had been carefully chosen because he died two years earlier and therefore could not contradict what was on the papers.

There were a few minutes of chaos before the pounding on the door started again as *Mutter* and I found Paul a small knife and fork, a bar of soap, and whatever scraps of bread we had. *Mutter* took a deep breath, opened it and immediately began pleading that Herr Albrecht was a sick man with a heart condition and could die suddenly so—

"Lucky him," snapped the tall SS man standing behind Dick and Doof, "He'll die from natural causes before the Russians get to him. Let's go!"

And then suddenly, Paul was gone.

I ran to the rooftop and looked down on the street as he was marched out to join a group of confused looking, mostly older men. He was by far the youngest and had to help several of the men up into the back of an army vehicle, load several bicycles the SS man handed to him and then was shoved onto the truck as it drove away. I watched it, desperate to do something, to hold that ugly army truck in my sight until it was lost in the distance.

Standing there in my own confusion I realized something was different this morning. It was not just that the Russian artillery sounded closer. It was that it did not sound the same. It was no longer just a low rumble. It was a quick succession of terrifying howls. None of us had ever heard the sound before but everyone instantly knew what it was. On the street, women stopped and looked in the direction of the distant *bawoosh-bawoosh-bawhoosh.*

"Stalin's Organs," said *Mutter* standing in the doorway. We had all seen photos of them, *Katyushas*, rocket launchers mounted on trucks that fired in volleys. "We're in for it now," she said.

It was a tribute to German technology. The phones continued to work, even in the middle of all the destruction. Once in a while they would go dead but then miraculously an hour or two later, they would be working again.

It was something the Russians discovered as soon as they were in the northern areas of Berlin. Even from the outer parts of the city, in places like Wedding whenever they found a telephone they would dial random numbers, wait for a nervous German to answer and then yell things like *Ivan is here!* before laughing and hanging up.

We had only two calls, both of them for me. The first was from Paul three days after he left. *Mutter* answered, looked as if she touched an electrical wire, and then thrust the phone in my direction. "It's me," he said sharply and quickly. "I'm not supposed to do this. We're going to the Tiergarten. It's complicated. But I'm okay. I love you." Then the line went dead.

I decided I would get the bicycle out of my old room and ride to the Tiergarten. "And what on earth are you going to do when you get there?" *Mutter* asked, knowing better than to try and stop me from going.

"I have no idea."

"Well you'll need this," she said putting a small, sealed jar of her stew in the pocket of my coat as the phone rang again.

This second call was from Karin. She was calling from Babelsberg and for a moment I thought she was living on a different planet; she talked about everything except what everyone else in Berlin was living and dreading. She talked of the studio and how her costumes were not right; and the film was behind schedule; and the director was an ass; and the dressing rooms were too cramped and the makeup was-

"Karin!" I interrupted. "Are you not aware of what's happening all over the city?"

"Well?" she said, instantly becoming defensive. "We have shortages too you know. They can't even build sets anymore."

"I'm talking about the war. And the Russians, And—"

She interrupted me: "You should see what we have to put up with. We have some SS man here now. Very young, but *yechh* you should see his face. Part of it got blown off and god, looking at him while we're eating is—"

Another air raid siren suddenly sounded.

"I have to go." I hung up.

The Tiergarten was, for as long as I could remember, almost sacred ground in the middle of Berlin. For centuries the immense park has been the verdant, living heart of the city. Every schoolchild knew that it was first bequeathed to the people by Frederick the Great and had enchanted generations in all its many kilometers of different guises: forests, meadows, trails, streams and ponds. So profound was it in all of our psyches that we could describe the Tiergarten perfectly from memory. We would tell you of its lushness, its green vastness, its beauty.

Which is why I stood there beside my bicycle, clutching it for support, my legs barely supporting me.

Our Tiergarten was gone.

Where it had been, there was … what? Hectares of mud. A treeless bog. A wasteland from here to the horizon. Axed and smoldering tree stumps. Bomb craters. An endless desolation stretching on into an infinity you never wanted to reach.

I saw it—but for a moment my mind refused to accept the information my eyes were providing it. I burst into tears. Which was absurd. Surrounded by pain and death, and I was weeping over what? Trees? A meadow? I had no idea. I still don't.

It took me hours to find the *Volkssturm* unit that Paul had been made part of. About two hundred men, some in suit coats and street shoes were stumbling through the mud positioning a battered tramcar in an attempt to make a barricade across a road that ran next to the wreckage of the Tiergarten. When it was in place, horses hitched to the tram strained against ropes and pulled at it until it toppled over onto it side.

There were other women who joined me, watching on their bicycles. One of them shook her head and said *"Der Führer zieht Opas ein."*—*The Führer has called the Grandpas up.* But it was not only the *Opas.* There were middle-aged men in shiny shoes, men who looked as if they'd never been out of their offices.

And what was strangest, even from a distance, was that it was young boys who looked as if they were in charge. While the men were shuffling, a dozen or so Hitler Youth were striding around. They were boys, filled with a chilling and childish fury, yelling while the men were mostly silent.

Even from a distance, I could see Paul blending in anonymously with the others and staying in the back or the center of clusters of men, many of them hobbling. I saw him in that way you glimpse something that you flash past in a train. Somehow he knew I saw him as he moved across that road where they were building the barricade. He flashed me a look that I translated instantly: *Stay away! Do not make contact.*

The boys were a feral pack, laughing and ordering the men around. None of them noticed three other men arriving out of the mist. These men were dressed differently, in *Wehrmacht* army coats and none of them moved when one of the boys yelled at them.

One of these men stopped, turned and looked almost curiously at the boy who was yelling at him. Then he smacked the boy so hard that his helmet flew off and he lay in the mud blubbering. The other boys reacted as the pack, training their rifles on the man who stepped toward them bellowing, "You treasonous little shits. I'll have you shot, all of you."

The boys faltered. "Are you a soldier? A *real* soldier?" one of them asked in an uncertain little voice.

The boys suddenly seemed to realize that two other men in torn *Wehrmacht* uniforms were heavily armed and had positioned themselves on either side of their group with rifles pointed at them.

"Stand at attention, all of you shitheads," yelled the first man. None of the boys had to ask again if these men were real soldiers The first soldier walked back and forth among the suddenly nervous boys.

"Join us," said a different little voice.

"*Us?* Join *you?*"

"Yes," said this little voice. "How else are we going to defeat the Ivans?'

"Have you ever even seen a Russian?" the soldier snarled. "They'll wipe their asses with your face. And then they'll shoot you."

Outburst of blubbering could be heard.

The soldier continued, pacing among the boys. "Do you have any idea what *we* did to *them* when we were in their country? And what they are doing to us now? Have you heard about Neubrandenburg two days ago? And all the throats that were slit by the Russians? And the women raped over and over. Even nuns."

"Especially nuns," said one of the other soldiers. "Before they killed them."

"Go back to your mommies you little fools. If they haven't already been raped because you are out here playing stupid soldier games,"

Because of the way the wind was carrying, the women I was with had heard every word even from a distance. One of them murmured. "Nuns too?" Another almost moaned "What hope is there for us?" Another was crying softly.

From within the ragged group of men I saw Paul again flashing a look that said *Leave.*

I got on my bicycle. But I rode not toward Mutter's but northwest. Toward Babelsberg. "Stop!" called one of the women "You're going in the wrong direction. The Russians are up there." For a few dozen meters I bicycled onward but then something stopped me.

From somewhere nearby there was a scream that repeated and grew louder.

The group of women hurried up to me and all of us moved forward holding our bicycles in front of us like shields for some danger we couldn't quite identify.

One of them stopped abruptly. "Oh no, no, no," The words choked out of her.

Behind another wrecked tram barricade was a terrified young soldier under a lamppost. He was teetering on a small wooden box with a noose around his neck; the other end of the rope was tied tightly to the top of the lamppost. Around him were more of these boys, some so young that their Army helmets were several sizes too big for them and bounced all over whenever they turned their heads. All of them were filthy and seething with an untested and feral savagery. They had the faces of little boys into which the eyes of wolves had been implanted. And all of them had rifles aimed at the young soldier.

"No, no, no! Please! I am not a deserter," he screamed.

A sign had been hung across him written in childish script, *I AM A COWARD. A DESERTER WHO WOULD NOT FIGHT FOR THE FUHRER* The young soldier was crying, pleading, "No please, I was not deserting. My mother is dying and—"

One of the women I was with called out "No! This is not right."

The leader of the boys whirled around, his eyes like tiny beacons of fury. "Mind your own business, you stupid women," he yelled.

Then he spun around and ordered, "Do it!"

Two other boys kicked the box out from under the young soldier who screamed and kicked at the air. These boys, some of them little boys, alternated their weapons, some pointing at us, others pointing at the dying young soldier.

I almost collapsed over the handlebars of my bicycle. One of the other women helped me keep my balance

After several minutes the kicking stopped. The young soldier hung dead from the lamp post as the boys looked at what they had done, not sure what to do next.

I thought I would faint.

The leader of the boys took a piece of chalk and drew a circle on the pavement below the dead young soldiers' dangling feet. He divided the circle into sections each with its own number. The boys each put some cigarettes on whichever sections they chose. Then the leader made a chalk arrow on one of the dead young soldiers' shoes and began turning the corpse around and around until the rope that had hanged him was a series of tight coils. Then with a whipping motion he let it go. The dead young soldier spun like a top, round and round until finally coming to a slow swinging halt.

The boys laughed and fell to their knees staring at the chalked arrow on the dead young soldier's shoe. Finally it stopped swinging and settled above one of the chalked sections. One of the boys erupted in cheers and scooped all the cigarettes that had been put in the chalk circle beneath the dangling feet.

I was trembling and trying not to be noticed. I had pulled my scarf around my head, And I tried not to be noticeable retching into what was left of some shrubs. I did not have a choice.

The leader of the young boys was Max.

I fled.

48

FATHER WAS NOT ALONE.

They were killing themselves all over Berlin.

With high-ranking Nazis, it was obvious why they would nuzzle the gun. Their choice was either the swift certainty of their own bullet or the agony of waiting to dangle from the enemy's rope when the war ended in days, or at most, weeks. But more curious, were the mid-level bureaucrats and the minor officials who would have survived and gone onto some variation of the certainties that had always made up their lives. But they cannot face a future without the certainties the Führer has given them; the certainties that have filled the gaps within them, giving them this gift of an identity under his rule. So, around dining room tables, or on park benches, they arrange themselves, and sometimes their children, in ways that will make it look as if they are sleeping when their bodies are found.

What is now known:

The most intense and spectacular episodes of self-destructions are concentrated in the bunker under the grounds behind the Fuhrer's chancellery. It is where the last remnants of the Reich are wracked with fierce oscillations of hope and despair as the sound of Russian guns draws closer.

And no calculation of existence is more high-pitched than that of Magda and Josef Goebbels. Magda had often said that seeing Josef for the first time she had felt she might almost burst into flames. And now, in the last hours of the war she will indeed burst into flames in his presence.

Minutes after they have both killed themselves.

As SS-Hauptsturmführer Günther Schwägermann watches over what is left of her to make sure the flames do their work.

On that bright first day in May, having just murdered all six of her children, with the sound of the Russian artillery just over there! Josef, her husband, her great love, her tormenter, will fire a bullet into Magda's head just to make sure—in case the cyanide capsule she bit into has not totally done its work. Then he will point the trigger at his own head and pull the trigger.

Which leaves Goebbels' trusted aide SS-Hauptsturmführer Schwägermann to douse them both in gasoline and light the match.

Magda does burn—far better than Josef! Her flames are raging, incinerating all they can reach and destroy. But her husband is far less combustible, leaving more of him in his charred state for Russian soldiers to find.

It is all that is left of the pageantry.

The grandeur.

With the film's director lying dead in front of us, a circus is all I can think of.

Yes, a circus, the part where the clowns come running in all at once, falling all over one another. Because what is happening up there around that massive tank rumbling through the Babelsberg studio toward us is an eerie and terrifying clown show. Wildly dressed figures stumble and run in bizarre circles like overgrown children. Some are trying on women's wigs and gowns, and one is wearing a brassiere on his head and a cowboy outfit with others dressed as Napoleon or Caesar or the Kaiser, circling and falling from bicycles or running into each other. There are dozens of Russians, maybe more, the 'Asiatic Hordes' that Goebbels had been shrieking about in his last radio broadcasts.

No one understands what is happening until there is a shriek and a large woman bursts from the side door of the big sound stage, yelling at the clown show, barging in among them and tearing at Napoleon's coat.

It is Frau Haller, the famous head of the UFA costume department. Even from a distance you can hear her yelling, "These clothes do not belong to you!"

More Russian soldiers tumble out of the studio doors,

For us they are just called the Ivans. Some of the Ivans are now dressed as gladiators, others as Prussian kings and even one in a clown costume. Frau Haller is almost hysterical, pawing and tugging at the costumes. "I created these! You are defiling them! Stop! You are pigs!"

Caesar grows tired of it all and smacks Frau Haller with such force that she topples backwards. Then Caesar and the clown fall onto her ripping and tugging as she shrieks and slaps at them, trying to cover herself as her clothes are being torn off. From where we are, it looks like a feeding frenzy.

She is pulled by one arm, enormous in her mud-smeared, jiggling nakedness into the grass where the Kaiser takes down his pants and falls on top of her while Caesar and Napoleon laugh and wait their turn.

A few feet from where Karin and I stood, gunfire ripped through the big movie camera, almost blowing it up and sending those close to it diving for cover. The Russians who had fired right at the camera were shorter than the others and built like a barrel on legs. Filthy black hair fell across his forehead and down around his wide, flat face. He had come out of the sound stage dressed in a cowboy hat, big leather chaps that movie cowboys wore on their legs, and a holster, the kind that those American pistols fit into. It didn't matter to him that all he had to put in the holster was a German style Luger pistol.

His dark eyes narrowed as he practiced his gunslinger act yelling "Me Tex. Tex! Okay? *Pow! Pow!*"

He looked around for someone to be the Bad Guy, saw the accountant staggering to his feet beside the camera and yelling "Tex! Me." the Russian took aim and fired. The accountant slammed into the ground with blood gushing from his mouth. It was when Karin ran to the accountant that Tex knew what he wanted next.

"Frau! You, me. Wife," he yelled with his Luger pointed at Karin, as he did his herniated cowboy walk toward her.

On sheer instinct I yelled "No!" and ran toward Karin. He yelled what must have been a stream of angry Russian curses, waving the Luger all around until he fired again and I felt my arm catch fire. A thin bloom of blood seeped onto the upper sleeve on my left arm. He cursed more and walked toward us, raising the pistol.

But something almost hit him.

It fell out of the air, landed not far from him. It was shiny and caught the light of the sun in a reflected silver glint. Instantly he lost interest in Karin and me, running over to this shiny object.

It was a watch. He picked it up as if was an insect. Then his face erupted with delight. He yelled to the others, holding it up as a trophy. But as he was brandishing it, another watch flew through the air, this one landing between him and Caesar who was jostling with Napoleon over Frau Heller.

High above them, in the upper loading door of the studio sound stage was a thin, older man with little round glasses. He stood on the edge of this open doorway holding a box from which he had just taken the cheap wristwatches used as part of film costumes. I recognized him as the film's property master who I had seen an hour earlier arranging the decoration for a dining room scene that was to have been filmed later in the day.

Trying to distract the Russians, he stood up there flinging the cheap watches where they did the most good.

The one that landed between the three Ivans set off a stampede. Tex, Caesar and Napoleon all raced toward it and were joined by a dozen other Russians, all of them in outrageous costumes, elbowing and clawing their way toward the watch. Cursing and punching, they fought one another until a watch was ripped from its straps.

Another watch arced through the sunlight and landed near the remnants of the SS man. Then another, as Tex staggered to his feet and looked up to see where these shiny things were coming from.

The old property manager was just about to throw another watch when one of the five shots fired from the Tex's Luger hit him. For a moment he stooped slightly forward. Then he bent further until he plummeted the four or five stories to the ground, surrounded by a shiny torrent of watches flying all around him.

The pavement around his body was covered in watches, setting off the wildest stampede yet. Thrashing and fighting each other, they forgot about everything else around them.

I grabbed Karin by the hand and ran.

What is now known:

Watches.

They are spilling out through the air as a platoon or more of Russian soldiers fight for the watches.

But just a few kilometers away, so close that it if you were standing where the old property master was before he was shot, you would see it. Just over there beyond the trees:

The charming little city of Potsdam.

You could look over there to Potsdam and count off a mere seventy-five days from now.

Because in seventy-five days the war will have been over for over two months; there is no more fighting; it will be a warm July day, and other Russians are arriving, flying in from Moscow, travelling to Potsdam in luxury. The victorious Russians are led by the Soviet leader Josef Stalin. For years Stalin has been Adolf Hitler's only rival in the rarefied category of most-millions-of-people-murdered. But now that Hitler is dead, Stalin can claim the title all to himself.

No one does mass murder and death like Stalin. For decades he has been a master at it. He keeps millions of Russians in constant terror, many of whom are executed for no rational reason in the purges.

Stalin has explained:

"I trust no one, not even myself."

Or eight years earlier, executing, with bullets in the back of necks, almost his entire, loyal, military leadership?

His rationale?

"The easiest way to gain control of a population is to carry out acts of terror."

But now sitting in Potsdam, just a few kilometers from the bunker where Hitler and Goebbels fired bullets into their own heads eleven week ago, Josef Stalin looks genial and at ease, wearing his cream-coloured military dress jacket with its five brass buttons and its Marshall of the Soviet Union shoulder boards. He is there for a meeting of himself, American President Truman and British Prime Minister Churchill.

The three leaders are in Potsdam to meet as conquerors. In an elegant old palace, they will spend two weeks around a large circular table covered with green, billiard table baize. They will make momentous historical decisions about carving up Europe, war crimes trials and even this new military toy, the Atomic Bomb. All this will be discussed, debated and decided.

But strangely there is something else that concerns the Russian leader, something seemingly out of proportion to the vast issues being discussed across that green baize.

Watches.

Josef Stalin is obsessed with them. He sees wrist watches as a mortal threat.

Since the very last days of the war—mere weeks ago, he had become fixated on the subversive effect of the watches that ordinary Russian soldiers had discovered while conquering the Nazis. Before the war these soldiers, many barely educated and from impoverished villages in places like the Asian republics of the Soviet Union, had only known watches as those awkward metal things that important comrades in the cities wore on their wrists. The Russian watches were made by the First Moscow Watch Factory and were as ugly as a Soviet tractor.

But then when these same soldiers first saw watches on the wrists of the conquered Germans they went into a frenzy of confusion—these watches were shiny. Sleek. Stylish. The opposite of what was clunking out of the First Moscow Watch Factory. And everyone here, not just rich comrades, was wearing these shiny things. How could this be? When everything was supposed to be better under communism?

Could it be that we have not been told the truth?

A sudden lust for watches obsesses what seems like the entire Russian army in the last days of the war. Looting, robbing at gunpoint, ripping off wrists—whatever it takes to get one of these shiny things. It's as if every Russian soldier has to have not just one watch but as many as he can fit on his forearm. Cheap silver plating or pure gold, it's all the same as long as it's sparkles in the light and will attract the envy of other Ivans who want to be like the big-shot comrades.

And when they suddenly discover these all these bright shiny watches, they are momentarily conflicted. Because even the cheapest, watches will make them forget about everything else.

Even rape.

Which is why Stalin is so concerned with these alien trinkets, these watches.

Anything more powerful than sex is something to be feared.

It was the watches that saved us.

We ran while the Russians fought over the watches. For once Karin questioned nothing, asserted no standards of the way the world should work or behaviour that had to be observed. She just ran as I did. We got to the S-Bahn station and amazingly there was a train that was still running. It was packed with refugees from Silesia clutching remnants of a life bombed out from under them. For some reason they had thought Berlin would be a safer place. They were all almost dazed, without any understanding of where they were or what had happened to them.

None of them even noticed the blood dripping down my arm from where the bullet had grazed me like the shallow cut of a knife. For these people such things were now entirely ordinary.

The train stopped between stations somewhere in Charlottenburg where the tracks had been bombed into tangled metal spaghetti. With the trainload of people we walked toward the center of Berlin. I didn't hear what Karin was saying;o I was too busy debating with myself if I should say anything about what I had seen earlier that morning.

The brutality of Max and the other boys.

But the closer I got to the Tiergarten the more desperate I became to find Paul. The Tiergarten was now deserted except for a few old *Volkssturm* types stumbling through the mud and debris. Not far from the Brandenburg Gate I asked one of them where the others had gone. He was a heavy older man with a mane of dirty white hair. He looked confused and then waved his hand in a palsied non-directional manner and said "The river. The Spree. I think."

'You think? Don't you know?" Karin said.

"I'm too old for this."

I said, "Where? Where on the Spree?"

He drifted from confusion to indignation. "The Moltke Bridge. Please. Don't ask me anything else," he said shuffling away. He turned back and stared at Karin. And then adjusted his glasses, peering at her more closely.

"Aren't you in the movies?"

You could tell something terrible was happening over at the Moltke Bridge. Hidden from view by the shattered shells of buildings on the other side of the Tiergarten, the noise was not like the snap, thud and crash of guns and artillery that we had almost gotten used to. These were shrieking sounds, not from human throats but from metal surfaces shredding one another as great iron beasts snarled and thrashed at the bridge.

I stood frozen, staring across the Tiergarten. "Paul," I said. I didn't mean to. I just blurted it out.

Karin needed no explanation. "Do you want to go?" she said looking from me to the shrieking noise. I was already walking toward the terrible sounds.

We hurried across but it felt as if we were somehow descending because for an instant I thought of Dante and his circles of Hell; the closer we got to the awful, grating noise, the more wreckage, burning vehicles and bodies we were among. And I thought of the zoo on the night it had been bombed and the bellowing and screeching of the animals. Now it was machines making their own bellowing and shrieking sounds.

And they were no less terrible.

I stopped, suddenly afraid that in another hundred meters I could not be heard over the noise. "Karin!" I shouted. I needed to say it, to tell her. She turned like a cat that has heard a sound that should not be there. "Max. I saw Max today. He was with the men who are fighting. He may be at the bridge."

"But he's a boy."

"They are using boys. And old men."

"Boys? Max? Impossible."

"It's not."

She was already storming away. Then she stopped, turned again and came back to where I had remained standing. "You're sure?"

"Yes."

"Thank you."

"For what?"

"For telling me this. So I can go over there and stop it."

"Stop it?"

"I'm getting my son out of there," she yelled pointing to the bridge.

"Are you crazy?"

"Any mother would understand what I'm doing now."

"No they would not!" We were screaming at each other over the screeching roar of the battle just ahead. "There is a war going on!"

"Exactly! And finally! Finally my son will have a chance to see me as the mother he always knew I was. I was always there for him. It may not have looked like it but I was, And this will show him."

She was already hurrying toward the bridge and calling out. "Stop this madness! My son is here!"

Through the smoke and the twisted remnants of trees the Kroll Opera House loomed to our left like a gigantic masonry corpse. Shell wounds pocked its façade leaving large mouth-like holes in its standing walls as if the building itself was crying out in pain.

I almost caught up to Karin as she was clamouring over rubble ahead of me. "Karin, stop! You'll just get yourself killed."

She turned indignantly, "Are you stopping a mother from seeing her son?"

It was then that I wondered if it was really her talking to me. Or if she was now an actress delivering her lines in this, the latest great role of her life—the maligned, misunderstood mother.

Or even better, the tragic mother.

Someone was swearing at us, yelling through the roar of war. It was a heavily bandaged SS man carrying an artillery shell toward the bridge. He stumbled through the smoke past skeletal remains of vehicles. "Get away! *Away! Now!*"

Other SS men appeared, lurching toward the roar, carrying ammunition and yelling words that were sucked into the din from what lay ahead. Bandaged, filthy and desperate they all had the look of men who knew they were about to die.

The little river Spree was ahead, and between the walls of dead buildings we saw the Moltke Bridge. It lay smoldering, a rust-coloured stone gateway aimed like an arrow at the heart of Berlin. For an instant nothing made sense: the bridge itself still stood but its five stone arches spanned an elegance that lay in pock marked ruins. Its intricate carvings had been shot off and the mighty stone griffons that had stood guard in winged defiance at either end of the bridge now were mere stubs presiding over desperately constructed barricades and the overpowering stench of explosives.

An SS soldier grabbed Karin by the arm, leaving a smear of grease across her as he shoved her back. "Are you crazy?" he screamed.

"Are you stopping a mother from getting to her son?"

"What? Go away! They're going to blow up the bridge!"

"Where are the boys?"

"What boys?"

"The ones who are fighting."

"Most of them are dead. A few are left. Somewhere over there."

She shook herself free and stumbled forward. I screamed with all the force I had in me: "You could die!"

The strangest look came over her. It was pure defiance, the kind of look I hadn't seen from her since she was a child, defying our own mother. "Yes I know. But I am a mother."

An SS soldier stumbling next to her reached out with a filthy hand catching her around the waist. "We don't have time for this," he said pushing Karin to the ground and hurrying back toward the bridge,

Karin lay there dazed.

"You can't change what is happening there," I yelled. "You can't make the past go away."

She was screaming over the roar looking up at me through those wolf eyes she sometimes possessed. "I've done it all my life."

"Yes. And everyone else pays the price."

"Don't you talk to me like that. A mother who—"

"Oh stop!" I yelled as my voice was drowned out by the artillery.

From a loudspeaker somewhere came *Fünf!...*

"So now I will clear up my debts."

"Oh right! In the middle of a battle?"

"Yes!"

"Madness!"

...Vier!...

"No *this* is madness." She swept her arm across the entire vista of death and destruction, "And I am going to stop it."

"Stop it? You think you can stop *this*?"

"Yes!" she shrieked over the violence." All I have to do is talk to those Russians over there and tell them that we the German people do not want war. We are done with war."

"You're mad."

"That's the trouble with you. You can only think about war."

What? I was the one who was screeching now.

Drei!...

"I will do it for my son. My son needs—"

"He's not your son. You gave him up."

...Zwei!

"Well now he'll see what a good mother I am."

Eins!—and instantly a bone-jarring roar knocked me to the ground. Followed by a cascade of smaller explosions erupting from the bridge. Smoke and dust blasted out in stinging clouds that obliterated everything, choking the voices into a few seconds of silence.

Before the clouds blew away, other voices were heard: "It didn't work!" someone yelled.

"What?" someone else screamed "The bridge! We didn't blow the fucking bridge. It's still standing."

The smoke cleared. Karin was gone.

I stumbled over the debris, vaguely aware that gunfire was stitching the earth and the debris around me.

From the other side of the Spree, a Russian tank hidden in the wreckage of a building emerged slowly from its hiding place and began rumbling toward the still-standing bridge. And then it stopped.

Someone was on the bridge.

Karin. She turned one way and then the other. "I am telling you to stop!" she shrieked at the tank.

Even from where I was, I could hear other voices spitting out rough guttural bolts of a language I did not understand. The tank had stopped, its barrel pointing right at Karin. Russian soldiers emerged from behind it.

She put her hand out in a *Stop!* motion but the Russians began running toward her. She spun around, looking for me through the smoke.

"Bella!" she yelled.

I stood and watched from a lifetime's distance away.

"Bella!" she screamed again.

With the same cry, adamant, indignant, "*Bella!*" that had woven through the years.

I turned and walked away.

I only know part of what happened to Karin.

There was the one final glimpse of her when she was bizarrely lecturing someone, with fingers pointing and gestures back to where she had come from—until a Russian soldier raced out and grabbed her, dragging her screaming with flailing arms as gunfire exploded all around.

And then she was gone.

I limped back to Neukölln as the sun was setting. Everything in me ached and with my stinging eyes it was hard to tell what was fading sunlight and what was the glow of the fires burning in the west as the Russians surrounded the city. In the east, the battle for Tempelhof airport was sending columns of smoke into the darkening sky. Everywhere refugees were hurrying in search of air raid shelters, often stepping over bodies on the streets. The facades of many buildings were either strewn across streets or clinging to existence.

I got to the end of the long block looking straight down to what was left of *Mutter's* building. It was still one of the luckier ones; there were now gaps on either side and debris was spilling onto the street that was almost deserted as I got closer. A few women scurried in and out of doorways and once an older man could be seen tearing off his *Volkssturm* armband before vanishing inside.

I stumbled into *Mutter*'s and found her beside the stove. Before I could say anything else *Mutter* had sat me in a chair and pressed a warm, towel on my face. "Shh," she said before I could move. "You look a wreck."

"Karin is with the Russians." I gasped. "If she's even alive."

Mutter stopped what she was doing. shaking her head slowly and looking at the floor. "Oh," was all she said.

Or maybe that was all I was capable of hearing. I sank into the fog that had rolled through my mind like something viscous and clinging. I was too exhausted even to fight through it and form words. I remember nothing of those hours but the dreams, the flashes of Karin that startled me momentarily awake with images that came at me. Mother was there. She was standing right beside Karin on the Moltke Bridge while she lectured the Russian tanks, that sunny, smiling child waving as she left the house and the cool beauty unshakable in her own view of almost everything. Was this where it all had been leading? To that folly on the bridge?

Had her whole life been leading to the Russian who seized her and dragged her between the tanks?

Was I the one who had shone the light on the path that led her to that bridge?

Was it me all these years?

Mother? Tell me.

The next morning: I told *Mutter* what had happened.

She sat in her chair and stared into the little fire she had made in the stove. "Why are you surprised? It was always going to be like this. Your sister always flew too close to the flame. You know that."

"I told her about Max."

"So?"

"I shouldn't have."

"Of course you should have. For every reason why something happens there is the unreason. Unknowable, invisible and overpowering."

"I did something I've never done before. I turned my back on her. And walked away."

"And what exactly would the difference be if you hadn't?"

"Nothing."

"And it's been that way since you were a girl. You just didn't know it."

For a long time I could say nothing as Mutter waited for me to respond. Finally she held her hands out in front of her. "What?" she said exasperated.

"I knew it," I said. "I always knew it."

"Jah," she said quietly. "We always know what we don't think we know."

49

MUTTER HAD DECIDED THAT MOST of the men she knew were now useless.

Without all their puffed-up power, their uniforms, their swastikas and jack boots they were just like everyone else but less so, like balloons after the air rushes out.

When the Russian guns had first been heard in the distance all the big-shot Nazis decided this was not the time to do their stomping around and *Seig Heiling.* Almost immediately they began throwing away anything that would identify them as a member of the Nazi party. Most of them were confused and sometimes even whining about how unfair it all was.

Especially Doof.

After Dick was killed by an artillery blast a hundred meters away on a narrow street, Doof was close to hysteria. When Doof ran to him it looked as if Dick was sleeping in the middle of the street. Doof shook him several times and when nothing happened, he started wailing. When another blast hit a few streets over, Doof began ripping off the swastikas on his jacket, and when one of them wouldn't come off he threw the whole jacket away.

Mutter was watching. "Doof have you heard what the Ivans are doing to any Nazis they catch?" she said. *Mutter* had no idea what the Russians were doing. Which was part of her plan for Doof.

"Please, please you have to help me."

"You know Doof, I mean Günter, there might be a way I can help you."

"How?"

"That photograph. The one of you prancing around naked with Gisela. Where you're wearing that communist banner and Russian hat. You can show the Ivans that photo to prove that you have been one of them for years."

"You were supposed to give me the photo!"

"I already told you: No."

"You promised!"

"Not until you trade me for it."

"Trade? For what?"

"The Syphilis signs."

"What are you talking about?"

"From your old office in that clinic. I want all those signs written in Russian and German."

"Are you crazy? That place has been bombed. And the Russians will be here any day now."

"Do I care? No signs, no photo."

One day later Doof stumbled desperately into *Mutter's* carrying three signs, all of them from the German-Soviet expedition to Mongolia in the late 1920s. Before she would give Doof the photograph, she made him help her nail the signs up in precise locations that she chose. In the middle of the night as the Russian guns drowned out the sound of the hammering, they hung over the front door the sign written in German:

Quiet please SYPHILIS WARD

Just inside the front entrance she put up:

Осторожно—сифилис заразен

I asked her what it said. *Caution—Syphilis Is Contagious* she grunted as she reached up to nail another sign onto the stairway beside the door to our floor:

Не трогайте зараженные трупы.

My favourite, she said; *Do Not Touch Infected Corpses*. She was beaming like a craftsman, admiring a fine piece of work.

Mutter had already decided that this was another place where gossip could be useful so she gave Doof orders. He was to casually tell everyone on the street that *Mutter's* building had been taken over by a Syphilis Clinic handling female syphilitics. And most importantly he was to talk about the infected corpses inside awaiting burial.

In the chaos of those final days everyone believed everything. Wild stories swirled through the battered population and the more extreme the story, the more believable it was.

"Yes, yes," said Doof and then left as *Mutter* told him to.

The areas of Berlin were toppling like dominoes. Zehlendorf was overrun in three days, Zossen and Bernau held out for two days, and then it was like an avalanche with Wedding and Pankow lasting barely more than a day before the Russian tanks rolled through them.

"This morning I talked to Elsa in Pankow," *Mutter* said that night as she sat next to the stove with me. "The Russians raped every woman they could find. Her daughter is hysterical. There is no counting how many of them had her today. And even an old woman. Her too. And on and on."

"And you think the signs will protect us?"

"Maybe. She said a lot of the Russians are from Mongolia. We will see."

Mutter had given strict instructions to the few people remaining in her wrecked building never to use the front door. With the Russians closing in, that door must look unused and unwelcoming she said. Only the back door was to be used and when the Russians come let them puzzle over what was happening behind all these *Infected Corpses* signs.

The Russians showed up on our street a day later. One of their tanks parked itself at the opposite end of the long block. It turned and swiveled like some dull inquisitive beast that wanted to know where the *panzerfaust* projectile that barely missed it had come from. The turret turned and turned some more. Then it belched fire and across the street, about a hundred meters away, an entire building crumbled.

After that, all was quiet, even for the first few hours after the Russian troops moved in and set up headquarters in the abandoned butcher's store.

Then horses and vehicles were moved into the street. Feeding stations were set up and *Katyusha* rocket launcher trucks were positioned. There was a lot of yelling, like a storm rolling in, gradually building in both noise levels and intensity. One of the Russians had an accordion that he played with the same fervour whether drunk or sober. Soon the looting began as the Russians kicked their way into any residence they could find and soon the street was filled with lampshades and Russians holding up light bulbs as trophies. Wristwatches were seized off any man foolish enough to walk along the street, Jewelry followed with necklaces being waved around in all the yelling and celebrations.

Then the screams came.

Screams from women, some coming like muffled echoes and others ripping through the night in bloodcurdling shrieks that were instantly snuffed out. For three days and nights the screaming grew into a terrible chorus from dozens of female voices. It went on and on. And then faded for a while on the fourth morning only to resume again.

Mutter and I could see the street only by creeping out onto our rooftop patio area. Several times we saw Russian soldiers come up to the door of our building, looking at the *Syphilis Is Contagious* sign and then leave. The drunker the Russians were, the more they seemed to want to disregard the sign and barge in.

But none of them took the chance. There were just too many other easy targets all around.

But it was Jürgen, whoever he was, who almost did us in. In her frequently delusional state, the Swabian on the ground floor must have woken up one morning and seen a Russian who she thought was sure was Jürgen. Over the years of war she had decided several different men were Jürgen and every one of them had been treated to a volley of profane curses and accusations of destroying her life. So many of her clients reminded of Jürgen that she ran out of business as a prostitute.

Mutter had long ago accepted that she would never see any more rent money from the Swabian and allowed her to become a permanent yet almost invisible resident. We had sometimes heard her but the last time we had seen her was over a year ago.

Her re-entry into our life came with a medley of filthy Bavarian songs sung at the noise levels of a brass band. We were at the kitchen table when we were suddenly treated a screeching rendition of Jürgen having sex with a goat.

Mutter rose up like cat dropped into a dog kennel. "She's going to get us all killed."

Russian soldiers, many of them barely men, but with ancient faces, gathered in a confused group whose mood swung from laughter to mocking and then to angry taunts. One of them threw what looked like a brick toward the screeching. Glass shattered somewhere and the Swabian curses instantly stopped. The Russians laughed and soon turned away losing interest in our building because someone had found wrist watches in a store at the end of the block.

At night I slept in one of the hiding places Paul and I had made, telling myself it was what would save me. But wondering if I was really there because for a few hours, I could not hear the cries of women echoing in the night,

But sometime during the night I left the hiding place and went to my room, sleeping with the pillow over my head.

The next morning I awoke to find *Mutter* sitting on the edge of my bed. She had never done that before and when I was able to sit up in the bed, she still had not looked at me.

"What?"

"Your sister," was all she said, getting up, still not looking at me. "She's alive."

Before I could even respond she had left my room. I hurried to the kitchen where Mutter sat staring off into something only she could see. "My friend Lina." she said, talking in fragments "I finally got the phones to work again. Lina is older than me. Fatter than me. No Russian would touch her."

Silence. "So?"

"So Lina can go anywhere where she lives. Over near the Lehrter Bahnhof. Hear everything. See everything. And she did."

I waited.

"Your sister was passed around among Russian soldiers who each took their turn with her. What stopped her from being passed to the others waiting in line was a Russian officer, a Major who saw her. He knew her from one of her films. Don't ask me how."

"What happened?"

"She is his wife now."

"Karin? A Russian's wife?"

"A temporary wife."

"Karin? Never!"

"You think so? When her choice was either that or another thirty penises and then a bullet?"

What is now known:

Relatively speaking—very relatively, they are the lucky ones, these women of Berlin who somehow attract a Russian officer who has the power to order the others off her and make her his 'Occupation wife.'

Occupation wives are somewhere between geishas and sex-slaves, depending on the character of their new Russian 'husband'. For those finding themselves bound to a war crazed, brutal officer, their life becomes its own form of a lesser hell.

But for a few German women taken as 'wives', there are ways to endure. And Karin will find one.

She is barely able to survive by telling this swarthy Russian Major, this 'husband' whose smell she cannot bear, tales calculated to enchant him. They are wildly embroidered stories of the films she has been in, sometimes even acting out roles, keeping him drinking and toasting until he is too drunk to want more sex.

Day after day, night after night, she acts to save her life. And sometimes her acting works. And sometimes when no amount of liquor can stop him from dragging her to the bed, it does not.

All over Berlin, German women are raped by the thousands, many repeatedly by the Russians. Those who fight back are often shot. As are those who have simply been used up by dozens of soldiers.

In Moscow the reports of mass rape by Russian troops in Berlin become so urgent that a communist leader from another country protests about what is happening to the women. When Stalin is confronted by the remark he is indignant. "Can't he understand? It's our soldiers who have crossed thousands of kilometers through blood and fire and death and are having some fun with women. Or taking some trifles."

Stalin's trifles go on for days.

It was after the eighth night of jagged screams ripping through the darkness.

Mutter was the first to hear a different kind of cry. She hurried past me toward the wrecked entrance of what was left of our rooftop patio. "This is bad," she whispered. "Very bad."

Even before I followed her out past the splintered walls, I knew it was the Swabian's rage that had erupted. It had driven her into the middle of the crowded street staggering past amused Russians and raging at whoever she had decided was now Jürgen.

We were peering down through rooftop debris at the Swabian woman lurching across the street. It was the first time I had seen her in months. She was now enormous, teetering on swollen legs, covered in dirty bundles of cloth and raging from a grimy face framed by filthy cascades of matted hair.

"That poor fool," *Mutter* whispered as the crowd of Russian soldiers again swung between hostility and revulsion.

"She doesn't know it but she's doing us a favour," *Mutter* whispered. "They think she's syphilitic. No way they'll ever come in here now."

As she raged closer to the Russians they backed away in waves, the Swabian being the one woman none of them would touch. But soon the taunting gave way to anger.

"Not good," said *Mutter*. "Not good at all."

It quickly became obvious that she had picked the wrong Jürgen. As the crowd of soldiers backed away from her, the Swabian stalked a hulking dark haired Russian junior officer who retreated with the others. But he wasn't laughing as she kept stalking him. He yelled at her, holding out his hand but still she pursued him like some demented banshee, crooking a stubby finger in his direction, her clothes flapping behind her and strands of filthy hair falling across her face.

"Jürgen you bastard, " she screeched.

The Russian, stumbling backwards took out his pistol and fired a single shot into the Swabian. She lurched and collapsed in the middle of the street, her swollen legs and arms splayed. The Russian walked back toward her holding the pistol above her head and fired again.

It was as if some game had finished. There was a moment of stillness and then they all shuffled back to the horses, the Katyusha rocket launchers or the wrecked apartments they had colonized.

The Swabian's body lay in the street for hours until the junior officer returned and ordered several soldiers to clean up the street. We watched as they used shovels and poles to avoid touching the Swabian woman's body as they loaded it onto a horse-drawn cart.

"Your word is a lamp to my feet and a light to my path," *Mutter* said.

"What?"

"Psalms," *Mutter* said. "It about redemption. I have the feeling she'll qualify."

For two more days it went on. And for the first time in my life I said prayers from the Bible because I didn't know what else to do when *Mutter* started reciting them. I wanted to yell at her to stop all that, but I didn't. I couldn't. So I joined in. Somehow, saying prayers felt good.

And I wondered if Karin was saying prayers.

On the tenth day we watched Doof being marched down the street holding up his photograph as if he was pleading for his life. We never saw what happened to him.

And then suddenly, the Russians moved away, The screaming stopped. There was a terrible stillness that overcame the street. For hours, almost an entire day there was the feeling that it was somehow a trick. No one dared go outside. And then it all changed merely with the sound of a vehicle driving past, one that made a slightly different sound than what we had heard before. It drew everyone to the windows.

It was an American army jeep.

It was so unexpected, so outside what our minds were capable of absorbing from our what our eyes saw that it could have been a spaceship from Mars.

But it stopped at the far end of our street where Dick used to sit. We kept watching expecting to be some magic trick, some mirage and vanish in a puff of smoke. But it didn't vanish.

Nor did the two American soldiers who were in the jeep. One of them got out, looked around, lit a cigarette and then took a photograph of the destruction. He walked around the jeep talking and laughing with the other soldier. Another American jeep drove along the street and stopped where the first one was parked. The four Americans talked and laughed some more as if there was nothing that was wrong with the world. Then one of the jeeps drove away leaving the other two American soldiers to set up a checkpoint.

That was all it took for us to begin to live again.

Later that day *Mutter* called to me to come and look. Out on the rooftop area, she pointed off to the distance and handed me the binoculars she had found left behind by the Russians. At first I saw nothing in the wobbling image of the binoculars. Then a man came into focus. Ragged and disheveled he was pushing a large wheelbarrow. Across one side of his head he was heavily bandaged. In the wheelbarrow was someone else, someone smaller who was strangely contorted and covered by a bloody sheet.

The breath left me. I raced down the quavering stairs and out onto the front steps still clutching the binoculars. I looked through them again, not believing what I had just seen from above. I was terrified that my eyes or my mind were playing tricks on me. *It couldn't be.*

But it was.

Paul could not see me. He was too distant, and he faltered several times pushing the wheelbarrow, then stopping until he had the strength to move ahead.

I ran.

I ran as fast as I could. Weaving through the people on the street, walking stiffly as if they had never seen daylight before. Horns honked at me; a motorcycle came out of nowhere, swerving around me with curses trailing in my wake.

I ran until I stopped as if I had hit some invisible barrier. The sheet on the wheelbarrow Paul was pushing had flapped in the wind and then flown away.

In the wheelbarrow, lying crumpled and contorted was Max.

I could not tell if Max was alive or even conscious. Where his right arm should be there was only an empty and bloody sleeve. His young face looked as if it was sculpted from marble, hard and lifeless and staring at the sky. Then he moved his head like a blood-soaked puppet, as if it was attached to nothing but invisible dangling strings. He raised his head ever so slightly with eyes that seemed unable to focus. He burst into tears, raging and sobbing like a child.

"Mama!" he shrieked.

The word exhausted him until he began thrashing the air with his one remaining arm. "*Mama! Mama!*"

Paul saw me.

He stopped, letting go of the handles as Max collapsed back into the filthy container that held him. Paul walked forward, leaving him behind in the wheelbarrow, visible only as a single, bloody arm slashing at the skies in blubbering indignation.

In a moment that went on forever, Paul and I stood facing each other. On either side of us was the chaos with carts and people and cars flashing past on the street.

Overwhelmed by what had led us back to this, our beginning, neither of us could move for that moment, and all our words fell silent.

AUTHOR'S NOTE

BECAUSE OF QUESTIONS FROM EARLY readers of this manuscript, for the first time in anything I've written, I'm including an Author's Note.

The questions basically came down to:

Did the incidents in this book actually happen?

They did. The scandalous gossip in this book centers around one of the most powerful and murderous Nazis, Josef Goebbels, and his affairs with actresses while Hitler was trying to keep the focus on his conquest of Europe.

Bizarre incidents including everything from Hitler playing marriage counsellor, to Nazi invasion plans being derailed by Goebbels' outrageous affairs, to a lethal Nazi SS brigade being ordered to dress in drag for a movie chorus line and to Goebbels running movie studios and becoming a big-time producer.

And many more.

They all happened.

ABOUT THE AUTHOR

MARTYN BURKE HAS PUBLISHED SIX highly acclaimed novels; he has won the Peabody Award and the International Press Academy Auteur Award. He has also been nominated for Emmys and Writers Guild awards. He often researches his novels by making documentaries which have included the Academy Award-short listed Under Fire: Journalists in Combat and as well as other topics ranging from traveling carnivals to terrorism and wars.